Detective Karen Sweeney recognized him the minute he climbed out of the cab in front of the crime scene.

Senator Grant Lawrence was sometimes referred to by the media as the next John Kennedy, and Lawrence really *did* have that magic. Karen, a lifelong Republican, somehow always found herself voting for Grant Lawrence, Democrat. He made sense.

She liked his attitude. And it didn't hurt that he could give a younger Robert Redford a run for his money.

And that bundle of talent, looks and potentially huge problems was walking her way right now, being passed through the police cordon as if he were king. Nobody even asked him to wait.

This was Lawrence turf, even for the cops.

RACHEL LEE

WITH MALICE

MIRA

ISBN 1-55166-658-8

WITH MALICE

Copyright © 2003 by Susan Civil-Brown.

MIRA and the Star Colophon are trademarks used under license and registered
in Australia, New Zealand, Philippines, United States Patent and Trademark
Office and in other countries.

Visit us at www.mirabooks.com

Printed in U.S.A.

WITH
MALICE

Prologue

Abigail Reese was dreaming of passionate sex. She was not the woman in her dream, however. The woman in her dream was someone else, someone she knew, but whose face she could not quite place. The woman grunted and moaned, making sounds of mock resistance, her body bucking on something hard.

Then the dream shifted, in the way of dreams, and it was no longer passionate sex. It was no longer sex at all, and the woman was struggling, kicking, crying out in a weak, strangled voice. Abigail was paralyzed in her dream, unable to help the woman, nor even to open her eyes to see her face. The woman's struggles grew more frantic and less controlled, panic and terror in the face of imminent death. Somehow gasping in a ragged breath, the woman's voice screamed out her name.

"Abby!"

Abigail shuddered awake. For a moment she fought her body's urge to drift back to sleep, knowing the nightmare would return. Her thin cotton nightgown clung to her damp skin like a shroud. She threw the covers off as the woman tried to call her name again.

"Ab—"

The sound died away in a gurgle.

It was not a dream.

Had she been fully awake, Abigail might have done the smart thing. She would have remembered that the children were with their father this weekend, locked her door and dialed 9-1-1. But in the manner of a woman who had cared for children for sixty of her seventy-five years, her first thoughts were not for self-protection. Adrenaline surged into her system, and she bolted out of bed with a fluid strength that would have surprised someone who looked upon her wiry, slightly bowed frame.

The horrible sounds continued, not at all passion but stark terror, and she grabbed for the first thing she could find, a heavy glass ashtray, the last remnant of a long-dead habit, before opening the door and moving toward the screams that were growing fainter by the moment.

Bile rose in her throat as she came to the bottom of the stairs and rounded the corner into the living room. The sounds from the woman reached a new if almost silent intensity, the nylon stocking—nearly invisible in the flesh of her neck—choking off all sound. But her eyes...

Abigail had seen a lot in her three score and fifteen years of life. She had watched a young boy scream as the doctors tried to reset the shattered bones in his lower leg, ending his dreams of college football. She had seen the boy grow into a man and the pallor in his face as he asked her whether he should propose to the woman he loved. She had watched him nearly faint at the news that his new wife was pregnant, and beam at the birth of their first child. She had watched his face, his entire counte-nance, sink like a gutted ship when he heard that his wife had been killed. She had seen children quiver in fear of punishment, in fear of shots, in fear of first haircuts. But she had never seen eyes like this.

They bulged from the sockets, blotched with red from burst capillaries, and they were looking into the face of eternity. The bloodied lips beneath them mouthed a word: "Abby."

It was only then that Abigail noticed that the woman was naked, her shredded nightgown protruding from beneath her back, apparently wrapped around her wrists. Her legs, though free, made only futile kicks, easily resisted by the man who was bent over her breast. With an ugly, wet, ripping sound, his face rose from her chest. He spat, and a chunk of flesh landed on the woman's face. Then he seemed to see through her eyes and turn to Abigail.

His was the face of a monster, smeared with the woman's blood, white teeth and eyes glistening in a red mask of rage and fury.

Abigail's nostrils flared with the fight or flight response. She should have flown. Instead she charged him, the ashtray raised high in her hand, the lioness protecting her pride. She closed the distance between them in four steps, swinging the ashtray down at his head with all her still considerable strength. But she was an old lioness, and her reflexes were not those of the younger woman who had snatched children from the throes of danger for decade upon decade.

He turned and caught the blow on his shoulder, grunting in pain, and then his arm flashed up. It was only then, in that last instant, that she saw the gleaming blade in his gloved hand, in the last instant before it plunged into her throat and savagely ripped across.

For a moment she thought he had missed, for there was no pain. But then she saw the pulsing explosion of red splash over his face, and in the fast-dimming light she realized it was her own blood.

She dimly heard a voice. "I'll get *him*, too!"

Abigail Reese was once again dreaming, running through a tunnel, trying to escape the gurgling, wet sound that propelled her. The light at the tunnel seemed to dim, then exploded into brightness and swallowed her.

1

Senator Grant Lawrence grunted in disgust as he paged through the proposed amendments to Senate Resolution Fifty-Two. Whenever he thought about the bill he'd sponsored, he forced himself to think: *clams have lips.*

That reminded him of the first time he'd snorkeled in the Florida Keys, as a teenager, and had seen the beautiful coral through water so crystal-clear that he'd felt he could see forever. On that bright April day, during Easter vacation, he'd been gliding through the water when he'd seen a squiggly, bright red line in the sand beneath him. He'd reached down toward it, and the line had split down the middle, the clam opening its shell to test the disturbances around it. Apparently deciding his finger was not appetizing, it had closed its shell again, leaving only that squiggly, bright red line.

Clams have lips. And, Grant had decided, they wore lipstick.

He forced himself to remember that day because he could not repeat it. The water of the upper Keys was now cloudy and thick with sea grass, choking out the coral, hiding or chasing away the clams. The grass was the product of nitrogen in the water, the runoff from fertilizers used by sugar growers in the Everglades. The problem was not limited to his native state, of course. All along the eastern seaboard and Gulf Coast, nitrogen-laden runoff was feeding sea grasses that had replaced the native underwater flora and displaced fisheries.

S.R. 52 was an attempt—a feeble attempt, his critics said—to slow the damage. It wasn't perfect, but it was based on the best scientific evidence and advice his staff could assemble. And it would be reasonably cost-effective to implement. Many of his colleagues in the Senate agreed, and his staff had negotiated with, cajoled and arm-twisted enough of the others that the bill seemed likely to pass.

Thus, he was not surprised by the pork amendments that had grown like barnacles on the hull of an ocean liner. Most were only vaguely related to the bill itself but would instead funnel some money into authors' home states. Some of them were amendments he'd pledged to support, bartered in order to secure a colleague's vote on the primary bill. However distasteful it might seem, it was the way of politics, and he accepted it as a necessary and sometimes beneficial fact of life.

Others were not so benign.

Amendment Nineteen, for example, would strike the paragraph that authorized additional funds to the EPA to monitor and enforce S.R. 52. Creating unenforceable law was an old political trick. The idea was to allow lawmakers to pad campaign literature about how they'd voted on popular issues without sacrificing campaign contributors whose interests ran the other way. To the voters: *I voted to protect your environment.* To the contributors: *But I knew this bill wouldn't upset your apple carts.*

And he knew who was behind *that* amendment. Randall Youngblood, head of the cane growers' association, now lobbying for a loose coalition of agriculture associations nationwide. Randall Youngblood, old friend, now nemesis.

Clams have lips. Grant used that image to maintain his focus as he waded through the swamp of cynical motives and opaque language. He scrawled *NO!!!* through the text of A.19, then tossed the folder aside. He would slog through the rest of it later.

He took another minute to flip through the news digest, circulated to members of Congress by e-mail. Compiled daily from wire services and newspapers from around the world, it offered a quick précis of the day's events. A humanitarian relief convoy had been ambushed by guerillas in Colombia, the second such ambush in a week. Two Americans were among the thirty-one casualties.

Grant scanned the rest of his e-mail. The only one that mattered was the notice of a meeting of the Central and South American Affairs Subcommittee of the Senate Armed Services Committee. The meeting was set for 10:00 a.m. He had no doubt that the situation in Colombia would be first on the agenda. He logged off and shut down. Colombia would have to wait. It was two in the morning, and he'd promised to take his daughters to breakfast.

While he loved having the girls in D.C. with him when they were off from school, they did make for longer days. Still, burning the midnight oil was a small price to pay for the time he had with them. He switched off the desk lamp and took a few moments in the comfortable darkness to massage the hair at his temples.

At least in the darkness he didn't have to notice that his formerly raven black hair was turning gunmetal gray.

His advisors had turned to an image consultant, who had pronounced it "statesmanlike" and "dignified." Grant thought it simply made him look old. But within a week the advisors had tromped in with focus group research. His daily jog, trips to the Senate gym and a healthful diet had kept him trim and lean. The focus group felt that the gray streaks softened his otherwise chiseled, youthful face. "The energy of youth, tempered with the wisdom of experience," one woman had said.

That sounded much grander than he felt about himself. He'd spent the day in the company of the energy of youth, chasing his girls around the Smithsonian. They had speed-walked him into the ground, giggling when he'd begged them to "slow down for the old man." Energy of youth? Not.

Letting out a sigh, he rose from his chair just as the phone rang. It was his private line, and the caller ID display flashed the name.

"What's up, Jerry?"

Jerry Connally's voice was thick with tension. "Grant…shit, I don't even know how to say this. It's Abby. She's…dead."

"Oh no." Grant felt the bottom fall out of his stomach and sagged back into his chair. "Oh no."

"She was…murdered."

Abby? Murdered? Shock froze him, caught him in an endless instant of incomprehension and disbelief. He had known the day would come when her body failed her, but this…this was beyond imagination. "Oh God. Oh God. This isn't…it couldn't have…"

Jerry's voice softened. "I'm sorry, Grant. I am so, so sorry."

Abby had been his nanny, raising him practically single-handedly while his parents had rubbed shoulders with the wealthy and powerful. It was Abby who'd taught him the difference between glitter and gold, that the wealthy were not always worthy of the privilege they enjoyed. And when his wife had died, it was Abby who'd stepped in to raise his girls. It was simply not possible that she was gone.

He had to lean forward, to put his head between his knees as he clung to the phone. The world around him swirled, and there was a faint buzzing in his ears. "Where? How?"

"She was here at home, Grant. Stabbed."

No. It was not possible. His mind rebelled, even as the words came out on autopilot. "A burglary?"

"I don't know," Jerry said. "It gets worse."

"Worse?" Grant asked. He gripped the phone so tight that his fingers ached, but that pain was a distant thing, barely scratching the surface of his horror.

Jerry paused for a moment. "They killed Stacy, too. It was...it was really ugly."

The room spun in the darkness, shadowy images swirling, closing in on him. Grant reached out, turned on his desk lamp to hold them at bay. He had to lift his head to do it, and the room spun a little once again. The light seemed to pierce his eyes. "What was Stacy doing there?"

"Don't worry about it. I...took care of it."

"What? How?" He wouldn't have thought his horror could have grown any deeper, but it did.

Jerry's voice grew chilly. "Senator, you don't want to know."

Karen Sweeney looked at the body in the alley again, then looked away. "God, what a mess."

Corporal Terry Ewing nodded in agreement, his face ashen. "Someone was really pissed at this woman."

"Looks that way," Karen said. She tore her focus from the horror in front of her and found a procedural routine. "Okay, Corporal, start logging the scene. ID anyone who's been in this alley, starting with whoever found the body. Seal the scene. Nobody comes in except the M.E."

"Should I call for the P.I.O.?" he asked.

She shrugged. "You can try, but he's already up to his ears in College Hill."

It would be better if the public information officer handled the press. But that wasn't going to happen here tonight, not with a black woman and her two children gunned down in a drive-by. The College Hill project had convulsed under escalating street gang violence, the ironic and tragic aftermath of a major drug bust that had left the formerly dominant Dark Angels decimated and leaderless. Three other gangs had flooded into the void, warring over control of the lucrative turf, where ecstasy, crystal meth, crank and smack flowed like deadly, golden water in neighborhoods where hope was dim and life was cheap. The P.I.O. would be there, trying to sound cool and authoritative as he dispensed what little meaning could be found in such mayhem. Detective Karen Sweeney was on her own.

She sighed and looked at the patrolman. "Who's your backup, and where is he?"

He nodded toward the end of the alley. "Patrolman Stan Barnes. Fresh out of the academy and he walked into this. He's in the car." Ewing pointed at a pale yellow puddle splashed down a wall opposite the body. "He lost it."

Karen looked at the stain on Ewing's cuff and realized

he'd been standing with the other cop when it happened. Unlike the horror that had been visited upon the woman at her feet, Karen could see that scene clearly. Ewing standing there, patting the young cop's shoulder, offering whatever supportive words there were, while the man lost both his dinner and his pride. "Tell him it's okay. It happens to most of us the first time or two."

"I did," Ewing said simply.

Karen nodded. "Okay. You're logging. Tell...Barnes, is it? Tell Barnes we'll use his cruiser as a command post until downtown gets us a crime scene van. I'll be out to brief the press when I know something. In the meantime, all he knows is that we've found the body of a young, white female, and the investigation is ongoing."

"The usual spiel," Ewing said. "It'll give him something to do. Good idea, Detective."

"Thanks." He nodded, jotted her name and badge number on a clipboard, and strode to the end of the alley.

Karen unslung the bag on her shoulder and set it atop the lid of a crusty Rubbermaid trash can a few yards down from the body. She pulled out a dozen of what looked like dinner place cards and numbered each with a black magic marker. She then stooped and put the card numbered "1" on the yellow stain and spoke into a microcassette recorder.

"Item one, yellow-brown stain at base of north wall, opposite victim, vomit of Patrolman Stan Barnes."

She continued in a slow, methodical pattern, first working her way to the end of the alley along the north edge, marking and noting an oil stain, two sodden and faded cigarette butts, and a half-dozen other bits of debris, all of them probably meaningless. Once at the head of the alley, she pulled out a fat yellow piece of chalk, drew an arrow pointing back into the alley and crouch-walked her way back to her evidence bag, dragging the chalk on the concrete in a wavy, sometimes broken, but clearly visible line. This demarked the "safe" path into the alley, so the medical examiner and any other officers who responded could get to the body without disturbing evidence.

With that first task completed, she had banished the horror from her mind, at least temporarily. Now she could turn her attention to the body and its immediate environs with cool, professional detachment. She lifted the recorder to her lips as her eyes swept the scene.

"Victim is a white female, apparently early- to mid-twenties. Bruising and diffuse ligature marks on wrists indicate that the hands were bound at some point, although no matching material is immediately visible at the scene. Nylon stocking tied around the victim's neck, along with pitecchia in the eyes and teeth indicate strangulation as the probable cause of death. Missing tissue on breasts, lower abdomen and upper thighs, with torn edges. Probably bitten away. Extensive bloodstains on skin and partial clotting indicate this was probably pre-mortem."

Forcing herself to take a mental step backward, she took in the overall impression of the victim. No prostitute, she decided. This woman looked too well-conditioned for that, and in no way blowsy. That helped, because it was likely she would be reported missing before too long.

She turned away again as humanity pushed aside objectivity, took a slow, deep breath, and forced herself to continue. She looked again, clinically. Something was wrong. "Lividity is noticeably uneven, greater on the left shoulder, arm, hip, outer thigh and calf, although victim was found on her back. Victim may have been…''

Switching off the recorder, she called to the end of the alley. "Ewing. C'mere a minute.''

The patrolman approached along the path she had marked. "What's up, Detective?''

"I think the body was moved. Have Barnes clear the street around the end of the alley and photograph any tire tracks. Make sure he shoots my car, yours and his for negative comparison.'' She looked up at the overcast sky. The Florida air was thick with humidity. "And tell him to hurry it up. It looks like it's going to rain soon.''

Ewing nodded. "Yes, ma'am.''

Karen then returned to her bag, tore off a long strip of waxy paper towel and laid it over the left side of the body, weighting it at each end with spare boxes of film. She carefully pulled the paper back a bit and studied the ruddy skin of the woman's left hip and shoulder. The dimples were faint but visible, fading down the arm and thigh. Atop the woman's thighs, Karen saw faint blood smears that mirrored those on her abdomen. She switched the recorder on.

"Remind the M.E. to check for carpet fibers. Victim was probably transported to the scene in a fetal position, on her left side. Probably in the trunk of a car.''

Two hours later, Karen watched as the M.E. techs zipped up the black vinyl body bag and hefted it onto a stretcher. The crime scene techs had arrived a half hour ago, and she had long since determined that the homeless woman who'd stumbled over the body was too disconnected from reality to offer any useful information. There was little left for her to do, and she walked back to her Jeep Wrangler, took a long swig from a lukewarm bottle of water, and began to scan Ewing's and Barnes' initial reports for anything they might have caught that she had missed.

She was still reading when her cell phone rang. It was the familiar voice of Sergeant Laura Aranchez, the overnight dispatcher for robbery-homicide.

"You're going to hate me, Karen."

"Don't even go there, Aranchez."

Karen heard the sigh and knew what was coming before the woman spoke.

"Afraid so, Detective. Black female, Tampa Palms." Aranchez read off the address.

Karen fought down the anger. Yes, College Hill was important, but so was the single white female, mid- to late-twenties, whose mutilated body lay ten yards away in an alley. "I'm still working this scene, Aranchez. Can't they free up someone from the gang-banger?"

"The lieutenant says you're it," Aranchez answered. "And he wants you there an hour ago." There was a pause. "That address is Senator Lawrence's house."

Well, shit, Karen thought. *That explains a lot.* "I'm on my way."

It was going to be a long night.

Karen surveyed the bustle of activity with more than a bit of disgust. It had taken her ten minutes to reach the Tampa Palms address, and the crime scene techs were already unloading their van as she pulled in. Death might be the great equalizer, but the rank of the living still held sway in the passage of the dead.

A middle-aged man in blue suit pants and a white dress shirt intercepted her on the way to the door and extended his hand. "Jerry Connally," he said, as if the name ought to mean something.

She shook his hand briefly and stepped aside. "Detective Sweeney, TPD. If you'll excuse me."

He didn't step into her path, didn't move at all, yet his posture said *I'm not finished with you yet.* She met his eyes. "What is it you need, Mr. Connally?"

"I'm special counsel to Senator Lawrence." He nodded over his shoulder. "You're aware this is his home."

Oh God, she thought. *So it's starting already.*

"Yes, I am. It's also a crime scene, and I'm the lead detective. And I've just been yanked off another homicide scene because they wanted me here in a hurry. So again, if you'll excuse me…"

He moved aside, as if to give her entry, but his posture was such that she paused and looked at him again. He reminded her somehow of a broody hen protecting a chick. It was as if he wanted to tower over her, tower over everyone and everything to protect his charge. She wondered if Senator Lawrence liked that…or if he was even aware of it. But something clicked in her mind, making a note she was hardly aware of.

Then she dismissed him with a glance and brushed past him into the foyer.

These were the houses of the rich, out here, and space was generous. The foyer was large, tiled in green marble that framed the sweeping rise of a staircase. The activity she was interested in, however, was in a room off to the right. She could see the criminalists poring over the scene like a hive of ants with a fresh kill. The kill lay on the floor, covered by a sheet. Arterial spray across one wall and the sofa, along with the huge puddle on the floor around the covered corpse, told a great deal of the story.

The room itself was very much not Florida. It might

have been taken from the home of British nobility of the eighteenth or nineteenth century, except that it was dominated by cream and ecru. Cream everywhere. And blood. As least half the blood that filled an average human body. Red on cream. Screaming.

With the criminalists all over everything, there wasn't much she could do except ask to see the body and find out what they knew so far. She raised an eyebrow in the direction of Millie Freidman, the lead technician on the scene. Millie nodded, spoke a few words to one of her team members, and came over to her, taking care to stay within the taped-out pathway.

"What have we got?" Karen asked.

"Ugly. Very ugly. The senator's seventy-five-year-old nanny had her throat slashed."

Karen winced. Violence against the elderly always seemed so inexcusable. How much more harmless could a human being be?

"Yeah," said Millie, reacting to Karen's expression.

"Robbery?"

"It doesn't look like anything else was disturbed. I have some people checking the rest of the house, though."

"Any other wounds on the body?"

"None that I can find."

Karen nodded, feeling like a fifth wheel. "Who found the body?"

Millie showed her teeth in an unpleasant smile. "The senator's watchdog."

"Connally?"

"You got it."

Karen glanced at her watch. "This early in the morning?'' She hated the very idea, but it appeared she was going to have to go talk to Jerry Connally.

One of the many reasons she was getting bone weary of this damn job.

He was careful not to show it, but Jerry Connally was as nervous as he'd ever been in his life. He was a man totally in control of himself and most of the world around him, but at this moment he felt his control might be slipping.

In law school he'd taken an advanced prosecution clinic. The professor had told him something he'd never forgotten. Criminals don't get caught because cops are brilliant. Criminals get caught because they're stupid. *For every one thing they think of,* the professor had said, *they forget five others. And those five others bury them.*

Jerry had tried to think of as many things as he could in moving Stacy's body. And he thought of himself as a smart guy. But that only meant that for every one thing he'd thought of, he'd probably forgotten two or three or four others.

The bottom line, though, was that Grant Lawrence was worth the risk. And if Jerry's neck ended up in the noose to save Grant's...that was just how things would have to be. Grant deserved no less.

He waited in the foyer for a few moments, glancing in the large, ornate mirror near the door to make sure he looked like himself and not like some criminal with something to hide.

His open, Irish face looked back at him, unnaturally somber but otherwise normal. A little edginess, he assured himself, was okay under the circumstances. After all, he'd discovered a brutal murder. So it didn't matter that his tie was loose or his remaining hair disheveled. It fit the moment.

Then, shoving his hands in his pockets to still their sudden inclination to fidget, he stepped back outside. He didn't want to hear what the crime scene people were telling that detective. What was her name? Swanson, Swenson, something. Sweeney, that was it. Someone he had a feeling he wasn't going to be able to control all that easily. He might have to do something about that.

Just then she appeared at his side. Damn, he hadn't been paying attention. He offered a smile.

"What can I do for you, Detective?"

She regarded him with gray eyes that seemed devoid of any color whatever, save for the tiniest slivers of green around the pupils. Predatory eyes.

"I understand you found the body?"

He nodded.

"It's, what, 3:00 a.m.? What were you doing here?"

This part was easy. It was the truth. "The senator left a message for me last evening. I was out with my wife at the time. He needed some papers faxed up to his office, for a bill that's pending. We got home around 1:00 a.m. I got the message and came right over."

"Couldn't it have waited till morning?" she asked.

"Yes. It could have. But I was planning to take my kids fishing today. I wanted to wrap it up tonight so I'd have the day to myself." He sighed. "Best laid plans."

The woman seemed to look right through him. "I'm sure Abigail Reese didn't plan on getting killed, either."

It was at best a sarcastic remark, and he could have argued the point. But for the moment, at least, she held the power. Better to let that lie, wait for her to realize she'd stepped out of line, and be ready to take advantage when she apologized.

"Point taken, Detective."

But she didn't apologize. She didn't even seem to care that she might have crossed a line. Dangerous woman.

She continued looking right through him and asked, "Weren't you afraid that coming into the house this late at night would wake the nanny?"

He shook his head, fists clenching inside his pockets. "Abby didn't have the best hearing. She wasn't stone deaf or anything, but I've come and gone before while she was sleeping."

"And you have a key, and you know the alarm code."

"Yes, exactly for purposes like this. The senator has an office at the back of the house."

She didn't say anything but simply turned to look at the brass dead bolt. Damn! He hadn't thought of that. There was no evidence of tampering. *Shit!*

She turned to him again. "Was the alarm on when you got here?"

He thought rapidly, then decided the truth was best on this one. "No."

"Did you find that odd?"

"Not necessarily. Abby sometimes forgets about it." That, too, was true. Grant had complained about it once, because he was concerned that she forgot it when his children were home.

"And you know that how?"

"Because the senator complained to me about it once."

She nodded, for the moment giving him the feeling she was accepting his explanations. "How did you enter?"

"Through the front door. As I always do."

"And then?"

"I turned on the foyer lights and headed back toward the office. But as I was passing the living room—" He broke off, and this time he wasn't pretending anything.

His throat tightened, and his face stiffened with the memory. "I...smelled it."

She nodded again. She knew what he meant, apparently. "Then?"

"I turned on the lights, and...my God..." He couldn't continue. He honestly couldn't continue as he recalled those first few minutes when he had stared into an abattoir and tried to make sense of what he was seeing. It had been so alien to his experience that for a while the images wouldn't even resolve into anything recognizable. And then...

He turned sharply away from the detective, forcing himself to draw steadying breaths, not wanting her or anyone else to see him break down. The ugliness. The horror. There were no words.

"Mr. Connally," said the woman behind him, "how long was it before you called us?"

2

Grant watched the water drip from his face into the sink. The bitter taste was still strong in his mouth, despite two rinses of mouthwash. The face he saw in the mirror had neither the energy of youth nor the wisdom of age. It was pale, drawn, eyes red-rimmed.

He drew a deep breath. He had to *do* something.

What would he tell the girls? They'd called Abby last night, before bed, just to say hi, they'd said. He couldn't remember a night when they'd been away from Abby and hadn't called her. It was as much a part of their bedtime ritual as hugs and brushing their teeth and him tucking them in. What would he tell them?

He had to get back to Tampa. That much was certain. Call his parents. That was the next step. Tell them what had happened and ask them to take the girls. One thing at a time, he told himself. One thing at a time.

His father's voice was thick with sleep.

"Dad," he began, and stopped. Saying that one word broke the last wall of reserve. Sobs tore from his chest.

"Son? What's wrong?"

"Abby...Abby."

His father knew. His father had always known. "Oh, son. Oh."

In the background, Grant heard his mother stirring, asking what was wrong. "Dad, can I bring the girls home?"

The answer was immediate and reassuring. "Come home, son. Bring the girls. Your mother and I will start getting ready now."

"I loved her," Grant said, his voice breaking.

"We all did, Grant. Bring the girls. We'll be ready."

Jerry Connally shook his head. "I honestly don't know, Detective. I mean, I know it's the wrong thing to do, but I looked through the house first, to see if he— I'm guessing he's a man—was still here. I could tell she was dead, but I checked anyway."

"Before or after you checked the house?" Karen asked.

"I think before. I'm not sure." He paused. "It's funny. I've seen in a hundred TV shows where someone finds a dead body and panics and does something stupid. I always thought it was a bad plot device. And I guess I went and did the same damn thing."

"So you approached the body?"

"Yes. I tried to find a pulse." He looked down at his hand and shuddered. He met her eyes. "You check the pulse in the neck. That's where it's strongest. Easiest to find. I…"

Karen watched his ashen features. It wasn't hard to see what had happened. Looking at a horrific wound was bad enough. Touching it would turn even the strongest of stomachs. She merely nodded and let him talk.

He seemed to study the floor for a moment. "I guess I checked her and then the house. Those footprints would be mine. Some of them, anyway. Maybe some of his, too. I just don't know, Detective. I wish I did.''

He was a man transformed, Karen thought. Either he was a hell of an actor or the scene really had horrified him. Neither would prove his guilt or innocence. But the emotions rang true.

''You checked the house and then called?''

She saw the pause flicker over his face. Something he was keeping back. Something he wasn't sure he wanted to say. ''I think I tried to call Senator Lawrence first. I don't know what time that was, but my cell phone records would show it.''

''You called the senator before you called us?''

He threw up a hand, a gust of breath escaping him. Even to Karen's alert gaze, there was no question that this was a man in distress.

''I may have. Detective, I'm not real clear on the order of events. I remember hardly being able to comprehend what I saw. I remember checking the house. I remember checking Abby to see if she was still alive. And when I knew she was dead... All I could think of was Grant and his children. They love that woman. They've loved her all their lives. And when I knew she was dead...well, it's possible I thought of telling him first.''

His gaze suddenly fixed on her, intense with emotion. ''What difference does it make, Detective? The woman was dead. Abby was dead.''

Karen refused to give him even a moment to collect himself. Instead she pressed him. ''It made a difference in how fresh the crime scene was. We might have found the killer in the vicinity.''

He shook his head, his eyes growing hollow. ''Like I was even thinking of that. A woman I'd known for years was dead, brutally killed. And people I love were going to be torn up by it. Do you think I was even thinking about what *you* might need?''

Then he turned and walked away, making it clear he was done with her.

Karen paused, thinking, then decided to let him go. There were questions yet to be asked, but something about Jerry Connally... Some instinct told her he wasn't the killer. She pushed away the niggle at the back of her brain that insisted Connally was withholding something and went back into the house. Unlike many cops, she had never believed that the most obvious suspect was the likeliest one in a case like this. She wasn't going to allow herself to get misled. She would find the killer, but she wasn't going to close off *any* avenues by making assumptions.

Karen found Millie dusting a heavy glass ashtray. Millie glanced up. ''From the floor by her feet. Looks to have prints. Probably the vic's.'' She turned it over. ''There's a bloody smear on the bottom, but that's from the carpet fibers.''

''So okay,'' Karen said. ''She's in her nightgown and a bathrobe. The ashtray doesn't have bloody fingerprints. Only smears from the carpet. Sounds to me like she's asleep or falling asleep, hears something, grabs an ashtray from her bedroom, comes down and surprises the killer.''

Millie nodded, her trained eyes sweeping the room. ''That would fit, yeah.''

''So what was the killer doing when she came downstairs? Burglary? So far as Connally can tell, nothing's missing.'' Karen nodded toward a lacquered end table where a sectional serving dish held jelly beans and other candies. ''That's silver. There's other stuff right here.

Even if the perp panics after he kills her, why not grab stuff that's right here in the room?''

"I'm a criminalist, Karen." Millie shrugged. "Not a profiler. Don't ask me to explain how criminals think. I just look at what they leave behind."

"Your people photographed the spatter patterns?''

Millie nodded. "And logged the footprints and all the rest."

Karen checked her watch. It was nearly five-thirty. "I'm going to go canvas the neighbors. Maybe somebody saw something." She shook her head. "This case is going to suck."

Millie smiled sadly. "They all do, Karen. They all do."

Out on the street, though it was still dark and most people ought to be in their beds sound asleep, a crowd had begun to gather. It wasn't a big crowd; after all, this was an upscale neighborhood where gawking at misfortune was probably a solecism.

But the ghouls had gathered nonetheless, a handful. All looking as if they had climbed out of their beds and dressed in a rush. Probably the nearest neighbors, and most likely concerned that their own families might be in danger. That was the rational explanation.

But something else stirred inside her, the memory of a Ray Bradbury short story, *The Crowd*. In the story, the same group of gawkers had appeared at every fatal traffic accident. And in the pre-dawn stillness, Karen could almost see that story taking place. The faces before her, concerned and questioning and peering as if to look through the darkness and the crime scene tape and even the walls of the Lawrence home, could have been the same faces she'd seen around dozens of homicide investigations before. The face of society's collective guilt and shame and morbid fascination with the depths of evil.

She'd seen too many of these crowds. Crowds around a house where a drunken husband had finally beaten his wife into eternal silence. Crowds around a playground where a drug deal gone sour had ended in gunfire. Crowds around a bar where fists and bottles had flown in the wake of angry words. Always the crowds. Always the same faces. Always the same questions.

Karen shook her head to clear her thoughts. It was late and she was tired. This was no time to let herself get spooked. These weren't phantasms. They were just people. Curious, worried people.

Sliding her hands into the pockets of her slacks, she ambled in their direction. The houses here were on large lots that were carefully landscaped to provide the illusion that the residents were alone in the universe. These people might or might not have been friends and acquaintances before, but right now they were drawn together by a tragedy.

"Hi," she said as she reached them. They had gathered by the tape barricade, politely out of the way. "I'm Detective Sweeney."

"What happened?" one of them asked her, a man who was probably in his midforties, with the well-coiffed, well-built look that came from a combination of money and the time to spend with a personal trainer.

"Who are you?" she asked him.

"Wes Marlin. I live across the street. And I want to know what happened."

"I'm sure you do." Karen gave him a polite smile and pulled out her pad and pen, scrawling his name. "Phone number?"

"Why? I didn't see or hear anything. I'm just worried. I have a wife and kids, you know."

"Yes, of course. I can get your phone number, you know."

So he gave it to her, along with his address. Then she turned to the others. "Did anyone hear or see anything at all?"

Most of the heads shook negatively, almost in unison, as if the crowd had become one entity. Muted calls of "What happened?" rippled out, indistinguishable one from the next.

Then another man spoke. "I heard a car," he said.

Immediately Karen's gaze snapped to him. "Your name?"

"Art Wallace. I live next door." He pointed over his shoulder to the right. "The Lawrences are like family to me. We've been friends for ten years, at least. Our kids play together. So could you please just tell me if Abby is okay?"

"Abby?"

"The nanny. Oh, hell, she's not a nanny anymore, she's part of the family. Grant took the girls to D.C. with him, so she's the only one home. Is she all right?"

He was a good-looking man in his midforties, a little thin in the hair, and wearing an expensive pair of glasses, but he had the kindest face among all the plastic faces around him. "Do you know Abby well?"

"Of course! Like I said, she's part of the family."

"When did you hear a car?"

"Hell, I'm not really sure. I was asleep and woke up a bit. It had one of those noisy mufflers that some people like so much. I remember thinking that if the driver lived around here, I was going to have some words with him.

Then I fell back to sleep until I heard all the commotion out here. What about Abby?''

"I'm sorry, Mr. Wallace.''

He looked at her; then his face seemed to crumble. "Oh, God,'' he said, his vice tight. He turned away and walked off into the darkness.

Karen let him go for now. She looked at the others. "Did any of *you* hear a noisy muffler?''

She was answered by more shakes of the head. She could see the crowd wasn't really attending her anymore, though. They were—it was—thinking about the fact that a neighbor had been murdered. Piece by piece, person by person, the crowd broke apart and melted into the dawn.

Grant eased Belle, his six-year-old daughter, into his father's arms. Behind him stumbled his nine-year-old, Catherine Suzanne, carrying Belle's teddy bear and her own secret vice, a fuzzy blanket from her babyhood. Both children were utterly exhausted, having been rousted out of their beds at three in the morning to catch a red-eye flight home.

Belle had finally fallen asleep fifteen minutes before landing, running out of the nervous energy of excitement at the strange situation. Cathy, older and a little wiser, seemed to sense something was wrong, but so far she hadn't asked. And she hadn't slept. But that was Cathy. She kept things inside, not exactly brooding, but more reflecting and waiting.

Bryce, Grant's father, reached out with an arm and squeezed Grant's shoulders before accepting the small burden of the sleeping Belle. "What have you said?'' he asked Grant, his eyes filling in the unspoken, *what have you told the girls?*

"Nothing. Later. The girls need sleep, Dad."

Bryce nodded, hugging Belle tightly to his chest. He smiled at Cathy. "How's my pumpkin doing?"

"Fine, Grandpa." The answer, tired as it sounded, carried Cathy's usual reserve.

"Well, let's get you home and snuggled into your comfy beds," Bryce said heartily. "And later, Grandma's planning pancakes."

Melinda Lawrence drew her son aside as Bryce tucked the girls into the car. Her eyes were red-rimmed, too. Abby had been as much a fixture in their lives as she had in his, and they felt her loss every bit as deeply. He felt his face sag.

"Mom."

She drew him into her arms. It was a familiar embrace, despite the media stories of his having grown up at the shadowy fringes of his parents' glittery world. Yes, Abby had raised him. Yes, his parents had worked long, grueling hours, often on location, producing films. They'd wanted him to have the stability of attending the same school, living in the same house, replacing Lego castles with posters of sports figures and, eventually, his own high school trophies. Of having a home. So Abby had always been there.

But they'd been there, too, in their own ways, and as often as they could. As Grant had entered his teens, his parents had cut back to a movie every other year, telling the media they wanted more time to devote to each project, when in fact they simply wanted more time with their son. His mother's embrace had never been uncomfortable, had never been unfamiliar. And now he found some tiny measure of solace in her arms.

"Abby's learning angel songs," his mother whispered in his ear.

"And teaching them how to make corn bread."

"Yes, son. And teaching them how to make corn bread."

She held him at arm's length and studied his face. "You need sleep, too, Grant."

He nodded sadly. "I know, Mom. But I also need to know what's going on. Jerry's holding down the fort, but I need to...I need to see."

Her grip on his arm tightened a bit. "Jerry Connally can see for us. He's a fine man. You come home and get some breakfast, at least."

He started to speak, but she cut him off. "I don't want to hear it. None of us is hungry. But you need food, son. And by God, you're going to eat."

The glint in her eye told him it was okay to smile, that he didn't have to fall and keep falling forever. He struggled to make the corners of his mouth lift a bit.

"No, Mother. I'm going to the house first. I'm going to speak to the police first. Then I'll come over and talk to the girls. In the meantime, make sure they don't see or hear the news."

She nodded, giving him the space to make his own decisions, which she still sometimes found hard to do.

He watched them drive away, then went back into the terminal, heading for the taxi stand.

Action was what he needed now, more than food, more than sleep. Even if action would save no one and nothing.

Karen Sweeney recognized him the minute he climbed out of the cab in front of the house. She almost sighed. She'd been about to leave the scene, to go home and grab a couple of hours of sleep. Now she had to do another interview and probably answer questions herself, questions for which she had no answers yet.

Grant Lawrence was sometimes referred to by the media as the next John Kennedy, and Lawrence really *did* have that magic. Karen, a lifelong Republican, somehow always found herself voting for Grant Lawrence, Democrat. He made sense. But more than making sense, he made the impossible seem possible, made the heart soar with hope that the world could be a better place. Like Kennedy, he never said it would be easy. He admitted to all the obstacles, then made you feel as if surmounting obstacles was the entire point.

She liked his attitude. And it didn't hurt that he could give a younger Robert Redford a run for his money in the looks department. Dark hair dashed with gray, perfectly chiseled features, a determined jaw, and a stride that said, *you can knock me around but you can't knock me down.*

And that bundle of talent, looks and potentially huge problems for her was walking her way right now, being passed through the cordon as if he were king. Nobody even asked him to wait.

This was Lawrence turf, even for the cops.

It struck her that all she thought she knew about him was public image, and that all her admiration for him wasn't going to make her job one iota easier. She suddenly wished someone else had been called on this case.

One of the cops pointed her out to him. Otherwise she was sure he never would have noticed an Irish wren with colorless eyes and her dark hair drawn impatiently back. Karen Sweeney had always been one to blend and never one to stand out.

But he was looking at her, straight at her, with electric blue eyes, bluer than she ever would have guessed from seeing him on the news and in the paper. He was also thinner than she had thought, and while tall, not quite as tall as he looked on the tube. He looked...not quite as imposing, yet somehow more powerful. Weird. And she needed to focus her sleepy brain before this politician ran roughshod over her and got information she wasn't supposed to give out. Before she forgot that *she* was the one who was supposed to be in control of the scene.

"Senator," she said simply.

"Detective," he answered. Then said nothing, as if waiting for her to fill in the missing pieces.

This close, she could see the fatigue and sorrow weighing down his features. The raw eyelids and cheekbones. In a moment he was no longer Senator Grant Lawrence, leading political light.

He was simply a man broken by violence.

"Jerry Connally told me he called you. I'm very sorry."

"Thank you," he said quietly. "Can I see her?"

She shook her head. "They've taken her away already. I hate to ask this, but I do need to go through the house with you. It looks like she surprised a burglar. Mr. Connally didn't notice anything missing, but...it's your house."

He simply nodded, and she continued.

"We can do it later. But it would help the investigation to know as soon as possible. If there was something stolen, finding it might help us find out who did this. A homicide trail goes cold fast."

"I understand, Detective." He glanced around. "Is Jerry here?"

He wanted the comfort of a familiar face, she could

tell. And she couldn't offer it. "I'm sorry. He went downtown to fill out a statement. Procedure."

"Yes. Procedure." He ran a hand through his hair, momentarily appearing utterly lost. Then he squared his shoulders. "Okay, Detective. Show me my home."

3

Grant Lawrence paused in the doorway and realized
his house had become an alien land. It wasn't just the
strangers who were everywhere, the police in their uniforms, the technicians with their cases and clipboards.
No, it wasn't that his house was full of strangers. For
Grant Lawrence, a stranger was merely an opportunity
to make a friend or an ally, and he met with many new
people right here in this house.

But the house was changed forever. It was no longer
his home. It had become the place where Abby had died.
It felt different. It smelled different. He stepped into it
as if stepping in a mausoleum.

He had been so shaken by the news of Abby's and
Stacy's deaths that he hadn't given much thought to how
they had happened. He wasn't spared the knowledge for
long. He turned toward the living room, that large, over-
decorated space where he often entertained, the creation
of his late wife's opulent taste, and he saw.

The sight knocked the wind from him, and he spun
away. It wasn't that he'd never seen bloody horror before. The memory of jagged white bone protruding from
his right shin, of bright, hot blood pulsing between his

fingers as he grabbed the wound, was still vivid. He knew *exactly* what he was seeing. But this time it had been Abby, his lifelong second mother. And Stacy, a woman he had once thought he might be in love with.

Oh, God! He leaned against a wall, hot and cold by turns, pressing his forehead against cool plaster, closing his eyes, trying to banish the image of what he'd just seen.

A hand touched his arm, a small hand with surprising strength. It gripped him. "Senator?" said the smoky voice of Detective Sweeney. "Do you need to sit?"

"I'll be all right." He had to be all right. As had happened so many times in his life, he had no choice but to be all right.

He drew a steadying breath, regaining his self-command. A line from one of his father's favorite poems floated unbidden through his consciousness. *If you can meet with triumph and disaster/And treat those two imposters just the same.* Rudyard Kipling's idealized "Man" would have known how to handle this.

"I'm sorry," she said. "I should have warned you."

He raised his head, pushed himself away from the wall and looked at her. "Why? That would have deprived you of the opportunity to see my initial reaction."

He thought she flushed faintly, but if so, it was nearly invisible. "Senator, you were in Washington. You're not a suspect."

He knew better. Jerry had found Abby and Stacy, and had called him before he called the police. This detective didn't look like the type who would overlook or ignore the obvious possibility of complicity.

He had to be careful not to mention Stacy, at least until he knew what the hell Jerry had done. He wasn't going to betray his friend over something that was relatively unimportant. If it *was* unimportant.

He shook himself. He would have to deal with Jerry later. That would be then. This was now. "How did it happen?"

"Her throat was cut."

"My God!" He closed his eyes for a moment, absorbing the enormity, trying not to think of Abby's last few moments. *Abby.* Far more important to him than Stacy in so many ways. But both were dead. *Both.*

"Look," said Detective Sweeney, "you don't have to go into that room. It's obvious the valuables in there weren't taken. But I need to know about the rest of the house."

He nodded, clamping down on the horror he felt. "Fine, let's go." He would have time later for feelings. He'd learned that long ago. There were a lot of things better put on hold until he had privacy to think about them and feel them. Otherwise, it was as his mother had once said: if there's one other person who can see you, you're on camera.

Why hadn't Jerry warned him about what he would see?

The rest of the first floor was undisturbed. The farther he got from his living room, the more he could almost lull himself into thinking everything was normal. Until he reached his office. A file drawer, almost but not quite closed, a discrepancy that most people might not have even noticed, alerted him.

"Detective, those cabinets were locked."

"Mr. Connally said he came for some papers."

He looked at her, noticing again that her eyes were almost colorless, but now they had taken on an almost preternatural focus. As if she had picked up on something. He wondered if he imagined the way her delicate nostrils seemed to flare, testing the breeze.

He spoke. "I called him last night to pick up some things for me and express them to Washington. But he wouldn't have left the files open."

She nodded and moved forward, coming within inches of the cabinets. "It looks like this lock was picked." She faced him. "What's in here?"

"Background information on a conservation bill I authored. Scientific reports, mostly, the stuff I brought down from D.C. to study while I'm here. Some from independent research firms, some from the EPA."

She looked at the lock again, then moved down the row of file cabinets. "They've all been jimmied. By someone in a hurry. Who would want these papers? Sugar growers?"

He gave her marks for environmental awareness. "They're opposed to the bill, yes. Among many others in agriculture. But I find it hard to believe they would kill to get a look at these documents."

"Maybe, maybe not." She looked his way again, her gray eyes opaque. "Anyone else who might be on the list?"

"I don't know." He sighed and rubbed his eyes, and tried to focus on what she needed, reminding himself it was all he could do to help Abby and Stacy now. "I have all kinds of political enemies, Detective. Any man in my position does. But it's hard to imagine them committing murder."

"I agree. But the murder may have been purely incidental."

Something in him flared, and his voice grew deadly quiet. "There's nothing incidental about what happened here."

Her expression never wavered. "Poor choice of words, Senator. I merely meant that murder was probably not the intention, but rather the result of panic on the part of the intruder. Except…"

Her voice trailed off, and she began to walk around the room, studying the bookshelves, the neat desktop, the view out the back window over well-tended gardens, now a riot of fresh April color. What a sorry ending to his daughters' spring vacation.

"Except what?" he demanded when she said nothing further.

"Except," she said finally, "I wonder how it was that Ms. Reese came upon him in the living room."

His head snapped up a bit as he realized what she was saying. "I don't keep anything of importance out there. Nothing of political importance, anyway."

"I would think not. Well, it might have just happened that way. Maybe he heard Abby coming and darted in there to hide."

Or maybe not. Grant felt his neck chill with a premonition of ugliness yet to be found. Stacy had been here, too. But he couldn't tell her that. What if Stacy had had something to do with the break-in? What if she'd brought someone here to give them access to his papers, then had been killed to keep her silent? And what if *that* was what Abby had stumbled into?

He felt, suddenly, as if he were standing on the narrow tip of a very windy precipice, barely maintaining balance. He understood from Jerry's cryptic remark on the phone that Jerry had removed Stacy from the house. He could have meant nothing else. And so far the police had only mentioned Abby, so they knew nothing about Stacy. God, he didn't want to think about the legal ramifications of that for Jerry.

But it also put *him* in a precarious position. He had information that might be relevant to the investigation, information he couldn't share without getting his closest aide into trouble, without exposing his children to the kind of scandal he'd been protecting them from for years. And protecting his daughters came first, came before everything else. Including his presidential aspirations.

"I'm going to have the file cabinets dusted for prints, Senator. Afterwards, I'd like you to tell me what, if anything, is missing from them."

"Very well."

"What's in the desk?"

"Just stationery, pens, pencils, pads, things like that. All my papers are in the file cabinets."

She nodded and gave him what he supposed was meant to be an encouraging smile. "Could your computer have been tampered with?"

He shook his head. "I wouldn't think so. It's password protected. But even if it were...I don't keep much on it. Drafts of speeches I'm thinking of making, little things like that. When I'm in town, Detective, I'm usually busy with constituents, and any private time I have is largely for *thinking,* not doing. That computer is full of a lot of quick notes and thoughts, but little else. If someone were going to commit electronic theft for political gain, he'd be better off hacking into the network server at my office, in Washington. That's where we do the real grunt work."

She looked at the monitor and keyboard sitting on his desk. "Then I doubt anyone got into it. I'll have someone check to make sure it hasn't been physically tampered with. But given that our perp was clearly in a hurry, it's not likely."

She turned to him again. "Let's take a look upstairs now."

He followed her up the sweeping staircase, one of the features that Georgina, his late wife, had loved about this house. To him it had always seemed pretentious, something better suited to an antebellum mansion. But Georgina had had her eye even more firmly fixed on the presidency than he had. Sometimes he thought this house had been his wife's rehearsal for the White House.

He dreaded what he might find up there. Signs of Stacy's presence? What had she been doing here? They'd broken off months ago, in mutual realization of the cost. Stacy had been a wonderful woman, but both he and she had seen the handwriting on the wall.

He'd met her on the rebound from his wife's death—strangely enough, not at the club where she worked, but in his local office, when she came to help stuff envelopes during his last campaign. But rebounds can only bounce for so long. Their parting had been amicable. Understanding. And he'd long since quietly found a way to make sure Stacy could open the dance studio she'd always dreamt of, rather than baring her body for strange men in a dark, noisy, impersonal bar.

He had thought their relationship had been secret from everyone but Jerry. What if it hadn't been? What if someone had staged this murder simply to ruin him? Somehow that seemed more believable than that someone had committed two murders over S.R. 52.

He had the worst urge to tell the detective all of this, to clear his conscience, to remove himself from this terrible position of obstructing an investigation. Damn Jerry for putting him between a rock and a hard place.

And then he remembered his daughters. He couldn't expose them to the scandal. He'd been through media feeding frenzies before. It had been by the skin of his teeth that he'd kept the press from discovering the truth about the auto accident that had killed his wife. Where she'd been coming from. Knowledge that, if made public, would have done nothing but cause more pain.

So he'd managed to protect the girls that time. They still remembered their mother as an angel who'd been stolen from them. They deserved that memory—however inaccurate he knew it to be—and he would do anything to protect it.

God, he hated this.

His room was first, to the right. A suite from which he'd erased all vestiges of his wife. It was spare now, with white walls, heavy brown velvet curtains and lots of dark wood. Masculine, almost monastic. His own eyrie. No woman set foot in here save the cleaning crew and his daughters. A wave of relief crashed through him when he saw the bed was carefully made. He'd feared he might find the brown duvet tossed back, evidence of Stacy's presence.

The children's rooms were undisturbed. They had a bright airy space, a playroom full of toys, with their bedrooms opening off it to either side. Then there was the formal guest room, untouched for years.

And to the rear, Abby's room. Her own retreat, filled with tatting and embroidery, flowery cushions, curtains and bed linen. The rocking chair, in which he would forever see Abby, stood still and empty.

The bedcovers were tossed back, indicating that she had left her bed to go downstairs. No light was on except the night-light Abby kept so the children could find her if they needed her during the night. Her bathroom was neat as a pin, as it always was.

The photos on her dresser were of him, at all stages

of his life, from infancy on, and of his growing daughters.

When Grant saw them, he could no longer contain himself. He sat in the rocking chair where he had been comforted so many times as a child and began to weep.

Karen was discomfited by Grant Lawrence's breakdown. It wasn't that she hadn't seen them often during her years on the force, especially since it was so often her job to break the bad news.

But Grant Lawrence was different. To her he had somehow always seemed a magical being, his footprints gilded as he strode through life. She knew about his wife's tragic death, of course, and remembered how he had emerged from that period with the first gray showing in his hair. The story of the horrific childhood injury that had left him with an almost imperceptible limp was the stuff of political legend. But these potholes in an otherwise star-kissed life had only seemed to strengthen him.

Now she was faced with the fact that the mythical being, the possible next president of the United States, was only human after all. His grief was deep and raw, and she had to battle an urge to put an arm around him and try to comfort him.

Instead, she did what she was trained to do. She walked away, looking out the sliding glass doors of Abby's room onto a balcony that had a view of the gardens, delicate and vital, carefully-sculpted paths among splashes of azalea and bougainvillea, orchid and mum, bamboo and palm, disparate and yet melding together into a whole that spoke volumes about the man who sat behind her, sobbing.

These people, she thought, had more money than she

could imagine. Most of it had come from his film tycoon parents, although she knew he had managed to make some of his own fortune, both before and since his ascension to the Senate. But regardless of where it came from, it was more than she could imagine having.

It was a world so different from hers that she found it difficult to connect with. Unlike many, she didn't begrudge the wealthy their good fortune; she simply couldn't imagine what their world must be like. Standing here now, she felt she was looking through a window into places where the ordinary woes of life never intruded.

But that wasn't true. The roses in that garden had thorns, and she had no doubt that a gardener had to pull the same kinds of weeds she struggled with in the tiny plot beside her own home. Behind her a very powerful man was weeping like a baby over the death of his nanny. Reality intruded here, too, in its ugliest forms.

"I'm sorry."

His voice, sounding raw and thick, reached her.

"Don't apologize, Senator," she said, without turning. "You're entitled to your grief."

"Yes, but I'm sure your job is already difficult enough."

She started a little, surprised by his perception. Surprised by his kindness. Very few people in his position were ever aware of hers. Very few considered that she might find it almost as difficult to be the bearer of bad news as they found it to receive it. But this was the quality she'd always found admirable in him, she reminded herself: his ability to put himself in the shoes of others.

"It's okay," she said, a little too quickly. "I'm used to it."

''Really? Somehow I doubt it.''

She heard him blow his nose. Then the rocking chair creaked. He must be rising.

''I don't see anything disturbed here,'' he said. ''It's...obvious she climbed out of bed when she heard something.''

''So it would appear.'' She turned to look at him again and felt a tug on her heart when she saw the redness of his eyes. ''Tell me about Abby.''

''What do you need to know?''

''The kind of person she was.''

Grant came to stand by her at the doors and looked out on the garden. ''Tough. She was very tough. When I was a child, she protected me fiercely. I remember once she chased some *paparazzi* away from the windows of my parents' house.'' A faint smile curved his mouth. ''She grabbed up a broom and went after them. They never came back.'' He turned his head, and their gazes met. ''She protected my children the same way.''

''She was getting old.''

''Yes. But she was family. I know people tried to make an issue out of her race years back, but she'd come into this family when she was fifteen years old, and by the time I was born, there was no question but what Abby was family. Part of us, made so by love.'' He paused for a moment. ''You know, a former advisor once said I should get rid of her. Said her presence in my life harkened back to an ugly period in the history of the south. I fired him on the spot. I'd sooner have thrown out my mother.''

''What about *her* family?''

''She had none. She was an orphan.'' His gaze grew distant and drifted back to the garden. ''Do you know how she came to my family?''

"No."

"My grandfather took Abby in after her entire family was killed in a church bombing. The Klan. The bomb killed seven people, including Abby's parents and her older brother. Abby was sick that night. She'd stayed home.

"So my grandfather took her in. At this late date, I'm not sure of what he intended, but I *do* know he was outraged by the event. Anyway, my dad was five, and Abby seemed to take to caring for him. And that's where it began."

"And she never wanted to leave?"

"She never gave any indication if she did. She had a romance once, this really dapper guy my dad still has pictures of. But then one day she announced he was shiftless, and that was the end of that."

"Why was he shiftless?"

His gaze saddened, and he closed his eyes. "I guess I'll never know now."

"Thank you, Senator," Karen said after a moment. "You've been a great help. Where can I reach you when I need to?"

"At my parents' place." He gave her the number. "I'd appreciate it if you'd keep that under your hat. My girls are there, too, and I don't want them…exposed."

"I understand."

She watched him leave the room and thought that his shoulders looked less square and his limp a bit more pronounced.

It was sad.

4

"**J**erry, where the hell are you?"

Jerry Connally's hand shook as he held his cell phone to his ear and heard Grant Lawrence's voice. "I'm in the car, Grant. On the way home from the police station."

He heard the pause before his friend spoke. "What have you told them?"

"I told them the truth. I came over to pick up the files you needed and found Abby. I checked out the house, called you, then called them. Straight, simple and to the point."

And true, although not the whole truth. He had, of course, left out the part about lifting Stacy's lifeless remains, fighting back the sheer revulsion at what had been done to her, gagging at what he himself was doing, carrying her to the trunk of his car and placing her in that alley.

He hadn't approved of Grant's relationship with Stacy, but he couldn't help but admire and even like her. She was a tough, no-nonsense woman who'd fought off the demons of an abusive childhood. Some would say she hadn't gone far, working as a stripper. That was how she'd made her living, but it hadn't been who she was.

She would have been death for Grant's career, and still might be, but there was no way she deserved what he'd done to her, to be left without dignity in a dark, dirty alley. He would live the rest of his life with the memory of that. But he'd done what he had to for his friend.

"What about Stacy?" he heard Grant ask.

Yes. What about Stacy? "She wasn't there. And I won't say anything more. For your sake."

"Plausible deniability? Jerry, you know I've always thought that was bullshit."

"And you're right. It is. But sometimes bullshit is the best option available." Jerry stopped at a red light and realized his arm ached from the tension of his grip on the wheel.

Grant Lawrence was as brilliant a man as Jerry had ever known. But sometimes even the most brilliant men needed a trusted friend to lay it out for them.

"Look, Senator, here are the facts. If it comes out about you and Stacy, there'll be a Grade-A shitstorm. Forget your chances for president. They'll be ancient history. But let's put that aside for a moment. S.R. 52 will die a quick and painful death. Right now, we need three votes in the House and one in the Senate, and it passes. And it's *good* law, Grant. It's *important* law."

Grant sounded impatient. "I know that, Jerry."

"No, sir, I don't think you do." He hated to play this card, but sometimes it mattered. "You're a hell of a man, Grant. Smart and honest and strong. But you also had a hell of a head start in life. For you, this bill is about snorkeling in the Keys when you were a teenager. Beyond that it's about abstractions. Economics, numbers and the world your children will inherit. And yes, that's important.

"But I didn't snorkel when I was a kid. I watched my dad's hands bleed as he hauled in crab traps on a smelly, oily dock on Chesapeake Bay. I got out because I could run and catch a football well enough to get a scholarship. But my brother's still there, in a town that's dying because the crab traps are coming up lighter and lighter, year by year. His hands are still bloody, and he has less and less to show for it. He's the human face I see on S.R. 52. If you go down, he goes down. My hometown goes down."

He heard the honking behind him and realized the light had turned to green. A car flashed around him as he pulled into the intersection, the driver yelling an obscenity as he passed.

"Grant, right now you're still golden under the law. You don't know anything, and you're under no legal obligation to say anything. And as much as it may raise your moral hackles, that's the way it has to stay. My brother and my hometown and thousands of other hometowns just like it, they need you. So if this hits the fan, I'll take the fall. Not you."

"Drop by my parents' house this afternoon and we'll talk about it."

Jerry suppressed a sigh. "I'll be there, sir. But this one is non-negotiable."

"We'll talk about it," Grant repeated.

The squad room was curiously quiet as Karen walked in and sagged into her chair. She was alone but for Dave Previn, who seemed to be trying to bury his head in his hands as he talked on the phone. Karen switched on her computer and spread her notes on her desk. She needed to get the initial reports in while the information was fresh, but her mind rebelled at the thought of anything but sleep. Previn finally hung up the phone and leaned back in his chair with a heavy sigh. When their eyes met, he spoke.

"You wouldn't think planning a boy's tenth birthday party would be this frigging complicated. But Linda wants to go all out. And it has to *matter* to me whether the picture on the cake is a Buccaneers' helmet or their flag."

"And good morning to you, too," Karen said simply. "Go with the helmet."

"You think I'm going to call her back?" He shook his head. "Uh-uh. Not this little gray duck."

His face said what everyone in the office knew, but no one talked about: his marriage was a mess. She looked around. "So where is everyone?"

Dave gave a disgusted look. "Task force meeting. Apparently the College Hill drive-by opened up a whole can of worms. The civil rights caucus says we're not doing enough to stop the violence in the projects. The mayor has egg on his face. Now it's top priority and all that. Like we wouldn't care about murder otherwise."

Karen nodded. "To protect and to serve, right?"

"Whatever. Oh, and the lieutenant wants to see you about the Senator Lawrence thing. Probably another task force in the making. We ought to form a task force on task forces."

"The lieutenant's not in on the College Hill thing?"

"Sure he is. He wants you to interrupt him. So congratulations, Karen. You're front-page news."

She rose from her seat. "Just what I always wanted."

The task force had taken over the largest conference room on the floor. From the sounds she heard outside the door, tempers were fraying. She considered going back to write her reports, to let Lieutenant Simpson calm down before she met with him. But he would probably be even angrier if she did.

With a brief knock, she opened the door and stepped into a chaotic swirl of voices and a view of Fred Lowery gesturing at a dry-erase board scrawled with multi-colored threads of preliminary evidence. Warren Simpson sat at the near end of the table, paperwork inter-mixed with the foam-boxed leftovers of McDonald's pancakes and sausage, syrup-dappled paper napkins and an extra large coffee mug that was his office trademark. The voices quieted as she entered—a brief symphony of terse "Hiyas" and "What's ups?"—and Simpson turned to look.

He reached for his mug. "Excuse me, y'all." His bar-itone voice poured out like molasses, thick and rich. Without another word, he rose and led Karen out and to his office, closing the door behind them. His eyes swept over her briefly. "You look like you need to sit down."

"At least," Karen said. "A few hours' sleep wouldn't hurt, either."

He nodded. "Seems to be an epidemic around here. So what's the deal on the Lawrence case?"

Cases were usually referred to by the victim's name. In almost any other situation, this would be the Reese case, but Abigail Reese was as subsumed in death as she had been in life.

Or maybe not. Maybe it was simply that she really was part of the Lawrence family. That option left less of a bitter taste in her mouth.

"Apparently she surprised a burglar. He may have been after some of the senator's files." She gave him a quick rundown of her morning. "But there's more to it.

Jerry Connally—the senator's chief of staff or some such—was holding something back.''

Simpson grunted. "Hardly surprising.'' He leaned forward. "Okay, here's the deal. We have two messes in the making, and the media are going to be all over both of them. Any other month and I'd put a half-dozen detectives on this with you. No stone unturned and all that. But if I do that, the civil rights caucus will play the race card, saying we're more worried about a rich white senator than we are about poor black kids dying in the streets.''

"Never mind that Abigail Reese was a black woman,'' Karen said.

"Right. And never mind that cleaning out the projects would take a hell of a lot more than just busting the gang-bangers. Regardless, the mayor has spoken—and loudly.'' He paused for a moment, drawing tiny circles on his desk blotter. "And you know what? In the big scheme of things, the mayor might be right. So College Hill gets as much as we can put there. Which means you're on point with Senator Lawrence.''

What he said made sense on a lot of levels. And it was true that, in the big scheme of things, it might well be better to focus the city's efforts at trying to bring some measure of safety and hope to the bleak lives in the projects. Abigail Reese's murder, however ugly and awful, did not seem to be a symptom of a festering cancer in the city. The College Hill murders were, without doubt.

She nodded. "Yes, sir.''

"So what's your caseload right now?''

"Not too bad. I have six active cases, plus the two from tonight. The state attorney says he'll probably get pleas on four of them. The Hart case goes to trial next month. And I'm still waiting on ballistics on Vance. If they come back positive—and they will—that'll plead out, too."

"So you're clear except for Lawrence."

"And the girl in the alley," Karen said.

"I'll pull you off that. Previn can take it."

Karen shifted in her seat. "I don't think that's a good idea, sir. Previn's only been here three months. He's not ready to solo."

And the unidentified white female deserved better than to get swept aside onto a rookie homicide detective whose marriage was crumbling before his eyes. The sight of her torn body still lingered in Karen's eyes.

Simpson studied her face for a moment. "Okay. So you keep an eye on Previn on the alley thing. But you need to keep your focus on Lawrence. You're going to get a lot of attention. Don't fuck up."

"Yes, sir."

Randall Youngblood scanned the e-mail once again. Like any prominent businessman, he'd had his share of dealings with the media. Some good, some not. Over the years, he'd made a practice of cultivating friendships with reporters whose views or stories were sympathetic. In return, he would slip them advance notice of any news from his industry. One hand washed the other.

He had known the reporter from whom he'd received this e-mail for twelve years. It wasn't the first time the man had given him a heads-up on a story that might affect him. The story would break on that day's television news, but the TV folks wouldn't mention the jimmied files or their contents. The newspapers might, but probably not for a few days. The immediate coverage would focus on the senator's lifelong relationship with his nanny. Vague possibilities of political maneuvering, or worse, would be unseemly. So he had a few days' lead time.

He tapped the intercom button on his phone and entered a three-digit extension. "Michaels, are you busy? Well, you just got busier."

Four minutes later, Bill Michaels strode into his office. Michaels never walked. He strode. He'd been an Olympic gymnast in college, and his smallish but solid frame still moved with a dancer's grace. More than one opponent in a courtroom or across a negotiating table had taken the wrong first impression from that. It was not a mistake to be made twice. Bill Michaels was as savvy a legal predator as had ever hefted a briefcase.

"Grant Lawrence's nanny was killed last night," Randall said without preamble.

Michaels nodded. "I heard something about it on the radio news."

"Well, you didn't hear this part. Apparently someone broke into his office files. Including his S.R. 52 files. We had nothing to do with that." If that was a question, it demanded only one answer.

"Of course not, sir."

"Fine. I'll stand by that." Randall leaned back and propped his feet on the bottom drawer of his desk. "So…how can we take advantage of this?"

Bill considered. "We've got a few days before that breaks."

"I'd think so, although with the goddamn piranhas in the media, I wouldn't book odds on it."

Michaels nodded. "Very well, sir. I want to refresh my memory on all circumstances surrounding Lawrence's life and political activities. I'll return with a report in two or three hours."

Randall Youngblood nodded. Then he put his feet firmly on the floor and faced Michaels. "Grant Lawrence and I go way back, Michaels. Sometimes we agree, and sometimes we disagree. I don't hate the man."

"I understand that, sir."

"Be sure you do." Then he waved a hand, dismissing Michaels, and propped his feet up again. It was a damn good thing he had a piranha of his own.

Breaking the news to Belle and Catherine Suzanne proved to be absolutely, without question, one of the most painful experiences of Grant Lawrence's life. It had been bad enough when he'd been told he might need to wear a brace or use a crutch for the rest of his life— he'd beaten that one pretty good, thank God—and it had been really tough to try to explain to a five-year-old Cathy that her mother would never come home again.

But this one was infinitely harder. In the first place, Belle was no longer a baby, so he had two pairs of horrified, disbelieving, stunned blue eyes looking back at him, innocent blue eyes that were unable to fully grasp one of the world's greatest evils: death.

And there was his own emotional devastation. Grant had loved Abby in a way he had loved no one else. It hurt to speak of her death, hurt to try to explain to the daughters he loved beyond life that one of their mainstays was gone forever. It hurt like *hell*.

But he got the words out, forced them past a throat so thick and tight that each one was squeezed. He managed to remind them that when people died they went to live with God and the angels, and that even now Abby was looking down on them and watching over them, even though they would no longer see her.

Belle, in all seriousness, wanted to know what angel song Abby was probably learning right now. For several moments, Grant couldn't even speak. He bit his lip hard and closed his eyes against a tidal wave of anguish and loss. What song would an angel sing?

All he could think of was a section of the liturgy of the Catholic Mass.

"Well," he said, clearing his throat and trying to smile at Belle, "I imagine the first song she's learning is *Glory to God in the highest, and peace to his people on earth....*"

"But, Daddy, we sing that in church."

"I know, sweetie. I think the angels taught us, too. But Abby went to a different church. I don't think she knows that song, so they're probably teaching it to her. I mean, she already knows so many hymns that they'd hardly teach her one she knows."

Belle nodded, satisfied. "I'll sing it, too. Abby will sing it with me."

Grant's heart fractured along a fresh fault line, but he held the ache inside. "Abby would like that." Then he looked at Cathy Suzanne, who had so far not said a word. She looked back solemnly at him, her gaze conveying a wider understanding of death than Belle's. But of course. She was older, and she still remembered her deceased mother.

Finally Cathy spoke. "She was getting old, Daddy."

"Yes." He didn't want her to know yet that age hadn't been the demon.

"She told me once that she might die before too long because she was getting old. She said she'd be sorry to leave us, but she was beginning to ache for her home in heaven."

"She did?"

Cathy nodded, still solemn, and turned away. "I know Abby didn't believe in our church," she said quietly, "but I think I'll say a rosary anyway."

"Me too," said Belle, racing to get her rosary beads.

Once her sister had left the room, Cathy looked into her father's eyes. "Daddy? It's okay to cry."

And as soon as he was alone, that was exactly what he did.

Jerry arrived about one-thirty. On any other day, Grant might have noticed just how worn, jumpy and unhappy Jerry looked. On any other day he might have been concerned for his old friend. Today they were both pole-axed, and there didn't seem much unusual about Jerry's state.

He took his aide out into the gardens. Grant's parents lived far more opulently than he did, and it was possible to get lost on their estate, built long ago when Florida land was cheap and the snowbirds hadn't begun to arrive in large numbers. The days when the Don CeSar hotel had been *the* place for Hollywood types to vacation. In the gardens of the elder Lawrences, it was possible to disappear.

Which was exactly what he did with Jerry. He guided him to the farthest reaches of the gardens, to a place where there was a nook with a stone bench beneath a trellis covered in roses.

"Okay," Grant said when they were sitting side-by-side, a gentle onshore breeze reaching them. "What did you get me into?"

"I didn't get you into anything," Jerry said firmly. "I got myself into something, and we're going to leave it that way."

"What about Stacy?" Grant's voice broke on the name.

"She was dead, Grant. What the hell difference does it make, as long as your chances for the presidency, and S.R. 52, don't get derailed? Dead is dead."

Grant didn't speak. He couldn't speak. "Jerry, tampering—"

"Don't say that word. I'm a lawyer. I know the situation. What I *don't* want is for *you* to know it, so will you just stop badgering me? For all you know, I heard of Stacy's death elsewhere."

Grant hesitated, looking down at the pebble path, at the gleam of his polished shoes, thinking he'd been wearing this suit for two straight days and he was probably beginning to stink. Thinking about irrelevancies in order to avoid the bigger issues.

"Sometimes," he said slowly, "I just want to tell that detective everything."

"Everything? What? Just what is the *everything* you think you know? Believe me, Grant, you *don't* know, so just shut up about it."

Jerry rarely talked to him that way. It was a sign of his distress, and Grant recognized it. He looked at his friend, taking in the tightness of Jerry's face, the sagging of his mouth, the wariness of his eyes.

"All right," he said finally. His heart was heavy with it, but he knew it was time for compromise. Politics had taught him that there was very little room in the world for sheer altruism. One hand washed the other. Compromises were the means of achievement, and some things were better left unsaid.

Whatever Jerry had done, Grant had to keep his mouth shut about it. He had to protect his friend; he had to protect himself and his children. He had to protect his shot at the presidency.

There was too much at stake here to indulge in an orgy of soul-baring that wouldn't help a damn thing. It certainly wouldn't bring Abby or Stacy back.

"You're safe with me," he told Jerry.

Jerry's hollow eyes looked back at him. "I hope you know you're safe with me, too."

Grant nodded, but given what had happened overnight, given that there was now a secret between them that he could only guess at, he wasn't as sure of that as he might have been only yesterday.

Shortly after Jerry left, Randall Youngblood called. The call might have gone unanswered except that the weekly maid was there and picked it up.

Grant took the call in his parents' study, sitting in the deep leather chair that over the years had become contoured to his father's body. "Hello?" he said.

"Grant." The use of his first name was a signal that this was to be a personal conversation. Grant relaxed a shade. He was not up to a political discussion right now. "I'm sorry," Youngblood continued. "I heard the news a little while ago. I am so sorry."

Grant had to swallow before he could answer. It surprised him how painful an expression of sympathy could feel. "Thanks."

"I just want you to know…well, I'm laying off for a week, okay? I won't lobby until you get back in the saddle."

"That's very good of you." And only slightly surprising. In this game, nobody burned bridges lightly, because you never knew when you might become allies. He and Randall Youngblood were opponents right now, but there had been times when they'd been allies, and there would be again.

"It seems like the right thing to do," Youngblood said. "You've got enough to deal with right now. Just let me know if I can do anything."

"Thank you. I will."

But after he hung up, Grant sat a while, thinking about how important blocking this bill was to Youngblood and his cohorts. And wondering what Youngblood would be doing during this hiatus on public lobbying.

Because he knew Youngblood and company weren't going to halt completely.

As Cathy Suzanne would say, "No way, Jose."

5

Randall Youngblood was rarely an impatient man. He'd been in agribusiness, and on the cane growers' association board, too long to have remained impatient. All things developed in their own damn time, and pushing and pulling rarely accomplished anything.

But this day he was impatient. He smelled blood. The question was whether it was *his* blood, his and the rest of the cane growers, or whether it was Grant Lawrence's blood. He knew which way he needed to tip the scales, but waiting for Bill Michaels to come back to him was proving very difficult.

Standing at his window in the penthouse office of a tall building in Miami, he looked out toward the Glades and considered his situation. The simple fact was, the death of Abby Reese, a figure who was known to the public to be well-loved by Grant Lawrence, was going to create a firestorm of sympathy for the senator. Hell, he felt an aching sympathy himself. But that sympathy had to be stemmed somehow, or S.R. 52 might sail through the Senate and House as an act of political compassion. Even if it was enough to tip the scales just a little bit more toward Grant, it could wind up being a done deal.

As a cane grower, Randall Youngblood knew very well how too many environmental restrictions were going to kill both his business and much of the most important business of south Florida. Depriving the growers of their right to use fertilizers and insecticides, demanding that large areas of the river of grass, now dry, be gradually returned to their previously flooded state, thus wiping out massive acreage now in production, would be an economic disaster.

Because if the Florida growers couldn't keep their prices down, foreign supplies of cane sugar would become the cheaper alternative.

It wasn't that Randall Youngblood didn't care about the coral reefs along the Keys, or the state of the water and fisheries out there. He did care. But he also cared that he and his colleagues not be wiped out in a headlong rush to undo eighty years of draining, reclaiming and planting.

S.R. 52 would cause reclamation to happen far too fast. It would wipe out lives and livelihoods beyond anything he figured Grant Lawrence had even imagined. Things like this needed to be taken very, *very* slowly. And Lawrence didn't seem to understand that.

The senator didn't understand the economic ripple effect that would occur when, lacking fertilizers and pesticides, per-acre yields plummeted and the layoffs began. The ripples that would run through other south Florida businesses, sinking them when they had no customers. Then it would spread out in ever-widening waves, because the businesses that would fail in south Florida would no longer be buying supplies from businesses elsewhere. Randall Youngblood could see that as clearly

as he could see his hand before his face. And because
S.R. 52 covered all of agriculture, the disaster that would
stem from south Florida was only a small part of the
overall picture.

Then there was the truly major issue of America's
position as a beacon of hope in an ever-hungrier world.

It wasn't too much of a stretch to say that the Soviet
Union had been brought down by the Randall Young-
bloods of the United States. People who lived in per-
petual near-famine looked with envy upon the opulence
of American life, and nowhere was that opulence more
apparent than in the ordinary supermarket. Fresh vegetables, meats, breads, all manner of foods, readily available, at affordable prices, on any given day.

And that was, in large part, a function of chemical
fertilizers and pesticides. Lawrence might not see it, but
the birthday cake he would have at his daughter's party
was a byproduct of the very industries his legislation was
trying to undermine. And Randall, for one, did not want
to pay ten dollars a pound for sugar, or five dollars a
pound for tomatoes. That was the alternative S.R. 52
would make inevitable.

The simple fact was that Americans liked to live
above their means, and the agriculture industry helped
to make that possible by producing a comparative abun-
dance of food. Yes, the cost of that was being passed on
to future generations, in the form of environmental
changes that would have to be dealt with. Grant
Lawrence and others seemed to view that as a moral
issue, but it wasn't. It was a political issue, a choice
made by the citizens of a democratic society. And they
made that choice every time they went to the supermarket and bought ordinary produce rather than the more

expensive, "all natural" items that were never more than a niche market.

Senate Resolution 52 had to fail. Not to make Randall Youngblood rich—he was already rich—but to keep America fed, fit and strong.

He was ruminating on that thought when Bill Michaels knocked at his door.

"So where do we stand?" Randall asked.

Michaels had that look in his eyes again, the look of a lion on the fringe of a herd of gazelles. "I think we have an angle to play."

Randall nodded for him to continue.

"The media's going to spin Lawrence as the victim of yet another personal tragedy. They'll bring up his wife's death. Hero conquers adversity and all that."

"Right," Randall said.

"Well, there's a rumor that the public didn't get the whole story when Lawrence's wife died. They don't have anything specific. Just that certain lines of inquiry were deflected, very obliquely, very discreetly."

"Could be something," Randall said. "And it could be nothing. And it could be something that'll make him even more the hero."

"That's true. And obviously we don't want to open that can of worms before we know what the worms look like. But I've got a man looking into it."

"Anything else?" Randall knew something that vague wasn't enough to get Michaels' blood pumping.

Michaels, ever the performer, let the moment hang for just a beat longer. "Yes. My source also says there's something fishy about the nanny's death."

"Fishy how?"

"He doesn't know yet," Michaels said. "But the lead

detective—a woman named Karen Sweeney—doesn't like the smell of it.''

"Stay on it," Randall said. "And stay invisible."

Michaels smiled. Randall hoped he himself would never be the object of that particular smile.

"I'll handle it, sir."

Grant Lawrence called the homicide squad himself in the late afternoon. It felt strange to do it, rather than have someone else handle it for him, the way so many things in his life were handled for him, by people who seemed to be in a conspiracy to protect him from the ordinary details of his life.

He had secretaries, both in Washington and in his public offices here. He had Jerry Connally, his right hand. All of them seemed to want to handle everything for him, sometimes even including his political duties. Occasionally he felt hemmed in. Mostly he was grateful to be able to keep his focus.

But today he made the call himself. A supplicant, which wasn't a familiar position for him anymore. But he sure as hell didn't want to bring Jerry into contact with the police more than necessary, and he knew if he called his secretary at the local office, she would have a ton of messages from the press, constituents and colleagues. He wasn't ready to deal with any of that.

So he called robbery-homicide and asked to speak to Detective Sweeney. Much to his amazement, she was there.

"Yes, Senator," she said. "What can I do for you?"

"I was wondering if I might be able to get into my house. There are some things I want for my daughters. Frankly, Detective, they need the comfort of the familiar right now. Their own clothes, their own toys, their own pillows and blankets. I left Washington in such a hurry this morning that I didn't even pack for them, other than bringing Belle's favorite stuffed animal and Catherine Suzanne's blanket.''

"I understand." Her voice remained detached. "Let's see…I'll be leaving here in about an hour. How about I meet you at your house in an hour and a half?"

"That would be fine. Thank you, Detective."

"No problem, Senator."

But as he hung up, he realized it might be a problem for her. Through the detachment of her voice, he had sensed great fatigue. Well, she'd been up most of the night. He brushed away the concern that he was imposing even more on her limited time. His girls came first, and he wasn't going to let their needs go unmet.

The phones at his parents' house had been ringing most of the day, and the line he had been on rang as soon as he hung up. The family wasn't answering. His parents' assistant, Keith Fairfield, was taking all the calls and messages in the office four blocks away, through the magic of call forwarding. Poor Keith. He was probably ready to tear his hair out…as were his own secretaries, now that he thought about it.

He was going to have to speak to the press at some point. There was no escaping it. At the very least, he needed to issue a statement. He realized without guilt that he was trying to avoid what had happened, unwilling to address it head-on.

He shook his head as if trying to clear it, feeling the fatigue of a sleepless night and the unbearable weight of grief trying to bend him, break him. It would be nice to let go, but it wouldn't do any good. Nor could he afford to.

The girls were outside with their grandparents, splashing in the pool, resilient as only the very young could be. He watched them for a few minutes through the glass doors, a faint smile lifting the corners of his mouth. His daughters were his *raison d'etre,* even more than the political career to which he devoted so much of his time and energy. It did his aching heart good to see them enjoying themselves, to see that they could escape the grief that had haunted their lives, even for a little while.

Then he went to dress for his meeting with Karen Sweeney, well aware that the press would be there, and would demand an answer to the stupidest question in the world: "How do you *feel,* Senator?"

He shook his head again, feeling as if cobwebs clung to his brain, and dressed for television because he was going to be on television whether he wanted to or not.

So he wore dark slacks and a dark shirt. He took a few minutes to shave, but he would be damned if he'd put on a suit. They were just going to have to take him as he was.

Karen Sweeney awaited him inside the house. The criminologists were still working the scene, although their number had shrunk considerably since the early hours. Now they were down to Millie and her team, working the two rooms they were sure had been invaded, leaving no dust ball unturned. Millie's thoroughness was famous, though there weren't many dust balls. Apparently Abby's thoroughness had been famous, as well.

"How's it going, Millie?"

The taller woman straightened and rubbed her lower back. A grimace creased her features. She was in the senator's home office, checking out the carpet. "I think we'll be done in a couple of hours."

"Find anything that sticks out?"

"Well, I've got enough latents to start my own fingerprint bureau. God knows how many people go through this house on a given day. The file cabinets were jimmied with a crowbar, though. It's like somebody tried to pick the locks, gave up in frustration or because of time, and just laid into them with a metal bar. The senator needs better cabinets."

"I got the impression that the stuff here is mostly copies of things for his personal use. He probably isn't worried about anyone getting into it. He said there was nothing important there."

"Somebody sure had a different opinion." Millie sighed and pulled off her rubber gloves. "I'm going out for a smoke. If any of my team start looking for me, they can find me out front."

"Okay."

Left alone in the senator's office, Karen walked around, taking in more detail than she had that morning. A stereo and TV were hidden in an armoire on one wall. Putting on gloves, she opened it all the way and looked inside.

Apparently the senator enjoyed thrillers. He had a stack of DVD movies, among them *All the President's Men,* a film about the two *Washington Post* reporters who'd exposed the Watergate cover-up. Interesting choice for a man well on his way to the White House.

He also had a copy of *The Contender,* a movie about all the ugly maneuvering around the nomination and confirmation of a woman for the vice presidency.

Cautionary tales, perhaps?

His choice in music was eclectic, from Jimmy Buffett to Beethoven. She almost smiled at that. Her own tastes were also eclectic, a little of this and a little of that.

"Karen?" called a voice from the front of the house.

"Yes?"

"The senator's here."

"Let him in. I'm coming."

She met Grant Lawrence in the foyer. The first thing she noticed was how grave he looked. How somber. But also how well controlled.

He shook her hand. "Please thank the officer out front for me," he said. "He kept the press at shouting distance."

She half smiled. "I wish he could keep them in Timbuktu, but I don't have the authority for that, so we'll settle for shouting distance."

He responded with a faint smile of his own.

"Do you just need to go to your children's rooms?"

"Well, I could use some of my own clothes, if that's okay. And I've got a couple of spare suitcases in my closet to put things in."

"That's okay. I'll go with you, if you don't mind."

It was not a request, and she saw that he realized that. He nodded. "Any idea when I get my house back?"

"Criminology has to release it. It might be a few days."

They began ascending the stairs together.

"It's not," he said, "that I'm eager to come back here. In fact, I'd rather not live here ever again. But my daughters…they're going to need the stability. So I guess I have to come back, at least for a while."

She reached in her pocket and handed him the business card of a cleaning service. "These people will get rid of the mess."

He paused on a step and looked down at the card. "Thanks. You know, it never would have occurred to me that this kind of business exists."

"It's an ugly world."

He didn't answer, and she looked at him from the corner of her eye. His face had become stony, as if he was fighting some terrible internal battle. Then he shook his head and tucked the business card in his slacks pocket.

They went first to his bedroom, to get the suitcases. She stood diffidently to one side as he pulled them out and threw a few of his own clothes in them, suits, shirts, underwear, some casual clothes.

Then she followed him to the girls' rooms, where he emptied drawers and closets of every wearable thing. The suitcases full, he carried them downstairs and put them by the front door. Karen stood on the landing and watched.

When he returned upstairs, his face seemed even grimmer. He pulled out duffel bags from the closet in the playroom, stuffed their pillows in one, then began to go through the toys, deciding which to take.

That was when Karen, unwillingly, began to feel her own heart ache for this man and the burden he bore. He lingered over each toy, as if remembering some special moment.

For the first time she realized that even his children's toys held memories of Abby for him. Saddened, she looked away.

"Okay," he said. "I'm all set. I'll get out of your way."

She helped him load the duffel bags and suitcases into his car. The determined reporters, who had lingered all day, shouted questions their way. Karen looked at Grant and saw in his eyes that he'd come prepared to speak to them, like it or not.

"Shall we do it together?" she asked him.

"Are you allowed to speak for the department?" he

asked. Obviously he was familiar with the ins and outs of official spokespersons.

"I only wish they'd give me a P.I.O. on this," she said. "Unfortunately, I'm it. So yes, I can speak for the department. Whether I want to or not."

He smiled, a brief flicker of the smile that half of America knew so well. It was even more impressive face to face, warm and open. Then the smile died. "I guess we're both here, whether we want to be or not."

Karen signaled to the officer at the police line, and he raised his hands to get the reporters' attention. Once Grant's bags were in his car, she accompanied him to the cordon. A flurry of shouted questions greeted them, but she merely looked on in stony silence until they quieted.

"As you're aware," she began, "Abigail Reese was murdered in the residence of Senator Grant Lawrence last night. Ms. Reese lived in the residence, and had lived and worked with the Lawrence family for sixty years. This is obviously an ongoing investigation, and I'm not going to discuss details, except to say that we have a number of leads and we are pursuing them. Senator Lawrence has agreed to say a few words, but please understand that he will not discuss the details of the case, either. And keep it brief. His family is grieving, and he'd like to get back to them."

She turned to him. "Senator?"

The change was almost palpable. He was still the same wounded, somber man who'd walked into the house a few minutes before. But he was also Senator Grant Lawrence. He spoke with calm, quiet dignity.

"Abby Reese was at the very heart of my family. When my parents had to be away on location, Abby was there. Whenever I had a heartache or a joy, Abby was there. She was there when I graduated high school and college. She was there when I married Georgie. She was there when my children were born. She was there when Georgie died. And the very last thing my daughters did, before going to bed last night, was to call Abby to say good-night. There are no words to describe our loss. And frankly, I'd rather not have to find them. Suffice it to say that I have lost a lifetime mentor, friend, surrogate mother and companion. And I will miss her always.

"I will, of course, cooperate fully with the Tampa Police Department in their investigation of this brutal and senseless murder. I have no doubt that they will find the person who did this terrible thing. And now I'll try to answer a few of your questions, but as the detective said, my family is grieving and I want to get back to them."

"How was she killed?"

Karen spoke up. "Again, I won't discuss details of the investigation at this point. The medical examiner and criminalists are still gathering and reviewing evidence."

"Was it a burglary?"

"It's too early to tell," Karen said. "Burglary is one possible motive we're looking at, yes."

"Senator, will this affect your intention to run for the presidency?"

She saw him bristle. "I haven't announced any such intention yet. And that's the furthest thing from my mind right now."

"Will you hire another black housekeeper?"

Now his nostrils flared. "There would be no way to replace a lost family member."

"And that's enough," Karen said.

"Is this related to your wife's death?"

The senator drew a breath, as if calming himself, then

locked eyes with the reporter. "I won't even dignify that with a response. My wife died in an auto accident."

"That's enough," Karen said again, slipping an arm in front of him to drive the point home. "The department, and I'm sure the senator, will discuss further developments as they arise. Thank you."

She pivoted on her heel and drew him toward the car. "I'm sorry, Senator."

He nodded. "I'm used to it. It is, unfortunately, part of the price of holding public office. And perhaps, in some way, part of the beauty of the American system of government. Secrets are dangerous things."

"Maybe so. But so are ugly rumors."

As he was about to climb into the driver's seat, he looked toward a small knot of people gathered under a tree. He turned to her. "May I have a moment, please?"

"You're a free man, Senator."

"Thank you, Detective Sweeney. For everything."

She watched his shoulders sag a bit as he stepped toward the group of neighbors.

Grant needed a familiar face, and he found it in Art Wallace. He extended his hand as Art walked toward him, leaving the other neighbors behind as he crossed the cordon.

"I'm terribly sorry for your loss," Art said.

"Thanks, Art. The jackals don't make it any easier, but I guess I have to deal with them."

Art nodded, then angled his head toward the detective. "Do they know anything?"

"Not a lot. It looks like a burglary." Grant closed his eyes for a moment. "Jeez, Art. She probably died for some files that anyone could have had for the asking."

Art shook his head slowly. "I don't know what to

say, Grant. If there's anything I can do, anything at all…"

"Actually, I came over to ask, are your daughters home with you?"

Art nodded. "Yes. My ex is getting married again, so I've got them for three months."

Grant reached out and squeezed his shoulder. "I'm sorry, Art."

"It was bound to happen." Art's wife had left him just over a year ago, and his pain was a palpable thing, even though he never referred to Elizabeth in any other way than as his ex. "So yes, I've got the girls for a few months. I can't tell you how grateful I am for that."

"I can imagine."

Art nodded, then smiled. "We should be grateful for our blessings as they come. Now, what can I do to help you out?"

"This is going to be hell for the girls. They need a few days to adapt, but then they're going to need to get back in school. And I don't know how long it'll be before they'll give me the house back. Or how long it'll take to…" He couldn't speak the words. They stuck in his throat.

"They're welcome to stay with us, Grant. They've always been welcome. You know you don't need to ask."

"I know, Art. It shouldn't be for long. I hate to impose."

Art took his hand firmly. "Grant, we've been neighbors for ten years. You're not imposing. I'd be glad to help, and you know Lucy and Jessie love your daughters like sisters."

Grant managed a chuckle. "And they fight like sisters."

"That's part of the package," Art said, smiling. "It's not a problem. Really. That's what friends do."

"You're good people," Grant said. "Look, I need to get back home. I'll call you when I think the girls are ready to get back to school."

"We'll look forward to it," Art said. "Take care of your family."

Grant looked up into a graceful live oak, as if trying to divine the secrets of the universe from its gnarled limbs. "I don't know if it's a matter of me taking care of them or them taking care of me."

Art clapped a hand on his shoulder. "I know, Grant. I know. Get on home to them."

"Thanks, Art."

"A friend?" Karen asked when he returned to the car.

"A friend."

"You seem to make close friends, Senator."

He studied her eyes for portents of an ulterior motive but saw none. "I do, I guess. In the end, what else is there but those we love and the memories we make with them?"

She nodded, glancing toward Art Wallace as he walked back around a copse of trees toward his house. "That's a beautiful sentiment, Senator. Do you ever disagree with any of your friends?"

"What are you suggesting?"

Those clear gray eyes of hers returned to him. "I just wondered if you ever had any disagreements with your neighbors. People are human, after all. This neighborhood can't be Eden before the fall."

"No, it's not. Of course we don't all see eye-to-eye on everything. Fortunately, we're all too civilized to get nasty about it."

She nodded. ''What kinds of things do you disagree about?''

He gave her a crooked smile. ''Politics, mainly. Given my position, I'm a lightning rod for such discussions. But they're my constituents, too, so I listen. Matt Witherspoon, across the street, cordially dislikes my position on gun control. I have no doubt he votes against me.''

She nodded. ''And the guy you just talked to?''

Now a look of faint amusement brightened his gaze, momentarily erasing his grief. ''Art? Art and I have been close friends for about ten years now. It doesn't bother me in the least that he volunteers for Randall Youngblood.''

''Youngblood?''

''The head of the cane growers' association. He's lobbying against my environmental bill.''

''And your neighbor volunteers for him?''

''Why not? It's his constitutional right to oppose legislation.'' He cocked his head. ''You know, Detective, it's entirely possible for gentlemen to disagree and still be friends. In fact, I don't believe Congress has settled legislation at gunpoint once in its entire history.''

Her face revealed nothing. ''It's my job to ask these questions.''

He felt a twinge of embarrassment. ''Of course it is. I'm sorry. It's just that I've never had a disagreement with any of my neighbors that's even reached the level of raised voices.''

She nodded, still expressionless.

''Thank you for your help, Detective.''

''It's my job, Senator. I'll keep you posted.''

He drove away, headed back to grief, but for the moment feeling only shame at his overreaction to Detective

Sweeney's questions. He usually displayed more self-control than that.

But there had been enough ugliness in the last twenty-four hours, and he was damned if he was going to start suspecting everyone he knew.

At least not until he had evidence.

6

After the senator disappeared down the street, Karen decided it might be a good time to try to interview the neighbors again. This morning, by the time she'd sent some uniforms around to ask questions, everybody appeared to have gone off to work. Or maybe they weren't answering their doors. But now it was late afternoon, and surely some of them would be home.

Unfortunately, most still weren't. She worked her way up and down the street, and managed to talk to only two women, both of whom denied having seen or heard a thing. That left the senator's next-door friend, the guy who said he'd heard a car. He'd been gone, too, when they'd gotten around to trying to question him.

But he was home now, and he invited her inside pleasantly. He even offered her a cup of coffee. Ordinarily she would have declined, but she decided instead to accept, wanting to make this interview as comfortable and friendly as possible in the hope that this friend of the senator's would relax enough to grow chatty.

As he gave her a mug of coffee and sat facing her across the coffee table between two sofas, he said, ''I suppose you want to know if I know anything more about that car I heard last night.''

''That's one of the things, yes. Delicious coffee.''

He beamed. ''I can't take credit for that. It's a Starbucks blend.''

Of course. Starbucks. In this neighborhood she was rather surprised it wasn't something even more exotic. ''Well, you brewed it perfectly,'' she said, and smiled.

''Thank you.'' He managed a look of embarrassed pleasure to perfection. She found herself wondering if it was real or practiced. Then she chided herself for being unnecessarily suspicious.

''But about the car,'' he said. ''I'm not sure it had anything to do with what happened to Abby.'' His lips trembled a bit at the outer corners, and he paused a moment, clearly gathering himself. ''I mean, how would I know?''

''Of course you don't know,'' she said reassuringly. ''But I have to follow every possible lead.''

''Of course.'' He nodded and put his own coffee mug on a coaster on the highly polished table. ''Well, I don't really know anything except what I told you. I think it was about one o'clock. I seem to remember glancing at the digital clock on the headboard. Anyway, I can't be certain of the *exact* time.''

She nodded and pulled a pad from her jacket pocket, making notes. ''You said it had a loud muffler.''

''Yes. One of those things some people seem to like. But it *did* have a muffler. I've heard cars without one. There's no mistaking *that* sound.''

''No, there isn't.'' She nodded pleasantly. ''Did it start or stop?''

He cocked his head, thinking. ''No, I don't think so. Or at least I didn't hear it. What woke me up was the gunning of the engine." He nodded to himself. "Yes, that's what it was. The car's engine gunned at least a couple of times. Then it drove away down toward Mulberry."

Karen scribbled a few more notes, then glanced at the toys in one corner of the room, a dollhouse with dozens of pieces of furniture. "Did your wife hear it, too?"

He seemed to jerk, an almost spastic movement. His face grew as rigid as a mask. "My ex-wife," he said shortly, "is taking a world cruise with her new husband."

"I'm sorry. I assumed, because of the toys..."

He glanced toward the corner, then nodded stiffly. "It's all right. It's a natural assumption. My daughters are staying with me until their mother returns."

She nodded, making another note, although it didn't seem relevant. "I understand you disagree with Senator Lawrence over S.R. 52."

He looked a little startled, then laughed. "Oh, yes. I suppose Grant told you that. We've disagreed about quite a few things politically over the years. But people can disagree about politics without becoming enemies."

"That's what Senator Lawrence indicated."

Art Wallace nodded. "In fact, I'm volunteering for Randall Youngblood right now. You know, the group lobbying against the bill? Grant knows that."

Again she nodded. "Why are you opposed to the bill?"

"Because I think it will devastate farmers. It's just that simple."

Karen slipped her coffee, smiled at him again. "Since you know Senator Lawrence so well, I was wondering if you know his enemies."

His eyes widened a shade, and he chuckled. "He's a

politician, Detective. He probably has hundreds of enemies.''

"Of course." She smiled deprecatingly. "I just wondered if you know of any who might go this far."

"To kill that wonderful old woman? No way. Politics can get dirty, Detective, but not to that extent. I can't imagine that anyone I know would do such a thing under any circumstances."

Just then twin girls of about seven bounced into the room, trailed by a middle-aged woman in gray.

"Daddy, Daddy!" they bubbled over. "Nanny took us to the zoo. And we saw lions!"

Karen waited while Art Wallace hugged his daughters to him as if he never wanted to let go. They beamed and chattered, utterly oblivious of her presence.

Finally, quietly, she excused herself, not wanting to interrupt the happy scene. And not at all sure she needed to ask Art Wallace another single thing.

She had something else to do, anyway. Something equally important, at least to her.

Karen drove back to the alley where the unidentified woman had been found. As expected, Dave Previn was nowhere to be seen. Not that there was much he might have learned by staring at this alley.

Still, it seemed wrong that the trail of the woman's death would be left to grow stale, so she paced the alley and remembered the horror that had been visited upon the woman whose body had been found here. *Found here.* She'd all but let that slip out of mind in the flurry over the Lawrence case. This woman's body had almost certainly been moved. Had she even put that in her report?

Suddenly it felt as if a lead weight were pressing on

her heart. She couldn't remember. She probably had. She remembered making extensive notes of it, here in the alley, and she would have referred to those notes as she made out the report. So of course those observations would be in the report.

Still, that she couldn't remember including them showed just how far the Lawrence case had driven this one from her mind. From *her* mind, and she had seen the woman's body lying broken and torn in an alley, something no other detective would see except in photographs. If she had to press herself to remember what she'd included in her report, what hope did that leave for Dave Previn giving this case the attention it deserved?

Karen let out a breath and shook her head at her own feelings. Raised in an Irish family, she sometimes missed the days when she had been a practicing Catholic. Back then, she would have gone to a priest, dumped her load of guilt in the confessional and received absolution. She would have had no reason to go on kicking herself. *Mea culpa mea maxima culpa. Teo absolvo.* Get on with life.

Alternatively, she missed her early days in the department, when she would have lit a cigarette, affected the diffident shrug of someone who is too ignorant to realize how little she knows and figured it would all come out in the wash. *Life sucks, and you deal with it.*

Instead, she'd quit going to church, and she'd quit smoking, and she'd come to believe that cynicism was simply the ugly twin sister of idealism, both born of ignorance. Which left her with no psychic defense against her feelings of inadequacy and sorrow as she stood in that alley and remembered the horrible images she'd seen.

"I'm sorry," she said to the chalk outline on the pavement. "I'll try to do better."

It wasn't confessional, but it was what she had left.

She returned to the office to find Previn pouring the dregs from the office coffeemaker into a mug that read *I'd rather be thinking*. The mug had been given to him when he'd left the fraud squad and moved up to homicide. It was a cop joke. Previn was always thinking. Thinking about his wife. Thinking about his kids. Thinking about some article he'd read that week in *Science Weekly*. Thinking about the fact that he thought too much. The book on him was that he had no instincts and tried to make up for it by spinning his mental wheels until he dug his way through to the bottom of a case. The approach worked, but the people around him had to dodge a lot of flying mud.

"Where are you on the woman in the alley?" she asked without preamble.

He smiled. "If it isn't the TV star. They just ran a teaser for the evening news."

Karen would rather they had lost the videotapes, but that was too much to hope for. Lawrence was front page, film at six and eleven news. Which meant that, for a while, at least, she was, too.

"How lovely. So where are you on the woman in the alley?" she repeated.

"I reviewed your files and notes this morning," he said, plunking his mug on his desk. "I put a call in to the M.E., but they're ass deep in everything else. Said they hoped to get to the autopsy this evening. The crime scene techs will call back later or tomorrow, they said. Missing persons has no one recent who matches the general description, so we're dead in the water on an ID. I walked the scene this morning, knocked on doors. Zero, zip, zilch, nada.''

"Keep pushing it," she said. "I don't want her to slip through the cracks."

"There's not a lot to push until I hear back from the M.E. or the lab, or we get an ID. I don't want her to slip through the cracks, either, Karen. But right now I've got nothing to push against."

She nodded and picked up the phone, stabbing numbers by rote memory. "Yes, this is Detective Karen Sweeney. You have a Jane Doe of mine. Any idea when you'll get to her? She's in now? Thanks. We'll be right over."

Previn looked stung, resentment smoldering in his dark eyes. "They'd have called me when they were done."

"Maybe, maybe not. They're busy, like you said. And we're not going to wait for them to finish. We're going to be there as it happens."

"I've never…"

"Then get used to it," she said, grabbing her jacket and purse. "Welcome to homicide."

Previn was a weasely looking young man of about thirty, with a long, narrow nose and thinning hair. His normally ruddy skin went utterly pale the instant they stepped into the autopsy room.

The smell, of course. Even now, Karen wasn't completely used to it, but at least she expected it. Previn didn't. White, he turned away immediately from the sight of a corpse opened from collarbone to pubic bone with a Y incision, but that wouldn't get rid of the smell.

Nothing got rid of the smell. There was something about a dead body, even a relatively fresh one that had recently been in the cooler, that smelled just plain awful when you opened it up. Fishing around in her purse, she found a small jar of Vicks VapoRub. She'd carried it for years but hadn't used it in a long time.

"Here," she said to Previn. "Rub some of this right under your nose." He might even manage to do it, if he didn't lose his lunch first.

His hand was shaking as he accepted the small jar. A second later he bolted. Karen shrugged and stepped nearer to the table.

It wasn't that she was hardened to it; she was just accustomed to it—very different things. It was never pleasant—it would never *be* pleasant—but she no longer had to fight to maintain control in here.

"What have you got so far?" she asked the M.E., Dr. Caleb Carter, when he'd finished dictating something into the microphone that hung from the ceiling on an adjustable arm. Right now it was close to his mouth.

"Female Caucasian, approximately twenty-eight years of age…"

Karen had already pretty much figured that much out, but she let him run through the stats: height, weight, general health.

"Diseased right ovary," he continued, "and evidence of at least one not-too-good abortion. I'd say that was a long time ago, though."

"Okay." She had her notebook out, ready to write down anything that seemed particularly relevant, things she wouldn't want to forget before the report was issued.

"Proximate cause of death appears to be strangulation from a nylon stocking wrapped around her throat. There are four separate bite marks. From their locations and depth, I'd hazard a guess that there was a lot of rage involved in this act."

That was worthy of note. "Not ritualistic?"

"Well, there's always that possibility," he said, looking across the table at her. "I'm not a profiler. But…my guess is this was an act of rage, an instant response to some kind of provocation."

"Was she raped?"

"From my external examination, I'd say no. The swabs might say differently."

"Anything else?"

"Oh yes. She's got plenty of skin under her fingernails. She must have put up a fight before he got her hands bound behind her back. My guess is that someone is running around with some pretty deep scratches, probably on his arms."

"So look for a man in an overcoat, huh?"

Carter chuckled. "Or at least long sleeves."

Outside, Karen found Previn standing in the hallway, watching from behind the safety of the window.

He flushed when he saw her. "Sorry."

"It's okay, Previn. The first one is always hard. Just give me back my Vicks in case I need it."

Sheepishly, he passed her the small jar. "It didn't sound like he had much."

"Actually, he gave me a great deal."

"How so?"

"He gave me a picture of how the crime was committed."

"I didn't hear anything."

Karen looked at him. "Think, Previn. He said she probably scratched his arms."

"So?"

"That means he probably came at her from behind, so she couldn't reach his face and had to scratch at his arms."

Previn nodded slowly. "But how can he know that?"

"My guess is he's already looked at some of the flesh under a microscope. I'd further guess that he didn't find any sign of beard in the flesh. More likely he found body hair."

"There's a difference?"

She looked at him. "Previn, do you ever read?"

He flushed again. "All the time."

"Apparently not the right stuff. Read a little about the technical side of the business. You'll get a lot more out of the criminalists' and the M.E.'s reports that way."

Then she left him, determined to go home and get some sleep. She'd last sighted her bed at nine yesterday morning. She would be lucky if she got home without falling asleep at the wheel.

Grant collapsed into bed as soon as the girls were asleep. It was the same room he'd slept in after he'd outgrown the "nursery" area where his daughters now slept. Although it had been redecorated—his parents weren't the sentimental type, certainly not the type to keep a museum of their son's high school life—it still felt warmly familiar. He wondered why that was. Had he left some sort of imprint here, some sort of vibration he could now sense?

Because the room looked nothing at all as it once had. The twin bed had given way to a queen; the walls were now a dusty rose to match the curtains and comforter, which boasted cabbage roses. Even the carpet was new, a deeper rose.

It was a very feminine room, one that spoke of his mother's touch. Maybe that was what made it feel so comfortable after all this time.

Back when he'd lived here, it had been very much a

boy's room, decorated in blues and golds, almost nautical in style, though not quite. His mother had never been one to lack subtlety.

Lying on the bed, he closed his eyes and let the bone-deep fatigue fill him. Now he didn't have to be strong. There was no one to see him. Turning his face into the pillow, he let the tears come. Abby was gone, never to return. And he didn't think he could bear the pain.

Stacy was gone, too. Not that she'd been a big part of his life lately. It had been months since they'd slept together. But he could still remember her scent, gently musky, and her warm, smooth skin. He had no idea how she'd died, and if Abby's death was any indicator, he didn't want to know. He did, however, want to know why Stacy had been in his living room last night.

Last night.

So much had happened so fast. But it was only last night, at right about this time, when his daughters had called Abby. Abby had probably gone up to bed, after checking the front and back doors. She would have left the dim light on under the kitchen cabinet, as she always did, even when he wasn't home and wouldn't be trundling in there for a late-night snack or a glass of juice. She would have walked up the stairs right about this time, and curled up with her sketchpad and a charcoal pencil, graceful curves and shadows emerging onto the vellum. Deer, most likely, as they were her favorite subject. Soon enough, her eyelids would have grown heavy, and she would have put the sketchbook and charcoals on the nightstand, curling up beneath the handmade quilt and the knit afghan.

Sometime after she'd fallen asleep, Stacy would have arrived. But why? And then the killer. Had they come together? Had the killer found out about her, found out about their relationship, and forced her to let him into Grant's home? That seemed hugely unlikely. Anyone who knew him well enough to have discovered Stacy would also know he didn't keep sensitive files at home, wouldn't they?

Stacy had come in, using the key he'd let her keep. They'd planned to maintain the friendship, and she'd said she intended to volunteer for his next campaign, so he'd seen no reason to take the key back. It had struck him somehow as a crass thing to do.

So she'd let herself in. Maybe the killer, too, or maybe the killer had broken in later. The detective hadn't mentioned any signs of a break-in, though, apart from his office. Maybe Stacy had left the door unlocked. Somehow, anyway, he'd come in. And the horror had begun.

Abby was gone. Stacy was gone. Georgina was long since gone. Death seemed to follow him, although he wasn't a superstitious man. The press had, more than once, compared him to John Kennedy. He didn't especially like that, for any number of reasons. Not the least of them was that he didn't feel worthy of such a comparison.

But now, crying in the darkness, he thought about how much that family had lost. Joe Junior, killed in the war. John, killed in Dallas. Bobby, killed in California. Ted, ruined by the fiasco at Chappaquiddick. Bobby's son losing his leg to bone cancer. Jackie too had gone to cancer. Then John-John, crashed in the sea. So much promise. So much loss.

Would that be his legacy, as well?

He was no John Kennedy. But he had earned his own battle scars. And yes, he was ambitious. It had been said that anyone who ran for president of the United States must be blessed with charisma and cursed with arrogance. Was he arrogant enough to think his country needed him? Yes, he had to admit, he was.

And as so often happened, ideas for a speech began to roil around in his head, and he let them, for they distracted him from a grief he could not yet either bear or absorb.

He sometimes thought of himself as a product of the Generation of Apathy, those whose parents had fought the good fight for freedom abroad, whose older siblings and cousins had marched for freedom at home. His generation had had no war to fight and little to protest. They'd had few illusions to lose. They'd watched a president resign in disgrace, another crippled by senility, and another smeared by his own lust. Communism had collapsed under the weight of its own inefficiency, and religious fanaticism had inflamed the world. News had become a commodity, bought and sold and tainted by corporate moguls with little commitment beyond their own golden parachutes. People were living longer than ever, but also working longer hours, feeling more isolated, brought together only by anger and grief, when their children were gunned down in schools or their landmarks blown up live, on television, with their morning coffee.

When was the last time his country had been drawn together by a common hope, rather than a common fear? By a shared dream, rather than a shared nightmare?

Could he help them find a common hope, a shared dream? Perhaps it was sheer arrogance that he believed he could. Or perhaps it was simply that someone had to step forward out of a generation that had been not so much apathetic as biding its time, waiting its turn.

Abby was gone. Stacy was gone. Georgina was long since gone. But each, in her own way, had helped to shape his vision for his nation. So long as he held true to that vision, nurtured it, shared it, they would never be truly gone from his world.

He pulled a corner of the pillowcase up and scrubbed the tears from his eyes. He would press on. Those he had loved and lost, those who had loved him, deserved no less.

Across Tampa Bay, far from the Belleair home of the senior Lawrences, in the old-money realm of South Tampa, Jerry Connally sat in his home study and drank bourbon, trying to erase last night from him mind. Trying to numb the creeping sense that he had, in an instant of decision, become nearly as evil as the man who had killed Abby and Stacy.

He would do anything for Grant Lawrence, because Grant was his lifelong friend. Because Grant had a chance at the presidency, a chance to do all those things that Jerry so passionately believed were for the good of the nation. He truly believed that Grant could pull the nation back from the precipice over which it hovered: the precipice of an oligarchy run by big business, with democracy an illusionary sop for the masses.

He *believed* that.

But he was also a moral man, a man with a family of his own, a churchgoing man. He was a lawyer, trained in the most stringent of professional ethics, which, unlike too many of his colleagues, he took seriously.

Yes, in the world of politics, compromise was necessary. And sometimes things weren't exactly perfect as one hand washed the other. But never in his life had he done something so *unclean* as he had done last night.

And right now, telling himself that he had saved Grant

and the nation from a huge scandal wasn't easing his conscience any.

Nor was the bourbon wiping away the horrific memories that now stained his mind and soul. He had obstructed a police investigation by creating false evidence, by moving a body from the scene of the murder....

Oh, *God!* The memory of Stacy's limp body, bloodied and torn... With a shaking hand, he poured more bourbon into his glass and promised himself that he would get a grip soon, because he had to. And he'd always done what he *had* to. But he also promised himself these few hours of remorse, guilt and self-loathing, of grief and fear and disgust. He had to let it blow through him so he could be strong tomorrow.

Just then the phone rang. He stared at it, locked in fear and anxiety. Never before had he feared the ringing of the phone. Now it threatened him.

But the booze hadn't taken hold yet, and he knew if he let it ring, it would rouse his wife and she would answer it. He didn't want that, precisely because he feared what might be on the other end of the line.

"Jerry?" It was Sam Weldon, a quiet, almost invisible man whose job it was to keep tabs on the political activities of opponents so the Lawrence camp didn't get caught by surprise. And Weldon was very good at his job.

"Yeah, Sam." If his brain had fogged in the least from the bourbon, the fog was gone now. Jerry gripped the receiver tight.

"There's a leak at the police department," Sam said. "I don't know who. But I know they've been talking to Youngblood's people."

"Shit!"

"Wait, there's more. The word is that the detective on the case is suspicious of the scene."

"Suspicious?"

"Yeah. Things aren't adding up."

Jerry felt his stomach plummet. "Anything else?"

"My contact in Youngblood's group says they're looking into Georgina's death again, trying to rake up those rumors that got quashed. You remember that?"

Remember that? He'd had a big hand in quashing them. "I remember."

"Well," said Sam, "it seems they're going to let things ride for a few days. Then they're going to take off the gloves and hit us any way they can."

"That's hardly surprising. They always do." He sounded more confident than he felt. Far more confident. Because for the first time in his life, he was in the wrong. "Thanks, Sam. Keep me posted."

"Always."

Jerry hung up the phone and pushed the bourbon away. He couldn't afford to indulge. Not now. The storm clouds were getting bigger by the second.

7

"**S**tep-ball-point-and-side-in-*pivot,* turn-and-push-and-step-step-*point!*"

Alissa Jurgen called out steps with the precision of a drill sergeant, watching the nine girls try to copy her body movements. They were improving. Whether they would be ready for the performance next weekend was yet to be seen, but now it at least looked like they'd all heard the same music in the same place at least once before.

Perspiration flew from the ends of her short bangs as she whirled into a pirouette, halting the movement by kicking her left leg out to the side. Shifting her hips to the left, she moved her weight onto that foot, arched her right toe and planted it with a solid *thunk,* her hands flashing to her hips, face turned up in exultation. Then her eyes dropped to the mirror, to see the girls behind her.

"No, no, *no!*" She dropped the pose and turned. "Fay, your back is too soft there. You've just climbed to the top of the wizard's tower and confronted his magic. You've *won.* You have to *feel* that. And your body has to say it."

The twelve-year-old girl's face sagged, then crumbled. Alissa turned off the music and walked over to her. "Fay, what's wrong?"

"It's my ankle," the girl said, ashamed, almost too quietly to hear. "It still hurts on the jumps."

Alissa nodded. She'd been pushing the girls hard. Too hard. They seemed to push themselves harder for Stacy, but Stacy wasn't here. Stacy hadn't been here in nearly a week. Alissa knew it was unfair to dump her frustration on the girls. They would be ready enough.

"Okay. That's enough for today. Great work, girls." As they started to break ranks and head for water bottles, towels and gym bags, she took Fay's hand. "Let's have a look at that ankle."

It was swollen, despite the tight wrap Fay wore. The sprain wasn't healing. Alissa took a chemical ice pack from her bag, popped the membrane inside and shook it. In moments the bag chilled. She pressed it to Fay's ankle and secured it with a few turns of tape.

She studied the girl's face. "Fay, it's only been three weeks. You need to rest it."

Liquid brown eyes glistened back at her, brimming with tears. "I want to be in the show."

Alissa nodded. "I know you do. But is one show worth limping for the next six months, or maybe even for the rest of your life?"

Fay's face hardened. "I'm going to beat this, Miss Alissa. I'm going to dance next weekend."

The girl had grit to spare. Perhaps it was that her mother pushed her too hard. Or perhaps she was driven by inner demons. Regardless, Alissa knew enough about human nature, and dancers, to realize what would happen if she pulled Fay from the show. The girl's ankle mattered, but so did her spirit.

"Then you're going to have to keep it up at school, Fay, and wear the brace at night. Like the doctor said."

"I hate the brace."

Alissa set her jaw. "It's wear the brace or miss the show. Your choice."

Fay nodded. "I'll wear it, Miss Alissa. I'm not going to miss the show."

As the girl grabbed her bag and limped to the door, Alissa's heart squeezed. She'd been that way once. Still was, truth be told. The body was an instrument. If it was out of tune, you didn't put it on the shelf. You tuned it. And you pressed on through the pain. Dance was a discipline, every bit as demanding as any sport. Fay would succeed, if for no other reason than that she wouldn't accept failure. If only some of the other girls, some of them more talented, had the same attitude.

Alissa took a long drag from a bottle of water, then toweled her face. She missed Stacy. The girls missed Stacy. The show missed Stacy. But the show must go on.

"Alissa Jurgen?" a voice called from the door.

Alissa flinched at the unexpected presence, then turned. "Yes?"

The woman smiled. "I'm sorry. I didn't mean to startle you. I'm Detective Karen Sweeney, Tampa PD. I wonder if I might have a few minutes?"

Eyes like a snow wolf, Alissa thought. Eyes that brought back chilly memories of Minnesota winters. She suppressed the urge to shiver. Somewhere deep inside, she *knew.* "Is this about Stacy?"

The detective nodded. "It might be. I'm not sure. You filed a missing persons report, and the description is similar."

Oh no! "Similar to what?"

The woman drew a photograph from a manila envelope. The look on her face said everything there was to say. "I'm sorry, but if you could look at this. Tell me if you recognize her?"

Alissa's hand quivered as she reached for the photo. A lifeless, bloated face, photographed in the harsh, sterile light of a morgue, a sheet up to the neck. Alissa clapped a hand to her mouth, fighting the urge to retch. "Oh God no. No. Not Stacy."

"Is it her?" the detective asked.

Alissa nodded stiffly, trying to catch her breath. *Not Stacy!* "What...what happened?"

"I'm so sorry," the woman said. She reached out with a warm hand and grasped Alissa's shoulder. "Stacy was...she was murdered. I'm so sorry."

"Excuse me," Alissa said, gasping for breath. "I...I need to..."

She dashed for the rest room, racing the bile that rose in her throat.

Karen didn't need to hear the sounds to know what was happening. Instead, she paced the studio, forcing herself to take in details that were probably irrelevant, trying to give Alissa what privacy she could, even in her own thoughts.

Part of her thought she should have pulled rank and made Previn do this while she waited in the car. Part of her knew he couldn't have done it. His wife had given him the word last night. She was leaving. He was in no shape to deal with someone else's loss. So he'd stayed in the car, and she was doing this alone. God, she hated this job.

But Jane Doe now had a name. Stacy Wiggins.

She turned at a sound and saw Alissa sagged in the

door frame, wiping her mouth. "I know this is an awful time, Ms. Jurgen. But if I could ask you just a few questions?"

"Alissa."

Karen arched a brow. "Excuse me?"

"Just Alissa, please. My mother is Ms. Jurgen."

"No problem. Are you up to talking?"

"No," Alissa said. "But Stacy would be. How can I help, Detective?"

Karen watched the young woman's back stiffen, watched her set her jaw and blink away tears. True determination. The kind of determination Karen supposed was common to dancers and other athletes, if they wanted more than a weekend hobby.

"I need to know a little bit about Stacy," Karen said. "Her friends, her habits, that kind of thing. So maybe we can get a lead to the killer."

Alissa swallowed hard and nodded. "Okay. I can't sit just yet. I'm still cooling down. So can I pace?"

"Sure. I'll pace with you. I've been in the car too much lately."

Connections. Rapport. Essential to her job. Karen watched that first connection show in Alissa's eyes, followed by a nod and a weak smile. A good start. But sometimes she hated herself for being so calculating about these things.

"Okay," Alissa said on a deep breath as they paced before the mirrored wall and *barre*. "You want to know about her."

"Anything you can share. Who'd she hang out with, did she have a boyfriend, was she worried about anything? What places did she frequent?"

Alissa nodded, wiping her face once again with the towel that hung around her neck, taking a small sip of water from her bottle. "I'm sorry. Would you like some water?"

"No, thank you." Postponement. Karen was familiar with it, this holding off of the pain. Everyone did it.

"Well," Alissa said finally, "Stacy kept pretty much to herself. I think she had a boyfriend a while back, but I don't know who he was. I got the impression it evaporated maybe six, seven months ago."

"Did she seem upset?"

"No. Actually she didn't. It was like whatever happened, she considered it a natural end. But I don't know much about it. She never mentioned the guy in any detail, and I don't even have any idea who he might have been."

"Do you know the kinds of places she might have gone with him?"

Alissa shook her head. "Not a clue. Stacy was very private about a lot of things, but especially private about that."

"Did she seem worried or frightened at any time after the breakup?"

"No." Alissa paused. "Well, that's not exactly true. Just recently she complained that some guy she used to know as a client was bugging her, but she sent him away. That was…maybe a month ago. She never said any more about it, so I thought he was leaving her alone." She faced Karen, her face losing the last color from her recent workout, growing truly ashen. "Do you think…?"

Karen shook her head. "I don't think anything right now, Alissa. I'm still at the point of collecting information. When I've got enough information that I can put some pieces together, I start thinking."

Alissa squeezed her eyes shut and released a sharp sigh, as if battling another round of tears. "Okay."

"Now, you said this guy was a former client. What do you mean by client? A dance student?"

Alissa shook her head and bit her lip. "Oh, hell," she said, her face reflecting an internal struggle. "Oh, hell. I guess it doesn't matter anymore. She didn't want anyone to know, but she was an exotic dancer until about two years ago. She gave it up so she could start this studio. I think she was referring to someone she knew from those days."

"Did she say so?"

Alissa shook her head. "I don't think so. But when she referred to him as a client, I assumed it. Because she talks about *our* customers as students."

Karen nodded, scrawling a note on her pad, noticing how Alissa referred to her employer in the present tense. The news hadn't yet sunk in. It might not for a while.

She looked up from her pad. "Were the two of you close?"

Alissa nodded, rubbing her eyes with her towel. "Yeah," she said, her voice thick. "Yeah. We...did all kinds of things together. Took trips. Went out to plays and concerts."

"Even when she had a boyfriend?"

Alissa's wet, dark eyes met hers, and she nodded.

Curious, Karen thought. Curious indeed. Most women with boyfriends didn't take trips and go to concerts with female friends. At least not to the degree that Alissa was suggesting. "You did things together a lot?"

"Sure. All the time."

"What about the boyfriend? Why wasn't she with him?"

Alissa opened her mouth, then paused. "I got the impression he traveled a lot."

"Did she say so?"

"Not in so many words." Alissa leaned against the *barre* and patted her face again with the towel. She was wet with sweat still, beads of it were running down her forehead. "Detective, she never said much about him. I told you. I just got impressions."

Karen nodded. "Would you mind sharing those impressions?"

"I *am*. I got the feeling he was away a lot. I got the feeling she was lonely when he was."

"And you didn't mind standing in for him?"

Alissa smiled sadly. "I'm lesbian. I had a crush on my boss. What can I say?"

Karen nodded, undisturbed. She'd heard this kind of thing many times. "Was it reciprocated?"

"Hell no. Stacy's compass pointed straight all the way."

"Did she know about your feelings?"

"I hope not. I didn't want to make her uncomfortable."

Karen made another note, wondering if Alissa might have been more jealous than she was letting on. If she might have been jealous enough to do something. "It must have been hard for you."

"Being lesbian is hard from the word go, Detective. There's nothing easy about it. Lifestyle choice?" Her voice turned heavily sarcastic. "Yeah, right. I volunteered for this. I couldn't ask for anything better."

"I'm not criticizing you, Alissa. I'm just trying to understand."

"Yeah, it was hard. It's been hard before. Our emotions don't yield to reason. Straights fall in love with gays, gays fall in love with straights, and it's hard, but that's the way it is. We live with it when it happens.''

Karen nodded. "So you were there for her a lot?''

"I was always there for her—when she'd let me be. She said we were like sisters." Alissa shrugged. "That was good enough.''

"But she still didn't share anything about her boyfriend.''

Alissa shook her head. "No. I felt bad about that. Sometimes I wondered if it was because she suspected how I felt about her and she didn't want to hurt me.''

The dancer looked down at the polished wood floor, then raised a haunted face. "She had a heart of gold, Detective. Find the bastard, will you?''

8

The day of the funeral, just over a week after Abby's murder, dawned with the grumble of thunder and racing clouds that seemed to touch the treetops. A late cold front had blown in, making spring feel inauspiciously like autumn.

The little church that Abby had attended most of her life wasn't big enough to hold the number of people who showed for her funeral. There were all of Abby's friends, of course, a lifetime of relationships cultivated at church and home, some young, some elderly, and every age between.

But Grant's friends came, too, although, seated in the front row with his parents and his daughters, he didn't see them at first. His attention was partially focused on the closed coffin, but mostly it was focused on the girls on either side of him, dressed in their Easter outfits, outfits that Abby had chosen for them only a few weeks before.

No black. Abby wouldn't have wanted that. So the girls wore lavender and pink, and Grant himself wore a blue pinstriped suit that Abby always said made him look so good it was a downright sin. How many times had she said to him, "You gonna wear that sinful blue suit today?"

He might never wear it again after this.

We are…climbing…Jacob's…Ladder….

It was a hymn of hope. Hope for Abby. Hope for everyone. The choir was robed in royal blue with gold trim, their black sashes the only bow to the sorrow of the moment. As they slowly swayed side to side, their voices seemed to rise up and dance in the thick air.

We are…climbing…Jacob's…Ladder….

"Sister Abigail was an orphan," said the preacher, Ralph Anderson. "But we are all orphans here today."

The choir continued to sing softly as Anderson's rich bass voice rolled forth from a broad, deep chest within his white robe.

"We are all orphans in this world. We can't see our Father, or our Mother. The light of their radiance would blind us all, down here in our darkness. We are all orphans in this world. And yet we are not alone. *Not* alone."

A staggered chorus of "Amen" rippled through the congregation.

We are…climbing…Jacob's…Ladder….

"We can't see our Father. We can't see our Mother. But we can see our brothers and sisters." Anderson spread his arms. "And we are *all* brothers and sisters here today. Amen. Amen."

Soldiers…of the…cross…

"Amen," Grant heard himself whisper. The word translated as *I believe*. And he did believe.

Belle squirmed beside him, eyes wide, taking it all in as if to store away forever these last moments with Abby. On his other side, Cathy was still, the barest nod of her head indicating that she was hearing Anderson's words.

Every...rung goes...higher...higher....

"Sister Abby was orphaned by sin, but she was redeemed in love." His eyes swept over the congregation. "Every face here is a living testimony to that love. Abby loved her flowers. And every tear I see here today waters the flowers of love she's growing in heaven's garden. Amen and amen."

Belle curled tighter against Grant.

"We can't have our sister back. And glory be, if we listen to the stillness in our hearts, we don't want our sister back. For who among us would take Sister Abby out of her Father's arms? And yet we hurt. We hurt, not because she's gone. We hurt because it's not yet our time to go with her."

Every...rung goes...higher...higher....

"Because every time Sister Abby said 'I love you,' we could see, we could feel, just for a moment, the reflection of our Father's love."

"Amen," Grant whispered. This time he heard Cathy whisper it, too. *I believe.*

"And it's not Sister Abby we miss so much as that reflection we saw in her eyes, that reflection we heard in her voice. The reflection of our Father's love."

Every...rung goes...higher...higher....

"Sister Abby brought each and every one of us closer to God by the way she loved us. By the way she drew love from us." Anderson's voice dropped to a whisper, and he dabbed his brow with a white handkerchief. His eyes swept the congregation again. "Sister Abby was an orphan. Orphaned by hate. But I tell you, she was a sister of love. And every one of us will carry her love forever."

Soldiers…of the…cross…

"Amen," Grant and Cathy said in unison.

On either side of him, Grant's daughters stirred uneasily, and a sniffle escaped Cathy Suzanne. Grant reached out with both arms and cuddled the girls close, offering what comfort he could. Small comfort, he thought. Abby had been with them even more than he had, and her passing had left a gaping pit in their hearts and lives.

We will…see Him…in His…glory….

"Today, brothers and sisters," the preacher continued, "today we need to keep in our minds that our dear sister Abby is walking with the Lord.

"He has lifted her up from all the sorrows of this world. He has taken her hand and called her home to glory. We shall miss our dear sister, but we cannot grieve for her. She has gone to live with the Lord. No, we grieve for ourselves. For *our* loss."

We will…see Him…in His…glory….

"And that," said the preacher, leaning over his pulpit and stabbing his finger at the congregation, "is why we are here today. To share our sorrow with each other. And when it hurts too much, when it makes you want to weep and wail and gnash your teeth, brothers and sisters, remember that Abby weeps no more. We may still walk in this valley of tears, but our sister stands in the presence of the Lord Jesus, wreathed in glory, surrounded by a love greater than we can imagine."

"Amen."

We will…see Him…in His…glory….

"When you think of Abby, brothers and sisters, smile and celebrate her joy!"

Soldiers…of the…cross.

A stirring on his left side made Grant look down at

Cathy. She was looking up at him, her solemn face wet with tears. "She really is singing with the angels?"

He tightened his arm around her, wishing he could pull her close enough that all the pain would be squeezed out of her. "Didn't I say so?" he whispered. "Didn't the preacher just say so?"

She nodded, and the smallest of smiles came to her mouth. "She's happy."

"She's happy. Very happy."

Cathy nodded. "But I can still talk to her?"

"Just close your eyes and tell her whatever's in your heart, Cathy. She'll hear."

"Okay."

Cathy's teary eyes closed, and in that instant Grant could have sworn he felt Abby all around him.

A couple of Abby's friends from the congregation rose to share remembrances of her. Then it was Grant's turn.

Standing in front of the congregation, he was strangely unable to make out any faces except those of his daughters. For a few moments he couldn't even speak. When he did, his usually clear voice was thickened with grief.

"For the first time in my life," he said, "I don't have a prepared speech."

A rustle of kindly laughter passed through the church, and in the sound he could imagine Abby laughing that deep laugh of hers. It strengthened him.

"I couldn't write a eulogy," he said, "because for the last week I've been hurting too much. Every time I picked up a pen and tried to put down a few words, the pain overwhelmed me. But Brother Anderson is right," he said, with a nod in the preacher's direction. "We need to celebrate Abby's life, and her reward."

He drew a deep, audible breath. ''Words will never be enough to say what Abby meant to me. What she still means to me. What she means to my two daughters. What she meant to my father and mother.

''You see, Abby was a gift from God to us. She came to us from terrible loss, a loss many of us can't begin to imagine. But coming to us, she took up residence in our hearts, filling a very special place in all our lives. There is not a doubt in my mind that God plucked Abby out of the ashes of her old life and set her in ours to fill a place that could have been filled by no one else.''

''Amen.''

''When I was small and scraped a knee, she was right there to dry my tears, clean my cuts and cheer me up with a cup of hot chocolate or a game. On rainy days she turned my playroom into a fantastical world where anything could happen. When I got older and my problems became more serious, she was always there to listen and guide me. She had a lot of wisdom in her, hard-won wisdom, and even when I sometimes rebelled against it, in my heart I knew she was right.''

He looked at his daughters. ''This morning, when I got up, I didn't even want to get dressed. I didn't want to face this day. But then I heard Abby saying, the way she said so many times, 'You're gonna wear that pin-striped blue suit that looks so good it's a sin.' ''

A ripple of quiet laughter ran through the room.

''Abby is part of me now,'' he said. ''It's never been clearer. I'll hear her voice whenever I'm not sure what to do, whenever I need guidance. I may not be able to see her anymore, but she's part of me forever.''

He looked down a moment, then lifted his head and smiled quietly. ''She also told me the girls should wear the Easter outfits she picked for them. Because this is Abby's Easter.''

Amens followed him back to his seat. The moment he was in the pew again, his daughters curled close to him. He hugged them and held them close, because that was all he could do.

The cortege was a long one. The Lawrence family's limousine was followed by many others, as well as a huge line of cars belonging to Abby's friends. The quiet street was lined with cars, so many that the police department had evidently decided two motorcycle officers wouldn't be enough. The two that had been there when he arrived had expanded to six, with the addition of two patrol cars.

Thunder continued to rumble, but rain fell only in brief spatters as they made their way to the cemetery.

Karen Sweeney was in one of the nondescript cars that followed behind the limousines. She wasn't there to mourn Abby, though she could have. But she was more interested in who had come to this funeral and why. And more interested in watching the reactions at the gravesite.

Somebody who regretted his actions might show up out of guilt. Or, if the killer was another type, he might show up to gloat. Or to enjoy all the attention the murder was getting. It took all kinds of sickos to make a world.

So far the main thing she had noticed was that Grant Lawrence had a great many friends, a surprising number of them from both sides of the aisle in Washington. While she didn't recognize every member of the Senate or House, she recognized enough of them to know that a lot of politics had been put aside in sympathy today. Even Randall Youngblood, whom she now knew a great deal about, was there. And Art Wallace, standing near Grant and his daughters, looked about as grief-stricken as the Lawrence family

That made the senator a pretty special man.

Randall Youngblood hadn't attended the funeral. It would have been inappropriate to deny someone else a seat in the small church. Instead, he'd waited in the cemetery, watching the hearse pull in, followed by the limousines carrying Lawrence and other celebrities. As he saw the senator, ashen-faced, holding his daughters' hands, Randall couldn't help but feel for the man. Whatever their differences politically, Grant Lawrence was a good and decent man.

"Senator," he said, quietly, extending a hand. "I'm sorry for your loss."

Lawrence looked at him with eyes that brought back echoes of when Randall's mother had died. "Thank you for coming, Randall."

The senator moved on to the gravesite, and Randall took a discreet place at the fringes of the congregation. Trees whispered in the chilly breeze. The rainy season would be here soon, but for now the rolling fields of tombstones still stood amidst pale grass browned by the arid Florida winter.

Randall had lived here his entire life, save for a brief stint in the air force during the sixties. While a war had sputtered and lurched its way to failure in Southeast Asia, he'd been stuck at the Pentagon. At first he'd resented missing out on the combat zone duty time that everyone said was essential for officer promotions. But then he'd grown accustomed to his post in procurements, to working the corridors of power, buttonholing members of Congress to gain support for this new fighter or that new missile system. He'd learned how the game was played, and that education had served him well when he'd returned to his native state and his father's sugar business.

As Grant Lawrence knelt and prayed at the woman's grave, Randall found himself regretting that their interests were so at odds. Politics was a dirty business, where reputations were made and broken by people who looked not at the man but at the vectors of interest that guided every word, every thought, every breath. It made heroes—and villains—of ordinary men. Men like Grant Lawrence.

What a shame, Randall thought. But that was how the game was played.

As the coffin was lowered and the crowd filed away, Jerry Connally found himself joined by the junior senator from Delaware. They'd gone to the same college and even dated briefly, kept in touch through the years. Now her firm hand gripped his elbow.

"We need him back in Washington," she said quietly. "The rumor mill is starting, and it's not pretty. Falden came by my office yesterday. He's wavering. And if we lose him, we lose Mitchum, Rice and Galloway. Grant has to get back to work."

"What are you hearing?" Jerry asked.

"Nothing specific," she said. "And that's probably the worst part. People are filling in the details for themselves. But our golden boy is taking some dings."

Jerry nodded. He knew about the rumors, but he'd wanted to see if she'd heard anything more than he already knew. She hadn't. But that wouldn't last long. As she'd said, people would fill in the details, and those fictions would carry all the weight of fact after a few repetitions.

"He's flying back tomorrow," Jerry said.

Her eyes seemed to lose focus for a moment. He knew the look well. The wheels were turning. Finally, she spoke.

"Mitchum's getting married next week. I'll set up a small party for him tomorrow night. My town house. Eight o'clock. The right people will be there. Will he need directions?"

"He'll be there," Jerry said. "I'll get a gift."

"Mitchum's from Louisiana," she said. "His bride-to-be is from Baton Rouge."

Jerry nodded. "I'll get them season tickets to the LSU home games."

She smiled. "Go, Tigers."

"Go, Tigers," he echoed.

Lucy and Jessie Wallace tumbled out of the house like twin whirlwinds, giggling and bubbling as Belle and Cathy ran to hug them. For a fleeting moment, Grant almost forgot all of the mess that had happened, enjoying his daughters' enjoyment. He pulled the larger suitcase from the trunk and rolled it along behind him as he made his way through the gaggle of girls to the door.

Art Wallace bent down in the doorway to do his patented "Gorilla Art" routine, scratching his sides and making "oooh oooh oooh" sounds, which sent the girls into even more peals of laughter.

"They're going to wake up the whole neighborhood," Grant said with a chuckle.

"Tooh Tooh Tooh brad," Art said, still in gorilla mode. "Rooh Rooh Rit's rix-rirty ranyway."

"And I have to be at the airport at seven," Grant said. "Sorry I'm late."

"Rot rate," Art said, now reaching his arms out with feigned clumsiness to take the girls' bags. "Right ron rime ror reakfast. Root Root Root Roops!"

"Fruit Loops!" Belle said. "My favorite!"

After the girls had scrambled inside, Grant extended his hand. "I can't tell you how much I appreciate this, Art. The girls need to get back into their routine."

Art's face grew serious as he took Grant's hand. "So do you. The work will do you good."

"It probably will, but I'm not sure my heart is in it right now. Not yet."

"Grant, your heart has always been in everything you do. Once you get back into the job, your heart will follow. That's who you are."

Grant nodded. "I suppose so. It'll be hard, though. For everyone. I gave the girls a calling card and showed them how to use it. Here are my private lines at home, my office and my cell phone. I also wrote down the number of their pediatrician, just in case."

Art took the slip of paper. "They won't need the calling card. I don't mind paying for the calls. And I'll have them in bed by eight every night."

Grant listened to the din from the dining room. The Fruit Loops were already in play, he surmised. He smiled. "Not that they'll go to sleep."

"They'll settle in," Art said. "The girls will be fine. And you need to get on to the airport."

"Last chance for hugs!" Grant called.

It seemed to take a moment for the sound to reach the girls, but then Belle and Cathy came tumbling out into his arms. "Mmmmmmm…tight hugs from my babies.

Daddy's going to miss you. You call whenever you want, and be nice to Uncle Art.''

"Gorilla Art!" Belle said. "I'll give him a banana!"

Grant laughed. It seemed as if it had been forever since he laughed. "Be nice to Gorilla Art. I'll talk to you two tonight."

He clung to them for a moment longer, soaking up their affection and love like a camel drinking water before a desert journey. Finally they let go. "Do your homework. And I'll see you this weekend."

"I love you, Daddy," Cathy said, squeezing his hand one last time.

She might as well have squeezed his heart. "I love you, too, Catherine Suzanne Lawrence. And I love you, Belle Marie Lawrence. Be good girls."

"I'm *always* good," Belle said with a nervous giggle. "Remember?"

"Then be you," Grant said, giving each of them one last kiss.

It wasn't enough. As he drove away, he watched them pile back into Art's house. It would never be enough. Next year he would move them to Washington with him, put them in school there. He didn't want them this far away. But for now, they needed the stability of their school. Their needs came first.

Even when it hurt.

9

Karen looked at her boss over the in- and out-boxes, the never-used ashtray, the stack of file folders, the paper-clip holder and cup full of pens. Lieutenant Simpson looked back at her with a world-weariness that could only come from too many years working homicides, too much disrupted family life and too much being shut off from the world of goodness.

Cops were pretty much an insular lot, because almost nobody who'd never worked the job could understand them...including their wives. But that took its toll, as Karen was finding. Because when you saw all the ugliness of the world and very little of its goodness, you started to get skewed. Or get soul-sick. She was beginning to feel soul-sick. She suspected Simpson had long since worked his way to numb.

"Okay," he said. "Given that the investigation of the senator's wife's death was a little...interrupted, what are you expecting me to do about it? The fact is, the woman was killed by a drunk driver. Where she was coming from and why is God's business and the senator's, not ours."

"I know that," Karen said. "I don't want to rake it

up. I don't even think it's related. Well..." She hesitated. "Let me put that another way. *Somebody* is raking it up. And it could prove to be relevant if someone is out to get the senator for some reason."

"If they're out to get the senator, why would they kill his housekeeper?"

"Because she got in the way. Look, the files were jimmied."

He didn't say anything for a moment, just leaned back in his executive chair with a creak of springs and pondered. "Okay, the files were jimmied. The murderer was there for something besides your typical money-jewels-electronics scenario. Most likely it was something political. But, bear with me, Sweeney. I'm not connecting that with the DUI death of the senator's wife."

Karen knew she was making a hash of it. Too little sleep had left her a little bleary, but not so bleary that she could ignore the snake of suspicion that was twisting around in the back of her mind.

"The way I see it is this, Lieutenant." She waited for his nod. "Somebody is raking up that DUI as if there was something ugly behind it. Something the senator didn't want us to know. Something that could damage the senator."

"Okay. Go on."

"It's my thinking that if we can find out who's behind this muck-raking, we might find out who was behind the break-in and the Reese woman's murder."

"Ah, the light goes on." He leaned forward. "Continue."

"Okay, so we assume a political motive and the involvement, therefore, of a political enemy. Then..." she hesitated. "I'm hearing other stuff."

"Such as?"

"The cane growers' association—most specifically Randall Youngblood—is involved somehow."

"Oh, hell. You *do* know how to make my day. The spotlight and headaches weren't already big enough on this case." He leaned back again, rubbing his chin. "Well, I do know that Youngblood is opposed to that bill the senator is trying to pass. But that's so obvious that it's too obvious, if you take my meaning."

"I do, Lieutenant. That's why I'm in here. Youngblood would be an obvious suspect for a political vendetta. And the indication is that someone in his group is behind the rumors. But I don't see him getting involved in burglary and murder."

"Nobody saw Nixon involved in Watergate at first." He rubbed his chin again and sighed. "Shit."

"Well, it might be that someone is taking advantage of what happened to taint Youngblood, as well." Karen allowed herself a sigh. "I don't like politics."

"Not when it gets this tangled. Okay, so you suspect that not only is the senator being tarred, but someone is trying to tar Youngblood, as well?"

"I'm getting that feeling."

"I can't imagine who would want to bring both of them down."

"Me neither," Karen admitted. "But something isn't right. And if it's not one person trying to bring them both down, then they're trying to bring each other down, and somewhere in that mess is the person who committed the murder."

"Maybe. Or maybe someone on each side of that bill is merely an opportunist."

Karen nodded. "Entirely possible. But we're still faced with the fact that the only apparent motive for the initial burglary was political."

"Yeah. Where's the senator?"

"He flew back to Washington."

"And Youngblood?"

"He's up there, too, to lobby against S.R. 52."

"Hmm." Simpson closed his eyes for a minute, thinking. "You know," he said finally, "if there's a politico involved in this mess, the best place to look would be Washington."

"Shall I contact the police up there?"

"Hell no," said Simpson, leaning forward so suddenly that his chair thumped against the floor. "You're going up there."

Karen was taken aback. Her heart thudded with sudden anxiety. "Why? I don't know anyone up there. I wouldn't be any good."

"What makes you think the D.C. cops know anyone in political circles? Hell, Sweeney, nowhere do cops move in circles like that. You wouldn't be at any disadvantage."

He stabbed a finger in her direction. "Yes, you'll be good. Because the senator is the center of this maelstrom, and I can't think of anyone better to introduce you around to the people who might be trying to sink his boat."

"But, sir, I have other cases...."

"For now they're on Previn's desk. I'll let you know when I've got this all arranged."

Karen left Simpson's office feeling more uneasy than she had in recent memory. When it came to Senator Grant Lawrence, she wasn't exactly detached. And she didn't see how hanging around with him in Washington was going to help her be any more objective.

But she also knew better than to argue with Simpson.

"What's up?" Previn asked as she returned to her desk.

"I got my marching orders. Simpson wants me to go to Washington and sniff around for a few days." Karen shrugged. "The Reese murder does look political. So I guess it makes sense for me to go up there. But hob-nobbing with the rich and powerful isn't my thing."

Previn nodded. "Linda would love that."

Karen watched his face sag. "Any chance you can work things out?"

"I don't know. I'm...let's see." He ticked off points on his fingers. "I'm too distant. I work too many hours. I bring my work home, emotionally if not actually. And I'm a lousy fuck."

"She actually *said* that?"

He picked at an invisible speck on his desk blotter. "She said she's been faking for years, just to get it over with. She's been talking to some guy online, she says. *He* knows how to satisfy a woman, she says."

"Geez, Dave. She doesn't hold much back, does she?"

He was quiet for a moment, then finally looked up. "So when do you go to D.C.?"

"I'm not sure yet, but it'll be soon. I need to go home and pack. Power suits, the lieutenant said. Like my off-the-rack stuff is going to look powerful among Brooks Brothers, Armanis and other tailored things."

He smiled weakly. "Knock 'em dead."

As she looked at the battered shell of a man, she won-dered whether he would find justice for Stacy Wiggins.

"The Wiggins case," she said after a moment, giving him something to sink his teeth into, something to make him feel useful and important.

"What about it?" he asked dully.

"Well, she owned a dance studio. Her one employee, a woman named Alissa Jurgen, was in love with her, but Stacy was straight."

Previn perked a little. "Hm."

"Exactly. Do a background on the school and Jurgen. Find out if Jurgen stands to gain anything from Stacy's death."

"Will do."

For the moment, anyway, Previn looked better than he had in days.

Elaine Pragle smiled as she opened the door for Grant. "Good to have you back, Grant."

"Good to be back," he said. From the sounds in the back of her town house, the party was already underway. "Just tell me you didn't hire a stripper for Mitchum."

She laughed. "Ahh, that famed Grant Lawrence wit. No, just lugubrious congeniality tonight."

"In short, drinks and business."

"Bingo," she said.

He'd been to her town house once before, in the whirlwind after his first election. They had both been freshmen senators, and both had campaigned on environmental issues. Jerry Connally had said she would be a good ally to have, and he'd been right.

If he'd authored S.R. 52 in his first year, it would have gone down in flames. But over the past eight years, he and Elaine had worked to collect a bloc of other colleagues from coastal states by maneuvering for shared committee assignments, co-sponsoring bills, offering a carrot here, a carrot there. It had been a long, slow road. And way too much work to let slip away this late in the game.

Elaine ushered him to the backyard, where she'd had

festive paper lamps hung around the pool deck. Underwater lighting added to the atmosphere. Along the stone walls that enclosed the freshly-cut lawn, spring flowers burst with fresh color and life.

"Our golden boy is here," she said by way of introduction as they stepped through the sliding glass doors. "Now the *real* fun can start."

Rick Galloway turned and lifted a glass of his favorite Irish whiskey. "Welcome home, Grant."

Oliver Falden offered a cautious smile. "Are you going to help us wrangle one last night of fun out of Mitchum before he goes and gets himself tied down?"

"That's the plan," Grant said. He turned to the senator from Louisiana. "Congratulations, Louis. I hear she's a Baton Rouge beauty."

Mitchum took his hand. "Thanks, Grant. Is there anything you don't hear?"

Grant chuckled. "It always pays to keep your ear to the ground and your nose to the wind."

"And you always were the master contortionist," Elaine said. "What can I get you to drink?"

"A glass of Baileys would go down well, thanks."

"My favorite," said Harrison Rice, lifting his own glass of the creamy liquid. Then his slow, Alabama drawl softened. "I'm sorry about Abby, Grant. She was a great woman."

Grant nodded. "Thanks, Harry. We were very touched by the flowers."

"That detective, the one on TV," Rice said. "Is she good? Abby deserves the best."

"She seems to know her business. I sure wouldn't want to be on her bad side."

"Good." Rice patted his shoulder. "Okay, enough

gloom and doom. Let's tell our friend Mitchum what he's in for in the way of marital bliss."

But of course, as usually happened at these "parties," it wasn't long before they settled around a table on the pool deck and the serious conversation began. The purpose of these affairs, whatever excuse was used for them, eventually came down to deal-making and problem-solving. As a rule, the senators were so tied up during the day that face-to-face communications came after hours. In fact, Grant sometimes thought that fifty percent of the real work was done in committee and the other fifty percent was done at social gatherings.

"Grant," said Falden, "I just wanted to offer my sympathies again. Tragic, about Abby."

"Thanks. We appreciated the flowers."

"Sorry I couldn't be there for the funeral. My wife had already committed us."

Grant nodded. "Thanks. I knew you were there in spirit." Which wasn't true. He knew Falden better than that, but polite fictions had to be preserved. But he also didn't want to spend the evening talking about Abby. His grief was a private thing, and if people kept bringing it up, it might become a public thing. And as he knew too well, tears were considered a weakness in men. There'd be a hundred sharks ready to pounce if Senator Grant Lawrence broke down in public, and some of them were here right now.

"Anyway," Falden said, "I wanted to talk to you about S.R. 52. You know, Randall Youngblood is making a very good case for rewriting the bill to slow things down."

Grant nodded. "I've heard." He knew Falden was speaking for Mitchum, Halloway and Rice, who were also wavering. He felt the same adrenaline kick as when he'd stepped into a courtroom that first time. The back-yard moved into softer focus as his eyes bored into Falden's face. Game time. This was his life, his milieu, his bread and butter.

Falden continued. "There are valid concerns. All of our states rely on agriculture. So does the whole country."

"I don't want to kill agribusiness," Grant said forcefully, yet still within the limits of the social occasion. It was a fine tightrope to walk. "And the effects of the bill would not be as dire as Youngblood would have us believe. Trust me, Oliver, I've had studies done. I'll be glad to send you some fresh copies for review." A veiled reminder that Falden already had the information in his files, even though he probably hadn't bothered to review it.

Elaine spoke, playing devil's advocate. "I read the studies, Grant. Some of the fertilizer-intensive farmers would be hurt. Production would drop. Prices would go up."

Grant nodded, and Elaine continued. "But we need to look at some other things, Oliver. Like the displacement of fisheries because of the fertilizer runoff. The increase in red algae blooms, which also cause high fish mortality, not to mention human health hazards such as asthma and severe allergic reactions."

Oliver nodded as if he'd read all of that, too. "But we can't just kill the farmers. Hell, farmers are like mom, apple pie and the American flag."

"I'm not proposing we kill them," Grant said, keeping his tone friendly and understanding. "You need to come down to my part of the world sometime, Oliver. I'd love to show you around. But until then, let me tell you what's happening."

Oliver nodded. "I'm willing to listen."

"At least as well as you've listened to Youngblood," Elaine said dryly. The others laughed warily.

Grant ignored the aside, keeping Falden pinned with his gaze. His heart was drumming the steady beat of battle. "The Everglades was once justifiably called 'The River of Grass.' Most of south Florida was covered by it. It was home to thousands of species, some of which are now facing extinction, like the Florida panther. It also provided freshwater runoff into the Bay of Florida and a huge section of the Gulf of Mexico. Then Lake Okeechobee was dammed, and huge tracts of the Glades were drained for agriculture. Goodbye, freshwater runoff."

Oliver nodded. "But…"

"Wait a moment, please," Grant said, aware that he had everyone's attention and unwilling to relinquish it. He had to hammer his points while their attention was fully on him. He leaned forward a bit, pressing the point by his physical presence. "The loss of that freshwater flow to the Gulf was bad enough. Add to it the nitrates from fertilizers—hundreds of tons of fertilizers each year, I might add—and you shatter a complex and vitally important ecosystem. The water is cloudy, the coral reefs are dying, and the fin fish and shellfish populations are plummeting."

Oliver nodded. "But we mustn't be hasty. These farmers, they tell me—"

"S.R. 52 is a very cautious bill," Grant said, sitting back, forcing himself to appear relaxed, when inside his muscles were screaming for action. "It compensates farmers for lost yields caused by the reduction of fertilizers. It has price supports for major crops. It defers wetland reclamation over the next twenty years. And it has

grant money for research into site-persistent fertilizers—
which will reduce runoff *and* be more economical in the
long run—and advanced hydroponics, so they can still
grow crops in reclaimed wetlands. We're not cutting
their throats, Oliver.''

"There are no price supports for tobacco," Galloway
said. "Say what you will, but it's a legal product, and
it's a big chunk of my state's economy. The growers are
getting crunched by taxes, and now you want to cut back
on how much they're allowed to fertilize. Not to put too
fine a point on it, but I'm up for re-election next year,
and I can't fight off Williamson without the tobacco
growers.''

Grant wasn't sure Galloway could beat Williamson
even *with* the tobacco growers, but he wasn't going to
say that. Truth was, Galloway was caught in a squeeze
between the far right and moderate wings of his party.
North Carolina, like other southern states, had both
gained and lost much in the transition to the New South.
Old-time power brokers had to vie with newcomers who
represented the high-tech industries—and with the pop-
ulation shift from the northeast, which brought educated,
more liberal workers along with those high-tech firms.

Williamson was a virtual lock for the districts in the
Triangle, named for the trio of top-notch universities in
the Raleigh-Durham-Chapel Hill region. Galloway
needed the agricultural and coastal districts, many of
which were still recovering from a spate of Atlantic
storms that had roared through and flooded last year's
crops. Emergency relief funds were stretched tight after
a series of tornadoes had ripped through Dallas and Ft.
Worth, and a moderate earthquake had shaken Seattle.

Grant knew exactly what carrot to offer Galloway.

He'd been holding it back as his ace-in-the-hole, one that he knew he had the power to bring off.

"Let's talk FEMA funding," Grant said, casting a quick glance over to Elaine.

She nodded and picked up the thread. "I have solid support for a nine percent increase in the FEMA budget. I can probably still push it through committee at eleven percent, but it'll be closer."

She looked at Galloway. "I'll go to the mat on that if you'll work with us. Go to your coastal fishing towns, Rick. Get a sound bite standing next to some guy whose nets came up empty and tell him you're working to protect his job. I'll bet you that'll change a few hearts in the Triangle. High-tech folks are strong on the environment, you know."

"And," Mitchum added dryly, "the yuppies love their fish and seafood. It's heart-healthy, in case you haven't heard."

A quiet round of chuckles greeted the sally, easing the tension, but only for a moment.

Galloway paused for a moment, as if calculating the voting districts in his head. "You get eleven percent on FEMA, and I'll push S.R. 52. But my farmers are going to need that emergency money. I have people who are still waiting to rebuild their homes. They've already lost one crop. I have to have something to take to them when I ask them to cut back on fertilizer and risk losing another."

Rice cut in. "Grant, when are you going to declare for the primaries?"

Now it was Grant's turn to pause. Part of him wanted to leap right into that fray, like the political fighter he was. Part of him feared the consequences, both politically and personally, if he failed. Presidential candidates were open season in the press. Reporters from all over the country would be digging through every moment of his life. The selection of a president was, as one commentator put it, trial by ordeal. Could he afford to inflict that on his girls?

"I don't know, Harry. Jerry's going to get back to me this week with a straw poll. I'll know more then."

"The party likes you," Rice said. "The people of Alabama like you. My numbers show you at nineteen percent over Phillips, and the others are barely a blip. My term's up next year, too. It'd be nice to have the next Democratic candidate for president shaking my hand."

Elaine smiled. "I think Grant would be happy to join you at a fund-raiser or two. Wouldn't you, Grant?"

Elaine had begun working on him to run for president within weeks of their last election. She was acting as if he was certain to run, and to win the nomination. As to the former, she was probably right. As to the latter, did she know something he didn't?

"I'd be happy to," he said. "We southern Democrats have to stick together."

Mitchum, although a Republican, was nodding now. Grant knew he was smart enough to see the handwriting on the wall. Only Falden remained stoic.

"I need better price supports," Falden said. "My farmers would go under on the soybean baselines you have. And like Rick, I'm hurting with the tobacco people. That's five percent of Maryland's agriculture, and S.R. 52 has no price supports at all."

Grant spread his hands. "The bill has to pass the budget muster, Oliver. And if we write in price supports for tobacco, I'll lose ten votes, guaranteed. But your own Department of Agriculture calls the Chesapeake Bay

'Maryland's great natural treasure.' That treasure needs this bill, Oliver. As much as the Everglades does."

"Maybe more," Elaine said. "This is the right thing to do, Oliver. It's the right thing for your state *and* mine. It's the right thing for the country. And if things do go our way next November, wouldn't you like to have a sympathetic ear in the Oval Office?"

Falden was a Republican, but he was also a realist. "Bring up the soybean baselines. Another two cents a pound. I can sell it at that."

Grant nodded. "I'll see what I can do."

"And while you're at it," Falden added, "get behind us on this mess in Colombia. The Bogota government needs to see unified U.S. support before they're going to go all out after those guerillas."

Caught up in his grief, with what little focus he had left given to his girls and S.R. 52, Grant had given only cursory attention to the deteriorating situation in the eastern highlands of Colombia. He was not about to get railroaded into supporting U.S. military intervention, and certainly not as a bargaining chip for his bill.

"The situation down there is too fluid for my taste," Grant said. "I want to see things coalesce a bit, give the Colombians a chance to clean their own house, before we go wading in with guns blazing."

"They're shooting up humanitarian convoys," Falden said, pressing the point.

Grant put up a hand. "Senator, I'll see what I can do about the soybean baselines. But as for Colombia, that's a different issue. My vote on funding for U.S. military aid will be on its merits."

Falden nodded. "I guess that's all I can ask."

Elaine smiled. It was a smile of cool satisfaction. She elbowed Mitchum. "Isn't this better than a stripper?"

The laughter broke the tension, and for the rest of the evening the drinks and conversation flowed freely. To Grant, it was also a blur. His body warred between the adrenaline rush of the deal and sheer exhaustion. After another hour, he excused himself.

It was time to go home and call the girls.

10

After he'd called his daughters and read *Horton Hears a Who* to them at long distance rates, Grant said the painful good-nights. He'd had to be away from them too many times to count, but still it seemed to tear his heart out when Belle said "Good night, Daddy" in that sleepy voice. He could see her pretty face, soft with sleep, stroking her cheek with her hand as she always did. Cathy held on for only a few minutes longer. It was past their bedtime, and he'd called too late.

It hadn't taken long for his job to step on his girls again. One night.

"The girls had a great time," Art said after Cathy had hung up. "They're super kids."

"How many gorillas did it take to feed them dinner?"

Art laughed. "Only two. I made batter-fried catfish and hush puppies for them. They kept saying 'Hush, puppy!' and laughing up a storm. But they ate well. And did their homework. I didn't even have to ask."

"I'm not surprised," Grant said, shaking his head. "Kids always behave better when they're away from their parents. But that will wear off in a couple of days."

"That's right. Once they start thinking of me as a parent, I'm sure I'll see all their hijinks."

"I'm sure you will, too." Grant glanced at the clock on the wall over his desk. "I have a couple of other calls I need to make tonight. Thanks again, Art."

"I'm glad to help out, Grant. Good night."

Art hung up the phone. It wasn't difficult to imagine Belle and Cathy thinking of him as a parent. They'd grown up with his twins, after all. He'd changed Belle's diapers more than once. And he often drove them to school when Grant was out of town.

Grant kept saying "Thanks," as if Art were making some major sacrifice. Truth was, it was no sacrifice at all. In the fifteen months since Elizabeth had left, his girls had become his life. Having two more gave him twice as much reason to wake up the next morning.

It was no sacrifice at all.

Grant flipped open the folder full of messages he'd picked up from his office in the Senate building that day. He sorted them into stacks, one for those that required a prompt phone call on Monday, another for those that required a letter in response, and another for the few he might need to reply to over the weekend.

And one he needed to answer tonight.

His heart slammed as he saw the message from Lieutenant Simpson, Tampa Homicide, with both work and home phone numbers.

Had they found Abby's murderer? Or—nightmare thought—had they found out that Stacy had been murdered in his house, as well? He felt guilty for even worrying about such a thing. But there was Jerry's future to consider. Most of all, there was the horrific scandal he didn't want to touch his daughters.

His hand shook as he reached for the phone and punched in the home number for Simpson.

"Lieutenant Simpson, please."

"This is Simpson."

"Lieutenant, this is Grant Lawrence. I just got your message. Sorry to call so late."

"No problem. Like yours, my job doesn't have regular hours."

Grant couldn't manage even a polite chuckle. "Have you learned something about Abby's murder?" His palm was sweating, he realized. He hated fearing what the police might find, and for an instant he felt a surge of anger against Jerry that shook him to his core.

"No, no, I'm afraid not, Senator," Simpson said. "Sorry I raised your hopes. No, I need to ask a favor with regard to the investigation."

"Anything I can do," Grant said. Anything except betray Jerry and hurt his daughters.

"I'm going to send a detective up there. With the break-in of your files, this is looking more and more like a political crime. We don't really have an eye on anyone in particular at the moment, but it makes sense to get a feeling for what's happening up there. It's not just the break-in, Senator. Someone's spreading nasty rumors."

Grant sighed. "Aren't they always?"

The policeman laughed. "I suppose so. But put it all together and…"

"Yes, of course," Grant said, impatient to get this conversation over now that he knew the cops had no real news for him. "What is it you'd like me to do?"

"I'd like you to let my detective follow you around a bit, give her a chance to talk to people in your circles."

"Her?"

"Well, I'm sending the lead investigator, Detective Sweeney."

Grant almost said no. He had a sudden memory of predatory, wise gray eyes, eyes that seemed to see too much. But it wasn't just what she might find out that disturbed him. No, it was his reaction to the thought of seeing her again. She intrigued him in a way that made him distinctly uncomfortable.

"I'll do what I can," he told the lieutenant. "When will she arrive?"

"I'm going to put her on the first available flight."

"Have her call me when she gets in. I'll have someone pick her up."

"Thanks. Just don't put her in a really expensive hotel. She's on a per diem." Simpson chuckled. "The department has a limit."

"I'll see that she gets a room somewhere suitable," he promised, straining to join in the chuckle. A room far, far away from his own Georgetown house.

When he hung up the phone, he felt as if he'd gone through the wringer. Now that he was learning to live with his grief over Abby and Stacy, he was realizing that he was in a real mess.

A really *big* mess.

"We have problems," Grant said to Jerry Connally.

It was Saturday. No need to go to his office, just a meeting later in the day with some constituents who were in town for the weekend. Ordinary people who had come to enjoy Washington and thought it might be nice to actually meet their senator.

They were having breakfast served on the terrace behind Grant's Georgetown house. It wasn't much of a terrace, but it was enough, with a bit of garden. The housekeeper filled the table with coffee in a thermal carafe along with a bowl of grapefruit and orange sections. On the side table, she had put a couple of chafing dishes holding grits and scrambled eggs. On a warming plate were sausage and bacon.

Enough to feed an army. But Grant's housekeeper was trained to provide variety whenever he had guests for a meal, even if it was only breakfast. When alone, he was apt to have only a bowl of whole grain cereal and a glass of orange juice.

"I told you," Jerry said. "Don't worry about it. I'm the only one who can take a fall on this. You don't know anything."

"And what's going to happen when they *do* catch the killer? You're not the only one who knows all of what happened that night."

Grant, aware that he could be watched from anywhere, though most likely only by his housekeeper this morning, was careful not to throw up a hand as he wanted to, was careful to keep his voice quiet and even, though turmoil made him want to get loud.

"They'll never make the connection," Jerry said quietly.

"Of course not. Unless the killer confesses."

Jerry's head jerked. Then he looked squarely at Grant. "Well, if he does, *I'll* confess."

Grant shook his head, feeling pain for his friend. "Jerry…Jerry, we've been friends forever. I don't want anything to happen to you."

Jerry's face hardened, a look Grant knew all too well. This was Jerry the fighter, a man who, for twenty years, had methodically overcome any obstacle in Grant's path, sometimes including Grant himself.

"If I go down, I go down. What's important is that we push the bill through and you get the presidency, Grant. This country needs a turnaround. People are ready for a fresh wind. *That's* what matters."

Grant's anger ebbed as he looked at his counselor and friend. It was humbling, more humbling than anything in his life, except the birth of his daughters, to realize how much Jerry was willing to sacrifice to put him in the White House. But it also disconcerted him. He suddenly wanted to bound out of the chair and pace off the agitation.

"Jerry, I don't need a fanatic on my staff."

Jerry gave him a half smile. "I'm no *kamikaze,* Grant. I'm not proud of what I did that night. But I'll have to live with the nightmares. I did the right thing for you, your daughters, the bill, my hometown and the country. If you need me to resign over it…"

"No."

Jerry shrugged. "Your call. I'm also clearheaded enough to realize that I'm in for a pile of shit, sooner or later."

Grant's heart ached for his friend. "Oh, I know."

"No, you *don't* know. You suspect. You can suspect all you want, but you don't know. And if it ever comes to it, I'll deny that you even suspected, because I sure as hell haven't told you anything except that Stacy died that night, too."

Grant gave up trying to maintain outward calm. He rose from his chair and started pacing the flagstone patio. Glancing through the French doors, he saw that his housekeeper was nowhere in sight.

He was lawyer enough to know that Jerry was right. If questioned in a courtroom, he would be nailed down to the fact that all he had were suspicions. That he knew nothing for a fact.

But that didn't settle the moral problem, not one little bit, and a bilious taste filled the back of his mouth. There were too many priorities involved here, too many people he cared about. Scandal had to be avoided for their sakes. For his. *Oh quit the nobility,* he told himself. *Give it up. You've got as much vested in silence right now as anybody.*

He hated himself for it.

Finally he spoke. "That detective's arriving in town this morning."

"What detective?"

He faced Jerry. "The Sweeney woman. Seems the TPD is following a trail in this direction."

Jerry nodded. He looked as calm as if they were merely discussing the weather. Maybe he was truly resigned to whatever might happen. Or maybe he was just good at hiding his feelings. Well, of course he was. He'd trained in a courtroom and had enough political experience to know how to hide what he was thinking.

"I said I'd have someone pick her up and establish her in a hotel," Grant said.

Jerry nodded. "I'll do it."

"Right into the lion's den, huh?"

Jerry shrugged. "I made the mess. I'll clean it up."

Karen walked down the jetway and into the cavernous, cockeyed, glass barn that was Dulles International Airport. She'd called the senator from the plane just before final approach. Lawrence had said that Jerry Connally would meet her at baggage claim. So the next step was to find baggage claim. This wasn't a matter of great detective work so much as simply following the herd.

It was, at least, a well-heeled herd. People for whom "weekend casual" meant designer polo shirts and freshly-pressed khaki slacks. Seriously relaxed faces. Seriously casual checks of pagers and cell phones. There seemed to be a pervading tension in the air. She'd read somewhere that New York was a city about money, while Washington was a city about power. She could almost see that.

Connally joined her as her bag came down the belt. She was a half step too far away to reach it, and he hefted it for her.

"You travel light, Detective," he said, with a hint of friendly sarcasm.

Breaking the ice. She smiled. "I didn't know if y'all might have a late cold snap. So I packed every warm thing I had."

"Good idea. It still gets chilly in the evenings." They made for the door, where he'd kept a car waiting. "I'll take you to your hotel. Then I guess you'll want to meet with Grant?"

"Sounds like a plan," she said.

Jerry climbed in beside her and gave the driver the name of a hotel. Minutes later, they were in the HOV lane of I-66, headed for the city. They swept past elegant new subdivisions, barely visible behind ivy-clad stone walls. Some cities wept. Some cities yelled. This city whispered. And every whisper mattered.

They crossed the Potomac on the Fourteenth Street Bridge and turned north, through Georgetown. Wisconsin Avenue teemed with European sedans. Embassies lined the streets until, farther north, they drove into another kind of elegance. Not a modern subdivision, but stately, residential homes that filled the northwest corner of the city.

"I could work my entire life and never afford one of these houses," Karen said.

"It's out of my league, too," Connally answered. "But there's a nice hotel up here that I hope the City of Tampa can afford. Have you ever been to Washington before?"

"Once. As a child. But that was years ago."

He nodded. "I'll teach you how to use the Metro. It's cheaper than cabs, and you can get anywhere."

"It's quiet up here," she said. "It's as if the entire city is quiet."

"It's a Saturday."

Karen cocked an eyebrow. "I know. I'd expect people to be out and about, free from the workaday grind."

He chuckled. "Not hardly. Welcome to Washington, Detective. Capital city of the most powerful country in the world. Weekends are just a different kind of work days."

"A different way of shuffling papers?" she asked jokingly.

"Something like that," he said casually, although his eyes darkened for a moment.

She'd offended him. "I said something wrong."

Connally shrugged. "Most people think it's that way. We shuffle papers and make speeches and collect big paychecks and bigger bribes. Truth is, the pace grinds you down after a while. Senator Lawrence is almost never *not* working. He reads three newspapers over breakfast, if he can get breakfast to himself. Lunch is shop talk. Dinner is deal-making. If he wants to hear the symphony play at the Kennedy Center, he's as much on stage as any of the musicians. I once had to physically block a reporter who was bird-dogging him while he was at the zoo with his girls. Grant was changing Belle's diaper, and the guy wanted to follow him into the bathroom.''

"God," Karen whispered.

Jerry nodded out the window. "And it's not just Grant Lawrence who lives that way. Everyone in this city is under a microscope. *Someone* is always watching. Political allies. Political enemies. The press. The intelligence agencies, our government's and others'. Everyone wants to know what's going to happen before it happens, so they can calculate their own gains and losses, nudge it along or block it. Washington belongs to the people who get up the earliest, stay up the latest, see the most, hear the most, know the most, ingratiate the most, piss off the fewest and work the hardest."

He turned to her. "And that's why I haven't seen my brother since a year ago Christmas. And he lives an hour away."

"I never realized," Karen said. "I mean, I never thought about it."

"Nobody does, Detective. Point is, it's Saturday. For most of the rest of the world, that means a weekend, a couple of days off. In the language of the press, those are 'slow news days.' So reporters are scrambling for anything to make copy. And no one wants to be fodder for a slow news day. That's why it's so quiet."

Karen could hardly imagine it. Yes, she'd worked on and around a couple of high-profile cases, where it seemed the press was all over every move the department made. But that was transitory. And, by and large, the scrutiny was limited to her professional activities. When she went home, she was just another private citizen, passing through life without much notice.

For people like Grant Lawrence, that never happened. There was no such thing as an idle trip to the grocery to stock up on nachos and a six-pack for a ball game. That, she suspected, meant whispered rumors about alcoholism or some such.

A college professor had, before his first class, explained that Karen and her classmates could use any kind of pen they wished on his exams. "You can use black ink," he'd said, "or blue ink, or even purple ink." Then he'd paused for a moment. "But if you decide to use purple ink, I'm going to notice it. I'll pay extra attention to that paper with the purple ink. So you might want to think twice about what kind of pen you use, and how confident you feel about this exam."

Karen had used black ink. If she could have, she would have used invisible ink.

Senator Lawrence, like the other movers and shakers in this town full of movers and shakers, wrote his life in purple ink. And people noticed every word, every comma, every space.

They pulled into the hotel, and Connally handed her bag to a bellman. He turned, smiling, and offered her a card. "If you'd like to shower and rest a bit, feel free. Senator Lawrence will send a car when you're ready."

Karen nodded. A movie line flitted through her mind: *You're not in Kansas anymore.*

11

The car Senator Lawrence sent for Karen deposited her at a row of concrete barricades a hundred yards from the steps of the Capitol, where she could see him halfway up, talking to a small knot of people and pointing toward the building. She wondered if he were suggesting they take a tour.

Dressed in the best power suit she had, scarlet with black piping, she waited at a respectful distance, not wanting to intrude.

She'd never been here before, and looking at the Capitol from its very steps, then back across the Mall toward the Washington Monument, filled her with a sense of awe. These were the structures and views that most symbolized her country to her, every bit as much as the flag. She'd often wanted to come here as a tourist, but so far had never managed both the vacation and the money at the same time. Besides, it was a heck of a lot cheaper to go to the Keys or St. Augustine when she needed to get away.

But here she could feel the weight of history, see the architecture that had turned this place from a swamp into one of the world's great capitals. Looking around, she thought of all the famous people who had climbed these steps.

Laughter caught her attention, and she looked up in time to see Grant shaking the hands of the men and women with whom he'd been talking. Moments later they turned to descend the steps. When they were a few yards away, Grant came over to her.

"Detective," he said, offering his hand. "Good to see you."

"Senator."

"Those people were from Florida," he remarked. "You might not believe it, but one of my favorite things is talking to my constituents. I especially like it when I have the time to give them the tour."

She smiled. "I imagine that doesn't happen often. Mr. Connally gave me quite a lecture on the way in from the airport about how hard everyone works here, even on weekends."

Grant surprised her with a laugh. "That sounds like Jerry. I guess he forgot that you probably work eighty-hour weeks, too."

Again that Grant Lawrence charm reached out to touch her. The man actually considered other people's lives, and the demands on them. "Sometimes," she admitted.

His blue eyes locked with hers as he continued to smile. "Looks to me like you're working a weekend right now, Detective."

"Please, call me Karen."

"Sure. If you'll call me Grant." He started leading the way down the steps toward the waiting car. "Your boss wasn't exactly clear about what I'm supposed to do. Introduce you around, I guess. Get you in contact with people?"

"Mainly I need to sniff around and find out who might have it in for you in a really bad way."

"Bad enough for murder."

"Something like that."

He looked down at her. "I hope you have something with sequins on it."

"Why?"

"The best thing I can think of to do is take you to a party tonight." He gave a mirthless chuckle. "It's a Party party. Take the measure of the man and all that."

"An audition?"

"Something like that."

Not only was she not in Kansas anymore, but she suddenly realized she might be in well over her head. This was not the kind of investigation she was used to running.

"Relax," he said, as if he sensed her trepidation. "They're all just human beings, for all they think they might be something more. And I usually bring a staffer or a friend to these shindigs. You won't be out of place."

Karen had never done undercover work. She'd spent a lot of the afternoon thinking about how she would handle it, what lies or half-truths she would tell to blend seamlessly into a crowd of schmoozers.

The rest of the afternoon she'd spent prowling Georgetown Park, searching for that elusive trifecta: her size, her style, her price range. She'd finally had to give a little on the price range to find a simple aubergine sheath that was formal without screaming *Look at me!* Undercover work meant keeping a low profile, or as much of one as possible, given the circumstances. Grant had described the party as "candidate under glass."

All of that planning had, of course, flown out the window five minutes into the party.

"You're the cop," the venerable representative from California had said after Grant introduced her. "I saw you on CNN, at the press conference."

He leaned in, offering her a whiff of breath mints and extra-dry martini. "Do you have any leads?"

Inspiration struck, and she flashed him a smile. "No. Do you?"

He guffawed. "Now isn't that just like a cop? Answer a question with a question." He shifted his attention to Grant. "Seriously, Senator, if there's anything I can do, just call."

"How very kind," Grant said. There was warmth in his voice, but also wariness. "If you'll excuse me, Fred, I need to get Karen a drink." He turned to her. "What would you like?"

"I'll just come along and see what they have," she said. "A pleasure to meet you, Mr. Rawlings."

"You don't trust any of these people," she said, after they'd stepped away.

"Not true." He smiled. "I just haven't introduced you to the ones I do trust. See, everyone here is trying to guess who's in everyone else's inner circle. Who do I listen to? Who listens to me? Whom do you call if you need my vote or my support?"

"Why not call you?" she asked. "Horse's mouth, and all that."

"Because if you call me directly, I might need something in return. Something you're unwilling to do. Or, worse, I might just say no. Then word filters out that you can't deliver me, and you go down a notch on someone else's list. No, it's much safer to talk to the people you know talk to me, the people I listen to. If you can convince them to convince me, you've still delivered. If they don't, *they* go down a notch. Wheels within wheels.''

''And you're creating a smoke screen,'' she said. ''Being seen talking to people, sharing confidential body language, but they're not in your inner circle. Making it harder for people to know what buttons to push to get to you.''

He smiled. ''Bingo, Detective. Part of John Kennedy's genius was that people couldn't be sure how they could push his buttons, who they needed to talk to. Except for Bobby, of course, and a couple of other guys, like Kenny O'Donnell.''

''Family, and friends he'd known for years,'' she said. ''Untouchables.''

''Exactly. Beyond that, in a crowd like this, you had no idea who could carry your water for you. So you had to carry it yourself.''

Karen nodded. ''Which put him in the driver's seat. Where *you'd* like to be.''

''The Oval Office isn't a passenger seat, Karen. So what would you like to drink? And you do look stunning, if I neglected to say so before.''

He'd delivered the compliment with such casual aplomb that it caught her off-balance. She felt herself blush and instantly regretted it. She knew she should have thanked him, but it was as if she couldn't find the right tone of voice. She settled for as wide a smile as she could manage without looking goofy. She hoped. ''Scotch and soda, please. *Very* light on the scotch.''

''I'll tell the bartender to wave the bottle over it.''

''That would be perfect. So,'' she said, pausing for a moment, ''now that you've explained the rules of the game, let's play.''

He nodded and handed her the drink. "Look interested, even impressed, but never awed. Remember, everyone in this room spent part of today sitting on the toilet."

She laughed. "Now that's an image."

"Keeps things in perspective, doesn't it?"

Of course, with her cover blown, there was no way she could hide any longer. Or so she thought. It was soon apparent that most of the people in this room hadn't recognized her, or even if they had, they figured that since she'd arrived on Grant's arm, she might have some influence with him. They certainly seemed intent on finding out.

The first inquiries were casual, wanting to know how long she'd known Grant. These came from a couple of Republican members of the House who introduced themselves politely. They drifted away when she admitted she'd known him only a week.

Realizing that wasn't going to get her anywhere, she pondered a different way to handle the inquiries. While doing so, she suddenly found herself face-to-face with Randall Youngblood.

"Detective Sweeney, isn't it?" he asked. He was a handsome man with steel-gray hair, warm brown eyes and just a couple of extra pounds on him, softening what might otherwise have been a harshly-chiseled face. He looked, Karen thought, comfortable. Comfortable with himself and the world. Comfortable to be around. And he did not look the least bit out of place in a roomful of image-conscious people.

"Just Karen, Mr. Youngblood," she responded promptly. "This is a social occasion."

"Is it indeed?" He lifted a brow but didn't ask any questions, unlike the others, who seemed to want to know the depth, breadth and length of her relationship with Senator Lawrence.

"Yes," she said firmly. "It is."

"Good…good. That makes you the only person here just to have fun. The rest are here to see and be seen."

She smiled. "That's what I was told."

"It's the price we all pay. They need to see and be seen, I just need to be here in case I can be useful."

"In what ways are you useful?"

"Oh," he said with a self-deprecating chuckle, "I'm a font of facts and information. If someone needs that during one of their conversations this evening, I can be summoned."

Karen nodded. "Why do I think you're more important than that?"

He shrugged. "You flatter me. But since the issue of the day is S.R. 52, which is sponsored by your friend Grant Lawrence, then I have to be present. Sort of like a human file cabinet."

"I see." She smiled again, hoping she looked suitably impressed. "What kind of facts are you providing?"

"Just the true impact of S.R. 52 in terms of economic and personal losses."

"That's very important."

"I like to think so. You know, you and I have something in common."

"What's that?"

He touched her upper arm lightly, briefly. Just a momentary contact that might have worked to create a feeling that they were in this together if she had not been a cop. Touch didn't work on her the way it worked on most people. On her, it worked as a threat.

"Well," he said, "not to put too fine a point on it,

we both work to prevent crime. Different kinds of crime, but crime nonetheless.''

How very interesting, Karen thought, while she nodded as if agreeing. Very interesting that he saw the senator's bill as a crime. She decided to pry into that perception a little further. ''And of course, there's self-defense.''

His face lit with a broad smile. ''See, we *do* understand each other. If the law can't protect us, then we must protect ourselves. Legally, of course.''

''Of course.'' But the reference to legality had sounded tacked on, an afterthought. Her heart quickened a little as she wondered just what lengths this man might go to in order to defeat the bill.

''Are you at all familiar with the bill?'' he asked her.

''Only vaguely. Very vaguely.'' Which wasn't true. Since the murder of Abigail Reese, she'd made it a point to learn everything about S.R. 52 that she could.

''Well, let me tell you a bit about it.''

She gave him a nod, trying to look ingenuous, and he was off and running. The interesting thing to her, though, was that he'd hardly said five words before others clustered around to listen to him hold forth. Under cover of listening to him, Karen watched the faces around her, trying to pick out those who agreed wholeheartedly, those who were indifferent and those who disagreed with him.

''Let me begin by saying that I care about the environment as much as anyone,'' Youngblood said. ''I'm a farmer by birth, a cane grower. And I can speak for all my fellow farmers when I say that we care about the environment, if for no other reason than that agriculture demands a healthy environment. You won't find a farmer or an agribusinessman *anywhere* who doesn't care about the environment.''

''Hear, hear,'' said a couple of voices. Karen made note of their faces so she could find out later who they were.

''You see,'' Youngblood went on, appearing to speak only to Karen, although she had no doubt he was aware of all the others gathering round him, ''we can't exist without a healthy environment.''

''I can see that,'' she said, to encourage him to move forward.

''We bust our backsides, literally, to return to the soil everything we take out of it. That's what fertilizers do, you know. They simply revive soil that would otherwise become spent.''

''That,'' the familiar voice of Grant Lawrence intruded, ''is a bit of an exaggeration, Randall. Or rather, an understatement.''

Youngblood smiled at the senator, as if they were the oldest of friends, but the smile never reached his eyes and couldn't quite conceal a flicker of displeasure. ''And *that* was a confusing statement, Senator.''

Grant eased closer until he was beside Karen, facing Youngblood. ''What I mean is, farmers don't only replenish the soil. You use fertilizers to enhance the soil, increase your per-acre yields. The excess runs off. And it's that excess that S.R. 52 addresses.''

''Well,'' said Youngblood, his voice as calm and confident as if the subject under discussion were the weather, ''I suppose that depends on what you mean by enhancement. After all, increasing crop yields is essential to this country.''

A number of heads nodded in agreement.

''He's right,'' said a short but lean man with a pleas-

ant face. "I don't know if you remember me, Senator, but I'm Representative Bill Olafsen, from Nebraska."

"Of course I remember you, Bill." Grant extended his hand with a warm smile, and Olafsen shook it. "It's been a while, but I remember when we sort of put our heads together on the grain support issue."

"Right." Olafsen actually looked mildly flattered that he was remembered. But flattered or not, he was undeterred. "The farmers, *my* people, my constituents, *are* enhancing the soil. No two ways about it. But neither they nor I are going to apologize for it. America wants cheap food, and plenty of it. Most of my farmers are barely making a living on the acreage they have, and they'd go under if their crop yields fell. But maybe that sounds like a selfish issue to you."

"Not at all," Grant said firmly. "I'm as worried about the American farmer as anyone. But I'm also worried about our fishermen, and worried about our children and grandchildren. We don't want to leave them seas that are devoid of fish."

"Oh, I doubt that will happen," Youngblood scoffed. "The oceans are huge."

"Right. And we still nearly fished cod into extinction. It's essential that we keep our coastal waters clean enough to sustain a healthy habitat." He turned back to Olafsen. "It's actually the same kind of problem you're talking about, Bill. Our fisheries are under the gun every bit as much as the farmers. But the fishermen can't fertilize the ocean. The only way their crops can be enhanced is to cut back on nitrate runoff."

Olafsen frowned. "So it's either-or?"

"I don't think so. The studies I've read suggest that we can find less polluting ways to keep crop yields up. What I'm proposing is that the government take it on the chin and support the farmers during the transition period, so we can bring our coastal waters back to life. So we can restore the wetlands that are so essential to so many species.''

Somebody else spoke, a woman in black velvet with large diamonds in her ears. ''Why should the government pay for all this, Senator?''

''Well, Ms. Reilly, it seems to me that the government is responsible for the present mess by ignoring ecological concerns for so many years. We seemed to think it was okay to plunder the land and seas any way that occurred to us, and we, the government, allowed a very bad situation to be set up. Now it's time for taxpayers and the government to solve the growing problems without causing any individual hardship that we can avoid.''

Youngblood shook his head. ''Somebody always pays, Senator. If S.R. 52 succeeds, Americans will be paying more for food, and more of it will be imported from countries that don't have your ecological conscience. And the American farmer will wind up on subsidies at taxpayer expense, and probably find it nearly pointless to go out and plant a poor crop that won't even return enough to pay for seed.''

''And I,'' said Grant firmly, ''think you're catastrophizing, Randall. I'm not talking about rapid changes, I'm talking about slow and cautious ones. I'm talking about developing alternatives to nitrates for fertilizing.''

''Like what?'' Youngblood asked, an unexpected note of humor in his voice. ''The heads of the fish that no longer exist, according to you?''

Laughs came from all around, and the sense of growing tension was eased. Grant laughed with everyone else, and Karen managed a smile, although she was annoyed by the way he was being attacked. Then she reminded herself that she wasn't here as a partisan.

"Well," said Grant, "I hope we can find something less smelly than fish heads."

More laughter.

"But," Grant said, his tone becoming once more serious, "we need to find a way to save our fisheries *and* save our farmers. I don't want to sacrifice either of them. And I'd *really* like to restore the climate in my state so that all of you don't have to go to the Caribbean for Christmas."

More chuckles. Karen, who was watching Youngblood closely, noticed that the tightness seemed to ease a bit around his eyes, as if he were letting go of the argument for the time being. But as the others drifted away, Youngblood remained. He seemed to want to speak with Grant, but not in front of Karen.

After a moment she stepped away, giving them privacy, although at that instant she wanted nothing more than to have a wire on Grant Lawrence. She found something about Youngblood to be distinctly threatening, although she couldn't put her finger on it. Perhaps it was that he seemed to have a lot of *negative* emotion vested in his arguments, whereas Grant seemed very positive.

She was mulling that over when Grant rejoined her. "Seen enough?" he asked.

"What did he say to you?"

He hesitated, then his electric blue eyes seemed to smile ironically. "He just told me he's going to bury me."

They didn't leave the party immediately, of course. They stayed on for several more hours as Karen watched Grant work the room, talking to as many people as he could, focusing on their interests and concerns, talking about the amendments they'd tacked on to S.R. 52 and how they might reach some compromise that would keep from burying the bill under its own weight.

But even as the discussions went on, she realized that Grant made no firm promises other than, "I'll look into it."

Very smooth. Very convincing. Almost like polite horse-trading, except there was nothing he could be held to.

Throughout the rest of the evening, she didn't sense anything else like the momentary animosity she had felt from Randall Youngblood. But his animosity might well be meaningless. He just might be the kind of man who took his cause very personally. Given that he was a cane grower himself, that would make sense.

And he might mean nothing at all by his threat to bury Grant Lawrence. Then again…the rumors that had been surfacing back in Tampa and the whole setup of the crime at Grant's house predisposed her to think a politically motivated break-in had gone wrong. She couldn't imagine Randall Youngblood as his own hatchet man, though.

Slowly, she worked her way back to Youngblood. When he saw her, he smiled, and after a moment he broke away from another conversation. "So," he said, "now you've heard both sides of the bill."

"Superficially, I suppose I have."

He laughed. "How much more depth do you want? I can bury you in paper."

The similarity of the phrase to what he had said to Grant seemed to indicate that he said things like that frequently. She wondered nonetheless.

"No thanks," she answered, smiling. "I have enough of my own paperwork."

"I thought you might." He sipped his drink.

"What's it like being a lobbyist?" she asked him, hoping she sounded ingenuous.

"Miserable, if you want the truth. I'm just one of hundreds begging for an ear."

"Then why don't you hire someone to do it?"

His look expressed humor. "We tried that. Unfortunately, he didn't care as much as we do."

"I can see how that might be a problem. Well, you certainly seem to be getting plenty of ears."

He shrugged. "Let's just say I'm getting the ears of people who agree with me. The others are harder."

She would have nodded, but she didn't bother, because he wouldn't have seen it anyway. His gaze was surveying the room, probably considering who next to buttonhole. She, after all, wasn't important to him in any way. He was merely being courteous to her.

But then his gaze lit on Grant Lawrence, and the way his expression altered, however subtly, caused every instinct in her body to go on full alert.

"Excuse me," he said, giving her a distracted smile.

She watched him work his way through the room until he reached the senator from Idaho.

"Interesting man, yes?"

She turned and found that Jerry Connally had joined her. "What do *you* think of him?" she asked bluntly.

He shrugged. "I think he's a desperate man."

"Over this bill?"

"Over the bill, over whether he'll lose his grip on the cane growers' association, whether he'll still be the front man for the agribusiness coalition he's built over S.R. 52."

''You think this is about power?''

He nodded. ''What isn't?''

''That's cynical.''

He shrugged with a smile. ''Maybe I've been hanging around this town too long. But power is everything, Detective. Without it, you're a nobody, just a simple cane grower from South Florida.''

''Just how far do you think he'd go?''

Connally hesitated. ''Do I think he's capable of murder? Is that what you mean?''

''It could be.''

He laughed. ''You're not fooling me. No, I don't think he's capable of murder. But I think people who work for him might be.''

Grant Lawrence ushered Karen into his limo and told the driver to go to her hotel first.

''It must be nice,'' she remarked, ''to be driven everywhere this way.''

''I'm lucky I can afford it,'' he agreed. ''It allows me to work on the way to and from my office, and considering the traffic around here at rush hour, that's a blessing. I'd just get impatient and nasty otherwise.''

''Worse than Tampa?'' she asked him.

He laughed. ''Far worse. It's the primary reason I chose not to live farther out.'' He turned in the seat, looking at her directly. ''Did you learn anything tonight?''

''I may have. Do you think that Randall Youngblood would be capable of starting rumors about you?''

''Hell yes. That's politics as usual. It's ugly, but a lot of people seem to consider it part of the game.''

''Do you think he hates you?''

He opened his mouth, then closed it and looked out

the car window at slowly passing buildings. "You know, until Abby's death, I'd have said no one hated me. Now, I don't know." He looked at her. "The thing is, Randall and I have always been friends, even when we disagreed. I don't think he hates me. But someone on his staff could. And we don't always know what our staffs are up to."

Then he said something that astonished her. "Believe it or not, this is the loneliest job in the world."

"How so?"

"Everyone's a piece on the chessboard. Ally or foe. No real friends. Everyone has an agenda."

Much to her surprise, she felt herself ache for him. It wasn't a place she wanted to be. It wasn't a feeling she could dare to have, certainly not while on an investigation. But she had the worst urge to reach out and hug him. "You must have friends who aren't in politics."

"Oh, sure. A few. But I tell you what. I could use a couple of brothers right about now."

There was an instant, just an instant, when she actually thought he moved toward her, as if he wanted to hold her, or be held. And for that instant, just that instant, she ached so hard for his touch that she thought she might shatter.

Then it was gone as if it had never been.

"Sorry," he said. "I must sound like a whiner. I chose this career, after all. And most of the time I love it."

She could have said that she understood, that people often chose to get into things without fully understanding what it would mean. After all, she'd done the same thing. But, at that moment, it seemed wisest to say nothing at all.

She heard the screech of brakes an instant before the impact. In the last moment before her head snapped back against the window frame and the world went dark, she heard Grant shout.

12

Grant heard, rather than saw, the popping of flashbulbs outside the open door of the limo. His eyes still registered only the blinding flashes that came from within, spurred by the tearing pain in his knee. In the fleeting moments of clarity, he realized he was on the floor of the limo, sagging to his side.

"Are you all right, Mr. Senator?"

The pain eased long enough for him to focus on the open door. A man stood there, one hand holding a cell phone to his ear, the other holding a microcassette recorder. Behind him, another man snapped photo after photo.

"Mr. Senator?" the man with the cell phone asked again. "Are you hurt? I'm on the line with the cops now."

"My knee," Grant said, fighting out the words.

"I think he's hurt," the man said into the phone. "His knee. Get an ambulance here. Fast. Please?"

The man closed the phone and looked at him. "Do you remember what happened, Senator Lawrence?"

Grant shook his head to clear it, then turned. "Who are you?"

"Stan Potter, *Washington Herald*. We heard the crash from around the corner. Is your girlfriend okay?"

Grant felt something warm against his cheek and turned. It was Karen's calf. As his thoughts cleared, he remembered where he was.

And what this looked like.

Oh shit.

Karen was unconscious, the left side of her hair matted and shiny in the dim glow of the overhead light. He reached up and felt the side of her head. His fingers came away sticky and wet.

"Oh no," he said.

The rising wail of the ambulance was soon matched by the world flashing red. But for Grant, that was far in the background. He could see only Karen's face, still and pale. He was still searching for a pulse as a paramedic wrenched open the far door.

"She's hurt," Grant said. "Her head."

"How about you?" the paramedic asked.

"My knee. But I'll be fine. She's unconscious."

"We'll take good care of her, sir."

He pulled Grant's hands away and touched her neck, first at the carotid for a pulse, then around to the back.

"We'll need a back board and a cervical brace," he said to his partner. "Call Sibley and tell them to prep for possible skull or spinal."

The words hit Grant like a sledgehammer. Abby. Stacy. Now Karen.

Karen was roused by the itching on the inside of her elbow. Her eyelids felt like lead weights as she opened them and reached to scratch.

"Can't do that," a woman's voice said. "And good morning, Ms. Sweeney."

The source of the itch came into focus, paper tape holding an IV needle in her vein. She looked up at a nurse in white slacks and a blue print top. *Mavis, R.N.,* the name tag read.

"Where am I?" Karen asked.

"Sibley Memorial Hospital," the nurse answered. "And don't worry about the IV. It's just a glucose drip, to keep you hydrated."

"My head hurts."

The nurse stifled a chuckle. "That's no surprise. You had a nasty concussion. You may have headaches for a few days. And the staple may itch some."

"Staple?" Karen asked.

The nurse touched the side of Karen's head gently. "Two of them, actually. Nice little cut you had there. But the doctors say you'll be fine."

Karen tasted grit in her mouth and tried to swallow. "Can I have some water? And a bowl or something?"

The nurse handed her a glass of water and a nausea tray. Karen took a swig of water, swished it in her mouth, and spat in the tray. Tiny white flecks floated in the water.

"You chipped some teeth," the nurse explained. "Like I said. Nasty hit on the head."

"I don't remember it."

"That's not unusual, Ms. Sweeney. Give yourself a few hours, or even a few days. The MRI was clear, so you should be fine. Just a little…"

"Scrambled," Karen said.

"Exactly."

She was still feeling scrambled when Jerry Connally walked into the room. "How are you?" he asked genially enough, although his face held no kindness.

Something in his eyes gave her pause.

"How's Grant?"

He smiled thinly. "He'll be okay—physically. They had to scope his knee again."

"Physically?" she asked.

By way of an answer, he handed her the tabloid he had tucked under his arm. The cover photo showed Grant on his knees in the limousine. Between her legs. *Crashing the Party?* the headline screamed.

"Oh shit," Karen said.

"Oh shit is right," Jerry answered. "The question is, how do we save Grant from this crap?"

She couldn't even answer. They'd been in a car accident as far as she could remember, and the tabloids had turned it into this? She stared blindly at the paper, then at Connally.

"Actually," said Connally, "there's no way to save him from this crap." He tossed the paper into a nearby trash can.

"Why not?" she asked, realizing for the first time that her jaw was sore, as sore as the scalp wound, which chose that moment to start throbbing.

"The tabloids say and do what they want. Grant's a public figure, and there's not much he can do about it. You, on the other hand, are not a public figure."

"Meaning?"

"You could hire a lawyer to sue them."

She let her head fall back on her pillow, wincing even from that light pressure. "Why? It would only keep it on the front page."

"True." He sat in the chair beside her bed. "Or you could sue Grant because you were in his limo when it happened."

"I don't want to sue anybody." God, her head was banging. "I just hope I don't lose my job."

"No reason you should. The real story is on the wires. The truth, as the cliché goes, is out there."

At another time, she might have smiled faintly. Right now, she was too uncomfortable. And besides, concussion or no, she was getting suspicious of Connally. "Why did you bring that for me to see? What is it you want?"

"I wanted to know how much trouble you're going to make for the senator."

Well, that was blunt. "I'm not going to make trouble for anyone. The world may not believe it, but I was on business. Accidents happen. End of subject."

"No," he said slowly. "Not quite end of subject."

Her eyes met his. "What do you mean?"

"It wasn't an accident."

She began to wonder if the concussion was making her truly crazy. "Of course it was an accident. Unless you're saying the driver tried to kill us."

"No. He was driving too slowly. Thank God he was driving slowly. But he remembers what happened. And he's saying a car pulled out directly in front of him, causing him to swerve. He hit the front end of the other car."

"Were the occupants hurt?"

"That's the funny thing, Detective. You see, there *were* no occupants in the car by the time anyone else got there. And it was a stolen vehicle."

Headache and concussion notwithstanding, Karen instantly understood the ramifications. "Who would want to kill him?"

"I'm not sure anyone does. But they might have wanted to cause him some serious embarrassment." His gaze drifted over to the wastebasket, where a corner of the tabloid still protruded.

"God." Karen couldn't believe her ears. "They might have killed us."

"No. Grant's driver always goes slow. They probably knew that."

"Or it could have been some joy riders with no agenda at all."

"Stranger things have happened. Except the press was there, right around the corner, because someone had called them with a tip. Only the tip turned out to be phony."

Karen tried to swallow, but her mouth was too dry. As soon as she reached for the plastic cup on the table, Connally was on his feet. He filled it and handed it to her.

"Thanks."

"My pleasure."

She sipped carefully, cautious because of her nausea. Her brain was still foggy, and she was having trouble coordinating her thoughts and reactions. "Is there something you want from me?"

"Yeah. Find out who's behind this shit before they kill Grant's candidacy."

Which, thought Karen as Connally walked out, was a long way from demanding she find Abby Reese's murderer.

Again there was that little click in her brain. Things were definitely not adding up.

"Yeah," said Lieutenant Simpson. "Mr. Connally called to tell me about the accident. How are you feeling?"

"Confused. What day is it?"

"That's bad," he said, assessing the situation. "It's Monday morning."

"I've been out that long?"

"Long enough to make one of the tabloids and the front page of the local papers. The tabloid picture isn't so good, but there's no mistaking you standing beside the senator at the party on the front page of the dailies."

"Oh, God." She sagged against the pillow.

"If this is your idea of being undercover, you better get plastic surgery to change your face."

"Lieutenant…"

"Forget it, Karen. You couldn't hang around the senator without anyone knowing anything. I'm going to send Previn up there."

"No! No. Please. I've got him working another murder. Listen, can you arrange for me to work with someone from Washington P.D.?"

He thought about that for what seemed like a lifetime. "Yeah, that might be a good idea."

"It would help with the investigation of the accident."

"What's to investigate? Connally said it was an accident."

"He just told me otherwise."

"Shit." Simpson fell silent again. Then, "What the hell do you think we're dealing with here?"

"The Reese woman may have been murdered incidentally. I think the target is the senator."

"I was afraid you were going to say that. Yeah. I'll get Washington to work with you. In the meantime, stay put in that bed until they say you can leave. Got it?"

"Yes, sir."

Alissa Jurgen poured herself another glass of wine and swirled the rich, golden liquid around in her glass. For an instant after the wine passed over the glass, it left a film. Then the film receded, as if it had never been. A memory, faded and gone.

Six months, two days, four hours.

That was how long ago it had been, and the memory hadn't faded yet. One kiss. A moment of weakness, Stacy had said. One kiss, and Alissa could still remember every moment of it. The look in Stacy's eyes, grief and gratitude, melded with curiosity and reluctance. The scent of her hair and her skin. The taste of her lips, still damp with Chardonnay. The sound of her own quiet sigh. A moment of magic.

Broken in the moment the kiss parted.

"I'm sorry," Stacy had said, sadness rich in her eyes. "I just can't."

Alissa had nodded and understood. How could she not? It wasn't as if she hadn't grown close to one or two men in her life. And always, at a moment just like that kiss with Stacy, she'd realized those feelings simply weren't there.

"It's not that I don't love you," Stacy had said. "I just don't…love you…that way."

"Please, stop," Alissa had whispered, not wanting to hear the words, not wanting to put the moment into the abstraction of language. It was what it was. "We are who we are."

Stacy had nodded. They'd hugged. Fiercely. But they'd never again been quite so close. Stacy had never again shared quite so much of herself. Her aching for the man she'd loved, even when both he and she had known it wouldn't work. Her dreams of children and family.

They had gone from soul sisters to…just for that one

moment, lovers…and then to business partners and friends.

She sipped her wine, the same Chardonnay they'd shared that night. She still had the memory, for as long as that winery bottled Chardonnay.

Fighting away tears, she returned her attention to the studio books. At least the studio was solid. It wouldn't make her rich, but she could afford a nice apartment and food. And she could do what she loved.

"Thank you, Stacy," she whispered into the darkness.

The stillness was broken by her doorbell. She rose from her chair and walked to the door, peering through the spy hole at the thin, sad-looking man on the other side. Latching the chain, she opened the door.

"Alissa Jurgen?" he asked.

"Yes. What is it?"

He held up a leather identification wallet. "Dave Previn. Tampa PD. Might I come in for a moment?"

"Is it about Stacy? Do you know who…?"

He shook his head, answering the question she couldn't bring herself to finish. "Yes, ma'am, and no. I just need to verify some information with you. May I come in?"

She closed the door, released the chain and opened it to let him enter. "Would you like something to drink?"

"No, thank you," he said. "I'm sorry about the hour. It shouldn't take too long."

He had wounded eyes. She wondered if he could see the wound in hers. "It's okay, Detective." She paused. "You are a detective, right?"

"Yes, ma'am."

He seemed at a loss for where to begin, thoughts playing through his eyes, half-starts and withdrawals. He was ill at ease, she thought. Probably new.

''What have you found out?'' she asked.

''Well, that's the thing, ma'am. I've read Miss Wiggins' will. She's leaving the dance studio to you.''

Alissa nodded.

''That doesn't surprise you?'' he asked.

''No, Detective. We'd talked about it. Stacy was the majority owner, but I'd put some money into it, too. When we set up the books, the lawyer suggested that we make plans to protect the business if either of us…'' Her voice trailed away. ''It seemed silly at the time. She was so young.''

He nodded. ''So your will would have left your interest in the studio to Miss Wiggins, then?''

Her eyes brimmed. ''I guess I'll have to change that now.''

''I know this sounds intrusive, but do you have a copy of your will?''

''Sure,'' she said. She pulled open the roll-top desk, a gift from an old flame, two months before the woman had decided she wasn't leaving her husband after all. The desk was neither a good memory nor a bad one. It was, she had come to believe, simply a piece of furniture. Taking a key from a small drawer in the top compartment, she unlocked the file drawer, moved past old tax returns and receipts, and found a folder labeled simply ''Me.''

She handed him the document, folded into a fancy blue cover sheet with what she considered ostentatious printing. Her lawyer probably did these things to impress clients. She ruminated on that thought for the few minutes it took the detective to scan the document itself.

He looked up. ''You'd have left your entire estate to Miss Wiggins. Not just your interest in the business.''

She nodded. ''I've no one else.''

"No parents or siblings?" he asked.

"They're…we're…not close," she said. "I'm not dating anyone, let alone in the kind of relationship where I'd put them in a will."

His eyes seemed to narrow. "So you and Miss Wiggins…you dated?"

"We were friends, Detective. It's like I told the other woman who came. I'm lesbian. Stacy was straight. I had a crush on her. She didn't have one on me. But we were close friends, regardless."

"Close enough that you'd have left everything to her," he said, without inflection.

It might have been simply repeating what she'd said, or it might have been a subtle accusation. There was no way to tell in his voice.

"Yes, that close," she said, trying to keep her voice as impassive as his.

"And now the studio is all yours. What are you going to do with it?"

"I'm going to work, Detective. Teach students. Teach my art and my craft. Maybe I'll get lucky and find the next Fred or Ginger, and they'll get rich and send me baskets of thank-you notes written on hundred-dollar bills, but I doubt it. So I'll work, like I've been doing. It's what I know. It's what I love."

"Nice to be able to make a living doing what you love," he said. His voice was still expressionless, but his eyes had narrowed. "Will you be changing the name of the studio? I mean, how can it be 'Stacy's Steppers Dance Studio' if Miss Wiggins is…gone?"

"I haven't even thought about it," Alissa said. "It's a known name. I may keep it."

"Or you may not," he said.

Anger and impatience finally flashed. "Are you going

somewhere with this, Detective? Do you think I killed Stacy to get the studio? Because if you do, you might look at the studio books. No one gets rich teaching children to dance, Detective. Maybe you've got us confused with some of the ballroom dancing businesses.''

"Maybe," he said, then paused for a moment. "But you can't keep emotions in a ledger."

She stood up. "I think we're finished, Detective. You can leave. Now. Please."

"Money's a strange thing," he said as he walked to the door. "People...do the most illogical things over money. They'll gun down a convenience store clerk for chump change, even though everyone knows the clerks don't keep much in the registers. Strange, strange things." He opened the door himself. "Good night, Ms. Jurgen."

"Good night," she said, closing the door behind him and turning the dead bolt.

She shook her head, fighting down the anger that nearly overcame her. She would not kick the door. She would not throw a pillow.

Instead, she simply picked up her will, reread it, then tore it to shreds. Fancy blue cover and all.

13

Tuesday morning, Karen was awakened by the gentlest of touches as a hand brushed her hair back from her brow. Even before she opened her eyes, she smelled the hospital odors, locating herself in space and time. Part of her wanted to sink into the tender touch, playing 'possum, but another part of her was disturbed that anyone should touch her that way in her sleep.

Her eyes popped open, and she looked into Grant Lawrence's face. Immediately, he dropped his hand from her brow and took a backward step. "Good morning, Karen. How are you feeling?"

She felt around in the bed for the control and raised her head, taking him in. He was dressed in a business suit, neat as a pin, and leaning on a cane. "I'm fine," she said. "I can leave today."

He smiled. "That's wonderful news."

"What about you? Your knee?"

"Oh, it's minor. I'll need a cane and a brace for a while, but I'll be okay."

"I'm glad to hear it." But looking at his familiar face, she saw that his eyes were pinched, despite his smile. The prickly, reserved part of herself warred with a sudden rush of tenderness and yearning...and won. It always won.

He spoke. "I'm very sorry about that photo in the tabloid. You must be horrified."

She shrugged. "No, I'm not. Not for myself. But I am for you."

He shook his head and gave a small snort of laughter. "If it wasn't this, it'd be something else. They will have their pound of flesh. Anyway, the real story went out over the wires, including the part about the press and paparazzi being called on a phony tip. Intelligent people will figure it out."

"You're very calm about it."

He grimaced. "I'm used to it. Or at least I'm getting used to it. Once people think you're nosing around the presidency, it's open season. There'll be a lot worse things rumored about me before all's said and done."

A sudden flash of humor lit his gaze. "Hell, I've been widowed for over two years. Why *shouldn't* I be found between a beautiful woman's legs?"

Almost in spite of herself, Karen laughed. "It sure isn't cheating."

"There, you see?" His smile broadened. "Now, do you want me to send a car for you?"

"No, I don't think so." The thought of seeing Jerry Connally today put her off, though she couldn't quite say why. Maybe it was because he stood between Grant and the rest of the world? That thought led to speculations about her own feelings that she didn't want to consider. "I'll just get a cab," she said. "I think I want to ride around a bit."

"Whatever suits you. I'll call you at the hotel this evening."

He smiled, started to lean toward her, as if he might

drop a kiss on her forehead, then stopped. His face changed in some indefinable way. Rigid now, he nodded, said goodbye and limped out.

What the hell was that all about? Karen wondered. She must have misinterpreted his intention. Most likely his knee had just twinged.

But much to her great relief, before she could think about it any more, the phone rang.

"Detective Sweeney?" said a gruff voice with a definite Philly accent.

"Yes?"

"This is Detective Tyson, Washington P.D. We got a request from Tampa to hook up with you. Are you about ready to march?"

"They're supposed to let me out sometime this morning."

"Okay. Give me a call when they discharge you. I'll be there within twenty minutes. Got something to write on?"

There was a small pad and pen on the bedside table, courtesy of Jerry Connally. She wrote down the phone number quickly. "Thanks, Detective."

"No problem, Detective."

If that was so, why did she feel as if it were going to be a very *big* problem?

Randall Youngblood's morning went to hell before he'd even crossed the sidewalk to the office door. He was accosted by a fresh-faced man of about thirty, who was holding a reporter's notebook and, poorly concealed beneath it, a microcassette recorder.

"Mr. Youngblood," the young man said insistently, "I'm Dan Weeks, *Washington Herald.*"

Randall looked at him, debating whether to make an

issue out of the recorder. Already he could feel his stomach going sour. It wasn't that he didn't like to talk to
the press; he actually enjoyed giving news conferences,
and he was good at it. But being accosted this way...
This guy wasn't after facts or figures about S.R. 52.

Finally he spoke, keeping his voice pleasant. "Do you
always tape people without telling them?"

Weeks slipped the recorder from beneath his notebook
and showed it to Randall. "It's not running, sir. I was
going to ask. Recording ensures I don't misquote you."

"Whether I have any comment depends on what
you're asking about."

"Yes, sir. I understand that, sir. But I thought you'd
want to respond to the accusation."

"Accusation?"

Weeks nodded. "I have a source who tells me that
someone on your staff was involved in the break-in at
Senator Grant's home."

For an instant, just an instant, Randall felt everything
inside him freeze.

"Who the hell told you that?"

"I can't tell you my source's name, sir."

Randall's shock gave way to a surge of anger so
strong it nearly blinded him. "So you fancy yourself the
next Woodward or Bernstein, do you?"

Now Weeks' face darkened. "I'm giving you a
chance to deny the story, sir."

"Well, I *do* deny it. Categorically. My entire staff
knows better than to indulge in shenanigans like that.
Politics can be an ugly business sometimes, but you
can't let it be personal. It can *never* be personal, because
once you let that happen, you end up with things like
Watergate."

Weeks nodded. The recorder was running now, and

Randall didn't care. Let this young news grubber record all this, and let him print it.

"Grant Lawrence and I have been friends for years," Randall continued harshly. *"Years.* Even when we're on different sides of an issue. We're able to do that because we don't let it get personal. So tell your cowardly anonymous source that he's got it all wrong. There's no Watergate in *my* camp."

Then he stormed into his office, wishing like the devil for a cigar, wishing he could get his hands around the throat of that anonymous source. Stories like this could destroy him. He stabbed the intercom button on his phone.

"Michaels? Get your ass in here."

At almost the same moment, Grant Lawrence was climbing out of his limousine at the Senate Office Building. He, too, was accosted by a reporter before he reached the door.

"Senator, may I have a moment of your time? Brigit Carter, *Washington Times.*"

"Certainly," Grant said, turning to her with a pleasant smile, even though his every sense was on high alert. Getting ambushed this way usually meant something unpleasant.

"Thank you, sir." She lifted pad and pen, smiling back at him. She struck him as a woman who went to great lengths to appear plain. "I was wondering if you have any comment on the story that someone on Randall Youngblood's staff was involved in the break-in at your Tampa house?"

Grant felt sheer astonishment. "Who in the world told you that?"

"I can't reveal my sources, sir."

Grant shook his head. "Well, I don't believe it. Not at all. And may I suggest we let the police reach the conclusions, based on evidence and not rumor?"

"Certainly, sir." In a practiced shorthand, apparently of her own devising, she seemed to get down exactly what he said. "And what about the rumor that there was a cover-up in your wife's death?"

This time he was more than astonished, he was angered. Yes, there had been a cover-up, but a cover-up of things that nobody else had a right to know. "I don't," he said carefully, "see what need there was to cover up anything. She was killed by a drunk driver, plain and simple. The facts speak for themselves."

"Yes, but sources in Tampa say the investigation was short-circuited."

"In what way? Tests showed she was sober. The other driver was not. *He* crossed the median and hit her nearly head-on. Read the police report."

"Yes, sir, I will. Sir, just one more thing."

He was already starting to turn away, sickened at the direction of the questioning, his thoughts leaping immediately to his daughters. If ugly things made it into the press, their schoolmates would hear about it from their parents or the TV, and then they would question and tease Belle and Cathy.

He forced himself to face her, forced himself to keep a pleasant expression. "Yes?"

"Senator, we have a tip that your daughters are…well, that you're not their biological father."

He looked at her so hard and so long that she finally stepped back. A black rage filled him, filled every corner of his heart and soul.

"I shouldn't even dignify that with a comment," he said shortly. "But I will. It's a lie. A damned lie. And if you print that damned lie, I will sue you on behalf of my daughters. Got that?''

Not waiting for her response, he turned and strode into the building.

The feeding frenzy had begun.

Before Grant arrived in his office, Jerry Connally brought Sam Weldon into Jerry's private office, next to Grant's. Out front, the staff was beginning to gather for the day's labors.

''Colombia,'' Sam said, taking a bite from a bagel that smelled as if it had just come out of the oven. ''We can't ignore it.''

Sam was Jerry's right-hand man, almost in the way he himself was Grant's right hand. No one man could keep his eye on everything, hence the need for a number of advisors.

But there was a major difference between the relationships. Jerry was Grant's friend from all the way back. Sam was an employee, hired away from a think tank. Jerry sometimes suspected that Sam cherished political aspirations of his own, because he sure wasn't making as much money here. Regardless, over the past four years, Sam had proved himself time and time again in foreign affairs—and a few other areas, as needed.

While they didn't always agree with his assessments, Sam had never yet failed to provide the facts and a reasoned course of action.

Jerry sighed. ''We're not ignoring Colombia, Sam. We just aren't ready to act.''

''The situation has changed, Jerry. It's not in this morning's papers, but it'll be on tonight's news. My source just e-mailed me an AP wire story.''

And probably e-mailed the same story to nearly everyone in Congress, Jerry thought wryly. Or maybe not. The exchange was a simple one: in exchange for the heads-up on news stories of national importance, Sam made sure his contact got news out of the senator's office sooner. And, on occasion, exclusively. Jerry suspected the exclusivity, when it existed, was all one-sided. But that was how the game was played.

"What happened?"

"You read that there's been an outbreak of hemorrhagic fever in two small villages in the Colombian highlands, right?"

Jerry leaned forward. "Wait, back up a minute. A couple of weeks ago, some humanitarian aid convoys were bushwhacked on their way into the highlands. This is something different?"

"Those convoys were bringing food. The fighting has wiped out farms. FARC guerillas fighting the government. Colombian troops—with some of our advisors, on the sly—fighting the drug cartels…and the guerillas. My source in the Pentagon tells me we tried to defoliate a cocaine crop and took out most of the vegetables for three villages."

"So this…illness…is new?"

Sam nodded. "In the last week. And, Jerry, it's not just any illness. It's a hemorrhagic fever. Nobody is sure what kind yet. But let me paint you a picture. Have you heard of Ebola?"

"Yes, of course. We had that flap a few years back when it appeared some infected monkeys had come in through Richmond or someplace."

"Well, it's a helluva bug, with a high mortality rate. Fortunately, Ebola isn't airborne, so it can be contained. This particular hemorrhagic fever is every bit as bad, and it spreads faster. One village has been wiped out. At least two others have been infected.''

''Okay. So the U.N....''

''Sir, that's what I'm trying to tell you. The U.N. sent in a World Health Organization team. It was manned in part by personnel from CDC, with an assortment from the European nations. Last evening the WHO team was ambushed. Two British nurses dove under a truck and crawled away into the bush. Colombian troops found them six hours later. As for the rest...eleven dead, including five Americans.''

Jerry sat back. ''Shit,'' he said succinctly.

''The situation is grave, Jerry. Very grave. The senator has to make a statement. He has to call for U.S. troops to protect the U.N. teams, so they can reach the infected sites.''

Jerry shook his head slowly. ''Sam, I know Grant. He's not going to sign off on that. Colombia is a mess...politically, economically, socially. All we'll do down there is kill and die and eventually walk, leaving the same problems we found when we got there. He's going to apply just-war doctrine. It's a moral issue for him, and he's not going to bend.''

God, he felt filthy even saying that, given his own recent crime. Inside, his very soul seemed to shudder.

''Jerry, listen to me. This is Grant's opportunity to appear presidential, forceful and strong. If he speaks out now in favor of intervention, nobody will doubt his guts just because he never served in the military.''

''Franklin Roosevelt never served in the military, either. Nobody doubted *his* guts.''

Sam spread his hands. ''Jerry, we can't afford to waffle on this one. That disease could put millions at risk.''

Jerry shook his head again. ''We're *not* waffling on

this. Not at all. The senator is taking a very strong, very difficult position. He is insisting that the Colombians sort out their own civil war. And that's what it is, Sam.''

"You hired me because of my ability to gauge public opinion and come up with rational foreign affairs policy.''

"Yes, we did. But Grant Lawrence isn't going to sell his soul for a few votes. Some things are too important.''

After Sam left, Jerry sat staring at the glass globe on his desk, a sour taste filling his mouth. *Some things are too important?* Yeah, right. Brave words coming from a man who'd done what he had.

Then he went in to tell the senator that he had to make a strong call for the State Department to step in and find a way for the WHO teams to reach the highlands safely. Maybe it wouldn't have to come to saber rattling.

Unfortunately, all he could see looming on the horizon was a bank of ugly, dark clouds.

14

Karen sat on a park bench in front of the hospital, waiting for Detective Tyson to pick her up. It was a pleasant spring morning, cooler than she was used to at home at this time of year, but comfortable. It seemed she had not been wrong to follow this case to Washington, given what Jerry Connally had told her about the accident.

The problem was, the accident could have been just that. An accident. It could have been utterly coincidental that those reporters had been right around the corner.

Although, in her business, she wasn't too inclined to believe in coincidence. The truth was usually obvious enough that it stood up and bit you on the nose. It usually *was* the husband, the wife, the lover.

And it was time to get back to work. She turned on her cell phone, and almost immediately the voice mail icon blinked at her. She dialed in and heard Previn's voice. He had news; she should call when she could. Closing the voice mail connection, she called him at the office.

"What's up, Dave?"

"I heard you got knocked around a bit, Karen."

"Minor concussion. The good news is that they did an MRI, and I do, in fact, have a brain."

Previn laughed. "Have the hospital send a copy down here. We'll put it on the bulletin board in the squad room, for when Simpson comes storming out asking 'Does *anyone* here have a brain?'"

"Not a bad idea," Karen said. "Although I can imagine the graffiti. 'Clean thoughts here,' with a tiny circle. 'Dirty thoughts here,' with a huge blob."

"What don't I know about you?"

It was her turn to laugh. "Nothing you're ever likely to learn. So…you said you had news?"

"Yes, I do. Turns out Stacy Wiggins and Alissa Jurgen had written each other into their wills. Jurgen gets the whole studio."

"Sounds like a typical business arrangement," Karen said. "Do you think there's something more?"

"Well, Jurgen's an admitted lesbian, and she had a case for Wiggins. It was not requited love."

He'd said "admitted lesbian" as if it were a crime. Karen bit back the urge to call him on it. "I knew that. Those things happen for everyone, Dave. Straights and gays."

"You're right," he said. "And I'd say the same thing if it were a straight situation. Jealousy and greed are two of the classic motives for homicide. Put them both together and it's worth a look."

"True. Although we don't know that Jurgen was jealous. We don't even know if Wiggins was seeing anyone. Jurgen only mentioned an ex."

She paused for a moment to rub her eyes and put on her sunglasses. The doctors had told her that bright light might bother her for a couple of days.

"I don't know, Dave. She didn't read like the type who could do what happened to Stacy Wiggins."

"Maybe not. On the other hand, she's a big woman. I'm guessing five-ten, at least. And she has to be in great shape, teaching dance and all." He paused for a moment. "And she has a temper."

"Oh?"

"I pressed her a bit. Love spurned. Now she gets the business. I didn't come right out and accuse her, but she got the message that I see her as a suspect."

Karen could imagine the scene. Previn still needed to work on his interviewing skills. "And?"

"And she threw me out. She kept it in check, but I could see the fire in her eyes. The look she gave me... Karen, I know angry women."

He did. Linda's outbursts were volcanic. She'd thrown a cup of punch in his face at the office Christmas party one year because he'd jokingly kissed Simpson under a sprig of mistletoe. The laughter had died in a heartbeat. On the other hand, perhaps his wife's rages had made him hypersensitive.

"Well, it's something to look into," she said. "See if you can find out where she was that night. But, Dave?"

"Yes?"

"Do it discreetly. Try to avoid the students and their parents, if you can. If she's innocent, I'd rather not have ruined her livelihood."

"We'll see," he said.

It wasn't the assurance she'd hoped for, but it would have to do. She had just hung up the phone when a car pulled up and a heavyset black man leaned across the front seat to the window.

"Detective Sweeney?" he asked. She nodded and

rose, gathering her discharge forms under one arm. He pushed open the passenger door and extended his hand. "Terry Tyson, D.C. Homicide."

"A pleasure, Detective."

"Terry is fine," he said. "It used to be just Tyson, until that idiot bit off Holyfield's ear. I'm not going to change my name, though."

"No relation, I'm sure," she said.

"Actually, I'm told we're third cousins twice removed or some such. Not that I give a frog's hair. And you'll want to change clothes, I'm sure."

She'd had nothing to wear out of the hospital except the dress she'd worn to the party. "Yes, I would, if you can spare the time."

He laughed. It was a hearty laugh that rolled from deep in his ample belly. "I can spare all the time you want, as long as you don't want more than twenty-two days."

"What happens then?" she asked, after telling him the name of her hotel.

"Then," he said, "I get my gold watch and look for retirement villas in Florida."

"Just what we need," she quipped. "Another retiree. God's waiting room."

"God's gonna have Him a long wait," Terry said. "I've quit smoking, got my blood pressure down. The wife, you know. She says she's waited thirty years for a husband, and she's damn sure not gonna lose me just when I'm available."

"Wives can be that way."

"Lord, tell me about it. I told her I'd quit smoking if we could...you know...every day. She told me if I quit, we could do it three times a day. I haven't touched a cigarette in three months."

"Congratulations," Karen said. "On both counts."

He laughed again. The ice was broken. They could work together. "So, Detective, what is it that brings you to this lovely city that I can't wait to get the hell out of?"

Karen took a moment to regard his eyes. Easy to miss in his jovial demeanor were the intelligence and activity in those eyes.

"I figured Simpson had briefed you," she said simply.

"Oh, he did. But I've been a detective too long to trust lieutenants. So…what do you know, what *don't* you know, and what do you think you'll learn here in D.C.?"

She took a breath, a moment to organize her thoughts. "I know Grant Lawrence is high on the list of potential Democratic presidential nominees. I know he's pushing hard for an environmental bill, the success of which would establish him as someone who can forge a bipartisan bloc to get things done in Congress. I know that Abigail Reese was his nanny, a lifelong presence, and she was brutally murdered. I know his home office files were broken into, although it looks like nothing else was touched. I know there are powerful interests that oppose his bill, and I'm sure there are interests that would oppose his candidacy. And I know someone is stirring the rumor mill, possibly to the point of staging the accident Sunday night to create a scandal."

He nodded. "That's a good start. What *don't* you know?"

"Now that's a *long* list," Karen said. "Who killed Abby Reese? Was it politically motivated? Was it a conspiracy, or just some druggie who broke into a rich man's house trying to score some cash? How far are Randall Youngblood and his confederates willing to go to block this bill? Who set up the accident? Who's planting the rumors? I could go on, but you get the idea.''

"Makes sense." He drew a deep breath, held it for a moment, then exhaled slowly. Then, glancing over at her, he said, "Something I learned that helps to quit smoking. Take deep sighs several times an hour. Anyway, your case. How long since the murder?''

"Two weeks." Karen knew that meant a largely cold trail. As a rule of thumb, a homicide that wasn't solved within forty-eight hours was going to mean a long, difficult and all-too-often stalled investigation. "There weren't any fresh leads to chase down in Tampa, so it made sense to sniff around up here.''

Tyson drew his hand over his chin in slow, rhythmic movements. "I've been a cop for just almost thirty years now. A detective for twenty-five of those years. Homicide for twenty. I've come up with a way of working a case. I look at the core of a case first, victim, crime scene evidence, family and friends, known associates and enemies. That's most of your murders, right there. When that doesn't work, I find the farthest piece of fringe there is and start fraying at it. Sooner or later, you get to the middle.''

Karen smiled. "I wouldn't have put it in those words, but that's pretty much how I work, too. You might say that coming up here is fraying at the fringe.''

"Maybe," he said. "But not if, while you're up here, you're sniffing around the big dogs. That part of the case isn't going to unravel yet. If it were, it would have already. No, Detective, we need to find us some *real* fringe and commence to fraying on it.''

"Like?''

He winked, though the rest of his features had settled

into a poker face. It was a grim wink. "Like who set up that car accident."

An hour later, Karen had showered and changed into work clothes: a pair of khaki slacks, a navy blue cotton top and a slate-gray blazer. Tyson was waiting in the hallway outside her room.

He nodded as she emerged. "The plainclothes uniform. It's the same everywhere, I guess."

"Pretty much. At least I don't have to wear a tie."

Tyson tugged his collar a bit looser. "Twenty-two more days. Now we need to get a late lunch."

Karen hesitated. Now that she was out of confinement, she wasn't eager to be delayed any longer. But she *was*, she acknowledged, operating as a guest of the D.C. police. "Sure," she said.

"I know you're champing at the bit."

She glanced at him. "It shows?"

"Hell no. You got a good poker face, Sweeney. But I'd be champing at the bit if I were you. Sorry, but lunch is essential. I'm diabetic."

"That's rough."

"My fault. Too many doughnuts." He patted his belly and let out that deep engaging laugh. "No more doughnuts for me, but I can still hit a greasy spoon."

Which was exactly where he took her, a place that served breakfast round the clock and food that would make the American Heart Association quail. And all of it was delicious.

While they ate, he slid a manila envelope across the table to her. "While you were showering, I did a little checking.

"Reports and statements on the accident. You'll want to read them, but here's the nutshell. Y'all were headed

north on K Street, crossing over Nineteenth, when a gray
Taurus driven by Walter Russell overtook you in the left
lane. At that point, a white Beemer came flying out of
Nineteenth from the left. Russell says he swerved to
avoid the Beemer and bumped your limo, but the
Beemer drove right on into him and slammed him harder
into y'all. The Beemer was stolen. The driver got out
and skipped the scene before anyone got a look at him.
That's what we know."

"Okay," she said. It pretty much fit what Jerry had
told her already.

"What we don't know is who was driving the
Beemer, and who called in the phony tip to the *Times,*
which put their reporters a half block away from, but
not in sight of, the accident scene."

"Convenient staging," she said.

He nodded. "Or coincidence, except the phony tip
makes me think it's not a coincidence. Which means
there was at least one more player. Someone to let the
driver of the stolen Beemer know when you were coming into position."

"Russell?" she asked.

"Nope. His cell phone hadn't been used all night, and
there was no walkie-talkie in his car. He was just in the
wrong place at the wrong time."

"So where does that leave us?"

"After lunch, we're going to the impound lot. I wanna
show you something."

Another hour passed before they even left for the lot,
and the drive was a long one. By that time, Karen was
really getting antsy.

Terry pulled into the impound lot and stopped in front
of a white BMW, the front of which was crumpled.

Flecks of gray paint were stippled over the bumper and right fender.

"That leaves us here," he said, walking over to the driver's side door. Black powder clung to the handle, window and door frame, and the rearview mirror.

"Any prints?"

He laughed. "Of course not. There are smudges, most likely from leather gloves, but that won't get us anywhere. We did, however, catch a break."

He pointed to the deflated air bag. A rectangular hole had been cut from it, near the top. "Seems it didn't fully inflate before he made impact. The way I figure it, he was leaning forward at the time. Trying to look around the corner for y'all. He didn't have time to lean back before the crash, so he hit the steering wheel as the bag was deploying. The lab guys found a couple of fragments of teeth, and cut out a blood smear."

"And of course you have a DNA database."

He nodded, and she continued. "Which means you can finger him. In four to six weeks. If his DNA is on file."

"That would be how it'd usually work," Tyson said.

"Except?"

"Except we've already found him. Or I'm pretty sure we have. Nat Olson."

"How?"

"He's in the morgue right now. Overdose. *Way* overdose. Turns out one of our lab guys is dating a woman who works at the M.E.'s office. She mentions this stiff who comes in, O.D.'d, with two front teeth broken out within the past few hours, judging by the blood around his gums. Our lab guy asks what he's wearing. She tells him."

"Leather gloves," Karen said, smiling.

"Bingo. Driving gloves. So our lab guy takes the broken teeth they'd found in the car over to the morgue, and sure enough…"

"They fit. Nice work, Tyson. You've found the driver of the stolen car. Of course, it'd be better if we could talk to him, but he jacked a needle in his arm and went night-night."

He grinned. "Sarcasm becomes you, Detective."

"Thanks. And just Karen, please."

"And you're right, Karen. Short of a séance, we're not going to be interviewing Nat Olson. But I'm not buying the accidental overdose theory. Nobody shoots up wearing gloves. No, someone helped him O.D., probably by giving him pure, uncut shit. And I'll bet that person was at the scene, to make sure everything came off."

"Olson became a loose end," she said.

"That's my read on it. Maybe they planned to kill him all along. Or maybe they thought he'd slip away during the commotion, unnoticed, no prints, no way to find him, no problem…"

"Until they saw the bloodstain on the air bag."

"Give the lady a gold star."

"Next stop, *Washington Herald* photo shop?"

He smiled. "My thought exactly. Maybe, just maybe, the camera-toting vulture who put y'all in the tabloids also got a shot of the handler peering in the car window."

Karen laughed. "I could get used to working with you, Tyson."

He shook his head. "Twenty-two days."

Randall Youngblood stood with his back to his office window and looked at Bill Michaels, who was sitting on the other side of the desk. It had taken the better part of the day for Michaels to turn up. He'd been out doing some work with some congressional aides. "Researching," as he called it.

Michaels was speaking. "Of course we didn't have anything to do with the break-in at Lawrence's home. It would have been too risky and potentially pointless."

Randall wasn't sure he liked Michaels' reasoning on that, but he left it alone. The important thing right now was the current situation. What Michaels might do under other circumstances was a subject they could get to later.

"Then why the hell are these rumors spreading?"

"Probably because the only thing tampered with at the house was the senator's files."

Youngblood reached for his chair and sat down. He didn't like the sound of this one bit. "Where did you learn that? The press is saying it was a burglary."

"It *was* a burglary. These burglars, however, only seemed to be interested in the files."

"Oh my God." Randall swiveled his chair and looked out the window, where the capitol dome was visible over the nearby roofs. "Watergate."

"No way. We didn't have anything to do with it."

Randall turned around again to face Michaels. "Are you absolutely positive of that?"

Michaels nodded. "My guys don't do anything without specific orders. That's why I picked them."

"But who else would…?"

Michaels' eyes took on a chilliness that made Randall wonder, *really* wonder, for the first time what this man was truly capable of.

"Sir," Michaels said, "you need to remember that while you may have taken the public position of lobbyist for the majority of agricultural associations in the country concerned over this issue, there are people besides you and the cane growers involved. And some of them are very, very big businesses.''

''Meaning?''

''Meaning, sir, that there are plenty of people *outside* our personal organization who could have been behind the break-in—assuming it had anything at all to do with S.R. 52.''

''I don't know whether that comforts me or not.''

Michaels' expression didn't change. ''You're merely the most public face behind which all the shadows are standing. You must have known that.''

Randall looked down at his desk. ''I hadn't thought of it quite that way before.''

''No, sir. But perhaps it's time you did. You're naturally the first person the press are going to ask about that rumor.''

''I wonder who the hell started it.''

''I'd almost bet it was someone in Lawrence's camp.''

''No. He wouldn't do that.''

''I didn't say the *senator* did it. But someone who works for him or supports him might have done so.''

''Christ, what a mess! How did you find out about the files, anyway?''

Michaels crossed his legs. ''From my source at Tampa P.D.''

''What else have you found out?''

''Only that Detective Karen Sweeney is up here to check you out.''

Ordinarily Randall didn't need antacids until later in the day, but this morning he needed one right now. Opening the desk drawer, he pulled out a bottle of Tums and popped a couple.

''Bill?'' he said as he chewed.

"Much better." She smiled. "The headache is almost completely gone."

"I'm glad to hear it."

"Your knee?"

He dismissed it with a wave of his hand. "It's been worse. This is only a minor inconvenience."

The *sommelier* appeared with the wine list. Grant looked at Karen with a questioning lift of his brow, and she nodded.

"Do you have any preferences?" he asked.

"I'm willing to try anything. I don't drink often."

The *sommelier* departed with the order, leaving them alone again, but only for a moment, as the waiter appeared with menus. Grant barely glanced at his, apparently knowing what he wanted. Karen scanned hers more closely, looking for the cheapest thing, something that wouldn't make her credit card smoke.

Grant seemed to sense her hesitation. "This is my treat," he said. "No obligation implied. I just didn't want to dine alone tonight, and right now there aren't many people I trust."

She looked up from the menu. "Are you sure you should trust me?"

"You're the force of law and order, aren't you? I could use some of both in my life right now."

"Did something happen today?"

His mouth twisted. "Other than the press asking if my children are my own?"

She felt her jaw drop as her heart slammed. "My God!"

"Whatever is going on, Karen, is getting very, very nasty. I don't know who is behind it or why, but it's far more than a simple break-in that went bad and cost Abby her life. It's a directed and concerted effort."

"Sir?"

"I want you to bust your butt to find out who's behind this. If I get tarred by that break-in and murder, however distantly, S.R. 52 is going to pass in a landslide."

"Yes, sir. One other thing, sir."

"Yes?"

"I found out why the investigation into the death of Georgina Lawrence was short-circuited."

Randall stopped chewing. "Why?"

"She was on her way home from meeting her lover. The senator apparently knew about it, and Jerry Connally stepped in to have the autopsy report skip over certain details...such as that she had just had sex, and that she was pregnant, presumably by another man."

"My God! How the hell did you find this out?"

"From someone in the medical examiner's office. Apparently Connally persuaded the M.E. that there would be no useful service performed by putting information in a public report that would only harm the senator's children and didn't have anything at all to do with Georgina Lawrence's death."

Randall looked down, shaking his head as he absorbed this information. "I have to agree with Connally on that one."

"Perhaps there's an issue you're not considering, Mr. Youngblood."

"What's that?"

"Senator Grant Lawrence is willing to tamper with the conduct of a police investigation to serve his own purposes. I think that's rather significant, don't you?"

15

It was too late to get anywhere with the *Herald* photo shop, so Terry dropped Karen off at her hotel.

"We'll get started again in the morning," he told her. "Doesn't hurt to take the first day out of the hospital slow, anyway. Pick you up at nine?"

"Sure. Thanks, Terry."

He grinned and drove away. That was when she first suspected he'd been taking it easy all day, including that long lunch break, for her sake. Smiling inwardly, she headed up to her room. There was nothing like the way one cop looked out for another.

A message from Grant Lawrence awaited her, suggesting they meet at a restaurant in Georgetown for dinner at eight. "I'll be there," he said. "If you can make it, great. If you can't, don't worry about it."

She decided she would make it. And as soon as the decision was made, she had to face the fact that she wanted to see Grant Lawrence for reasons other than the case. He probably wouldn't have anything to add—after all, he was the victim, of sorts, not the perp—but she wanted to see him anyway.

For the first time, a very real fear penetrated the de-

tachment she worked so hard to maintain. Fo[r] time in a long time, she wasn't simply a detecti[ve] [doing] a job, but a woman. A woman who felt very al[one] very vulnerable all of a sudden.

She didn't like that at all.

She gave herself a stern lecture, muttering unde[r] breath as she moved around the room, trying to de[cide] what was appropriate to wear to dinner with a sena[tor,] finally ordering herself to wear something businessli[ke,] so there wouldn't be any misunderstanding.

And realizing that the only misunderstanding was ap[t] to be on her part. In Grant Lawrence's world, she wa[s] merely a cop doing a job. He probably just wanted t[o] pick her brains.

Finally she settled on a navy blue suit, one with [a] skirt that reached to mid-calf, and black low-heele[d] pumps. Aside from her red suit, it was the only othe[r] piece of power clothing she owned. She wore it mainl[y] for testifying in court.

She suspected it would be apropos.

Grant was already waiting for her inside the rest[aurant] when she arrived. A pleasant maitre d' escorted [her to] the table in a quiet corner, a table somewhat shiel[ded by] leafy tropical plants. Most of the tables, she note[d, were] shielded in just such a way.

"Hi," Grant said, rising to greet her. He sh[ook her] hand and remained standing until the maitre [d'] seated her. They sat facing one another across [a] tablecloth, with a small bowl of floating candles [between] them, a little sprig of flowers in a miniature vas[e beside] it.

"How are you feeling?" he asked, his gaze [full of] genuine concern.

"Against *you*."

He nodded slowly. "But anyway, I didn't invite you here to talk business. I was hoping we could both forget our jobs for a few hours and just chat about anything else. Anything besides the fact that things are going to hell in Colombia and I may have to take a position on the matter that I won't like. Anything besides a press that knows no limits of decency."

"Sure." She managed a smile. "What shall we talk about?"

"What made you decide to become a cop?"

She cocked her head to one side. "Well, I suppose I ought to have some kind of romantic story about wanting to avenge someone I cared about, but all I've got is stubbornness."

"Stubbornness?" He grinned. "That's a new one. What set that off?"

"My father. When I was little, like most kids, I toyed around with the idea of being a cop. The difference was, my dad said I'd make a lousy cop. So I fixated on it. And the more he told me I couldn't do the job, the more determined I became to do it. The day I graduated from the academy I wanted to tell him, 'I told you so,' but he wasn't there."

His expression gentled. "Was your father that hard on you about everything?"

"Pretty much. He didn't have much respect for the abilities of women."

"What about your mother?"

"She left him when I was twelve. I never saw her again."

"Damn." His hand stirred as if he were about to reach out for hers, but then it stilled. "I'm sorry, Karen."

"It doesn't matter anymore. I've proved myself to my

own satisfaction, and that's what really counts, isn't it? My own opinion of myself?''

He smiled. ''I like to think so. But in *my* business, everyone *else's* opinion seems to count more.''

She tilted her head to one side, giving him her patented straight stare. ''That's not really true, is it? I mean, in terms of getting re-elected, it is. But that's not the most important thing in your life, is it?''

''No,'' he admitted.

''That's what I always figured about you. That your own morality took precedence over politics.''

His face shadowed a bit, pricking her interest, but then he nodded. ''You're right. At least mostly. But all of us have to make compromises to get anything done in this country. It's the beauty—and pain—of democracy. I wash your hand, you wash mine.''

''And you find that painful.''

''Sometimes, yes. But I'm also a realist. And actually, most of the compromises I have to make aren't that distressing.''

''But occasionally?''

''Occasionally it can be hell.'' He smiled. ''Now don't tell me your job is a bed of roses.''

''It's not. It's not at all.''

She was interrupted by the waiter, who came to take their orders, and was grateful for it. She didn't want to get into the doubts she was experiencing, or the anger that seemed sometimes to eat her alive.

But Grant wasn't one to forget where a conversation had been headed. ''What are the things you hate about your job?'' he asked when they were alone again.

''The ugliness. The unfairness. The murder of a prostitute won't get half the attention of the murder of a successful businessman. I was called off the scene of a woman found dead in an alley to come to your place. That irritated me.''

He nodded. "Why couldn't they send someone else?"

"Because everyone's tied up in the College Hill shootings. That's a headline case. You're a headline case. So the unknown woman in the alley was pushed onto the back burner."

"That's not right."

"Of course it's not right. It's justified as apportionment of limited resources."

His expression encouraged her to continue.

"It's not that Abby Reese's murder didn't matter to me," she said. "Don't misunderstand me."

"I don't. I can see you care very deeply."

"I do. Maybe that's the problem. Anyway, the woman found in the alley got moved from the back burner."

"By your efforts?"

"In part. I wasn't going to forget her. But then it turned out she wasn't just another prostitute."

"No?"

"No. She turned out to be the owner of a dance school. So nobody's going to forget her now."

Grant Lawrence grew very still. Karen, a cop to her very bones, didn't miss it. "What's wrong?"

For a second or two, he didn't answer. "Just...a twinge in my knee. Sorry."

Then he reached out and touched her hand lightly, briefly. "I'm glad you think that one victim matters as much as another."

"They do. They're all human lives." She still felt his touch, though it was gone, and realized that she didn't want to talk about her job anymore. Not tonight. Tonight she wanted...she wanted. Exactly what, she wasn't sure, but not this.

"This is depressing," she said, trying a smile. "There must be something more cheerful we can talk about."

The veal marsala had gone down well, as had the cheesecake with fresh strawberries and most of a bottle of cabernet sauvignon. The conversation had roamed over the usual superficial issues—movies his parents had made, war stories from her early years on the force, how he'd gotten into politics—and even as he slid his credit card into the leather folder in which the waiter had left the check, Grant realized he didn't want to simply say good night.

"Are you up for a walk?" he asked.

"I don't think either of us is safe to drive, but what about your knee?"

It wasn't a no. "The doctor says I'm supposed to walk a little, to keep it from stiffening. Besides, I don't intend to walk very far."

She smiled. "Sure. Why not?"

It was a beautiful spring night of the sort that Washington got too few of. Past the gray, drab chill of winter, not yet the clinging humidity of summer. Along the Potomac, cherry blossoms were in bloom. Around the Mall, vacationers would be strolling, standing in awe at the Washington Monument or in sadness at the Vietnam Memorial. On Fourteenth Street, streetwalkers would be hawking their wares. On Constitution, homeless men and women would still seek the warmth of steam rising from subway grates. Here in Georgetown, well-heeled young professionals emerged from brownstone town houses to stroll along the sidewalks, window shopping, talking quietly, sometimes laughing too loudly, often ruminating silently about the day's business.

It was, Grant thought, a curious place to call home.

Yet he *had* come to feel at home here, in a city where transience was the norm. It was a city in which one could put down roots quickly, because so few others had any. If you'd been here through two elections, you were a local.

"Funny," he said.

"What?"

He shrugged. "I grew up in Florida. Traveled some with my parents, but by and large they tried to give me a sense of groundedness there. And yet…this feels as much like home as anywhere."

"You've been here for what, eight years?" Karen asked. "Hardly surprising that you've made yourself comfortable."

"It's not that," he said. "It's…"

His thoughts roamed in rapid free-association. When he'd moved here, it had felt like commuting. Tampa was home. This was where he worked. When had that changed?

"…Georgie," he said. He let out a mirthless chuckle. "She *wanted* to be at home here, among the power elite. I didn't. Or maybe I did and didn't want to admit it. But Tampa was *home*. The house, the girls. Then she died, and…Tampa wasn't so much home anymore. I had the girls up here for summers, even when we were on recess. Georgie had always wanted this to be her city…our city…and it only became my city after she died."

He looked into her eyes for a moment. They were skeptical, probing eyes, yes, but they could also be full of so much kindness. At moments like this, for example. Perhaps it was the dilation of the pupils in the dim nighttime light that made them seem so much greener. Or perhaps the flecks of green grew when her mind softened and she wasn't in cop mode.

"Your eyes change color, you know."

She glanced away, as if unsure what to say next. When she looked back, the moment had passed. "So where are we walking to, Senator? That's Georgetown Park, across the street. That's where I found the dress."

"We're going right down that alley," he said. "Do you like the blues?"

Blues Alley was virtually an institution in a city full of institutions. Karen had heard of it, but somehow she'd expected something…else. What it was, was a smallish stage surrounded by a relative handful of tables, all taken, with a bar along one wall. The bar stools were also taken. There was nowhere to sit, and within five minutes, she didn't care.

Her mind was lost in the patient moans of a tenor sax, backed by a piano, a real bass fiddle and a drummer who played with dexterity and discretion. The song's vocals—a quiet, respectful rendition of Louis Armstrong's "What a Wonderful World"—had been little more than preamble to the sax solo, which conjured, better than words ever could, skies of blue and trees of green. No one danced. No one talked. There was nothing but the sax, and the band, and a world where, no matter what hardships lay at hand, one could find only wonder. The word "evocative" had been created for moments like this.

Karen hadn't realized she was pressed against Grant, intimacy born of necessity in the crowded room, until she felt him swaying to the music. She swayed with him, and it was as if they were leaves on one of those green trees, under that blue sky, caressed by the warmth of a summer breeze flowing through the music.

She should have been uncomfortable. She should have

been thinking about the case, and the tangled skeins of motives and agendas. She should have been wondering who would think so little of human life as to slash the throat of Abby Reese or dispose of Nat Olson like so many old leftovers. She should have, at the very least, been asking herself what possible point there could be in hitching her heart to a star whose background and ambitions were so far from her own. She should have been.

Instead, she was lost in the moment, swaying beside him, their hands somehow having become entwined, the mixed odors of beer, wine and liquor transformed into the bloom of hyacinth and heather, daisy and daffodil, leaf and loam. It was, she tried to tell herself, just a tenor sax and a piano, a bass fiddle and a drummer, a Washington blues bar and a Washington politician, a man for whom charm and charisma were stock in trade.

Enjoy the moment for what it is, she thought. She had hoped the thought would be rational, clearheaded, a wedge of pure, cold logic biting in to cleave an emotional spell. Instead, it, too, was swallowed into the spell. It was...permission. She tucked herself a bit closer to him and let herself squeeze his hand. He squeezed back. And they swayed on.

For a few hours she didn't have to be a cop, swimming in the worst of human ugliness. And he didn't have to be a politician, scheming to mate principle and possibility. For a few hours she could simply be a woman in the company of a man, swaying to the music of the blues, not dissecting, not analyzing, not predicting. Just...being.

Enjoy the moment for what it is, she thought.

And she did. For a few hours.

* * *

The band was in its last set when the throbbing in Grant's knee pushed its way past distant discomfort to intolerable. He didn't want to leave. They'd promised a reprise of "What a Wonderful World," and he wanted to hear it again. But his knee wouldn't let him. He squeezed Karen's hand to get her attention.

She seemed to read the situation in his face. "Your knee?"

He nodded. "I don't want to go."

"It's okay," she said.

They slipped back into the night. He tried to keep his stride even. It was a discipline he'd developed in high school, not wanting to be seen as the cripple. Most of the time he could keep the limp down to imperceptible. But tonight the knee was too sore, and he could feel the ungainliness in his step.

"You're really hurting," she said. "You should have said something earlier."

"I didn't realize I'd had too much until I'd...had too much."

She laughed. It was a beautiful laugh, light and delicate, but at the same time sincere and hearty. "That's how I am with Godiva chocolates," she said.

"This was...nice, Karen. I needed to be away."

"Yes, it was. And so did I."

He could still feel the way her body had melded into his. "You're nice to be away with."

"So are you, Senator."

"Grant," he said.

"Grant," she echoed.

They were back in front of the restaurant, where his car had acquired that ubiquitous bit of Washington litter, a parking ticket.

"I forgot to feed the meter when we went for a walk," he said sheepishly.

"I wouldn't worry about it. You *are* a senator, after all."

He shook his head. "In any other town, that might matter. It won't here. Besides, I parked illegally. So I'll pay the twenty dollars."

"Expensive parking."

"You're worth it," he heard himself say.

He hadn't meant to say it. Certainly hadn't meant to say it that way. It had been a lovely evening, and for the first time in a long time, he'd felt peace. But he couldn't afford to look at it as anything more than what it had been...a lovely interlude, a needed respite.

She rescued him.

"Well, I'm glad to know I'm worth twenty bucks," she said with a mischievous wink.

His hand found hers again. "Thank you for a wonderful night, Karen."

"Thank *you*, Grant."

"Do you need a ride back to your hotel?"

She shook her head, her eyes never leaving his. "I'll catch a cab. You need to get home and get that knee up."

"It's no bother...."

She smiled. It was a wistful smile. "It's better this way, Grant. Go rest your knee. I'll catch a cab."

He wanted to lean forward just that tiny bit he would need to for a good-night kiss. While they'd swayed to the music, he had actually thought about whether he should kiss her, and how. A gentle brush on the cheek. A thank-you. But now, at the moment of truth, looking into those pale, green-flecked, wistful eyes, he balked.

He gave her hand a squeeze.

"Good night, Karen Sweeney."

She squeezed back. "Good night, Grant Lawrence."

Then she released her hand and turned, lifting an arm to hail a taxi, which arrived with maddening timing.

"See you tomorrow," she said, as she climbed into the cab.

"Yes," he said.

And then she was gone, whisked away into the night.

He climbed into his car, groaning as he flexed his knee, turned the key in the ignition, put the car in gear and headed for an empty town house.

The red message light was blinking as Karen stepped into her room and closed the door. The maid had turned down the covers, even putting a mint on her pillow, yet the room that had felt almost homey that afternoon was sterile tonight. That afternoon she'd been a cop on a case. Tonight she was a woman, alone in a hotel room in a strange city. She picked up the receiver and pressed the message code.

"Turn on your cell phone," Previn's voice said.

That was odd. It should have been on. She pulled it out of her purse and opened it. Pressed the power button. No response. The battery was dead. Maybe there was a God, she thought. A God who had killed her cell phone battery so she could enjoy an evening away from the job.

She plugged in the recharger and set it on the nightstand. Then, in a silent act of defiance, she moved it to the desk across the room. A shower and sleep were the only business she intended to attend to. *Previn, you'll have to wait till morning....*

The room phone rang.

...or not.

"Hello?"

"Turn your phone on, Sweeney." Previn.

"It was on," she said. "The battery's dead. So what's so important that you're calling me at," she glanced at the clock—could it really be this late?—"one-fifteen in the morning?"

"We've got a problem. I'm looking at a black-and-white photo, which arrived in a plain manila envelope, addressed to your attention, unsigned, no return address, no prints."

"And this is a photo of?" she asked impatiently.

"Grant Lawrence. Walking through what looks like a park. Hand-in-hand with Stacy Wiggins."

16

꧁ ꧂

The line hummed emptily for a few seconds as Karen absorbed what Previn had just told her. She took a deep breath. This was the precipice. She would be risking her career, and Previn's. But it was the right call. She hoped.

Then she said flatly, "Bury it."

"Karen! My God, you can't…"

"Bury it," she said again, her voice as taut as a violin string. "Bury it. Put it somewhere no one else will see it."

"But…"

"Listen to me, Dave. Just listen. That photo doesn't prove a damn thing except that a widower dated a woman who has since been murdered."

"On the same night as his housekeeper? Karen, are you out of your mind?"

She paused, seeking inner stability, fighting for it. "Dave, just keep listening. It's enough that you and I know about that photo for now. It may be completely harmless. It may be that Lawrence had nothing whatever to do with these two deaths. It may be that someone who is after him killed both women. You follow?"

"I follow."

"After all, what does that photo say? Only that some-one is after his ass."

Previn made a muffled sound, as if he weren't happy.

"Dave, I'm not asking you to destroy evidence. I'm asking you to bury it until we find out whether it's relevant and what it means. Because we don't want to destroy this man's career if he's innocent."

Again the line hummed with emptiness. But finally Previn said, "Okay. Okay. You're right. If someone did all this to ruin him, we don't want to help."

Karen let out a sigh of relief. "Exactly. Where are you, and where is the photo? Did you show anyone?"

"Hell no, this is *our* case. Give me credit for some sense. I figured if anyone else saw that pic, we'd be off the case in a snap. Shit like that makes headlines."

"Good. Are you at the station?"

"I'm at my apartment." The apartment he had just moved into after separating from his wife.

"Where's the photo?"

"With me. I didn't want anybody scoping it till I'd talked to you." He sounded almost ashamed.

"I'm proud of you, Dave," Karen assured him. "I'm really proud of you. A lot of people forget, but part of our job is to avoid damaging the innocent."

"*If* he's innocent."

Her heart thudded. "Yeah. If. Hide it in the back of your closet or something. I want to think about this."

"Okay. But don't keep me out of your cogitations. I feel like I'm holding a red-hot potato."

Karen was shaking like a leaf when she hung up the phone. And then the rage began.

"What the hell is going on, Michaels?"

It was late, very late. Randall Youngblood had just

come back to the office after an evening spent buying dinner for men he didn't like, in order to have time to explain to them why S.R. 52 would be bad law. Too keyed up to go straight home, he'd decided to go through his inbox and see what tomorrow would hold. He wished he hadn't.

"What do you mean, sir?" Michaels asked sleepily.

Randall had awoken him. That was just fine. "I'm looking at a photo of Grant Lawrence holding hands with some woman in a park. Why is this in my inbox? Who is she?"

There was a rustling on the other end of the line, soon accompanied by a woman's sleepy moan. "It's okay, honey," Michaels said quietly. "It's Youngblood. Go back to sleep." Then, "I don't know, sir. I didn't send you any photos. Is the envelope still there?"

"It came in a courier pouch. The return address is our office down there. I assumed you'd sent it. Unless you have…someone else working on this."

"No, sir. You said to keep it close, and I have. Was there anything else in the envelope, sir? A note?"

"No note," Randall said. "Let me check the back of the photo. Maybe there's…there's a date, last fall, and a woman's name. Stacy Wiggins. Does that name mean anything to you?"

"Give me a moment, sir." More rustling, followed by the sound of a door being drawn closed. The beep of a computer powering up. The clacking of keys. "I'm checking the news database, sir. How is the name spelled?"

Randall spelled it for him. More clacking of keys. "What have you got, Michaels?"

Michaels summarized as he read. "There was a small story in the *Tampa Tribune* last week. Dead woman identified. Owned a dance studio. Body found in an alley, brutally murdered...hold on, sir. Let me check my calendar.'' There was a pause. ''Holy shit.''

''What?'' Randall asked, growing impatient.

''Sir, Stacy Wiggins was murdered on the same night as Abby Reese. Lawrence's nanny.''

''I know who she was,'' Randall said. ''I went to the interment. So Lawrence had, at least once, seen some woman who was later murdered. Coincidence.''

''Murdered on the *same night?*''

''Weirder things have happened.''

Michaels made an impatient sound. ''Sir, what are the odds that two people known by Lawrence would be murdered on the same night? Found within a relatively short time of one another?''

''It's still not proof.''

''We know Lawrence has manipulated a police investigation in the past, sir.''

Randall felt his stomach begin to burn. ''Just what kind of manipulation are you suggesting? You surely can't mean that he killed those women.''

''Of course not. But someone did. Maybe in an attempt to get at him. That's not what matters. What matters is that Lawrence knows both of these women are dead. And if he hasn't apprised the police of his connection to both of them, then he's obstructing a police investigation.''

Randall's stomach turned so sour that he started hunting in a drawer for a bottle of antacids. ''We don't know that. For all we know the cops already know about the connection and are keeping it private.''

''That may be. The point is, sir, that *we* now know. And if we keep it a secret, we're *also* obstructing an investigation.''

"Christ." Randall slammed the bottle of antacids on his desk with so much force that the plastic cracked. "You know, Michaels, you haven't seemed to grasp something very important about me. There are lines I won't cross."

"I've grasped it, sir. But concealing evidence is surely a line you don't want to cross."

"I also don't want to skewer Lawrence. We've got nothing here that proves he did a single thing wrong."

"Well, sir, if we don't act on this information, some-one else will. And they might also point out that you knew about it and kept silent. Besides, if you want to talk about what's in the best interests of this country, then you have to consider what it would mean to have a man in the White House who's already been involved in two cover-ups."

"We only know of one," Randall said. But he was weakening. And starting to feel angry that he could have been so mistaken in the character of Grant Lawrence.

"Take care of it, Michaels," he said finally, propelled by a sense of outrage.

"I will. And I'll be certain your name isn't involved."

When Randall hung up, he found himself wishing he could go back to being a simple cane grower, where all he had to worry about were the vagaries of Mother Nature.

Karen forced herself to calm down. It took a while. Seldom had she experienced anger so strong it nearly blinded her. Unlike some people, however, anger didn't clear her head, it clouded it. The objectivity she had learned as a cop was impossible to find tonight.

She had to settle for putting her anger in the back-ground, far enough back in her mind that she could think past her sense of betrayal, her feelings of disappointment and, worst of all, the dirty feeling of being used.

She had, she reminded herself, no proof that Grant Lawrence was using her in any way. No pressure had been applied to her. It had been *her* idea to come to Washington, not his.

Besides, he had been in Washington when both murders were committed. Yes, her mind was getting clearer. She was overlooking essential elements in this case.

Grant had been in Washington. There was no reason why he would have murdered the nanny he had loved all his life. On the other hand, if Stacy Wiggins had been threatening him in some way...

She shook her head, fighting for clarity again.

No, that was the wrong path. Stacy Wiggins hadn't been the threat. Someone *else* was. Someone who had sent that photograph to her. Someone who had arranged for a "car accident" and reporters to be on the scene.

Someone who was trying to destroy any hope of the presidency for Grant.

But was that worth two murders?

Picking up the phone, she called room service. She needed coffee.

Okay. She opened her suitcase and pulled out a legal pad to work on. What did she know? What did she suspect? Why had that photo turned up now and not right after reports of Stacy's murder appeared in the papers. Or even before Stacy had been identified? That would have seemed even more incriminating.

Stop. List only the facts she knew for certain.

Abby Reese had been swiftly murdered, apparently as a result of startling an intruder in the Lawrence home.

The senator's home filing cabinets had been pried open, but nothing taken.

Stacy Wiggins' murder was totally unlike Abby Reese's. Its savagery suggested a huge anger. Given that the senator had apparently had some kind of relationship with her, he would be an obvious suspect...except that he'd been in Washington.

Such unidentified prints as they had found couldn't be linked to anyone in the databases. Whoever had done these things had no criminal record, no fingerprints on file as a result of job-related requirements. Not even a military background. They might or might not belong to the perp. As often was the case with physical evidence, it was useless in identifying the perpetrator but would eventually be useful in proving a suspect had been present. Once they had a suspect.

But she was wandering again.

Stacy Wiggins' body had been moved. Nylon fibers clinging to her wounds might have been from automobile carpeting or from cheap household carpeting. There was no way to be certain. Rug burns on her buttocks, arms and heels showed that she had flailed mightily as she had been tortured and killed...on a rug.

Alissa Jurgen. The name popped to the top of her mind. The woman was strong enough to have killed Stacy, particularly if she had managed to tie Stacy up first. Not impossible.

Alissa. Alissa admitted she had a crush on Stacy. It probably went a lot further than that. Maybe she had followed Stacy to find out who the secret lover was and had taken the photo.

Yes, that was possible. Maybe she'd only intended to create a bit of scandal for Grant. Maybe she'd planned a little blackmail. Maybe the jealousy had worsened once she saw the couple. And maybe she'd lied to Karen in saying that the relationship had broken off a while ago.

Yes, a jealously enraged Alissa Jurgen could put the puzzle pieces together. It could explain the fury of the attack on Stacy. It could even explain the break-in and Abby Reese's murder. Maybe Alissa had gone to Grant Lawrence's home to kill him, too. Instead, she had encountered Abby Reese.

It would even explain the auto accident. Karen had known jealous lovers to kill the object of their love and then try to destroy the person they blamed for taking their love away.

Alissa might blame Grant for stealing Stacy's love and, by extension, for making it necessary for her to kill Stacy. If that were the case, she wouldn't stop trying to get at Grant.

But no matter how she put the pieces together, one thing still stuck in her craw:

Grant must have known Stacy was dead. And he hadn't told Karen that both women were connected to him, a piece of information that would have been significantly helpful to the investigation.

Instead, he had kept silent. She remembered the ''twinge'' he had claimed to feel in his knee, remembered that it had occurred just as she mentioned the murder of the dance studio owner.

The lying son of a bitch!

''Well, hell, Sweeney,'' Terry Tyson said as he picked her up in the morning. ''You look even worse than when they let you out of the hospital.''

''I didn't get much sleep,'' she admitted.

''Why not?''

"I had a call from my partner in Tampa. It kinda disturbed my sleep."

"Anything to do with this case?"

"A different murder," she said by way of evasion. Now even *she* was doing it. She loathed this case. If she had half a brain, she would ask to be taken off it.

But she couldn't do that. Mad as she might be at Grant Lawrence, angry as she might get at herself for not backing out of this, she feared what might happen if this case fell into another detective's hands.

At the very least, she was going to beard Grant before she did anything else.

"Well, let's go take a look-see at the *Times* photo shop," Terry said pleasantly, apparently deciding she wasn't going to be any more forthcoming and taking it in good part.

"Sorry, Terry," she said after a moment.

"No problem. Sometimes it's best we keep our own counsel."

If rush hour ever ended around here, Karen couldn't tell. Of course, it was getting harder and harder to tell in parts of Tampa, too. She supposed if traffic was moving at all, it wasn't rush hour. Certainly Terry didn't seem troubled by the snail's pace at which they were often moving.

One look at Terry's badge was enough to get them into the photo shop at the paper. The photographer who'd been present the night of the accident wasn't in, but another photographer was willing to dig out the CD that contained the digitized photos and set them up at a computer with a seventeen-inch screen so they could scan them.

Much to Karen's dismay, most of the photos showed

her sprawled on the floor of the limo, with Grant in various positions between her legs as he tried to rise.

"Saw that in the paper," Terry remarked. "I felt sorry for you."

"Thanks. Amazing how ugly they can make something perfectly innocent."

Terry glanced at her from the corner of his eye. "Seat belts. You've heard of seat belts, Detective?"

She flushed. "Mea culpa."

"You-a bet-a." He chuckled deeply. Then, "Here we go. God bless newshounds."

The camera had focused on the other vehicle. A skinny, way too skinny, guy was trying to climb out the passenger side. He could only be seen from the back.

"Damn," said Terry. "That's not enough."

Another photo, then another. The driver clambering over the top of the car and running toward the far side of the street.

More photos. A man standing near the corner, all but indistinguishable beneath a brimmed hat that shadowed his face from the streetlight. The fleeing driver came close to him. Passed him. Was gone.

"Back up," Karen said.

"Yeah." Terry backed up straight to the photo that showed the man on the corner. He turned to the photographer. "Can we enlarge this somehow?"

The man left his task and came over. "Sure. What do you want bigger?"

"The guy standing on the street corner. His face, if you can."

Leaning across them, the photographer grabbed the mouse, moving and clicking it. A box appeared around the face, then, with another click, it doubled in size.

"More?" Karen asked.

The box tripled in size. But now it was beginning to look fuzzier. "Can we clear that up any?"

"I can try. It's not something I'm good at. We're not supposed to alter news photos."

"Try," she suggested.

He was willing, but when he got done, there was nothing except a sense of familiarity that niggled at her. The face was still too shadowed to identify.

Terry looked at her. "What's up? I can feel something is up."

"I just get the feeling I know this guy."

"I'll have a boiled egg with horseradish sauce on the side, and a whole tomato, wedged," Terry said. As a diabetic, he'd explained, he needed to eat several small meals each day. "You have to try the tomatoes here. The cook grows them on his balcony."

Karen ordered a garden salad. Breakfast wasn't high on her list of daily needs. But greens were always good. On the way to the diner, they'd discussed whether to circulate the photo of Mr. Fuzzy Shadow. They hadn't reached a decision.

"I say we keep it to ourselves," Karen said, after the waitress had left. "Yeah, the guy looks familiar, but I could have seen him in the hotel lobby, or when I was out that afternoon buying a dress, or on the flight up here. He could just be Joe Innocent, standing on a street corner when an accident happened."

"Do you always second-guess yourself?"

"Isn't that the mark of a good detective? Second-guess everything, including yourself? *Especially* yourself?"

"To a point," he said. "On the other hand, you're a cop. You have cop's eyes. And a cop's mind."

She nodded. She didn't feel especially perceptive at the moment, after the news Previn had given her. In fact, she felt pretty damn stupid. She fiddled with her fork, dragging it over the paper napkin to create a grid.

"Okay," Terry said, breaking the silence. "What's the waitress's name and what's her hobby?"

She thought for a moment. "Sandi. And gambling. Unless she has a passionate love affair for air conditioning or alternating current. But I'd guess the 'A.C.' in the 'I Luv A.C.' button on her blouse stands for Atlantic City. Especially since it's money green."

"Now," he said, "what color were the tablecloths at the restaurant where we ate lunch yesterday?"

"Damned if I know," she answered.

"Same here. But if I'd asked you in the parking lot after we ate, you'd have known."

She shrugged. "And this proves?"

"That you notice what's going on around you, but you don't put obviously useless trivia into long-term memory. So if Mr. Fuzzy Shadows tickles your memory, it's probably because when you saw him, you thought he might be worth remembering. It's called trusting your instincts, Karen."

"I'm low on that right now."

"I can tell." He paused while the waitress brought their food. "Thanks, Sandi. Did you win or lose?"

"Excuse me?" she asked.

"In Atlantic City," he said, pointing to the button.

She laughed and shook her head. "I won two hundred dollars. Two years ago. I've never gone back. Figured I should quit while I was ahead."

"So much for trusting my instincts," Karen said, after she'd gone. "Wow, these tomatoes *are* good."

"Nothing like home-grown," he said.

He peeled his egg, dipped it in the horseradish and bit off a chunk. His eyes watered briefly, until his sinuses adapted to the bite of the spice. "Great stuff," he said, after a deep swallow of water. "I never get colds, you know."

"Your sinuses are pickled."

"Probably. So okay, where have you been since you got in town?"

She chewed her salad while she thought. "My hotel. The Capitol, briefly. A party."

"The one you were coming home from in the limo."

"Right. The hospital. Around town with you yesterday."

"And last night?"

It was probably an innocent question. So why did the answer make her feel guilty? "Dinner."

He studied her carefully, finishing his egg. "I can probably guess for myself," he finally said.

"Yes, you probably can."

He took a wedge of tomato on his fork. "I'm in an interesting situation. Three weeks from today, I'm an oil stain in the parking lot. Which means I can play a little loose on the rules. Keep things to myself, if I need to, without worrying about someone crawling up my ass about it. Because by the time they found out, I'd be lying on a beach, annoying my wife by watching the bikinis pass." He paused to eat the tomato, then continued. "I mention this in case it might be relevant. If, for example, there were something you were holding back because you didn't want it to end up in a report. Something like that."

She could see why he'd been a top-notch detective. He would be positively lethal in interrogation. Finally she decided another brain couldn't hurt. And, like he said, he could afford to be discreet.

"Yes," she said. "I had dinner with Lawrence last night. We went out to Blues Alley after. It was...a nice break."

He nodded, seemingly knowing there was more.

"Then I got back to my hotel and checked messages. And all hell broke loose."

"Mr. Connally?"

Jerry looked up from his desk. Fay, the phone receptionist, looked as if she'd been the subject of a wind tunnel test. "What's up?"

"I was going to ask you that, sir. I've had four calls this morning, all in a half hour. The *Post*. The *Times*. CNN and NBC. Something about a photograph of the senator with a woman."

Again? He'd put out that fire two days ago. "The senator has no comment beyond what he's already said, Fay."

"I think this is a new one," she said, tapping a pencil against her fingertips. "Something about a woman who was killed."

Oh shit. His stomach did a nervous flop. "The senator has no comment. Call Strickland at the *Post* and tell him if he wants a comment, we'd like a copy of this mysterious photo. Unless his paper wants to stoop to the gotcha tactics of the *Herald*."

She nodded, uncertainty in her eyes.

Jerry took a breath. It wasn't her job. Her job was to be nice. "Just say no comment. I'll call Strickland."

"Thank you, sir."

She left and he stabbed the phone. "Sam. Someone's

chumming. I want to know who and what they're using for bait. And I want to know in thirty minutes."

Weldon paused on the other end of the line. "I'll make some calls, Jerry. But thirty minutes, that's tight."

"Thirty minutes," he repeated.

That might give him time to figure out how to save Grant's hide. And, possibly, his own.

17

It was midday, and Grant Lawrence was staring at the faxed photo of himself walking hand-in-hand with Stacy Wiggins. Mixed feelings tore at him.

Part of him remembered that day with a smile. It had been a wonderful afternoon, sailing on a rented boat and finally taking a twilight walk on a deserted jogging trail in his gated community. At least he'd thought it was deserted. The photograph made him feel seriously betrayed.

But the betrayal didn't overwhelm the aching sense of loss as he thought again of Stacy's death. They had parted months ago. The love had never ended, but the spark had gone away. Her future was in Tampa. His was, he hoped, in Washington. The girls liked her, and she them, but there had never been the kind of bond that would have sustained a family. The girls had had that bond with Abby and had never seemed inclined to form it with Stacy. She had been a delightful companion, tender and warm and sincere. But as the months went by, they had both realized they valued each other more as friends and less as lovers.

Still, he grieved for her loss, grieved to know that he

would never again see her smile or hear her laugh. A dear friend had departed, had been taken away viciously and violently. Another woman in his life, gone.

But he also looked at the photo with loathing. It was going to appear in the press. It was going to turn his daughters' lives into hell. The press, encouraged by anyone with an axe to grind, would hound him over it relentlessly, beating the horse long after its death.

And just as S.R. 52 was about to come up for a vote.

But life, as he had long since learned, rarely made allowances for what was already on someone's plate. And now he had this in addition to everything else.

Then there was Jerry to consider. Jerry hadn't said a thing when he reported this fiasco, but Grant was sure he knew he was worried. Grant wished he could think of some way to save his friend from what, in all probability, was right around the corner.

But it was too late now. Whatever Jerry had done couldn't be undone.

Shit. To hell with himself. He was feeling sick at heart that he hadn't, and couldn't, protect the people he loved.

The phone rang, startling him out of his reverie. His private line. He wondered what new catastrophe Jerry had to report.

But it wasn't Jerry, it was Art. Grant's heart slammed into high gear. "What's wrong?"

"Nothing major," Art said easily enough. "I've got to take the girls to the doctor. Lucy's running a fever of around a hundred and two, and her throat is all red and swollen. And Belle's complaining that her throat is getting scratchy, too. So I'm taking them all, just to be safe. I just wanted you to know. But I don't think it's anything out of the ordinary."

"Thanks, Art." Grant felt his heart rate ease and slow. "Have my girls call me when you get back?"

"Sure. I'm not sure how long it will take, though. I'm going to one of those minor emergency clinics. The pediatrician couldn't get them in until five."

"Okay. Let me know when you know."

"I sure will. Take it easy, Grant. They'll be fine. We've both been through this routine before."

Grant managed a chuckle. "Countless times. I just hate it when I'm so far away."

"I know what you mean. I go through hell every time my ex tells me one of the girls is sick."

"I know, Art."

It was Art's turn to chuckle. "On the other hand, trying to manage four girls in a waiting room.... I think you got the easier job."

"Maybe so."

"I'll call when I know something, okay?"

"Thanks again, Art."

Another thing he had to do, Grant thought as he hung up. Find the girls a new nanny until he could move them up here with him. It was not a task he was looking forward to, but it was unfair to keep imposing on Art. Besides, the girls needed to be back in their own home just as soon as possible.

He needed to call a press conference to deal with the photo issue. He wished it would put the matter to bed, but he knew better. What he could do, though, was tell his side of the story, then shut up, buckle up and prepare to ride out the storm.

He paged Jerry. He would do the press conference soon. Immediately. That afternoon.

"You know what the worst thing about diabetes is?" Terry asked Karen as he ordered another cup of coffee and two more hard-boiled eggs.

"What's that?"

"You're supposed to lose weight. But the insulin injections make it just about impossible."

"So what do you do?"

"I walk a lot in the evenings." His eyes crinkled at the corners. "Life makes us pay for every pleasure eventually. I'm paying for doughnuts, cake, candy bars and mashed potatoes. And the million cups of java with three sugars."

She had to laugh with him. "You're probably right."

"Of course I'm right. All the good stuff I ate. Well, that and the patrol car. Sat around too much. Now I'm getting creaky and I have to take long walks. You pay, Sweeney. You pay."

She looked down at her own plate, her English muffin barely touched. "I'm afraid you're right."

"On the other hand," he continued, "some things are worth paying for."

"Maybe."

"No maybe about it." The waitress put his eggs in front of him with a fresh scoop of horseradish. "Okay, so you've got a bit of a mess on your plate."

Karen nodded.

"And you're thinking you're a bit…uh…too close to the senator emotionally. But that's okay."

"Okay?"

"Sure. He's not your perp. He's a victim."

"But…"

Terry waved a hand. "How long you been in homicide?"

"Five years."

"Then you ought to know you never get the whole

truth out of anybody. Everybody's got something to hide. The man's feet aren't any more clay than yours or mine. He probably didn't know his girlfriend was dead, at first. How long was it before you even ID'd the dancer?''

''Almost two weeks,'' Karen said.

''Okay, so it was a while before he found out. And the two murders were very different, and the bodies were found across town from each other. Sure, you and I get our antennas waggling because they were on the same night and he's the connection between them, but from his viewpoint, there's nothing to connect them *except* that he knew and loved both of them. So why should he bring it up?''

''So as not to obstruct an investigation.''

Terry nodded and took a bit of horseradish-slathered egg. His eyes watered while he chewed and swallowed. He didn't bother with a sip of water. ''That's the way it looks to us. We're cops. But he's a politician. He thinks differently. He *has* to. He's gotta wonder whether airing the dirty linen will be good for anyone at all, including himself. He's in a precarious position. This comes out and maybe he can kiss off the presidency.''

''You approve of him hiding it?'' Karen couldn't believe it.

Terry's face stiffened a bit. ''Did I say that? I know I didn't say that. *If* he knew the dancer was dead on the same night as the nanny and he didn't come forward with it, then he was wrong. Plain wrong. But I can understand where it came from, and I'm not going to make it a federal case. What's the point?''

Karen couldn't even think of a reply.

''You, on the other hand,'' Terry continued after another mouthful of egg, ''don't see it that way. You don't like compromises.''

''Not compromises like this.''

''Right. What's more, you're getting sweet on him.''

''I am not!''

Terry just laughed quietly, shook his head and started on his second egg. ''Keep your feelings out of it, Karen. Don't let yourself get sweet on him, 'cuz it might make you too angry to see the truth.''

''Truth? There's hardly any truth in this whole case.''

''Oh, there's truth, all right. Two women are dead, killed in entirely different ways, and you think it might have been the dance studio partner because she had a crush on the deceased.''

''It's a possibility.''

''Everything's a possibility, and that's where you're going wrong.''

''How do you mean?''

''You're limiting the possibilities, Karen.''

Her spine stiffened, primarily because she was good at thinking outside the box, not going for the obvious when there were other possibilities. She almost said something, then bit the words back. Terry had a lot more experience than she did. Maybe she *was* missing something.

Terry smiled at her as if he'd read her reaction, but he didn't say anything about it. ''Step back a minute,'' he suggested. ''I'm coming into this case fresh. Pretend you are, too. Now, let's start with the murders themselves. They say a lot. The dancer was strangled and mutilated. You say she was a strong woman.''

''Yes.''

''And there were signs of struggle.''

''Carpet burns. Some flesh under her fingernails.''

"Right. So whoever subdued her had to be stronger. Her partner isn't likely to be that much stronger than she was."

Karen hesitated. "Maybe."

He let that pass. "Regardless, that murder was an act of rage. Male rage. Women don't kill like that."

Karen's head snapped up. "There's always a first time."

"A jealous woman usually resorts to a gun. Or she'll do it while the vic's asleep. Nothing physical. Nothing mutilating. Just as quick and clean as she can make it without getting herself into a fight. Poison or gun. And this was neither."

"Okay. I'll accept that."

He smiled again. "So we're looking at a murder that was *probably* committed by a man. A very *angry* man. A very disturbed man."

She nodded, seeing where he was headed.

"Now, we also have the murder, the same night, of the nanny." He washed down the last of his egg with coffee. "Given that both victims are linked to the same man and that both occurred the same night, my guess is they were committed by the same perp, despite the difference in modus. I think you're right that the nanny was an unintended victim. I'll bet you both murders happened in the same house, probably in the same room. That's the intruder Abby confronted when she came downstairs. The killer probably figured that, with Lawrence and the girls up here in D.C., Abby would have taken some time away with family or friends. Didn't even expect her to be there."

Karen nodded. "If they were killed in the same room, there would be transfers. Blood, trace evidence. I'll tell Previn to have the lab check."

"You said the body was moved. You picked up on that right away."

"Yes," Karen said. "But that raises another question. Who moved Wiggins' body? I mean, if someone wanted to bury the senator, why not leave the body in the house, where it would be found?"

He paused for a long moment, his eyes darkening. "That's an ugly question, you know. There are only two possible answers. Either the perp loaded the dancer's blood-soaked body into his car, to make it *look* like the senator was trying to cover it up, or…"

"…or Grant Lawrence had it moved," she said. "And that goes beyond just keeping quiet when he might have told us about the connection. That's felony obstruction."

Grant stepped out his front door, made his way to the podium and looked out at the reporters. Their eyes were focused, cold and hard. He wasn't comfortable with a press conference held on his front lawn, but Jerry had insisted. Addressing it here, at his home, was symbolic: this was a personal issue, not a political one. The two would be linked, of course, but there was no reason to encourage that linkage by having the press conference at his office or on the Capitol steps. Jerry was right, of course. Still, Grant was uneasy about drawing attention in the presence of his neighbors. There would be suspicious looks every time he ventured out of the house. But that would probably have happened anyway.

"I'm going to make a statement, and then I'll take questions." He drew a breath and continued. "Yes, I knew Stacy Wiggins. Yes, we had dated. For several months. We met when she volunteered in my Tampa office. My wife had died six months before. We talked."

He felt as if he were betraying her memory and the

time they'd shared by talking about it this way. She deserved more than to be discussed and dissected with clinical detachment.

"Stacy was a marvelous woman. I loved her. Yes, she was an exotic dancer when we met, although I never saw her dance. Not that way. I did see her with her students, after she opened her studio. To watch her move was poetry. And she brought out that poetry in the young girls she taught. She was a wonderful teacher, dedicated and vivacious, and I'm sure her students miss her."

They were writing. What his words would look like after they'd rearranged them was another issue. And their responsibility.

"Stacy and I dated for just over a year. Over time, the relationship evolved into a deep friendship. As for the romantic side, we parted by mutual agreement. But we remained friends. I miss her."

He paused to draw breath, fighting within himself to quiet his emotions, to be calm and…presidential…when his grief ached to pour out. He would not wear his heart on his sleeve.

"We hadn't seen each other for about three months. I'd been busy here in Washington, and I'm sure she was busy with her students. I was…shocked…to hear of her death. It was brutal and tragic. The world was robbed of an amazing woman, who would have, I'm sure, blessed many lives for many years. She certainly blessed mine."

His face hardened. "It pains and angers me to have to explain, defend and justify what Stacy and I shared. That there are those who would use her death for political gain is…unconscionable. The country deserves better. The voters deserve better. But most of all, Stacy Wiggins deserves better. She was a human being, not a pawn on a political chessboard. And so, to those who are inclined to exploit this vicious act, I say this. Respect this great country. Respect the voters. And pay to Stacy Wiggins the respect that is due any human being, the respect you would want paid if she were your daughter, your sister, your wife. She earned that.

"Thank you. Now I'll take your questions."

Sitting in Terry's office, listening on the radio, Karen thought it had been a heartfelt speech. She doubted anyone else, besides Terry, had noticed the slight pause when Grant had talked about learning of her death. The pause, for her, had been pregnant with meaning. He had known. She fought down her anger and listened.

"Senator, when did you learn that Ms. Wiggins was dead?"

He had prepared for that question. "The police identified the body about a week ago. I read it in the newspaper."

That was true, albeit incomplete and misleading. But there was no reason to dive on his sword.

"Is it true that you financed her dance studio?"

Again, that had been expected. While the money trail had been discreet, by mutual agreement and for mutual benefit, he hadn't doubted the capacity of inquiring minds.

"Yes, I did. That happened about three months into our relationship. She had too much potential, as a dancer and as a woman, to waste herself in a strip club. She hated it, and hated herself for doing it. Having a dance studio was…her dream. I wanted to make that dream possible, and I was in a position to do that."

"How long did you continue dating after she opened the studio?"

"About six months. If you're asking whether she used me to get money, let me simply say that I didn't feel used. Not before. Not after. Not since."

"Did you use money to get her?"

"That question took some big cojones," Terry remarked.

"It's the one everyone is asking," Karen answered. It was one she was asking herself. Did this man use everyone?

"Stupid question," was Terry's opinion. "That man don't need to buy *any* woman. Anything he wants is ripe for the plucking."

Including me. With effort, Karen dragged her attention back to the interview. Grant was speaking.

"...insult Ms. Wiggins and you insult me with that question. Once again, I did *not* know Ms. Wiggins was an exotic dancer when I met her and did not find out about it until we'd dated a few times. At that point we had grown close enough that she trusted me with the information. My immediate response was to find a way to make that line of work unnecessary for her."

"Charity?" sneered a voice.

"You know, Bob," Grant said, recognizing the reporter, "if you check my financial statements, you'll find I give a great deal to charity every year. What I offered Stacy Wiggins was a mere drop in the bucket, especially as she and her business partner had saved up quite a bit already toward the dance school. All I did was make the dream immediately possible."

"Kind of convenient this happened on the eve of your making a presidential bid."

Karen gasped at that.

Terry looked at her. "Oh, they can get a lot nastier, Karen. They're trying to provoke him. You don't usually see that stuff on TV, though."

Grant gripped the podium tighter for a moment, then let the emotion pass into his carefully-calculated words.

"Convenient? Convenient for whom? I certainly don't find this *convenient*. Nor have I announced any intention of seeking my party's nomination for the presidency."

"Everyone knows you will."

"Everyone knows more than I do, then. But my point is this. I knew that eventually I would have to explain my relationship with Stacy should I ever be foolish enough to run for the presidency. I knew I would have to explain it, just like I'm explaining it now. And her being killed didn't and wouldn't have prevented that."

He paused, remembering all the times he and Stacy had talked about the secrecy, and her wishing they could be open in their relationship. "In fact, her death seems only to have made the explanations more difficult."

I'm sorry, my darling friend, he thought. *I'm sorry I could only acknowledge you after your death.* "Thank you, ladies and gentlemen. That's all I have to say."

A chorus of shouting voices was followed swiftly by the announcer, telling everyone what they had just heard. Terry reached over and switched off the radio.

"The vultures smell blood," he said with a shake of his head. "You better get out there and save the guy."

"Save him?"

"Do your job, Detective. And I'll help you."

18

Terry's belief that Grant wasn't such a bad guy at all did nothing to ease Karen's feelings of anger. She was going to talk to the senator, and very soon, but first she needed to call Previn.

"The story's out," she told him. "He just held a news conference. It'll probably be all over the evening news."

"Thank God," Previn said. "I don't like this shit."

"Neither do I. I want you to get the lab to compare physical evidence and blood samples from both Reese and Wiggins."

"What?"

"I want to know if Wiggins was murdered in Lawrence's living room."

"Jesus."

"Just do it, Dave."

"I will. But...maybe I better tell Simpson what's coming down. Or he's going to wonder if we're asleep at the wheel when he sees the news tonight."

"Okay. But tell him *I* told you about the relationship. The photo came to me after all. I don't want you on the hook for the delay in us bringing this out."

"Believe me, I won't be. Okay, I'll bring him up to date. And I'll pretend I just found out."

"Fair enough, Dave. You have enough trouble on your plate right now."

"No kidding. Hell, I'll pretend *we* just found out. Who's gonna know?"

When Karen hung up the phone, she stared at it as if it might bite her.

Terry spoke, his voice rumbling deeply and lazily. "It would be interesting to know who circulated that photo."

"The press doesn't like to ask or answer those questions."

"Depends," said Terry.

"On what?"

"On what you've got on 'em."

She swiveled the chair and looked at him. "Meaning?" But she had a good idea what he meant.

"Just leave it to me, Sweeney. There are some things you don't need to know about the underside of D.C. You're going home, after all."

"I want to know."

He cocked his head and studied her. "I don't like to burn a source. You're not exactly low profile."

She almost flushed, remembering that terrible photo of herself and Grant after the accident.

"It's time," said Terry, "for us to split. You go beard Lawrence in his den, and later tonight I'll get to my source."

"Why should I beard Grant?"

"Because you're dying to. And because you need to. For the case. For yourself."

* * *

"We've got him," Michaels said. "We caught the son of a bitch red-handed."

"Maybe," Randall answered. "If he made a mistake. If he didn't, we just smeared an innocent man, a decent man, over a very personal part of his life. If he didn't, we took something beautiful and made it ugly."

"He did," Michaels said. "I could see it in his face. And this isn't about something legally irrelevant, like where his wife was coming from when she died. This time, he can't hide."

Randall knew Michaels was probably right. But that didn't mean he had to like it. Or gloat over it. "Did I ever tell you how Lawrence and I met?"

Michaels shook his head. "No, you didn't."

"It was fifteen years ago," Randall said. "I was lobbying for the sugar growers, in Tallahassee, against a bill to tear down the Okeechobee dam and restore the Everglades to their original form."

"Things haven't changed much," Michaels said, chuckling.

"Haven't they? I hadn't hired you then. In fact, you'd have been what, sixteen, at the time?" Randall arched a brow to make his point.

Michaels glanced down, then nodded. Good. He needed taking down a peg. Randall continued.

"Grant Lawrence was in the state legislature at the time. Late twenties, first term, full of fire and drive. It was obvious he had a national future, even then. And he looked to be a key swing vote. So I went to see him. He was big on the environment from square one, but he wasn't one of the tree-hugging loons. I pitched him. I laid out what Everglades business meant to the state, financially, and in terms of ordinary farmers who'd spent the past forty years making their livings from reclaimed swampland.''

"You won him over?" Michaels asked.

Randall shook his head. "No. He didn't like the bill, thought it asked for too much, too fast. But too much, too fast was better than too little, too late, he said. He agreed to vote against the bill, if and only if I'd agree to back a more reasonable measure in the next session. I said I couldn't promise that. I wasn't about to buy a pig in a poke. We shook hands, and I left his office. The bill eventually died in committee.''

"So you won after all."

"You're missing the point," Randall said. "A month later, my wife died. Lawrence sent flowers and a card. I called him, to ask why. I was angry. She'd looked healthy when I left for Tallahassee. I got home after the session ended, and she had bruises on her arms and legs. We took her to the doctor. Leukemia. It tore through her like a forest fire. She was dead two weeks later. I told myself she had to have known she was sick and held it back, and it killed her. I blamed her. I blamed the doctors. Most of all, I blamed myself, for being too busy and preoccupied to notice.''

He pursed his lips, drew a breath. Steadied himself. "So I lit into Lawrence. 'What's in it for you? It's people like you who kept me away from my wife when she was sick. By the time you let me go back to her, she was too far gone.' What I said was ridiculous. Embarrassing. I let him have it for…must've been fifteen minutes. And you know what he said when I finished?"

"I've no idea," Michaels said.

"He said three words. 'You loved her.' I caught my breath. I was expecting him to hang up. Or tell me to go to hell. I'd have deserved that. He didn't. He just said those three words and went quiet. Finally I said 'Yes, I did.' He said 'Then don't be ashamed to grieve her.' And that night, after I hung up the phone, for the first time I got past my anger enough to cry.''

Michaels sat for a moment. Finally he spoke. ''Okay, he's a nice guy. Everyone knows that. That doesn't mean S.R. 52 is a good bill. And it doesn't mean he deserves to be president.''

''Maybe not,'' Randall answered. ''But next time you think about gloating over what's happening to him, try to show a little respect. He may be wrong about this bill. He may be the wrong man for the White House. But he's forgotten more about class than you'll ever know.''

Jerry looked across the patio table at Grant. Grant's face was drawn. ''I fucked up,'' Jerry said. ''That's the bottom line.''

''Yeah. You did. Things happen.''

''Don't lie to protect me, Grant.''

''I didn't lie. Plausible deniability, right?''

It had sounded almost sensible, in the abstract. Now, Jerry realized, it was indefensible. No, Grant hadn't lied. Not outright. Not yet. But to keep up his story, he would have to. And sooner or later the truth would out. It always did. And that would be the end of Grant Lawrence. That was not acceptable.

The doorbell rang like the sword of Damocles, drawn from its scabbard. It was only a matter of time before someone ringing that doorbell would confront them with some piece of evidence that linked Stacy's and Abby's deaths. Grant simply shook his head. Jerry rose and walked into the house, determined to hold the wolves at bay. He opened the door to find Damocles herself.

''Detective,'' he said.

Her eyes were like ice chips. "Is he in, Jerry?"

He thought for a moment, then nodded. "Yeah. He's out back, on the patio. C'mon in."

"Thank you," she said, almost silently, as he stepped aside for her to enter.

"Helluva goddamned day," he said as they walked back through the foyer to the kitchen. "Helluva goddamned day."

"Yeah," she said.

"Look, before you talk to him. He didn't know."

She turned to face him. Her gaze hurt. "You?"

His shoulders sagged. "He didn't know."

"That's not good enough," she said, cold and hard. "We need to talk. Right now. Let's go."

The first thing Karen noticed as Jerry escorted her onto the patio was Grant Lawrence. He was sitting with his back to her, suit jacket cast aside, the sleeves of his white shirt rolled up. He didn't even look around to see who was there.

There was a slump to his shoulders that troubled her despite her anger. Not even Abby's death had made his shoulders slump that way, as if defeat were a foregone conclusion. Yes, he'd wept and grieved, but he hadn't given up. Right now he looked like a man who wanted nothing more than to give up.

"Grant?" Jerry said, "it's Detective Sweeney."

He didn't turn his head. "I was expecting you, Karen. Have a seat."

She rounded the table, her ire tempered by a sudden awareness of what this was doing to him. She didn't want to feel that. She had to remember she was a police detective on a case, not a woman visiting a friend. She grabbed for her focus and stoked her anger, suddenly aware that with this man, she would never be coolly objective. For the sake of the dead, she had to choose anger over concern.

She pulled out a wrought-iron chair from the table, brushing Jerry away when he tried to do it for her. She sat, facing the two of them across a surface of decorative wrought iron, a thermal carafe and cups between them.

Grant leaned forward. "Coffee?"

"No. Thank you." Her voice was stiff, hard. "Stacy Wiggins was killed in your house, wasn't she? And don't bother lying, because I'm having forensics look for a blood match right now."

Grant's gaze met hers. His eyes were troubled but otherwise opaque. "I suspect she was."

"Suspect? Who do you think you're kidding?"

He gave a little shake of his head and sat back, saying nothing. Of course he would say nothing. He was a damn lawyer, and any lawyer knew better than to say something to a cop.

"He didn't know," Jerry said. "Honest to God, Detective, he didn't know. He *doesn't* know. Because no one ever told him."

She looked scornfully at Jerry. "You expect me to believe you'd do anything at all without approval from him?"

Jerry's mouth compressed, as if he were holding in some fury of his own. "I do things all the time without checking with Grant first. There aren't enough hours in the day for him to superintend every action taken by his staff members, Detective. That's why he has people like me, people he trusts, to take care of things. This time I failed him."

"But *you* knew, correct?"

He lowered his head a bit, then lifted his chin. "Yes.

I found the bodies. I found Stacy Wiggins dead in Grant's living room. And before I did anything else, I moved her body.''

Grant drew a sharp breath, and Karen looked swiftly his way. The anguish she saw written there pierced her own anger again. She grabbed once more for it. "But you *suspected,* Senator."

"Yes." The word was heavy but clipped.

"Then why didn't you tell me? Do you realize how this affected the investigation? I can't believe your career is more important to you than honesty."

"Wait one minute," Jerry said sharply. "His career had nothing to do with his silence. You'd better get that straight, Detective. If you knew this man at all, you'd know I put him in an intolerable situation. All he had were suspicions, and if he voiced them, I'd go to jail. It wasn't fear that kept him silent, Sweeney, it was friendship."

He seemed to catch himself, then said more quietly, "As a lawyer, Detective, I also need to remind you that Grant was under no legal duty to report a suspicion. And trust me, I made sure he knew *nothing* that put him under legal obligation of any kind."

With that, Jerry stood up. "You have all you need to know. You can arrest me right now."

"I'm not done here yet."

Grant spoke. "Jerry…could you leave us alone, please?"

"No! I'm not going to have her twisting your words in a way that somehow makes you responsible for what *I* did."

"Jerry. Just leave us. Karen won't do that."

Jerry's glare bored into Karen, a warning; then he turned on his heel and disappeared into the house.

Alone now with Grant, Karen felt her anger being transformed into disappointment, a disappointment so painful that for a moment she couldn't even speak. She had admired this man for years, had believed him to be a cut above the rest of the political world, and now this.

"I may not have had a legal duty," Grant said, his voice quiet, "but I suppose I had a moral one. Except that morals and ethics can get considerably muddied when speaking out would send a lifelong friend to jail."

Karen marshaled a small measure of scorn into her voice. "Don't worry, he's right. You can't be arrested for failure to report a suspicion. But I thought you cared more for honesty than that. I thought you cared more for *Abby* than that."

His gaze moved to the gardens, where twilight was slowly wrapping the plants in gloom. It was dark enough now that only a few brilliant blossoms stood out like beacons.

"I loved Abby," he said slowly. "At one time I loved Stacy. And I love Jerry. Maybe I haven't been thinking too clearly since the murders, but I was worried about a number of things. I was worried about what would happen to Jerry. I was worried about what a scandal would do to my daughters. And there *would* be a scandal, Karen. There *is* a scandal, the very one I hoped to avoid for the sake of my daughters."

He turned to look at her. "You see, Karen, my political career, while it is important to me, doesn't hold a candle to my girls. I would have sacrificed anything, including life itself, to keep them from harm or shame or embarrassment. I have failed to do that."

In spite of herself, she felt her throat tightening. Professional detachment was now utterly beyond her reach.

"I'm sorry," he said, "that you're disappointed in

me. But I will *not* apologize for protecting my daughters or my friend. Nor will I ever regret it, regardless of the outcome.''

''What was Stacy doing at your house?''

''I have absolutely no idea. We broke up months ago. I wondered if maybe somebody got to her and made her let them into the house to get at my files. But I don't know that was the case. All I know is that she shouldn't have been there.''

''Tell me about her,'' Karen said. It wasn't a request. She wasn't sure if she was asking for the sake of the investigation or for some other reason. It didn't matter. She had to know. And he had to tell her.

He drew a breath. ''Like I told the press, we met when she volunteered for my campaign. There's something else you don't know about me, Karen. About my past. About…Georgie.''

''I know that investigation was…quieted,'' she said. She spun between anger, disgust, pain and hope. ''You were behind that, I assume.''

''I was.'' He paused for a long moment, swirling a tumbler of Irish cream. His eyes looked as if gnats were landing in his lashes; he blinked in rapid-fire succession as he studied the fluid clinging to the sides of the tumbler. Finally he looked at her. ''I found out she was having an affair. It had been…we had been…distant for years. I felt as if no matter what I did, I could never quite reach her, touch her, hold her, fulfill her. She would look out the window and go inside herself, thinking of…I didn't know what. I was busy, of course. Campaigning for office, then serving in office. Talking to colleagues. Networking. Taking calls from constituents. Answering a lot of their letters personally. I suppose I left her alone so much and so often that she had to go…somewhere else.''

Karen listened, fighting between professional duty and her own feelings. The night was suddenly too dark, too damp, her blouse clinging to her skin.

''I tried to be everything for her,'' he continued. ''The perfect provider. The perfect husband. The perfect father. The perfect public figure. I performed for her. And it wasn't enough. After the accident, when I was at the hospital, the doctor told me she was gone. I was in shock. It wasn't possible that she was gone. And I did a stupid, stupid thing. I thought maybe if I read the emergency room report, if I could see something, anything, a way to bring her back… Or maybe I just needed to see it, in cold, clinical, medical terms, to believe it was real. I don't know. I asked to read the report.''

He paused, closing his eyes, the struggle evident on his pained features. ''The doctor refused at first. But I kept insisting. Finally he gave in. One of the nurses had made a notation. An irrelevant observation, she'd probably thought. Just something she'd seen because she was trained to look and had written down because she was trained to chart everything.

''There was semen in her panties.''

''Oh God.'' Karen's heart felt as if it were in a vise. ''Oh, Grant.''

After a long, shuddering breath, he continued. ''She was having an affair. Was on her way home from sleeping with someone else. And I didn't want the girls to ever know that. I wanted them to remember her as a beautiful mother, as the angel I'd always seen in her. Whatever she'd done, she deserved that. And whatever she'd done, the girls deserved that.

''So yes, Detective. I talked to the doctors, and later

to the investigating officers, and asked them to leave that part out of their reports. It wasn't relevant to how she'd died. Making it public would serve no purpose except to hurt my girls. They understood.''

Of course they had, Karen thought. It was the kind of decision good detectives often made. She would have done the same thing. But what he'd done this time, or what he'd countenanced Jerry having done, that was something else again. She wrestled back to her focus. ''And Stacy?''

''Georgie's death was a double blow. I'd lost my wife. And I'd also found out that I'd…already lost her. I was grieving for her. I was grieving for my girls. And I felt…'' He seemed to search for the right words. ''I felt like a failure. As a husband. As a man. And then I met Stacy.''

She nodded. She could see in her mind's eye how it had happened. A beautiful, young, vivacious woman, in his thrall to the point that she volunteered for his campaign. A new light. A new hope. ''Were you in love with her?''

He studied her eyes. ''I thought I was. For a while. Then we both realized we weren't. I helped her with the loan for her studio. It's…ironic. It's almost like we were closer after we stopped being lovers. I could talk to her. I liked listening to her. I liked what I felt when we went out to dinner or sat around talking about her next recital, or some deal I was working on or my girls or… whatever. I wasn't in love with her. But I loved her.''

''What you said in the press conference, about not having seen her for months. Was that true?''

He nodded. ''I'd been busy here in Washington, with S.R. 52. She'd been busy down in Tampa, with her studio. We'd talked once or twice on the phone, but not for a couple of weeks, I guess. And I honestly have no idea why she was at my house that night.''

Karen thought back to something Alissa had told her. ''A friend of hers said she'd said something about an old client who'd been bothering her. Did she say anything about it to you?''

He thought for a moment. ''No.''

''But you were close friends. Why wouldn't she tell you if someone were stalking her?''

''I don't know, Detective. Maybe she knew I'd get involved and she was trying to protect me. But I just don't know.''

It made sense. Stacy must have known how the press would have pounced if Senator Grant Lawrence had flexed some muscle on her behalf. Yes, Karen thought, that fit.

She wondered if she were trying to make things fit as a cop—or as a woman. Was she searching for the truth? Or for any tiny glimmer of logic and reason to reassure herself that she hadn't totally misjudged him, that her heart wasn't being taken for a ride? That he truly cared for her, and wasn't simply using his charm and charisma to short-circuit her investigation?

She fixed him with her eyes. ''What exactly did you know, Senator?''

His shoulders slumped. ''The night Jerry called me, to tell me Abby was dead, he told me Stacy had been killed, too. He didn't say where or how or anything, although I assumed she'd been there in the house, too. But I could never pin him down on it. And I tried, Detective. He's one of the few people I've ever met who is more stubborn than I am. And he was stubbornly determined to protect me, even at his own expense.''

She would have to arrest Jerry. That much was certain. Or was it? She realized that if she arrested Jerry for tampering with evidence, she would have to distance herself from Grant. If she didn't, people would notice. Simpson would notice. The press would notice. And they would ask the obvious question: Why had she believed Grant's assertion that Jerry had acted alone? And they would find the obvious answer: because she was involved with him. Subtext: because she was a woman, and she was leading with her emotions. Not cut out to be a cop. Just like her father had said all those years.

If she arrested Jerry, she would have to cut herself off from Grant. She was stunned to realize that thought hurt to her very core. As a cop, she had no choice. As a woman, she had to find one.

Because she believed him. And she believed *in* him.

He seemed to see the thoughts play over her face and reached for her hand. She drew it away, closed her eyes and shook her head.

"I have to sort this out, Grant."

He nodded. "I understand."

"I'm in an impossible position here."

He nodded again. "I'm sorry."

She looked at his face and felt the weight of her father's derision, the weight of her professional duty, the weight of her innermost hopes and dreams and fears, crush down on her.

"So am I, Grant."

"What now?"

Gone was the cool, confident statesman. Before her was a lost, hurting man, seeking redemption.

"I don't know." She reached for a kernel of false courage. "But I'll find a way."

19

Art Wallace called Grant Lawrence midafternoon and left a message for him that the girls were fine, that the doctor recommended only some Tylenol and another day off from school. He said he would have the girls call late that evening, after he took them to a movie they wanted to see. He didn't talk to Grant directly, and that was as he intended. He figured the man was up to his ears right now in the scandal of those photographs.

Humming, Art left the pay phone and returned to the car. He could have used his cell, but he didn't want the girls to know what he was telling Grant. Right now they appeared to be napping, but you could never be sure of them. Sometimes they slept like the dead, and other times a pin drop would waken them.

They were all excited and happy. As far as they knew, they were headed for a vacation at Art's cabin in the Catoctin Mountains in faraway Maryland. The excuse given was that Grant missed his daughters too much, so they were all taking a road trip. Even the school, which knew Art as a trustworthy father and stand-in for Grant when he was out of town, accepted the excuse of a few days off, especially in the wake of Abby's death.

Art would have preferred to fly, but with airport security what it was these days, he didn't want to be so easily traceable. Not yet. Sixteen hours to his cabin, half of them already behind him. By the time Grant realized his girls were gone, later tonight, he would be only hours away from the hideout. And Grant didn't know where it was.

The thought gave him a rare sense of satisfaction. Very little in life had satisfied him, and getting even with the man who had always been a step ahead of him, the cause of his misery, made him feel better than anything had in a long, long time.

He was grinning into the twilight as the ribbon of highway extended before him, unrolling like a carpet. Senator Grant Lawrence, the man who had turned Art's life into a disaster. The man who had been first with Georgina. The man who had taken Stacy away from him. The man who had caused Art's own wife to leave, because he couldn't measure up to a senator, for chrissake. The man whose life was blessed by all the beneficent gods.

The man who was about to learn that even the charmed eventually had to face the gritty misery of reality.

Art laughed, keeping the sound under his breath.

Just wait until he told Grant the truth. The truth about where Georgina had been the day she died. The truth about Belle and Cathy Suzanne.

Then he would have the pleasure, the utter sweet pleasure, of watching Grant Lawrence dragged down.

How sweet it was.

Jerry reappeared on the patio, his steps loud in the silence that had grown between Grant and Karen. ''Are you taking me in? Because, if you are, I'd like to get this over with.''

"I'm out of my jurisdiction," Karen said, her voice even. "I'm not taking you anywhere. Nor was the crime committed in *this* jurisdiction."

"I know that," he said. "I'm a lawyer, remember? I just want to know if you want me to board a plane for Tampa with you tonight."

Karen hesitated. For the first time in her life as a cop, she actually hesitated to arrange the arrest of a guilty man. Something about her own ethics was beginning to stink to high heaven, and she was feeling less and less like she ought to be casting stones.

"You're not a flight risk," she said after a moment, clinging to the dregs of her job. "And at this point, no one but me knows you were involved in any way. So we'll get to that part later."

Jerry gave a short nod. "Fair enough. I'm going to my apartment to call my wife. Grant knows where to reach me when you need me. Good night."

Karen watched him walk away, arguing with herself over what she had just done. Then, jumping up, she said to Grant, "Excuse me a moment," and ran after Jerry.

He hadn't even made it to the foyer of the house before he turned in response to the sound of her footsteps. "Change your mind?" he asked ironically.

"No." She halted two feet away. "I'll need to talk to you tomorrow. About exactly what you saw when you found the bodies."

His face darkened. "Believe me, it's branded on my brain. What time?"

"Early."

"I'll call your hotel around eight, then. Good night."
She stood there for a moment, watching him disappear

in the direction of the foyer. Grant's watchdog, she thought. And for that alone she liked him.

This case was a pile of shit that she had a feeling was only going to grow deeper. Squaring her shoulders, she went back onto the patio, to Grant.

The twilight had deepened considerably, bringing the world to the cusp of night. Traffic could still be heard— apparently it was a sound that was never gone around here—but it had grown quieter, less annoyed. Fewer horns honked. Somehow, in the past hour or so, it had found a comfortable rhythm, like a horse hitting its stride. Far away, a siren wailed.

"So where do we go from here?" Grant asked her as she once again sat.

"I don't know," she answered honestly. "I'll need to talk to Jerry tomorrow and see what, if any, additional information he can give me about the crime scene as he found it. I'm going to have to charge him, you know."

Grant nodded slowly, saying nothing.

He had to think she was going to charge Jerry, even if she wouldn't. She had to keep the pressure on. That was her job. She wanted to apologize but couldn't. Knew it would be wrong to apologize for doing her job, the job she had sworn to do, just as he had sworn his own oath of office.

Those oaths lay between them now, his still pristine, despite Jerry, hers beginning to look a bit...marred.

All of a sudden it burst out of her, shocking her. "This case is going to make me hate myself."

His attention fixed on her, making her feel as if everything else in the world had vanished from his awareness. His intensity thickened the air around them, and it left her unable to breathe.

"No," he said.

"No?" She could barely expand her constricted chest to release that one word.

"No, you're not going to hate yourself. Not because of this case, not because of Jerry, and certainly not because of me. You're going to do what you have to do and let the chips fall where they may. I don't want you weighing anything else in your thoughts about this case."

She stared at him, wondering whether to believe him, part of her fearing he was manipulating her, part of her knowing he wasn't that kind of man. *Don't let him be that kind of man.*

"There are times," he said, his voice as tight as piano wire, "when we have no other choice. When there is no option but to do the right thing whatever the cost. I've been forgetting that lately, getting confused between conflicting loyalties and values. But I don't want you forgetting it. I want you to find the murderer of Abby and Stacy. I *need* you to find the son of a bitch. And if that means my career goes down in flames, I don't give a damn. Find that demon and put him away for the rest of his natural life."

"Jerry..."

He shook his head. "Jerry acted without thinking, and he's confessed to it. I'll make sure he has the best lawyer in the country, but he chose to own up to his mistake, and there's nothing I can do now except get him through this somehow."

She waited, holding her breath now, suspecting that more was on the way. She was right.

"The thing is, Karen," he said, stabbing his finger at the table for emphasis as she had seen him do so often when making an impassioned statement, "the thing is, I don't want you drawn into this political mire. Enough good people have been hurt already, and I put Jerry among them. Do you think I want to watch you sacrifice your ethics? Can you possibly think I want any job that much? So much that I'd be willing to use people's lives and consciences as stepping stones?''

She didn't want to think that, no, but some part of her stubbornly insisted she needed to be wary. She couldn't even explain to herself why she was suddenly so sick of being cautious.

He leaned forward. ''I'd rather go down in flames than lay waste to one more life.''

''But…your daughters.''

He sighed heavily, letting go of the intensity, leaning back and passing a hand over his face. When he looked at her again, even in the almost-night, the sorrow on his face was evident.

''I can't protect them anymore,'' he said. ''The word is out about Stacy. It's going to get even uglier when Jerry's confession and arrest come out. It's going to get so ugly that short of taking them away to the depths of the Amazon rain forest for the next six months, I won't be able to entirely protect them. Somehow I'm going to have to help them deal with all this.''

He sighed again, this time more quietly. ''I wish I believed the media would let my wife's death alone. But they won't. They'll go back to it just because it's so juicy that *two* women I've been involved with have died. And they'll dig around until the dirty stuff is out on the front page. Belle and Cathy Suzanne are just going to have to deal with it somehow, and I'm going to have to help them. I'm just glad they weren't in school today and won't be tomorrow.''

''Why not?''

''Some kind of sore throat, Art says. Nothing major,

apparently. The doctor recommended Tylenol and another day at home.''

"I'm glad it's nothing major."

"Me, too. But if they had to get sick, they couldn't have picked a better time. I may even have Art keep them out another day or two. Give this mess time to settle down a bit."

A pang told her she was getting too involved. She ignored the warning. "I'm sorry, Grant. I'm truly sorry for your daughters."

"Just find the killer, Karen. That's all I ask. It's obvious now that whoever it is wants to destroy me, too. I don't care for myself, but I care for my girls."

Karen nodded, wishing she felt even one inch closer to solving this case.

"I'm sorry," he said a few seconds later.

"Sorry?"

"For disappointing you."

Her throat squeezed tight, too tight to speak, even if she had known what to say.

"It's okay," he said, misreading her. "You don't have to accept the apology. You don't have to forgive me or excuse me. God knows I'm finding it harder and harder to excuse myself."

The ache in Karen's throat now filled her entire body. She didn't want him to feel that way. At this point she couldn't find it in herself to condemn him for anything. Instinctively, almost needily, she reached out and took his hand. "Don't beat yourself up," she said, her voice husky with emotion. "Don't."

His fingers wrapped around hers, holding tightly. Their eyes locked. The world stopped. Karen hovered on the brink of something she couldn't name, a feeling that if she could just take one step, she would soar rather than fall crashing to the ground. But she dared not move.

Instead, he moved. He rose from his chair, and with a gentle tug on her hand, brought her to her feet with him.

"I should tell you to go," he said. But even as he spoke, he was drawing her closer and closer, until only the merest sliver of the night stood between them. Until his breath feathered her cheek and his body heat warmed her.

"I should tell you to go," he said again, "but I can't. I'm so damn lonely. Everyone I most care about is in a mess because of me, because I had the nerve to want to be president. God forgive me, because I can't forgive myself."

She waited, aching in every cell, though whether with sorrow or something else, she wasn't sure.

An inch. A half inch. No more. So close that the collision of worlds could no longer be halted. Her head tipped back as if by command of someone else. His head lowered, his eyes never closing.

Lips met.

It was as if her entire body sighed, having found at last what it had waited for so long. *Yessssss.*

As the kiss parted, he looked into her eyes. In the near darkness, they shone almost totally green, like twin emeralds beckoning him on. His voice was a mere whisper.

"Karen."

She was looking up at him, and then, for an instant, past him. A smile creased her face.

"Shh," she said, lifting a finger to point at the sky. "Look."

He followed the line of her finger, for a moment not

sure what she had seen. Then a golden-white flash flickered across the sky.

"See it?" she whispered.

"Yes. A falling star." He paused. "Like me."

He felt her fingers tighten on his shoulder. "Don't. I won't let you."

Another meteor flashed past. "I believe in signs," he said. "Call me superstitious."

"Then try this," she said, steel in her voice. "Stop looking at how quickly they wink out and think about how magical it is that we get to see them at all."

"True. Still..."

"What?"

He watched her eyes as if he'd never seen them before, for that was how he felt. These were softer eyes than he'd met a few weeks ago. Eyes he could get used to seeing first thing in the morning. Eyes he could trust talking to over dinner, or in the last moments before sleep came.

And it would never be.

She was a cop, and he was a senator whose career was about to crash and burn. Over a murder. Over Jerry's mistake. Over this woman's investigation. Over the press and their insatiable appetite for ugliness. Over his own hubris at the belief that he could run for president and, at the same time, protect his daughters from scandal. His was a life story that should have been written in Greek.

And she was a cop.

And the kiss had felt so...

"Grant?"

"Yes?"

"Just for a few moments...let it go. And kiss me again."

Yes. He felt the almost painful grip of her hand on his shoulder, not letting him slip away into his reverie, not letting him sink under the waves of his own thoughts and fears and regrets. Yes.

He sought her lips, letting his own trail them, slowly, softly, never closing his eyes. Sinking into the depths of hers.

He felt the tip of her tongue trailing over his lips, wetting them slightly. His breath quickened, and in the night air, a chill flickered down his back and out along every nerve, goose bumps rising, his nipples stiffening inside his shirt, his knees softening, until he was clinging to her, clinging to the kiss, clinging to the moment, clinging to whatever meaning life held, in this instant, in this flicker of a falling star, in this brief, shining moment when all that mattered was the quiet, soft caress of her tongue on his lips.

Her eyes went out of focus, and he felt a trickle on his cheek. She saw it, too, and broke the kiss. The very tip of a finger reached up and wiped the tear away.

"Yes," she whispered.

"Yes," he answered.

She touched the finger to her lips, then to his. He tasted the salty fluid of his own tear, shared with the lingering taste of her kiss. She let out a shiver.

"It's cold."

"Yes," he said. "Let's go inside."

"No," she answered, glancing over at the mist rising off the pool. "It's heated, right?"

"Yes, it is."

She stepped back, her eyes never leaving his, and slowly unbuttoned her blouse. Creamy Irish skin seemed to glow in the darkness. Her hands worked with practiced ease, unfastening another button, and another, and now the pale gold nylon of her bra came into view. He found himself fighting for balance as she finally pulled the bottom of her blouse from her slacks and shrugged it off.

"Well?" she asked.

"Beauty."

"Undress, Grant Lawrence. Swim with me."

"Yes."

He pulled off his tie as she unbuttoned her slacks and let them slowly slide over full hips and down, revealing slim, firm thighs, the dimples of her knees, the smooth curves of her calves. He began to fumble with his buttons, drawn on by the siren song of her silent smile. Another meteor arced across the sky, and it seemed to mate itself with the tumble of her bra to the pool deck. Her breasts were full, round, chocolate-brown nipples stiffening in the cool air. Now the night air washed over his own torso, his shirt having somehow found its way off and down his arms.

He reached for his belt buckle and stopped.

"What?" she asked, stepping closer, so that her warm breasts barely brushed his skin. "Grant?"

"It's...the knee. It's not..."

She touched her fingertip to his lips. "Shhhhhh."

She reached down and unfastened his belt, then his trousers. Sinking to her knees, she pulled them down. He closed his eyes, waiting for the horrified gasp. Instead, he felt her lips on the raised spider web of white skin at the bottom of his thigh. No one—not Georgie, not Stacy, no one—had ever kissed him there before.

A flash of memory, the screech of brakes, his father's muttered "Mary help us" waking him from sleep in the back seat, an instant before the oncoming truck turned everything to blackness. The horror of coming to, the smell of gasoline and oil and fear, and the coppery smell of blood, the white shards of bone poking out of his leg, the blinding, awful pain.

All of it washed away in the tender, seeking, needing, patient touch of her lips. He gasped.

"Does it hurt?" she asked.

"Not anymore."

He didn't remember stepping into the pool. Instead, he felt the warmth rising over his skin, her hand in his, until they stood face to face, the water lapping at their shoulders. Her hands were so soft, finding every nerve ending, gliding, pulling him closer. Their lips met again, parting fully this time, tongues dancing with increasing urgency. His fingers explored the smooth skin of her back, the narrow taper of her waist, the swell of her hips, the fullness of her breasts, the stiff nubs of her nipples. His tongue found her throat, and she gasped as he drew a tiny fold of tender skin between his lips.

Her nails dug into his back, dragging down lean, firm muscles, then stopped at his buttocks.

"Grant?"

"Yes?"

By way of answer, she lifted her legs and tipped backward slightly, then pulled herself onto him. Her ankles crossed at his buttocks and locked her to him.

"This," she said.

"Yes."

The heated water seemed to envelop them in a cocoon against the cold darkness of the night. Their hips began to undulate together, a slow, easy rhythm. He felt his breath quicken as her fingers entwined with his, and she let herself float back, until their arms were extended.

Her eyes opened, looking up into the stars, and in that

instant her face radiated more light than all the stars in the heavens.

"Yes," she whispered to another shooting star.

"Yes," he answered.

Her warmth and the warmth of the water melded in his senses, until the night was filled with her. Her beauty, arcing across the sky. Her wetness welcoming him. Her breath in the quiet kiss of the wind. Her lips in the trickle of moisture over his face and shoulders. Her scent in the sweetness of fresh blooms. Her quiet gasps in the lapping of the water against the sides of the pool.

He could sink into this woman forever, he thought as he drove himself deeper into her, his own need rising with hers in the motion of their hips, until he cast his head back and he heard a low, growling sigh as their muscles fluttered in unison. His sigh. Her sigh. Their sigh.

Electricity seemed to crackle along every nerve, until he felt as if every muscle in his body spasmed in rhythm with hers. Another meteor streaked over. Another. Another.

Until he was beyond knowing.

Karen laid her face on his shoulder, her arms tight around him, their legs entangled as they sat on the bottom step of the pool. The water fluttered at her throat, and she could still feel his lips, his teeth, his tongue. The world had seemingly taken forever to come back into focus, and now she heard his breathing.

"Are you okay?" she asked.

He chuckled. "That would be the understatement of the century."

She smiled. "Well, the century's still new."

He turned to face her, his eyes intense. "A lot of things feel new right now."

Yes, she thought, *they do.* There was, she knew, some reason why she ought to feel afraid or ashamed or anxious. But she couldn't for the life of her think of it in that moment. Deep within her, aftershocks still fluttered. It had been forever since she had felt this alive, and she was not about to surrender this feeling to return to a life of the dead. Not now. Later. But not now.

She heard her voice murmur something. His answering. The words didn't matter. What mattered was the way his skin felt against hers, the slight tickle of the hairs on his legs and chest floating across her breasts and thighs. She sought his lips again, sipping, grazing, nipping, her fingers clinging to his back.

The world was far away, beyond the mist rising around them, distant, fuzzy, out of focus. The world was here, in the way the stubble on his chin scraped over her cheek, in the way his strong hands supported her buttocks, holding her effortlessly close. The world was the taste of his lips and the soft smile in his eyes.

This was the world. No need to hunt for clues or evidence. No need to see how the pieces fit together or wonder what it all meant. A world to be experienced. Taken in. Savored.

His fingertips were pruned, and for some reason she found herself entranced by every tiny wrinkle and trying to smooth them with her tongue, her lips, her cheek, her hands. A giggle escaped her. Or him. She realized her own fingertips were crinkled, and now she tried to fit their fingers together, like a jigsaw puzzle, looking for just the perfect combination where his rises fell into her hollows, and vice versa. Finally she touched her left ring finger to the same finger on his left hand, and they fit.

Perfectly.

She was a split instant from sorting out what that might mean when he started.

"What is it?"

"It's late and the girls haven't called. I should call them," he said.

Later, she would ask herself what had snapped him out of the moment so abruptly. The time of night, perhaps. Or something more.

They disengaged, and he climbed out of the pool, still naked, his body glistening in the starlight. She watched his back as he dialed the phone. Watched the tension grow in his muscles. Heard the gasp, just before his hand sank and the phone slipped from his fingers to land with a clatter on the table.

"What?" she asked, already moving. Beside him now, looking into a face that, in the space of a minute, had gone from dreamy to numb. "Grant?"

He didn't answer, and she picked up the phone. Dead silence, then the three-toned squeal of a dying line. She pushed the hang-up button, then hit redial. The phone rang. An answering machine picked up, a disembodied voice.

"Art said you'd be calling. We have your girls. Don't call the cops—or else."

20

Karen released her white-knuckled grip on the receiver and put it back in the cradle. "I have to report this."

Grant shifted from shock to frightening rage as if someone had flicked a switch. Instinctively she stepped back as his face contorted and he snarled, "No!"

"Grant…"

"No!" He stepped toward her, looming, and the finger he usually stabbed downward for emphasis now stabbed in her direction. "My girls are in danger! If you do anything to harm them, I'll make you regret it forever!"

She told herself that his savagery wasn't personal, that he would have said the same to anyone, but the closeness of the past hour evaporated as if it had never been, and she felt she was standing alone, shivering and naked in a desert night. Without a word, she turned and gathered up her clothes, then dressed with swift, businesslike-movements.

She wanted to believe that she hadn't been used, but it was hard to feel anything else at the moment. When she faced him again, he had pulled on his own slacks. The stars still fell overhead, an omen indeed.

"I'm sorry," he said, his voice flat. "But you can't report this. You heard what the guy said. And I don't trust a bunch of cops I don't know to keep their mouths shut."

She didn't say anything immediately, giving him time to absorb his shock and his fury, giving him time to start thinking again. She certainly didn't tell him that she was scared sick for two little girls she had never met, had only seen at a distance. Forty-eight hours. They had to find those girls in forty-eight hours or the chances diminished exponentially.

The only ray of hope she could find in this was that they had been taken by people who wanted something. That meant they would have to contact Grant again, and each contact increased the likelihood that she could learn something useful.

She watched him pace the patio, his steps at first rapid with anger and anxiety, then growing steadier and more determined as the news sank in and he began to think about options.

Only then did she speak. "There are things that can be done without letting the kidnappers know the police are involved."

He spun to look at her, but this time he didn't immediately jump on her.

"Wiretaps and traces," she said. "We can do those without anyone knowing you've told us. We don't have to fill this house with officers. We don't have to inform anyone except a select group."

"What select group?"

"I'd like to inform my liaison here in D.C. You can trust him. And in Tampa…" She hesitated. Previn was her partner on the murder cases, but…something in her held back from wanting him to know this. On the other hand, with the College Hill shootings, there was no one else she could call on. Nor was there any escaping that this case was headline material, the kind of material some people wouldn't be able to keep their mouths shut about. "I'll get someone I trust in Tampa to check out Art Wallace's house for clues."

"They may not have been taken from the house. Art was taking them to the doctor." A sudden look of horror passed across his face. "My God, do you know what that call means? It means they have Art and his daughters, too."

There was no mistaking the look of guilt on his face, as if he were personally responsible for whatever was happening to Art and his daughters.

"First," Karen said as sternly as she could manage, "none of this is *your* fault. I realize it's a totally human thing to blame oneself for things like this, but the simple fact is, you didn't make the kidnappers do any of this. They're solely responsible for their own actions. Secondly, if they left a message on Art's machine, they were at the house."

"I didn't think of that. Shit." He pivoted sharply and began to pace again. "I don't know. I don't know. There are five lives in the balance. I don't want to put them at any more risk."

"That depends on how you look at risk," she said. "Statistics say if we don't find them alive in forty-eight hours, we're…" She didn't complete the sentence. She didn't have the heart to actually say it.

He swore again and ran his fingers through his wet hair, leaving it all spiky. "God, I don't know what to do!"

"Wait for the next call. Meantime, I'm going to get my liaison here to put a trap and trace on your phone.

We can keep that quiet, and if they call, we'll know where they are.''

After a moment, he nodded. ''Okay. Okay. But nothing else until they call. I can't risk it, Karen. I can't.''

''I understand.''

Before he could change his mind, she reached for the phone and called Terry. He answered promptly, although in the background she could hear cheerful voices chatting and laughing.

''Hey,'' he said when she identified herself. ''What's up?''

''I need your help,'' she said simply. ''And I need it on the QT.''

There was no hesitation. ''Where do you want to meet? And what do you need?''

''Bring a wiretap and trace authorization for a victim to sign.''

''Okay….'' There was curiosity in his voice.

''Bring it to you-know-who's house. And make sure you're not followed. Do you need the address?''

There was the briefest silence. ''No, I got it. Give me twenty or thirty. I'm a long way out.''

''Thanks, Terry.''

The click of the phone being hung up answered her.

Twenty minutes later Grant was still pacing like a lion that had scented prey. Karen reached for the phone and redialed Art's number. If the kidnappers were nearby, they might have changed the message, which would tell her a whole lot.

But no, it was still the same chilling, flat message it had been. She would have to keep checking.

Folding her hands, she waited with the long experience of a cop accustomed to stakeouts. Experience didn't make her any less tense, however, not over this case. Her heart was beating nervously, and her stomach quivered. Four young girls and a father at the mercy of someone ruthless was a nightmare she could barely force herself to contemplate.

"They'll call," Grant said, but it sounded almost like a question.

"I'm sure they will. There's no point to this otherwise."

He nodded. "I thought so, but…"

"But waiting is hell."

He gave a short nod and kept pacing.

The spring night was growing chilly, but he still hadn't put on a shirt. Her own clothes were damp from her body, and none too comfortable. "Let's wait inside. It's getting cold out here."

"Sure." He led the way indoors to the living room, spacious enough that he could continue pacing. Then, as if he realized how it would look if Terry arrived while he was shirtless, he disappeared for a few minutes and returned wearing a polo shirt. Karen doubted it would fool a cop of Terry's skill; they both reeked of chlorine from the pool.

Terry rolled in about fifteen minutes later, driving a beat-up old Toyota that looked out of place against the curb in this neighborhood. But as nearly as she could tell, as she watched from the slit window by the front door, no one had followed him.

He confirmed it when she opened the door for him.

"Nobody interested in *me*," he said. "What's up?" He followed her through the foyer into the living room.

Grant immediately offered his hand, acting automatically in the midst of his upset. "Grant Lawrence," he said.

"Terry Tyson, and I've heard all the jokes."

Grant managed a faint smile. "I'm sure you have."

"Okay," Terry said. "What's going on?"

Karen spoke, sparing Grant the necessity. "The senator's daughters have been kidnapped, along with a neighbor and his two daughters."

"Jesus H. Christ." Terry shook his head and looked to the heavens.

"At least I'm assuming the neighbor and his daughters have also been taken," Karen said. "The message on the man's answering machine is from the kidnapper. That leaves the assumption that the man and his daughters are also gone."

Terry nodded. "What do they want?"

"They didn't say. They just said not to call the police or else."

"They always say that," Terry remarked with the air of one who'd seen this before. "And the best thing to do is ignore them."

"No," said Grant flatly. "I absolutely do not want my house or the houses down there crawling with cops. I refuse to take the risk."

Terry looked at Karen. "Can I have a private word with you?"

Grant pointed across the foyer. "My study's over there. Help yourself."

Karen hesitated, afraid to leave him alone, he seemed so much on edge, but needing to get things going with Terry. It wasn't like she could do anything on her own here in Washington.

Terry firmly closed the study door behind them and folded his arms. "I'm not going to ask what you two were doing before I got here, but I've got a pretty damn good idea."

Karen managed not to flush.

"Regardless, I want to know if you're out of your mind. You can't expect to deal with this kidnapping without getting both our departments involved, if not the Feds."

"I asked you to get the authorization for wiretaps and traces, didn't I?"

"Yeah, but why do I get the feeling you haven't been pushing him to allow more? What I want to know is, are you too emotionally involved to handle this? Because if you are, I know a few good detectives who can fill in."

Karen bridled. "The only thing I'm emotionally involved with is getting four young girls back alive."

"Yeah. Right. Okay. Look, I said I could bend a rule or two, but there are limits. I'm not going to have five deaths hanging on me. So let me ask you this. Are you a better homicide cop now than you were when you took the job?"

"Sure," Karen said, not sure where he was leading.

"So am I. I've been doing this job for a long time. I know the streets. I live them. I know where to start kicking rocks. That's what experience is for."

Karen nodded. "Right. Your point?"

He looked at her. "How many kidnappings have you worked?"

Of course, she thought. "None."

"Neither have I. Why? In my department, we call the FBI in on every kidnapping, even if there's no evidence that the kidnapper has crossed a state line. They have experts in this. *They* have the experience. And you can stand there with those cold eyes and stare me down for the rest of the night, but you know I'm right. The *best* chance those kids have is if we bring in the Feds. They deserve no less, whatever the senator says.''

"Right," she said. And he *was* right, no question. "You're right. But it's his call."

"Then make him make the right call, Karen. For his kids' sake."

There weren't really any options. However used she might have felt at that moment, however unsure she might have been about Grant's intentions, one thing was sure. His kids were innocent. Art and his children were innocent.

"Do you know any Feds?" she asked.

He chuckled. "I live in Washington. If a cat gets stuck in a tree, we have to fight the FBI for jurisdiction to get it down."

"Okay, do you know any *good* Feds?"

"I know one."

Discretion would still matter. "Can you trust him?"

He smiled. "Let's say that if my cat were stuck in a tree, I'd call her."

While they were in the study, Grant tried to calm himself. He willed his muscles to relax, as he did before major public appearances, but again and again the tension crept back in. And he realized just how much he missed Abby.

Always, before, he would have turned to her when the girls were in trouble. She would have known what to do first. It would have been something simple, something that would have given him an initial focus in the first moments until the shock passed and he could wrap his mind around the problem. He loved his parents, and they loved him. But this was not their forte. They would be as shocked as he was, and in those first moments, they, too, would have turned to Abby for direction.

But Abby was gone.

Who was left? Jerry. The political version of Abby. This was personal, not political, but Jerry was all he had. He picked up the phone and dialed.

"What's up?" Jerry asked.

"Someone's kidnapped my girls," Grant said simply.

"I'll be there in twenty minutes. Is the lady cop still there?"

"Yes. And she's brought in her local liaison. She wants me to call the FBI."

"Do it," Jerry said. "She's good, but they're better at this. And they can lean harder on the press."

"Jerry…"

"I'll be there in twenty minutes. We'll talk about it then."

Jerry rang off without saying another word. Grant was just replacing the receiver when Karen and her partner emerged from the study.

"I called Jerry," he said in response to the question they were doubtless about to ask. "He'll be here in a few minutes."

Terry simply nodded. Karen spoke. "We've hashed it out, and you have to call in the FBI."

"Jerry said the same thing."

"They're the experts, Senator," Terry said.

"Your girls deserve the best," Karen added. "And Terry has a contact in the Bureau. He says she's good. And trustworthy."

He nodded. It was the right thing to do, but at this point he felt as if his life had been taken over by law enforcement. Adding another cop would only add to the feeling. And it wouldn't be just one more cop. The FBI would bring in an entire team. He would have someone with a badge grunting approval when he went to the bathroom.

He knew these considerations were childish. His girls had to come first. But he didn't have to like it. And he didn't have to surrender control of his life to yet another person he didn't trust. He looked at Karen.

"I want you in charge of the task force."

"Grant," she said, slowly, measuring every word, "I don't know if I'm the right person to—"

"I trust you," he said. He turned to the black man with the impassive face. "Detective Tyson, I'm sure you're very good, but I don't know you. And I don't know this woman from the FBI. I know Detective Sweeney. I trust her judgment. These are my girls. I can't just…"

"You're right," Terry said, much to Grant's surprise. And Karen's, to judge by the look on her face. "She's been working this case for weeks. And I'll bet my badge that this is related to the rest of it. The kids were taken in Tampa, correct?"

"Yes," Karen said.

"So until we know it's an interstate case, you have primary jurisdiction. You should be point on this. It…simplifies things."

Karen nodded slowly, as if dissecting the subtext in his words. It took Grant a moment longer, but he caught on. Apparently this cop knew more than Grant realized and was a decent guy to boot.

"So it's settled," Grant said.

Karen's eyes were distant for a moment. "Okay, then I need to call my lieutenant. And my partner. I'm betting this is the same perp who killed Abby, Senator. The whole pattern of events, the murder, the car accident, now this, it speaks of a concerted attack on you. If we catch the kidnapper, I bet we'll have our killer. So the kidnapping is top priority. I need someone to work the crime scene there. Senator, we'll use your study as a command post. How many telephone lines do you have?''

"Three," he said. At this point, it almost hurt to hear her call him *Senator*. "Home office, fax and my private line."

"That'll do for now," Karen said. "If we need more, we'll get them. Or the FBI will have secure cell phones. I'll need recent photos of your daughters. We'll make a half-dozen copies for starters."

"We can't go public...." Grant began.

"I'm not planning to," Karen said. "But kids attract attention. Witnesses will recognize the kids, even if they barely notice the perp."

"She's right," Terry said. "And, Senator, in terms of discretion, it would help if you weren't in the photos."

"Understood," Grant said. "I'll go find pictures."

It was a place to start.

While Terry called his FBI contact, Karen dialed Simpson's number. She explained the situation with as few words as she could manage. If he was reading between the lines, he didn't give any indication.

"Who do you want on it?" he asked.

"Who's available?"

He ran off a list of the best detectives, most of whom, she knew, had until that moment been committed solely to the College Hill task force. Kidnapped kids, apparently, ranked higher than murdered nannies. Once again she fought down the impulse to anger. It wouldn't solve anything and would only make more problems.

"I'll stick with Previn," she said.

She heard a grunt of surprise. Yes, Previn was still the least experienced detective in the squad. Two of the detectives on Simpson's list had even worked a high-profile kidnapping three years ago. But they'd developed a taste for seeing themselves on TV, and she needed discretion. Not only during the investigation, but afterwards. She didn't want to end up as fodder for reality shows.

"Previn will keep his mouth shut. There's been enough of a feeding frenzy already. Too much, if you ask me."

"Agreed," Simpson said. "But you know it's going to happen, Sweeney. We can't keep a lid on this forever, and when it comes out...well, he's a national figure. I don't want to come off looking like I didn't put the best detectives I had on the case."

Everyone had an agenda, Karen thought. Even her. "My D.C. liaison is calling in the Feds. Everyone thinks they handle these things. As far as public consumption goes, we have a supporting role."

"And that's what will probably happen," he said. "No matter what your friend the senator wants."

"If it happens, it happens. All the more reason not to pull guys off the College Hill team. 'All politics is local' and all that. And Previn's competent to work a crime scene."

Simpson let out a slow sigh. "Okay, Sweeney, we'll go with Previn for now. Will you need an inter-agency memo from me?"

"Probably. I'll let you know."

"Do you want me to call Previn?"

"I'll do it," she said. "I need to brief him."

"Then get busy, Detective. Find those girls."

''Yes, sir.''

As if she needed reminding.

She dialed Previn immediately. He sounded stressed and irritated when he answered. ''What's wrong?'' she asked immediately.

''If she gets the alimony she wants, I'm not going to be able to afford to live anywhere except under a bridge.''

Karen paused. ''Cripes.''

''I just opened the mail. I ask you, did I do anything to deserve this?''

Karen didn't know how to answer; she hadn't been on the inside of Previn's marriage. ''I'm sorry,'' she said.

''Fuck it. What do you need?''

''For you to get yourself and your wife into marriage counseling. Beyond that, I need you to get a search warrant.'' She gave him everything she knew, which wasn't much. ''And keep your mouth shut,'' she added.

''It's an ongoing investigation. Of course I'll keep my mouth shut.''

''Of course you will. You don't want to endanger those little girls.'' Why she felt it necessary to say that, she didn't know, but she trusted her instincts.

''I'll get right on it,'' he said.

''Don't be surprised if the FBI shows up.''

''Great. That'll be like having my wife on the job.''

''Previn…''

''Sorry.'' He sighed. ''I'll talk to her tomorrow about counseling, and I'll get the damn warrant within the hour.''

''Thanks. You know what needs to be done.''

He was silent for a few seconds. ''Thanks, Sweeney,'' he said. ''I appreciate the vote of confidence.''

She had the feeling that he really did.

She was just hanging up when Jerry arrived. He arrived alone, but he blew into the house as if he were at the head of the cavalry. Crisis management put him in his element, and it showed.

"Where's the FBI?" he asked.

"On their way," Terry said dryly. "Getting dressed takes them a few minutes longer." He extended his hand. "Detective Tyson, D.C. police."

Jerry shook his hand. "You're heading this up?"

Terry cocked his head toward Karen. "Detective Sweeney is. The crime happened in her jurisdiction."

Jerry looked at Karen and said something that stunned her. It was simple, but very much to the point. "I'm glad."

She managed a nod, wondering why his approval seemed to mean so much.

"Grant?"

"In the living room."

She watched him cross the foyer, heard voices from the living room.

"You ought to be in there," Terry remarked.

She swung her head around to look at him. "Why?"

"Because you're probably the most comforting thing in his life right now."

No, she thought, *Jerry is.*

21

Special Agent Miriam Anson arrived a few minutes later. She appeared to be about thirty-five, with dark hair, dark eyes and the confident stride of a man. She wore a dark slack suit that in lamplight could have been either blue or black.

"Terry," she said, shaking Tyson's hand. Then she turned to Karen. "You must be Detective Sweeney."

Karen shook her hand. "Yes."

She turned to Terry. "You point?"

Terry shook his head. "Detective Sweeney is. The kidnapping occurred in her jurisdiction."

Miriam Anson's gaze returned to Karen, measuring. "Good."

"Good?" Karen asked.

"Yeah." A surprising wink. "Women tend to think about the kids first and the collar second."

Under other circumstances, Karen would have laughed, but right now all she could manage was a smile, a sure indicator that this situation mattered more than it should, professionally speaking. Black humor was part of the way cops coped, and she wasn't coping right now. But Miriam didn't seem to be disturbed by that.

Miriam spoke. "Have we learned anything more?"

"Not yet," Karen answered. "I have my partner in Tampa getting a warrant to search the Wallace house, but at this point nothing more has happened."

Miriam nodded. "The kidnapper or kidnappers—you know, it has to be multiple kidnappers. The message said 'we.' Taking four children and an adult is biting off a rather large chunk, don't you think?"

"My feeling exactly," Karen agreed as Terry nodded. "And…I'm worried. If the senator is the target of this abduction, taking Art Wallace and his two daughters seems like raising the stakes unnecessarily, while enhancing the difficulty of the abduction."

Miriam's nod was approving. Not agreeing, but approving, as if she had judged Karen and liked what she heard. "My thoughts precisely."

"Which means," Karen said, "that Wallace and his daughters might already be…out of the picture."

"Maybe your partner will find them at the house. It's possible, and in this business we have to hope for the best. However…" She paused, frowning.

"However," Karen said, aware she was going out on a huge limb, "we also need to consider the possibility that Art Wallace is involved in this abduction."

Miriam's gaze fixed her. "Why do you say that?"

Karen shrugged. "Because it's possible. Because…I don't know. A feeling. He was the only one who heard anything the night the senator's nanny was killed."

"Ahh." Miriam nodded as if she found that significant. "Good point, Detective."

"Karen, please."

"My friends call me Miri," the other woman answered. "Okay, I'll get the tap on the lines. Meantime, I want that answering machine message checked every twenty minutes. It may take a while before we hear anything, because the kidnappers had no way of knowing when the senator might call. And with your permission, Karen, I'm going to get a colleague of mine involved in Tampa. Just let me know who to have him get in touch with."

Karen gave her the information on Previn, including his cell and pager, then announced, "I think I'm going to talk to the senator about Art Wallace."

She left Terry and Miriam together and returned to the living room. The scene was unbearably moving, Grant sitting in an armchair with his head down, Jerry behind and to one side, his hand resting on Grant's shoulder.

Grant looked up at the sound of Karen's footsteps. "They're not going to do anything stupid?"

She shook her head and sat facing him. "You'll like Special Agent Anson. She just said it's better for women to head up kidnapping cases because we care more about the kids than the collar."

The faintest of smiles lifted the sagging corners of Grant's mouth. "Does she want to talk to me?"

"Not yet. She's arranging for the taps on the phone lines and getting a colleague to help out in Tampa. But *I* want to talk to you."

Jerry spoke. "Need me to leave?"

"No. It's not private. I just need to know about Art Wallace. Everything you can tell me."

Grant nodded slowly. "Because it might help you find him and his daughters."

Karen didn't disillusion him. "Because every bit of information is critical right now. However unimportant it may seem."

He closed his eyes for a moment, as if focusing himself. When they opened again, they were gray-blue, a sad color. "The Wallaces have been our neighbors for ten years. They were in the neighborhood when Georgina and I moved in, just before Cathy Suzanne was born. Elizabeth, Art's wife, hit it off with Georgina, my wife, and we started getting together for backyard barbeques and things. When I was in town. I think Georgina knew them better than I did."

Karen nodded encouragingly. "Go on."

"Anyway, we both had kids, the kids grew up together pretty much, and it was like we were just one family, what with the girls running back and forth, taking turns sleeping over and all that. And Art and Elizabeth were always helpful when Georgie and I had to be out of town. Abby was getting older, and I was glad to have neighbors who were happy to keep an eye on things, just in case. Art and Elizabeth even picked my girls up from school in the afternoons, or took them in the mornings, to save Abby the trip."

"So Art and Elizabeth were allowed to pick up the girls from school?"

"Sure. And we were allowed to pick up their girls if necessary. I know Abby picked them all up any number of times until it started to get difficult for her to drive."

"Okay."

"Anyway, a little over a year ago, Elizabeth left Art. I don't really know why. I know it ripped him up that she took his daughters with her. It seemed to make him even more attached to Belle and Cathy Suzanne, from what I saw." His face darkened. "Not that I saw much. Not enough."

"It's not your fault, Grant."

He looked up at her. "No? Then whose fault is it? Abby's dead. Stacy's dead. My girls and my neighbor and his daughters are missing. You got smeared all over the tabloids. All of it seems to be about hurting me. So…whose fault is it?''

"The man who killed Abby and Stacy. The people who took your kids. That's whose fault it is. Blaming yourself isn't going to bring your girls home, or bring Abby or Stacy back. I need you focused, Grant.''

Jerry nodded approval. ''She's right. Someone's beating up on you. They're enough. Don't do it to yourself, too.''

Karen smiled. It was the type of thing she wished she'd said, and she was glad Grant had Jerry to say those things. He needed all the support he could get.

For now, though, it was time to get back on topic. ''You said you and Art disagreed on politics?''

He nodded. ''Sometimes. But you ask that as if it's relevant. You have to understand, Karen, I spend most of my time dealing with people who disagree with me. It's part of the price of admission when you're in politics. I don't take it personally unless it gets personal. It never got personal with Art.''

"And, of course, he took good care of your girls.''

"Like they were his own,'' he said. ''He once said they were the rest of his children. And he not only said it, he acted on it, especially when I couldn't be there to do it.''

"Sounds like a good friend,'' Karen said, although her mind was spinning a mile a minute. Perhaps it was the cynic in her, but she was distrustful of altruism. In most cases, in her experience, there was an ulterior motive. She'd seen too many kids molested by ''good friends.'' It was a sad commentary on society, or her view of it. ''So there was no animosity? No arguments?''

Grant cocked his head. "You sound like he's a suspect."

"I have to keep all possibilities in mind," she said with a shrug. Pieces of the puzzle were tumbling together in her mind, but she wasn't willing to say more yet.

"I see," Grant said. "Well, no. Not that I saw. He never...I mean...no. No. Nothing."

Which meant either Art Wallace was an innocent victim or a hell of an actor. She'd seen both. And the latter possibility worried her. The history of crime was riddled with charming, neighborly sociopaths. And, all too often, their crimes were horrific.

She turned to make sure the door was closed, then looked at Jerry. "Soon enough, the lab's going to tell me they found Stacy Wiggins' blood at Grant's house. In the meantime, I'm going to say I have a suspicion that she was killed there and her body moved. We've been told that someone from Stacy's...past...had contacted her. And that it was bothering her. If someone wants to draw the conclusion that the killer moved the body because he could be linked to her, well, that's a reasonable conclusion."

"That would be a lie," Grant said.

She nodded. "Yes, it would be. And if Jerry's having moved her body ever becomes relevant, I can defend it. Right now, the focus has to be on finding your girls. Arresting Jerry isn't going to help that, and what's more, the killer knows he didn't move that body. Maybe he'll want to correct the record. I've elicited confessions on less. I'm the lead detective, and it's a tactical decision." There was more to it, she knew. A lot more. But that was enough. She could deal with her own feelings later. She turned to Jerry. "In other words, a public confession isn't going to help anyone, and it could hurt the investigation."

He nodded. "I understand. Thank you."

"Don't thank me. Just help Grant."

"I'm trying."

"Keep trying. And if he gets any wild-haired ideas about trying to do something on his own, try even harder. Do you get me, Grant?"

"Yes. Jerry's my watchdog."

"Exactly. Don't make his life harder. These cases are all about managing the information and the actors. If you get heroic, it makes everyone else's job harder."

"They're my girls, Karen."

His face was firm. It was a pleasant change. But hers was equally firm.

"Until we get them back for you, they're *my* girls, Grant. You wanted me to run this. That's how it's going to be."

"Has anyone ever told you you're a tough cookie?" he asked.

"More than once," she said. "And right now, I'm HBIC."

"HBIC?"

"Head Bitch in Charge. The speaker of this house, if you prefer."

"HBIC works," he said. "I'll behave."

"And I'll make sure he does," Jerry added.

There was a knock at the door. Terry poked his head in. "Karen, we've got a new message."

It was the same flat, disembodied voice, no hint of inflection, difficult even to tell whether the speaker was male or female.

By now you know we have your children. This will be

the only means of contact. The ransom is three hundred ninety-six thousand dollars. Non-sequential, tens and twenties. You have twenty-four hours to raise the money. Payment instructions will be here tomorrow evening. Be smart. Do it.

"We've recorded it," Miri said, after pressing the hang-up button. "It sounds like a synthesized voice, but I'll have forensics try to pull something out of it. And I'll have a profiler listen to it. But I have some early impressions."

"I'm listening," Karen said. She had her own, as well, but wanted to hear the agent's first.

Miri nodded and glanced at a yellow legal pad before speaking. "The caller is male, probably thirty to fifty-five years of age. He's well-educated. And he has some other motive, besides the money."

"Because of the amount," Karen said. "Someone who simply wanted money would have named a round figure, in the millions. This amount is low, and very specific."

"Bingo," Miri said. She glanced over Karen's shoulder. "Senator?"

Karen turned. Of course. Grant and Jerry had followed her. Grant's face was lifeless. Jerry's was not. He was angry.

"You're the special agent?" Grant asked.

She stepped over to him and extended her hand. "Miriam Anson. I'm sorry to meet you under these circumstances."

Grant took her hand. "I was about to say the same thing."

"Everyone does," she replied, with a sympathetic but businesslike smile.

"And this is Jerry Connally, my senior aide."

Jerry shook her hand briefly and nodded silently, the fire still flashing in his eyes. Miri nodded a greeting, then returned her attention to Grant.

"Do you have any idea why this amount? Does the number ring any bells?"

He shook his head. "None."

"What's your annual income?" she asked. "I know it's an intrusive question, but…"

"My Senate salary is one-hundred-fifty thousand."

"And your personal income?"

His eyes almost found focus. "It goes into a trust. The trustee pays the bills on my home here and the one in Tampa. The rest is invested."

"What's the balance in the trust account?" Miri asked.

"I don't see where the details of the senator's finances are relevant," Jerry said, interrupting.

"They are," Karen said, meeting his angry gaze, hoping her face was the image of calm amidst the storm, because she certainly didn't feel that. "The ransom demand is strange. The kidnappers had a reason for choosing that number. We're fishing for numbers that might match up. Knowing how the kidnappers chose that amount might give us a clue as to their identity."

"Of course," Jerry said. "I'm sorry. We're all tense."

"Grant?" Karen asked. "Do you know the balance in the trust?"

He met her eyes for an instant. "No. Not offhand. I'd have to call the trustee. But it's been growing for ten, twelve years."

"So more than four hundred thousand dollars?" Miri asked.

"Considerably more," he said.

"Grant can get that information in the morning,"

Karen said. "In the meantime, let's talk about the rest of the message. I agree the caller is male. The clipped diction sounds male. As for the age, I think you're right. I also think, despite the pronoun, we're dealing with a single perp."

"Because the amount is too low to split among a gang?" Miri asked.

"Exactly. One guy in a gang of kidnappers might have a personal motive, but the others would be there for the money, and they'd demand enough to make it worth the risk. And it's no secret that Grant's family has money."

"Even if they didn't know about Grant's family money," Terry cut in, "people assume that senators and congressmen are rich. And this is a high-risk crime. Anyone involved would have to know we're going to throw everything we have at the kidnapping of a senator's kids. They'd want a big payday. Bigger than three hundred ninety-six grand split however many ways."

Miri nodded. "And the wording of the ransom demand, it's inconsistent with an experienced, professional perp. 'Non-sequential tens and twenties' is a cliché. A pro would know more about how we track ransom money and make a more sophisticated demand."

"They may get more sophisticated with the next call," Jerry said. He looked at Karen. "Just trying to keep an open mind, I guess. Both messages did say 'we,' after all."

"True," Karen agreed. "And there's some evidence of sophistication. Art Wallace must have an answering machine that allows remote control. And whoever planned this must have known that."

Which was another strike against Art, in her mind.

She would know more on that when Previn searched the Wallace house. Which he should have done by now.

"Excuse me," she said, dialing his cell number. He answered on the second ring. "Any news?"

"I'm just pulling into the driveway," he said. "It took a few minutes to get the duty judge for a warrant."

"Fine. I'm putting you on speaker." Karen pushed the button and replaced the receiver. "The whole task force is here. Terry Tyson, from D.C. Homicide, and Special Agent Miriam Anson from the FBI. Talk us through your search."

"Sure," Previn said. "I've parked at the curb. The house is dark, no sign of activity. There's no car in the driveway. I can't see any garage windows. No visible signs of disturbance in the lawn. Front windows are all closed, and no broken panes."

"Walk the entire perimeter of the house before you go in," Miri said. "We're looking for points of entry."

"Gotcha," Previn replied.

From the tone of his voice, Karen could tell he was already doing that and wasn't happy about being reminded of the obvious.

"There's dew on the grass, and no tracks except mine. But it would only have settled in the past hour or so, and we know they were gone before then. The windows on the north side are intact and closed. I'm heading around back now."

"He has two sliding glass doors," Grant said. "One off the kitchen, and one from the family room to the pool deck. The one off the kitchen was always left unlocked when he was home." He looked at Karen. "He said the alarm would go off if anyone opened it at night, and he hated fussing with the lock when he walked his dog in the mornings."

"Dog?" Previn asked.

"A Yorkie," Grant said. "Samantha's her name."

"Is she nice?"

"She's always been nice to me," Grant said.

"Are we afraid of dogs?" Karen asked, the chuckle breaking the tension.

"Only their teeth and claws," Previn said. "Their wagging tails are cute, though."

Karen smiled. "How about their kisses?"

Previn gave a one-word reply. "Ick. Okay, I'm at the back of the house. Both sliding doors are closed. Pool toys on the deck." There was a rattle. "Screen enclosure door is closed and locked. Windows are all closed."

"Check the sliding glass door to the kitchen," Karen said. She looked at Terry and Miri. "Call it a hunch."

"It's locked," Previn said.

Strike two, Karen thought. "Can you see inside, through the glass?"

"Checking now. No signs of disturbance in the kitchen, from what I can see. There's what looks to be an empty Dunkin' Donuts box on the table. Food and water bowls for the dog, by the door. Food bowl is empty, but there's water in the other."

"So where's the dog?" Terry asked. "You'd think she'd have heard him walking around out back."

"No teeth, claws or wagging tail," Previn said. "I'm headed around to the south side of the house. Looks like it's all closed up, too. There's a cracked pane, smoked glass, probably a bathroom. But it's cracked in place. No sign that anyone went in that way."

"Take a closer look at the crack," Miri said.

"Doing that now," Previn said. "There's some dirt in the crack, but not much. Looks like it's gathered since the last time the window was washed outside. I'd guess the window's been broken for a while.''

"Sounds like it," Karen said. She wanted to *be* there, to look at every detail herself. But she had to admit that he was doing a thorough job. "Okay, try the front door. Let's see what's inside."

"Yes, ma'am," he said. The impatience was evident in his voice.

"Sorry we're being mother hens," Miri said. She'd heard the tone of his voice, too. "You're doing fine, Detective. We're just a little tense here."

"I'd be doing the same thing on your end of the phone, I guess. Okay, I'm at the front door. No visible damage around the knob or jamb. Just routine wear and tear. I'm wearing gloves and trying the knob with two fingers. But I'll probably ruin whatever prints are here anyway."

"Not much we can do about that," Karen said. Not that she expected they would find any prints. Still, it was better that he try to preserve whatever was there.

"The door's unlocked," he said. "Might be a point of entry."

Probably only a point of egress, Karen thought. "Go on in. Be careful."

"Bet on that," he said. He called out loudly. "Tampa Police. I have a warrant." He paused and repeated the warning. "No answer. Okay, I'm in the foyer. Two pair of shoes inside the door, one male adult's, size eleven. One female child's, size two."

"Art and one of the girls," Grant said. "Jessie and Lucy. They're twins. Seven."

"Sounds about right," Previn said. "Remind me never to have girls."

"Why's that?" Karen asked.

"Because someone decided to play with glitter in the living room. Some of it is stuck to the arm of the couch with what looks to be paste."

"Kids," Grant said.

With no adult watching, Karen thought. "Let me guess, no signs of disturbance?"

"Well, if it were my couch, I'd be disturbed. But no, nothing. Dining room table has scraps of construction paper. More paste and glitter on the tabletop, and the chairs and the floor and a light switch."

"Got the point on the glitter, Dave," Karen said, a tense laugh in her voice.

"And on the curtains," he added. "And on the north wall. In short, lots of glitter."

"Describe what's on the wall," Miri said, suddenly alert. "In detail."

"You mean besides the glitter?" Previn asked.

"No. The glitter."

"Ummm...okay. Smears. Like finger-painting. At what would be a child's eye level and below. Shining the light from the side. Looks like a capital 'B' and a small 'e.'"

"Belle," Grant said, gasping.

"Where is that, exactly?" Miri asked.

"Maybe eighteen inches off the floor. Beside a window looking out on the house next door."

"Which side?" Karen asked.

"South."

"My house," Grant said. His face had gone ashen.

Karen's heart squeezed for him. One part of her wanted him out of the room, not having to hear this. Part of her recognized that his knowledge of the house was invaluable. Like the locked kitchen door. It was a wrenching tradeoff. On the other hand, he probably wouldn't have left ever if she'd asked him to. She certainly wouldn't have, in his position.

"There are dishes in the sink," Previn said. "All rinsed."

"Check the dishwasher," Karen said.

There was a pause. "It's full. Looks like it's been run."

"And he was rinsing dishes in the sink before emptying the dishwasher and reloading it."

"He always ran it after dinner," Grant said. "Said it was habit. Even when we had barbeques."

"What dishes are in the sink?" Karen asked.

"Cereal bowls. Glasses. Spoons. That's all."

"That fits," Karen said. "Okay, make a quick sweep of the bedrooms, but they'll be empty. Look for the answering machine and the dog. Other than that, you're not going to find anything useful."

"You sound like you know something," Previn said.

"I think I do. One quick thing. Check the bedroom and any hall closets for suitcases. You're not going to find any."

"Checking now." For a few minutes, there was nothing but the sound of doors opening and closing. "You're right, Karen. No suitcases. And to answer the next question, no car in the garage."

"Of course not," she said.

She turned to Grant. "Art Wallace took your girls."

22

They were within just a few miles of the cabin now. Art glanced in the rearview mirror and saw that the girls were still soundly asleep, wrapped safely in their seat belts with their heads cradled against the sides of the SUV on the pillows he'd had them bring. Samantha was asleep on the floor between the front seats. At the cabin they would probably wake just barely enough to stagger inside and fall on the cots in the bedroom. That was the great thing about kids this age. They could stay excited and awake just so long before they fell into a sleep so deep little could disturb them.

It made his life easier, for sure. And this wasn't going to take all that long anyway. As soon as Grant paid the ransom—the amount of child support Grant would have owed, under Florida guidelines, until the girls reached eighteen, plus a college fund for each—he and all the girls were going to disappear forever. He wasn't giving them up. Never. Not any of them.

It had hurt enough when his twins went to live with their mother, but now he was going to lose Belle and Cathy Suzanne, as well, because he was sure that at the end of the school year Grant was going to take them to Washington to live.

He couldn't allow that. He most especially couldn't allow it because Belle and Cathy were *his* daughters, the fruit of an affair with Georgina. An affair that had begun long before Belle was conceived. An affair that had made Georgina determined to move into the same neighborhood. An affair that, when Elizabeth found the letters Georgina had written to him, had killed Art's own marriage.

Art had never been stupid enough to think Georgie would leave Grant for him. No, Georgie had been too in love with the trappings of power, with the idea of eventually becoming first lady. But Georgie had also had sexual appetites that only Art had been able to satisfy. Her death had riven him as much as it had riven Grant. Maybe more so.

Well, he was going to get even. He brushed away all the unhappy thoughts of the past and focused on the future, a future that would allow him to keep all four girls and destroy Grant Lawrence for good.

He glanced in the mirror again and for an instant thought he saw a gleam from Cathy Suzanne's eyes. Awake? He watched, then decided he must have imagined it, some glimmer from a distant light.

But he felt a little less comfortable when he returned his attention to driving. Cathy had been making him uneasy for most of this trip. That solemn way she had of staring at him, as if she saw things deep within him.

That one might bear some watching, he decided. She was only nine but…a little caution might be advisable.

Then he almost laughed. He didn't need to be paranoid, because whether or not he got what he wanted, there was one thing for certain: Grant Lawrence would be destroyed.

"No!" Grant's eruption was loud and violent, compounded, no doubt, of all the strain of the last hours. "Art wouldn't do this."

Karen didn't even try to argue with him. It didn't matter whether he wanted to believe her or not. She was as sure as if she had a confession that Art Wallace was behind this abduction.

"You're letting yourself be misled," Grant accused her. "Art loves those girls. He wouldn't use them like this."

Miriam Anson spoke, saying the thing that was floating in Karen's mind. "Unless he hates you *more.*"

At that, Grant's anger evaporated. He looked away, cheek muscles working, mouth compressing. Finally he said, "I never would have thought so."

"Do you know how to get in touch with his ex-wife?" Karen asked.

"Elizabeth?" His gaze returned to her. "Yeah, sure. At home, anyway. But she's on her honeymoon right now. On a cruise."

"A cruise to where?"

"Antarctica, I think."

"Hoo boy," Terry remarked. "That's some money." Everyone looked at him, and he shrugged. "I wanted to do it so I priced it. I could buy a condo in Florida for that."

Miriam flipped open a cell phone. "Let's see if we can track her down. Senator, do you know her new married name?"

"LeMain. She married Girard LeMain."

Miriam began dialing, remarking, "There can't be that many cruises to Antarctica."

Karen's cell rang, and she answered it. It was Previn, of course. "I've got a feeb here," he said to her. "We're at the Wallace house. Name's Andrew Wicke. He wants to talk to Agent Anson."

"She's on the phone. Can you hang on a minute?"

"Sure." Previn hummed a few bars. "The house is too clean," he remarked. "I'd say they were abducted somewhere else except for one thing."

"Two things. The front door was unlocked and the alarm wasn't set."

"How'd you know about the alarm?"

"Because I didn't hear it in the background, and I didn't hear you swear about it when you opened the front door."

He laughed. "Okay."

"So I figure it was arranged to look as if someone had walked into the house when they were home. Except nothing was disturbed."

"Right. Which means we gotta find this Wallace guy. Agent Wicke agrees with me, by the way."

"I'm proud of you, Dave."

There was a pause. "Thanks." His voice sounded thick.

Karen figured he hadn't heard any praise in a long time, only criticism from his wife.

Grant's phone rang. Everyone in the room stilled for a moment.

"Here," Grant said, suddenly galvanized. He passed a headset to Karen, waited until she had it adjusted and the mike covered. On the fourth ring, he picked up the handset.

"Hello?"

Karen, whose heart had practically climbed into her throat, felt it sink as the caller identified himself.

"Grant, this is Randall Youngblood. I heard about…your girls. I'm so sorry…. If there's anything I can do…"

Karen broke in. "How'd you hear about this, Mr. Youngblood?"

There was a hesitation. "Who the hell is on the line?"

"Karen Sweeney."

"Detective Sweeney! Yes, I guess I should have expected you to be there."

"How'd you hear about this?"

"From my assistant, Bill Michaels. He apparently has a contact in the Tampa Police Department."

"Thanks. I'm off the line now." Karen pulled the headset off and grabbed for her cell phone. "Previn?"

"Yeah?"

"How the fuck did Randall Youngblood's camp find out about this?"

Previn didn't answer.

"You *did* get a sealed warrant?"

"Hell yes."

"Then how is it the news has already spread to Youngblood? He says one of his men has a contact in the department." No answer. "Previn?"

"Hell, I don't know, Karen. How the hell am I supposed to know?"

She didn't believe him. The anger that stirred in her stomach was of a new variety. "You listen to me, you got it?"

"Yes."

"These kids' lives are in danger, and flapping jaws getting this to the media could put this guy over the edge. Are we clear?"

"Yeah. I ain't talking. Maybe it's the feds."

Karen sincerely doubted that. A tap on her arm drew her attention to Miriam, who was holding out a hand for the phone. Karen passed it over.

"This is Miriam Anson, FBI…. Yes…. Hi, Andy…. Yeah, just walk it over one more time. If anything catches your attention, dust it, okay?"

They talked for a few more minutes, nothing that particularly interested Karen. She was more interested in the ashen look of Grant's face. He sat behind his desk now, staring at the phone, probably despairing because he had been warned not to call in the cops.

"Grant."

It took a few seconds, but he finally looked at her.

"Grant, it'll be okay. The leak will be plugged. As long as it doesn't get to the papers, Wallace will never know."

"You're still sure it's him."

"Yes. Grant, it's the only explanation that makes sense. The locked kitchen door was the big slip. He remembered to leave the front door unlocked and the alarm off, as if they'd been taken. But he locked the kitchen door, out of habit. A kidnapper would've been nervously watching the kids, making them keep still. Here we have kids who were being ignored while they spread paste and glitter all over the room. And who else would know that Art had a remote-controllable answering machine? Yes, I'm sure."

He sighed heavily. "Unfortunately, so am I."

"Grant, that gives us a big advantage. He doesn't know we know. He thinks he has time. He doesn't."

"He has my girls," Grant said.

Karen nodded. "Yes, he does. But he also has his own

girls with him. He won't want a fight. He'll take them somewhere they're all familiar with.''

"She's right, Senator," Miri said. "Have your girls ever gone on vacation with him?"

Grant paused for a moment, closing his eyes. Stress and exhaustion were wearing him down, Karen realized. His thoughts and reactions were slowing. He opened his eyes and nodded.

"Yes, they went to the mountains once."

"Who went?" Karen asked, walking him through the memory.

"Art and Elizabeth and their girls, Georgie and our girls."

"Which mountains? The Rockies?"

"No. Maryland, I think. Yes. Afterward Georgie brought the kids here to stay with me for a weekend. There was a budget brawl going on. Things were stalled, and we were trying to break the deadlock, so we'd put off the summer recess." He let out a long breath and looked at the couch. "Belle was just a baby at the time. I was changing her diapers on that sofa, with the phone on speaker."

"You must've had a number where you could reach them," Miri said. "Do you still have it?"

"I wouldn't even know. It was six years ago."

Miri and Karen glanced at his desk at the same moment. An appointment calendar was open on one corner. Karen spoke first. "Do you keep your old appointment books?"

"We do," Jerry said. "At the office."

"Get it," Miri said. "If he wrote that number in it, we can find the place with a reverse directory search."

Jerry nodded. "I'm on my way."

"I'll drive you," Terry said. "That way we don't have to worry about speeding tickets."

Karen didn't have to tell them to hurry. Once they'd left, she turned to Grant. "You need some sleep."

"I couldn't sleep," he said, almost angry at the very thought. "I can't sleep until they're back with me."

"That's not an option, Senator," Miri said. "You're the best source of information we have right now, but you're tired, and you're going to start making mistakes. Those mistakes could get your girls hurt. Or worse. We need you fresh."

He shook his head. "I can't go to bed."

"Don't go to bed, then," Karen said, almost snapping. She caught herself and softened her tone. "You have a sectional in the den. Crash out there for a few hours. We'll come get you if there's any news."

He ran a hand through his hair and sighed heavily. "I guess I can do that."

"Do it for your girls," Karen said.

"You convinced me already," he said, trying to feign the famed Lawrence humor. "I'll put on an old movie or an infomercial."

"Just not the news," Karen said.

"Definitely," Miri agreed.

He nodded and walked to the door, then turned and fixed his eyes on Karen. "You'll wake me if anything happens?"

It was a personal question. He didn't simply want to be awakened. He was asking if she would be the one to do it. She was, she realized, the only anchor he had left now that Jerry had gone. It suddenly struck her that, for someone who lived such a public life, he was an intensely personal man.

"Yes," she said. "I'll wake you."

"Good."

As he walked away, she could see the toll the day had taken in the degree of his limp. She couldn't bear to watch his pain and walked around to sit behind the desk. His desk. Her eyes swept it for anything that might help solve this mess, although she realized it was a pointless exercise, mental calisthenics to keep from thinking.

"He's a good man," Miri said, sitting on the sofa.

"Yes," Karen agreed. She didn't want to go there. "If Wallace has taken the kids to Maryland, I guess it's your jurisdiction now."

Miri nodded. "If he has. We don't know that yet, though. Regardless, the senator seems to want you on point. I haven't seen any reason to disagree."

"Thanks," Karen said. "But I feel like a butterfly in a hurricane."

"You are. I am, too. Do you really think Tyson offered to drive Jerry because he was worried about traffic tickets?"

Karen sighed. "No, I suppose not."

"I've known Terry Tyson for, I guess, eight years now. He's the best cop I've ever worked with. But like all of us, he doesn't do well just sitting around. He needs to be working the streets, making calls, doing *something*. Even if it's just being the chauffeur."

"He's going to hate retirement," Karen said.

Miri laughed. "He's been swearing he's about to retire for five years."

Karen looked up. "He said he has three weeks left. Then he's done with his thirty. He's going to move his wife to Florida."

Miri pressed her lips together and looked away.

"What?" Karen asked.

"Terry's wife is dead. Three years ago next month."

"But…"

"He met her in high school," Miri said. "Two days after they graduated, he married her. They had twenty-seven years together. Raised two kids. Then one night, while he was on duty, she went to the market for ice cream to put on top of the anniversary cake she'd baked. There was a robbery."

"Oh, God." The math seemed to do itself for her. "Thirty years, in three weeks."

"Right," Miri said. The look in her eyes said it all.

"I'm sorry."

Miri nodded. "Thanks. I've tried to get him into counseling, but he says he's not ready to let go. It's hard to compete with a ghost."

"I guess it would be."

Karen hadn't even considered that part. Grant had loved Georgie. And Abby and Stacy, albeit differently. Would she see their ghosts in his eyes? Did the question even matter? The pool had been a moment of need. A mercy fuck. Right?

He'd shown flashes of anger afterwards. Were they an anomaly, born of shock and fear and stress…and guilt? He certainly hadn't given the slightest indication that he was prone to violent outbursts. But she hadn't known him for very long.

Oh, stop it, she told herself. This was pointless. The pool was history. Right now she had to focus on getting his girls back. Then she had to find a killer. After that…

"Karen?"

Her head snapped up. "Yes?"

"You need to get some sleep," Miri said gently.

"I'm okay. I was thinking."

Miri laughed. It was a warm laugh. "You were snoring, Detective."

"No."

"Yes. And everything you said to the senator goes double for you. You won't do any of us any good if you're fighting your body. Terry's going to be a while. Even a half hour will do you good."

Karen slowly rolled her head. Miri was right. Everything in her body cried out to be horizontal.

"Take the other half of his sectional," Miri said. "I need to make some calls, and I'd keep you awake."

If she had an ulterior motive, Miri kept it hidden behind her warm eyes. Better to take her words at face value.

"Yeah. You're right."

"Get some rest," Miri said.

Karen nodded and made her way to the den. Grant was already asleep, one arm curled over his eyes, his breathing deep and even. She stretched out on the other wing of the sofa, curled onto her side and tried not to think about anything that mattered. The last thought she remembered was wondering whether the Devil Rays had won.

Art watched the girls flopped across the floor. Belle kept brushing her cheek in her sleep, soothing herself. She and the twins had dropped right back off, as soon as they had arrived. He'd had to talk to Cathy for a few minutes. She'd wanted to call her father. Art had told her he was working late, on the big environmental law.

"It's not a law yet," she'd said, nothing in her voice or eyes to betray her emotions. "It's a bill. It's not a law until both houses pass it and the president signs it."

"You know a lot about government," he'd said, trying to sound soothing.

"We read about it in school," she'd said, her eyes still unreadable. "And daddy talks about it."

He's not your daddy, Art thought, remembering the conversation. But, of course, he couldn't tell her that. She would learn the truth in time. And she would love him the way a daughter ought to love a father. It would all work out.

He rose from the chair and padded into the bedroom, careful not to wake them. The rifle was in the closet, in a cloth carrying case. He took it out and got the cleaning kit from the shelf. He went over the plan in his mind as he ran the cleaning oil through the barrel with a long-stemmed swab, then wiped down the action.

He'd give the ransom instructions. Grant must come alone to deliver the money. He wouldn't, of course. He would have called the FBI, and they would be trying to cover him. But they wouldn't have time to reconnoiter the scene. Art wouldn't give them time. And he had the perfect hiding place, the perfect escape route.

He sighted along the rifle and squeezed the trigger. *Click.*

One shot and his life would finally begin.

23

A gentle tap on Karen's shoulder woke her. She looked up into the face of Miriam Anson.

"Wake him up," Miriam murmured. "We got through to the cruise ship. They're going to patch us through to Wallace's ex the minute we're ready. The senator needs to talk to her."

Karen, instantly awake, sat up. Miriam walked quietly from the room.

Leaning over, Karen shook Grant's shoulder. His eyes popped open immediately, and his feet hit the floor almost as fast.

"What's going on?"

"We're patched through to Elizabeth's cruise ship. You need to talk to her."

"Me?" He passed a hand over his face, as if he might wipe away the last of the sleep.

"You," she said. "We've been talking. Elizabeth couldn't get back here in much less than two days. There's no point in scaring her needlessly. So you're going to tell her Art took the kids to the cabin for a few days, but you can't remember how to get there, okay?"

He nodded. "Okay."

They went into the office, where Miriam was holding the phone to her ear. She lifted a brow when she saw Grant, but handed him the phone immediately. Then Karen donned the headset and pointed to the extension phone across the room. Miriam picked it up.

"Okay," Miriam said to the person aboard the ship, "we're ready to talk to Mrs. LeMain now."

"One moment." A click, a hiss of static, then the faraway sound of ringing. After four rings, a man answered. He sounded barely awake. "Yes?"

Karen pointed to Grant. He nodded briefly. "Mr. LeMain, this is Grant Lawrence. I used to be your wife's neighbor."

There was a pause. "Oh, yes. Senator Lawrence. She's mentioned you. What can I do for you?"

"Well, I need to talk to Elizabeth, if you don't mind. I know the hour's unreasonable, but Art—her ex—took our kids to the cabin this weekend. Unfortunately, I can't remember how to get there, and I don't have the phone number."

"Oh. Yes. Of course. Just a moment please. She's just waking up."

There was some murmuring, occasionally washed out by static, then a woman's strong voice came on the phone. "Grant! This is an unexpected pleasure."

"You've been missed, Elizabeth," Grant said.

She laughed. "Not really. You were so rarely at home. What's this about the girls?"

"Art said he was taking them to the cabin. They were staying with him after…well, you heard about Abby?"

"Yes, I did." Her voice saddened. "I'm so sorry, Grant. She was a beautiful woman, and I know how much you loved her."

"Thank you." Grant cleared his throat. "Anyway, Art

said something about taking them to the cabin for a chance to recover. They just went up there. Stupid me, I didn't even ask for the phone number. I'm so used to Abby being on top of all that...." His voice cracked.

"I know," Elizabeth said soothingly. "Poor Grant. Your life has been such hell...." She sighed. "Unfortunately, I can't help you with the phone number. I hated that place and went there as rarely as possible."

Grant stiffened, as if this was news to him.

"It's just a couple of bare rooms, really," Elizabeth said. "But the girls always loved to go. And it's been in Art's family forever. Besides, I hate it for another reason. That's where Georgie and Art used to go for their trysts."

For the longest moment, dead silence filled the line. Then Elizabeth drew a sharp breath. "Oh, Grant, I'm sorry. You didn't know, either! I thought...well, when I found all those letters to Art from Georgie last year, I...guess I thought I was the only one who didn't know."

"Trysts?" Grant repeated, his voice as tight as wire. "I knew she was having a fling but..."

"But you didn't know it was Art. And it was more than a fling. As near as I can tell from the letters, they were having an affair for nearly ten years. That's what I couldn't take, Grant. The fact that it wasn't a stupid little fling."

"My God." His face was ashen.

"I'm sorry. You didn't need to know this. I should have kept my big mouth shut, but from things you'd said, I assumed you knew what was going on. Well. I really put my foot in it."

"It's okay," Grant said, his voice tense. "Don't

worry about it. It's just...I need to see my girls, Elizabeth. I need to get in touch with them at the cabin.''

"I'm sorry. I'm really sorry, Grant. I don't know the number. I might be able to drive you there, if I were up there now, but it's been so long and I went so rarely...I'd probably only get us lost. All I can tell you is that it's in the mountains in Maryland. Maybe he's in the phone book.''

"Thanks, Elizabeth. I'm sorry I woke you. My apologies to your husband.''

"It's quite all right. It was good to hear from you again. Don't be a stranger.''

Grant hung up, standing rigid, staring into space. Finally two harsh words escaped him. "The bastard!''

Miriam swore softly. "Forget the phone book. I already did a national directory search.''

"Besides, I don't want to call him," Karen reminded him. "I want to *find* him.''

Grant nodded and slumped into his desk chair. Karen wanted to comfort him, but they weren't alone. Besides, there probably wasn't any comfort in the world for a man who'd just found out his wife had been having a years-long affair with a mutual friend.

"The point is,'' Miriam said, "the number at the cabin, if he ever had a phone there, isn't in his name. That's the problem we're having. Whether we want to call him or not, the phone isn't in his name.''

"Shit.'' Grant closed his eyes.

"Jerry will find something,'' Miriam said, with more confidence than Karen believed she was feeling.

"Sure,'' Karen answered, feigning the same confidence for Grant's sake. "Jerry'll find it.''

After a moment, she called Previn. "Still looking around the house,'' he said. "Nothing.''

"Roust the judge again," she said shortly. "I want a tap on Wallace's phone line. I want a list of numbers that have called in within the last twenty-four hours."

"Oh, that's great. I can infuriate a judge only to be told the phone company offices don't open until eight. Tell you what. I'll roust the judge at seven and hit the phone company at eight. That's the soonest we can get the information, and you know it."

"We can't wait until the phone company opens!"

Miriam, who had been listening, said, "Put Wicke on, please?" She took the phone from Karen.

"Wicke, get me an emergency federal order. I want to know the originating phone number of every call placed to the Wallace home in the last twenty-four hours, and I want it PDQ. Interstate kidnapping."

"I can do that, but I don't think it's going to help us a whole lot," Wicke said. "He doesn't have an answering machine, or if he does, I haven't found it. It's probably the phone company's voice mail service. Which means he's not even calling here. He's calling the voice mail service number."

"Which would be pointless to trace," Miri said, annoyance in her voice. "Everyone in Tampa who has that service probably uses the same number. It probably gets hundreds of calls an hour."

"They might be able to screen for calls involving Wallace's phone number," Wicke said. "But who knows. I'll give it a try anyway."

Miri hung up. "He's either very smart or very lucky. Either way, we're stuck waiting for Jerry."

Karen rolled her head, trying to shake out the stiffness from sleeping on the sectional sofa. "It's almost a perfect way for a kidnapper to communicate. Using the phone company as a blind. If Grant hadn't known about the kitchen door..."

"He must've been thinking about this for a long time," Grant said. "And to think I trusted him. The bastard."

That made the cut even deeper, Grant thought. Betrayal by a trusted friend. All this time they'd been friends, and he and Georgie had been...

"Fuck," he said. Then, looking at them, "Sorry."

"No worries," Karen said. "You have every right to be angry. I'm angry, too."

"And you both need to keep that in check," Miri said. "But I didn't have to tell you that."

"Sometimes it's good to be reminded," Karen said. "So okay, how do we play it when Jerry calls with the number? You can get a hostage rescue team, I assume."

"All we need is an address and we move," Grant said. He wanted his daughters away from that man, and back with him. Where they should have been all along.

"Not necessarily," Miri said. "We need to know what we're doing before we go in there. It might be better to wait until tonight."

"What?" Grant asked. Wait to get his girls? "No way."

Miri's look was firm. "Think about it, Senator. We don't want to go in there with guns blazing. That may get your daughters killed. No, he's going to leave a new message tonight, with ransom instructions. I'm guessing he'll want to make the drop immediately. He's not a pro, but he's thought about it. If he gives us time, we'll be all over the drop site. He wants to make you move fast."

Karen nodded. "Right. And he'll have to leave the

cabin to go to the drop. It'll be safer to take him then, when the girls aren't with him.''

Grant couldn't imagine that Art would leave the girls behind to go to the ransom drop. Then again, he couldn't imagine Art doing any of this. The plan made sense. But the thought of sitting around while Cathy and Belle spent another day with that man galled him.

"The good news," Karen said, as if reading his mind, "is that right now the girls probably don't think there's anything unusual happening. So they're not scared. It's just an unexpected vacation."

"With a monster," Grant said bitterly.

"Yes. With a monster. But they don't know that. And it's better that they don't. They're probably having fun, or sound asleep. The point is, they're not in immediate danger, so we can afford to wait until the drop."

"I know, I know," he said. If Art hurt those girls, he would kill him. It was that simple. "We can find the cabin, at least, can't we? Put surveillance on it or something? Make sure the girls are okay?"

"Of course," Miri said. "Once we have a location, I'll have a team in the air in five minutes. Giving them a day to recon is a good thing. The more they know about the situation, the safer your girls will be."

"It's really the best way," Karen insisted.

"It is," he agreed. "I hate it, but it is. And like you say, the girls are blissfully ignorant. Even if I'm ready to chew the arm rests off my chair."

He looked at his watch. Two-fifteen. Jerry had been gone for an hour now. It shouldn't take long for him to find the old appointment books. Grant wouldn't have had a clue where to look amongst the office files. But Jerry would. He should be calling soon.

And then they would get his girls back.

* * *

Randall Youngblood woke in the middle of the night, an unusual event. Although he slept only five or six hours a night, and had for as long as he could remember, it was almost always sound, uninterrupted sleep. His late wife had said it was because he worked himself so hard. He saw it differently. He went to bed every night with a clean conscience, or tried to. Yes, over the years he'd done things he'd regretted, but who hadn't? He'd tried to learn from the experiences, to find ways not to put himself in the same situations again. Perhaps it was self-delusion, but he didn't feel the need to apologize to the universe at the end of the day, and he liked that feeling.

For that reason, when he awoke with a jolt at 3:00 a.m., with a sinking feeling in his gut from the moment his eyes opened, he knew there was a reason. He rarely had nightmares, and regardless, he didn't remember having been dreaming in the instant before he snapped awake. No, there was something wrong. Something for which he was somehow responsible. But what?

He lay there in the darkness, running through the events of the past few days. Yes, he'd been lobbying hard against S.R. 52, but it had been honest lobbying. He'd made no threats or insincere promises. It was stressful, frustrating, sometimes angry, but it was the business of politics, and he'd long since reconciled himself to that process.

He was almost ready to grant himself general absolution in the form of reading himself back to sleep when the thought wormed its way up from his subconscious. Grant Lawrence had been stunned when he'd called to express his sorrow and sympathy over the kidnapping.

Randall had assumed the story was already out, but apparently it wasn't. Yes, Michaels had sources who fed him information before it was general knowledge—like anyone else in the system, Randall knew how important it was to stay ahead of the power curve with advance knowledge—and Randall rarely asked or wondered where that information came from. There were always those whose egos or avarice overcame their duty of discretion. That, too, was part of the game.

But this was different. Grant's daughters were in danger, and leaked information could add to that danger. Michaels had a contact in the Tampa Police Department, that much Randall knew, but he doubted a cop would have talked about something that sensitive. There was, or should have been, a point where a sense of duty would again overcome ego or avarice. This was past that point.

Any thought of falling back to sleep was now gone. Randall picked up the phone and called Michaels. There was no answer. He tried Michaels' cell phone. Still no answer. That was odd. Michaels knew better than to be out of touch.

So where was he? The question suddenly made him feel ill.

"Cripes," Terry's voice said over the speakerphone, filling the study where Miriam, Grant and Karen all waited impatiently. "We had to go back six years. *Six years!* In case anyone is interested, the senator is one hell of a busy man."

Karen knew he was trying to lighten the heavy atmosphere for all of them, but this time it wasn't working. "Just shoot, Terry, before we all gnaw our hands off waiting."

"Yeah, we got it. I called the department and they're running a reverse on it. They'll call over there shortly with the address. Mr. Connally and I are on our way back.''

''Thanks, Terry.''

''Wait,'' said Grant, before Terry could hang up. ''Can I speak to Jerry for a minute?''

''Sure, Senator,'' Terry said, his deep voice calm and obliging. There was a rustle, a slight thud, then Jerry's voice filled the room. ''I'm here, Grant.''

''Jerry... I want to know how the hell Randall Youngblood found out about...what happened.'' He apparently couldn't even make himself say the word *kidnapping*.

''You mean *this*. He knows about *this?*''

''He called to express his concern. I want to know where the leak is.''

''I'll get Sam on it right away. Damn. I always figured there was something squirrelly about Michaels.''

''Michaels?''

''Youngblood's aide. His version of me and Sam.''

Karen jumped in. ''What do you mean by squirrelly, Jerry?''

''I don't think he's completely on the up-and-up, if you want the truth. He's as close to a hatchet-man as I've ever seen. If Youngblood knows something, it's because Michaels found it out. And he's not above dirty tricks, whether Youngblood knows it or not.''

''Well,'' Karen said, ''I don't care about Michaels' character or lack thereof, but I want that damn leak plugged before it turns into a flood.''

''That's easy enough,'' Miriam said. ''I'll have him picked up. He has knowledge of a crime that he shouldn't have.''

But something made Karen hesitate. Inside her, everything went utterly still. Then she said, almost before the thought formed, ''No. Don't pick him up.''

Miriam looked askance at her. "Why not?"

"I don't know. Just don't touch him. Jerry, if you can find out where the leak is without tipping off Michaels, fine. But...I don't want Michaels to know anything."

Jerry was silent for several heartbeats. "I understand. And I agree with you, Karen. It's too big a risk."

They disconnected the call, and the three of them sat in a room so quiet that the click of the air-conditioning thermostat could be heard.

Finally Miriam spoke. "You think Michaels is involved in this?"

"I think he might be. I could also be wrong."

Grant shook his head slowly. "Why would a man in his position get involved in something like this? He could ruin everything he's supposed to be working for."

Karen drummed her fingers on the console table next to her. "Maybe issues aren't important to him. Maybe he's driven by ego. It sure isn't money, not with what Wallace demanded."

"I agree," Miriam said thoughtfully. "To have any chance of pulling this off, especially the ransom exchange, there's got to be an accomplice. And it's pretty damn suspicious that Youngblood knew about the abduction. Particularly as quickly as he heard about it."

Grant's face tightened, his blue eyes darkening. "This just gets worse and worse. I at least had some hope Art wouldn't do anything to hurt the girls. Michaels is another kettle of fish."

"Maybe it's not so bad," Miriam said. "I can put surveillance on Michaels. It might help."

It was a thin straw, but all of them were willing to grasp at it.

Terry and Jerry arrived a few minutes later, carrying the appointment book in question, with the number circled in red. They had barely entered the study when the phone rang. Grant answered it, hope on his face. Then his expression sagged, and he offered the phone to Terry. "For you."

Terry grabbed the receiver. "Tyson. Yeah. Yeah?" He scribbled down the info. "I need a phone company map of the area. I know it's out of our jurisdiction. Damn it.... Okay."

He hung up and passed his scrawl over to Miriam. "This is what we've got. You Feds are going to have to locate it."

She looked down at it. "Oh, shit."

"What?" Karen asked.

"The bills are sent to a corporation in Florida." Then she laughed. "Oh, baby, we're on to you now."

She flipped open her cell phone and began to speak rapidly. Shortly, she hung up. "We're going to get the phone company maps of the area. That damn cabin is about to be pinpointed."

24

Terry arranged for his department to stake out Michaels' D.C. apartment and the lobby offices to start the tail. Miriam mobilized the FBI's local hostage rescue team, and now they were all waiting for the task force at the FBI offices to pinpoint the location of the cabin on a map of the Maryland Mountains.

"I'm going with the team to the cabin," Karen announced.

"You should stay with the senator," Miriam said.

"No. I'm point on this case, and I want to be there to ensure that no harm comes to those children. It's *my* responsibility."

"I want to be there, too," Grant said. His face was so drawn that he was hardly recognizable any longer as the handsome, youthful senator who might one day be president.

"No." The word emerged from Karen and Miriam at exactly the same moment.

"You can't, Grant," Karen continued. "You have to stay here and make the ransom call. He'll expect you to start the ransom instructions from here. You can't do anything suspicious. You can't disappear."

"My girls—"

"Your girls will be safer if you do your part. Your part is staying here so no one realizes that we're on to them. Got it?"

The struggle was written all over his face, but he finally agreed.

"And, Terry," Karen said. "You stay with Grant. When he starts to move, I want you to make sure he's tailed without anyone discovering that you're the tail."

"Obviously." He grinned as if he relished the assignment.

"I want Grant wired before he goes to deliver the ransom. That way we can know everything that happens. He can keep us informed, and we can hear any conversations he has."

"Good," Terry said. "That'll make tailing him easier."

"We also need a position locator in his car. Unless someone else would pick up on the signal?"

"No problem," Miri said. "We'll get him a rental, one with a GPS emergency system. We can track him that way."

Karen nodded. "That works."

Miriam's phone rang. She answered, listened intently, then disconnected. "Okay, they've located the cabin. We're moving out in thirty minutes." She looked at Karen. "We need to get out of here without making anyone suspicious."

"Easy," said Karen. "Drive me back to my hotel and say good night. You drive off. Have someone else pick me up at the rear service entrance."

Miriam nodded. "Are you sure you don't want to join my team? You'd be good."

Karen shook her head. "I just want those children back."

Miriam looked at her watch. "Let's go, then. Time's a-wasting."

The first pink streamers were just beginning to glow in the east when Miriam dropped Karen off at her hotel. Karen made a point of going around to the driver's side window to make casual conversation, as if the two of them were just friends.

Miriam surprised her. "Lean down and kiss me."

"What?"

"Lean down and kiss my cheek. It's the least professional thing you could do."

Karen caught on. She bent and kissed Miriam's cheek. "Night, sweetie," she said, a little laugh in her voice.

"Night, hon," came the response, and Miriam roared off into the dawn.

Karen watched her go as if she were reluctant to see her depart, but as she did so, she also took in her immediate environs. Nothing out of place. Feigning a yawn, she turned and entered the hotel.

No one followed her into the elevator. No one appeared in the hallways as she walked to her room. Inside, everything was exactly as she had left it.

Unfortunately, she hadn't brought her Kevlar vest. The thought struck her as ludicrous, and she swiftly changed into a dark green slack suit, the closest thing she had to camouflage, and a pair of jogging shoes that were entirely too white. Well, she would see if she could drag them in the mud a bit.

Then she left her room. No one in the hallway, no one in the service elevator. She didn't encounter a single soul until she stepped through the door onto the loading dock behind the hotel. Not a person was in sight.

Then a bundle of rags near a trash Dumpster stirred. "It's clear," said a voice. "Go for the black Taurus at the northwest corner of the parking lot. Heiland is waiting for you."

If there hadn't been so much at risk, Karen might have smiled at the extreme measures the Bureau was taking. As it was, she still felt exposed as she crossed the parking lot, weaving between silent empty cars that could have concealed almost anything.

Finally she reached the Taurus. A man was sitting behind the wheel, smoking a cigarette. When he saw her, he tossed the butt out the window. She heard the *thunk* of power locks being released.

"Climb in, Detective," he said quietly. "I'm Special Agent Heiland, and we have a chopper to meet."

They headed farther northwest and crossed the state line into Bethesda. "Where are we meeting the team?" she asked.

"Bethesda Medical Center," he said. "Their medevac pad. It's the closest secure location we could find."

She nodded. Perhaps it was because Miriam had taken charge of things from the FBI side, but she didn't feel she was living one of the jurisdictional nightmares for which federal/local relationships were so famous. Instead, she was glad she had someone along who would think of the things she didn't, and had the contacts and information she lacked.

Heiland flashed his badge at the base security gate. "Project Clam Lips," he said. The security guard nodded and glanced at a clipboard, then waved them through.

"Clam lips?" she asked.

"It's one of the senator's favorite sayings," he explained. "Something about seeing them in the Keys as a kid. Anyway, that's the Bureau's code name for this op."

Bethesda Naval Medical Center was, and looked like, any large, modern hospital complex. If Karen looked past the uniforms, she could have been at Tampa General. They pulled into the emergency room parking lot.

"You're sick," Heiland said. "But not too sick."

"Got it," she said, affecting a cough as they walked in the automatic doors and over to an elevator.

They stepped into a car. A woman with a child was about to enter, but Heiland stepped into the door. "You'd probably better not," he said, nodding at Karen. She let out another cough. He smiled at the mother. "I wouldn't want your son to catch it."

"Of course not," the woman said, stepping back as if from a rattlesnake. She looked at Karen. "I hope you feel better soon."

"Thanks," Karen said, drawing a wheezing breath before coughing again. "You too."

The door closed, and Heiland smiled. "You're in the wrong business, Detective. You should've been an actress." He pulled a walkie-talkie from his jacket. "Heiland here. We're in the elevator."

Without his pushing a button, the car began to rise. When it stopped and the back door opened, she saw they were on the roof. "Special access," he said, walking toward the waiting helicopter.

Miriam was standing in the doorway, a hand extended. Speech was difficult, if not impossible, over the rotor noise. Karen grabbed the hand and climbed in, then accepted the headset Miriam offered.

"Meet the team," Miriam said, her voice a bit hollow through the helicopter's intercom circuits. She nodded to the black-clad commandos in the aircraft bay. "Special Agent Phil Harrelson is the team leader. Agents Levin, Garcia, Rose, Maxwell, Suarez and Dateman."

The agents nodded as their names were called. Karen doubted she would remember them for longer than it took her to look away, but she had a day to get to know them. They were the men who would rescue Grant's children, and she needed to trust them.

"Detective Karen Sweeney, Tampa PD," Miriam said to Harrelson. "She's lead for the op."

Harrelson nodded, his eyes wary. "Have you ever worked with hostage rescue?" he asked.

"Not since I was a patrol officer," she answered. "And all I did that time was secure the scene. So I'm trusting you guys to know what you're doing."

"We do," he said, seeming to relax a bit.

Admitting her ignorance and acknowledging their expertise had been the right move, she knew. She hadn't worked with FBI hostage rescue, but she had worked with aggressive males for years. Patting their egos, especially when they were indeed the experts, was always good policy.

Miriam passed her a topographic map folded on a clipboard. The cabin, which looked to be nestled in a small clearing on the side of a mountain, was circled in red. On the other side of the mountain, a ranger station was circled in blue.

"That's our insertion point," Miri said. "The hill mass ought to mask the noise of our approach, and it's only about three miles over the ridge to the cabin." She checked her watch. "It's zero-eight-ten now. Flight time is about forty minutes. A little over an hour for the hike. We should be on scene by ten hundred or a little after.''

Karen nodded. They ought to have at least seven hours to recon the situation. ''Excellent.'' She turned to Harrelson. ''Our thought was to take him when he leaves for the drop. What do you think?''

''That's probably safest. We'll know more when we've had a chance to scout the scene. But yes, that's probably going to be our best bet to separate him from the girls.''

Over a decade later, the FBI still stung from the bloody sieges at Ruby Ridge and Waco. Macho heroics were out of vogue, and none too soon, in Karen's estimation. Harrelson and his team looked confident and determined. But she didn't see in their eyes an eagerness to wade in with guns blazing.

''Do you need a vest?'' Miri asked.

Karen nodded. ''As a matter of fact, I do.''

''We brought a couple of extras,'' Harrelson said. He nodded at her feet. ''We also brought some hiking boots. Seven, seven-and-a-half and eight.''

''Eight,'' Karen said.

''I was in the right ballpark then,'' Miri said. ''I didn't figure you'd have come to D.C. equipped for this.''

Karen nodded. ''I sure didn't. I do at least have my Glock.''

''You won't need it,'' Harrelson said. He smiled. ''You're here for your brains. We're the brawn.''

''Oh, I don't know,'' Karen said. ''I bet we could muster a brain between y'all.''

''We traded those in when we volunteered for hostage rescue,'' he said. ''Got extra brawn instead.''

Karen laughed. ''Sounds like the makings of a good team, then.''

"Sounds like it," he agreed.

She turned to Miriam. "Any news on Michaels?"

The agent shook her head. "They hadn't seen him leave his home when I checked in with Terry. I'll check in again when we land."

"He's gone to ground," Karen said. "Betcha."

"I won't take that bet."

"Roo-Roo-Roo-Root-Roops!" Belle said, her face exploding in a smile.

"Rat's right," Art said. "Roo-Roo-Root-Roops for everyone."

Belle and the twins dug in with relish, but Cathy was more subdued. "Can I call Daddy after breakfast?" she asked.

"We'll try," Art said. This girl was going to be trouble. "He may be at work already. You girls slept late."

"He'll want to talk to us," Cathy said.

Her voice was neither whiny nor confrontational. He could have dealt with either of those. Instead, she was unnervingly firm and matter-of-fact. He wasn't going to snow her. Not for long. But he didn't need to, not for very long. By tonight, she would be his.

Grant seethed in the inactivity. All his life, he'd been a doer. The grinding schedule of political life fit him to a T. Now he had nothing to do except to watch Terry make and receive phone calls, wait for reports from Karen and Miriam, try to make small talk with Jerry…and think. Way too much of the latter.

"They should be at the cabin in fifteen minutes," Terry said, seemingly reading the look on Grant's face. "Then we'll know more."

"Thanks," Grant said. "Waiting's hard."

"Of course it is," the cop agreed. "Anyone who says otherwise has never done it for a living."

"I almost forgot," Grant said. "You must have done more waiting than I'll ever know."

"Maybe so. It never gets easier, though. I'm waiting for this Michaels guy to make a move somewhere, and he's disappeared into the ether. I'd call Youngblood, but I don't want to tip him off, in case he's involved, too."

"He's not," Grant said. "I've known Randall for too long to believe he could have anything to do with this."

Terry shrugged. "Two days ago, you'd have said the same thing about Wallace. Are you willing to bet your girls' lives on being right this time?"

Could it be possible he was that bad a judge of character? He'd certainly misjudged Georgie and Art for a long time. He would never have believed Jerry would have been so headstrong as to move Stacy's body, even if he'd done it for all the best reasons. And he had let himself go in a moment of loneliness and weakness, and Karen had let him do it, something he never would have expected of her.

Or was there more to it than that? The more he thought about it, the more he realized he was asking those questions because of Karen. Not because she'd done anything wrong—he'd seduced her every bit as much as she'd seduced him, and he'd been growing more attached to her with each passing day—but because he *was* so attached. Was he grasping at emotional straws, looking for any sense of connection and stability he could find? Did he even have the judgment to know?

And there was the rub. Here he was, getting attached to a woman who gave his heart hope, at a time when people he'd known for years were turning out to be different than he'd believed. If his judgment was so bad, how could he trust anyone about anything, let alone trust a woman with his heart?

Jerry had gone into the den to call the office staff and explain the situation as discreetly as he could. They would stay in touch by cell phone for the day, if need be. He wanted to keep the land lines clear in case Art tried to contact him. Now Jerry stood in the doorway, holding the cell phone.

"Grant, you have to take this."

"Who is it?"

"John Kittinger."

The president's chief of staff, a man who did not take "No" for an answer and, when he had to, never forgot it. Grant nodded and turned to Terry. "I'll be in the den."

"John," he said, once he'd closed the door of the den. "What can I do for you?"

"Senator. The president sends his sympathies for all that's happened in these past weeks."

Right. And President Louis just happened to be sending along these sympathies when there was something he wanted. There was no way this was a simple social call.

"That's very kind of him," Grant said. "Please convey my gratitude to him."

"Will do," Kittinger replied. "Look, Senator, I know it's a bad time, but we have a situation, and the president needs to know he can count on your support."

I have a situation of my own, and you're damn right it's a bad time, Grant thought. "What's up?" he asked.

"It's Colombia. FARC forces just hit our embassy."

Shit. It never rained. "What happened?"

Kittinger's voice dripped disgust. "The early reports are that they fired some RPG-7's from a building across the street. It happened about an hour ago. We have three Marines down, not sure how bad yet. And a dozen or more administrative personnel.''

The RPG-7 was an old handheld rocket launcher, built in the Soviet Union as an infantry anti-tank weapon during the Cold War and since exported all over the world. That the FARC had them was no surprise. That they'd used them on the U.S. embassy ought to have been no surprise, either, given the recent talk of military intervention. Still, the notion of dead or dying Marines came as a blow.

''What's he considering?'' Grant asked.

''He wants to hit them,'' Kittinger replied. ''He's talking a special ops raid. We think we can get good intel on who did this. He wants to send a team in, snatch them, and put them on trial here.''

It was a dangerous tack. A lot could go wrong. If the raid were compromised, it could turn into a bloody firefight. Memories of Somalia flashed through his mind. This would be worse. Given the history of the drug war and the nation's reaction to the Al Quaeda attacks, there was no question what would happen if the networks flashed images of dead soldiers being dragged naked through the streets in Colombia. They would demand war and accept nothing less. Even if the war were unwinnable by any less than unthinkable means.

On the other hand, if the raid went well, it would send a clear message: the United States would treat terrorists as criminals and bring them to justice, even to the point of sending in troops to find and seize them. It was the approach Grant himself had advocated after the World Trade Center and Pentagon attacks. It was, he considered, a moral and just response.

If it went well.

"Senator," Kittinger said, "the president's in his last term. He'd like to know that the man most likely to have his job next is going to support him if he goes in. It would send a signal of continuity to the world."

"I understand," Grant said.

It was a clever pitch, appealing to Grant's ambition, talking in terms of "continuity" rather than "unity." It came down to the same thing, of course. But he had to give credit where credit was due, and Kittinger had framed the issue well.

"And this is the same response you argued for two years ago," Kittinger added. "We didn't think it was practical in Afghanistan. And it wouldn't have taken down the Taliban government, which had to happen. Colombia is different. This is the right call here. You know it is, Senator."

Grant didn't want to deal with this issue now. But it had come to a head today. And despite his disagreements with Louis in the past, the president was making the right call here. And a show of "continuity" *would* be in the national interest.

"Tell the president I would support bringing these criminals to trial, once we're sure we've identified them and we're sure we can get at them."

"Is that a yes?" Kittinger asked.

He wasn't buying into that trap. "It's a qualified yes. If he does the intel, takes the time to be as sure as he can be, then yes, this is the right response and I'll stand by him on it. Publicly."

He didn't have to say the rest: that if Louis went off half-cocked, Grant would make his objections known. Just as publicly.

"I'll tell the president," Kittinger said. "He'll be glad to know you're on board."

"Again, please pass along my gratitude for his sympathy," Grant said. Even if the gratitude was as hollow as the sympathy, courtesies must be observed.

He handed the phone back to Jerry and sagged onto the sectional.

"It was the right decision," Jerry said.

Grant nodded. "One right decision amidst so many bad ones."

"Don't do that," Jerry said. "Georgie made her own choices. So has Art. So did I, for that matter. You can't take responsibility for other people's choices. You're just not that powerful."

Grant looked up. Jerry's face was firm.

"That's what it comes down to," Jerry continued. "You're a hell of a man, but you're just one man. The rest of us have to muddle through our own problems, make our own choices. Make our own mistakes. You can't control everyone and everything around you. Which means you're not responsible for everything that goes wrong. You didn't make Georgie have an affair. You didn't kill her. You didn't kill Abby or Stacy. You didn't kidnap your kids."

"I left the kids with Art," Grant said. "That *was* my choice."

"And it was the best choice you could have made, based on what you knew at the time. Art betrayed you. But you didn't betray your girls."

"And I'm supposed to just flip a switch," Grant said, snapping his fingers, "and accept that?"

Jerry looked down for a moment. "No. No, it's not that simple. I know that." He met Grant's eyes again. "But it's the truth, whether you accept it or not."

Grant nodded. It was, but knowing the truth and believing it were two different things. And it would be a while before he trusted his own judgment with people. Even Karen. Especially Karen.

"She's a good woman," Jerry said.

Apparently Grant's face was an open book these days. Yet another reason to be cautious. "She's a good cop."

"At least. On the other hand, if she wanted to tear you down, I gave her every opportunity. She passed. That says a lot about her, and not just about whether she's a good cop. It says a lot about what kind of person she is."

"Maybe so," Grant said. "Maybe so."

Terry knocked at the door, then opened it and stepped in without waiting for a response. Adrenaline showed in his narrowed, sharpened eyes and his quiet voice.

"They're at the cabin."

25

The trees and brush provided adequate cover around Art Wallace's cabin. They couldn't get right up close, but they were definitely within easy range. Karen and Miriam hunkered down in the brush near some tall oaks, while the rest of the team encircled the cabin, making sure both doors were covered and all windows easy to observe.

"I wish we knew for sure the girls were in there," Karen remarked.

Miriam handed her a pair of binoculars. "The windows aren't covered." Holding her radio to her lips, she reminded the rest of the team to look for any evidence of the children.

It was Karen who made the first sighting. A pale face bobbed into a window toward the rear of the cabin. Cathy Suzanne. The girl rested her elbows on the window ledge and looked out at the glorious morning. The child was almost eerily still, like a statue. Then a muffled shriek of laughter escaped the cabin, a child's laughter. Cathy Suzanne turned her head for a moment, then resumed her contemplation of the outside world.

"They're in there," Karen said. "I wonder how he's managing to keep them inside?"

"And why," Miriam added, a frown creasing her brow. "Nerves? Or does he know something."

"I'm hoping he just doesn't want to take any chances." After a while, Karen passed the binoculars back to Miriam and rolled over on her back, looking up through a lacy pattern of leaves at a piercingly blue sky. "I hate waiting."

"Yeah. Well, if the asshole gives us an opportunity, we'll move on him. Otherwise, we don't know what's going on in there, whether he's armed, how much at risk the children are...."

"I know." Karen closed her eyes, squeezing back an unwanted rise of anguish. "I know, Miri."

"I know you do. I'm just reminding myself."

Karen rolled over again onto her stomach and looked at the cabin. "This is the hardest part. Damn it."

By noon, Grant was ready to chew nails and Terry wasn't doing much better. They'd found his kids, they knew where they were, and they couldn't do a damn thing yet. God, he hoped Cathy Suzanne wasn't getting scared. That child was bright, far too bright, and by now had probably figured out that something was amiss. His heart squeezed at the notion that she might be growing afraid and he wasn't there to comfort her. That she might think he didn't know what had happened, that no one was doing anything to come get them.

For an instant his hands clenched and he could almost feel them around Art Wallace's neck. It was probably a damn good thing he wasn't there, because he honestly didn't know if he could hold himself back. And if he couldn't, what horrors might his charge at the cabin unleash? He didn't even want to conceive of it.

But he would have given anything to get his hands on Art.

"No Michaels yet," Terry said, after yet another call to Youngblood's offices. "Hell. I'm gonna get a warrant on his apartment."

Grant couldn't stand it anymore. He had to do something. Without waiting for permission, he picked up his phone and called Randall Youngblood. In just a few seconds he was past the secretary and talking to Randall himself.

"Randall. Michaels told you about...what happened, right?"

"Yes. I thought I told you that." Something in Youngblood's voice sounded strained. "Grant, I've been—"

Grant interrupted him. "Where the hell is he?"

"I don't know. I honestly don't know, and that worries me. He's not supposed to ever be out of touch. Last night I woke up...well, I had this feeling about the kidnapping, and I tried to reach him and I couldn't. Not by phone or pager or cell."

"Shit."

"I mean, it's not out of the realm of possibility that he's off taking care of something and didn't want to be interrupted. He has a personal life of some kind. But..."

Terry was making signals, and Grant put his hand over the mouthpiece. "What?"

"I want a photo of Michaels. If he's got one, have him fax it."

Grant spoke into the receiver. "Have you got a photo of Michaels?"

"Yes. Yes of course."

"Fax it over to me, will you? My home fax." He rattled off the number. "Randall…we're pretty sure Art Wallace, my neighbor, is the kidnapper."

Terry made a face and shook his head. Grant ignored him.

"Wallace? He volunteers for me, I think. Well, for Michaels. Oh, Jesus." Randall fell silent.

"Just fax me the photo, will you?"

"Right away. And if there's anything else…"

"I'll let you know," Grant said. He hung up and swore savagely. "Son of a bitch. Son of a goddamn bitch!"

The entire team was wearing headset radios, so no sound would betray them. Karen's headset crackled to life in the early afternoon.

"Wallace is in the cabin," a low male voice said. "He just walked past a window on the north side. "He was carrying a child."

Karen spoke. "What did the child look like?"

"Girl, maybe six or seven, long reddish hair."

"That's one of Wallace's twin daughters. So we know they're in there, too." Karen looked at Miriam. "How the hell does that affect the equation?"

"Damned if I know. You'd think he'd want them to be safe, but after what he's done…"

"Yeah." Karen had seen cases where a parent murdered a child for no better reason than that he or she didn't want anyone else to have them. She sighed and looked down at her hands, knotted fists against dried leaves and dark green moss. "Any word from Terry?"

"I'll check."

The minutes couldn't possibly pass any slower. Nor had she seen Cathy Suzanne in a couple of hours now.

God, she hoped those children were all right. Because if anything happened to them while she sat on her hands in the woods, she was going to hate herself forever.

Art nudged the piece back with the tip of his finger. "Sorry, Cathy, but pawns only move one square at a time."

"But you moved yours forward two squares," she said, pointing to his pawn at king-four.

"That was its first move," he explained. "Pawns can move two squares on their first move only."

She looked at him. "That's a made-up rule."

"I didn't make it up, sweetie," he said. "Someone else did."

"It's still a made-up rule. It's bad enough these little prawns can only move straight ahead. Now you have a made-up rule that they can only crawl straight ahead. That makes them useless."

"They're pawns, sweetie, not prawns. And they're not useless. In the right situation, they can be the most important pieces on the board."

Her eyes fixed his. "I would rather you call me Cathy. Daddy calls me sweetie."

And there it was again. He'd hoped to distract her with games, and she'd promptly beaten him two out of three games in checkers before asking if there was some other game he was better at. So he'd spent the last half hour trying to teach her chess. He'd hoped for a father-daughter bonding experience.

Instead, once again, he had found that behind those intense eyes lay an equally intense will. He had no idea whether she was happy or sad, comfortable or frightened. She kept it all inside, showing him only what she wanted him to see, setting her rules for every conversation, every interaction.

He could kiss her cheek but not her forehead. She tolerated hugs stiffly but did not return them. She'd eaten breakfast, but not with the childhood relish of Belle or the twins. When Belle had asked if they could go out to play in the woods, Art had explained that he needed to wait for a phone call. Cathy had announced that she could watch her younger sister, and Art was forced to come up with some other reason to keep the girls inside. He didn't want to have to round them up if he had to move.

Now Belle was looking plaintively out the window, while Cathy passed judgment on the rules of chess and on how he addressed her. That would change in time, he was sure. It would change in time or she would have to go. That would be tragic, to be sure, but he'd had his fill of headstrong women whose first loyalty always lay with Grant Lawrence.

It wouldn't be the first time he'd had to deal with that problem. A drunk driver had taken care of Georgie after they'd had a huge fight that night. He'd wanted what every man wants, and she'd said she wasn't in the mood. That had become a common problem toward the end. He suspected she was once again sleeping with Grant and had said as much. She had fixed him with the cold, hard stare for which she was known and told him that was none of his damn business. But he'd shown her just exactly whose business it was, pinning her to the bed and clamping his hand over her mouth, fucking in anger rather than love. She'd lain there, limp and still, only afterwards announcing that she would see him rot for that. He'd known, right that moment, that she had to go. The drunk driver was a lucky break.

It was the first time Art had thought of the gods siding with him against Grant Lawrence. It had felt good.

The dancer was different. In a bizarre way, Art had introduced her to Grant. He'd met her often at the club, paying to watch her incredible body undulate in the near darkness, eventually just paying for her to sit with him and talk. It had come out that his neighbor was Grant Lawrence, the famous senator, and she'd brightened in an instant. She had become eligible to vote just a month before Grant's first election, and she'd voted for him. She had been thrilled to vote for a virtual unknown and watch the returns on election night, as he emerged the winner. Her vote had mattered, she'd said.

The next thing he knew, she was volunteering for Grant's next campaign. A few months after Georgie's death, she and Grant had started dating. A few months after that, she'd left the club, and him, to open that damn dance studio with that dyke. When Elizabeth left him, it had made sense to look up the dancer again, but she'd treated him like a fungus, an unwanted reminder of an unhappy time in her life. She wasn't that girl, stripping in a bar, anymore. She was what she'd always wanted to be…a dancer and a dance teacher. Go away, please. Don't come back.

She'd deserved everything he'd done to her. And that he'd done it in a way that would humiliate Grant Lawrence, well, that was a bonus. The old black bitch had wandered in, another Grant Lawrence devotee, and he'd taken care of her, too. The gods were with him, and it felt good.

He knew the gods were still with him when Grant asked if he could watch Cathy and Belle for a while. They had delivered his daughters—the daughters Grant had stolen—into his home. Now all he had to do was get rid of Grant and the justice of the gods would be complete.

And if Cathy Lawrence wouldn't accept him, well, girls got abducted and murdered all the time. It wasn't that difficult. He looked at her across the board, their eyes locked in a battle of wills.

"Your move," she said.

"You'll sit on him?" Terry asked. "I really need to be there to supervise this search."

Jerry Connally nodded. "Detective Sweeney made it clear. I'll keep him in line. Grant's my job. Go do yours."

"He's lucky," Terry said, extending a hand. "Not many men have friends like you."

Jerry shook his hand. "Keep in touch. I'll watch the phones here and call you if there's any news."

Forty minutes later, Terry knocked at the door of Bill Michaels' Crystal City apartment. It was across the Potomac, in Virginia, so Miri had put a word in here and there. There was no way he wasn't going to be there.

He knocked again, and again called out that he was a police officer serving a search warrant. There was no way this would get thrown out for failure to follow knock-and-announce procedures. Still receiving no answer, he nodded to the two officers holding the battering ram. With a deceptively casual swing, they turned the doorjamb to splinters.

Michaels certainly lived well. Dense pile carpeting, cream with an inlay of "GKM" in a decorative script of burgundy. The furniture was a blend of chrome and leather in the main sitting area, but Terry's attention went to the distressed maple roll-top desk. The warrant specified that they were looking for "documentary and/

or physical evidence related to the kidnapping for ransom of Catherine Suzanne Lawrence and Belle Lindsay Lawrence, and documentary and/or physical evidence related to the murder of Nathaniel Steven Olson.'' That was basically carte blanche to go into every nook, cranny, drawer and crevice in the apartment. And Terry intended to do exactly that.

He didn't expect to find much. Michaels was smart, and he was a lawyer. He should have been smart enough not to keep notes or to destroy them as soon as possible. He should have realized that a ballpoint pen would leave indentations beneath the top page of a legal pad, which could be read by lightly rubbing the paper with a pencil. He should have been too smart to keep four-point-eight grams of heroin, folded in a small square of aluminum foil, in the back of the locked top desk drawer. Michaels was smart, and he was a lawyer. But he was also arrogant.

Nat Olson's street name and address.

Logs of calls to and from Art Wallace.

Notes for a book exposing Grant Lawrence.

It was all there. Terry dialed the FBI communications center and asked to be patched through to Miri.

''We've got the son of a bitch,'' he said, quickly recounting the evidence they'd recovered. ''There's nothing to indicate Youngblood knew anything. Like the senator said.''

''Anything on the ransom drop?'' she asked.

''I'm not sure. It looks like there's a list of three or four locations in D.C., and a couple in Baltimore. They could be call stations. No way to tell for sure, though.''

''But you'll have teams out to cover them anyway,'' she said, a lilt of laughter in her voice. ''I know you, Terry Tyson.''

"Yes, you do. And yes, I will."

"Let me know," she said. "And stay safe."

"Anything I can tell the senator about his kids?"

Her voice dropped. "Nothing new. The younger one keeps looking out the window."

"If he hurts them…"

"You'll have to take a number and wait in line," she said. "But we won't let him hurt them."

"Okay, I'm headed back to the Lawrence house. I'll be on the senator when the ransom exchange starts."

"I didn't expect you'd be anywhere else," she said.

Something about the way she said that made him want to say the words she'd always longed for, the words he'd never been able to squeeze out. But this was an FBI frequency.

"Take care," he said.

"You too."

"Thanks," Jerry said, hanging up the phone. He turned to Grant. "That was Elaine Pragle. She'll get the floor vote pushed off a couple of weeks. She said, and I quote, 'I'll say the senator has a cold and is remaining home on the advice of his doctors.'"

Grant tried to find a chuckle but couldn't. Trust Ellen to find a subtle way to spin anything that happened. She was paraphrasing Pierre Salinger, who told the press Kennedy had a cold to explain the president's cutting short a visit to Chicago during the Cuban Missile Crisis. He had long suspected that Elaine was the one who had planted the seeds of the Kennedy comparison. He supposed there was worse baggage to carry.

Grant stuck his chopsticks into the box of lo mein and pushed it aside. Detective Tyson had insisted they eat something, and Jerry had agreed. Chinese was the least revolting of the delivery options available. Grant had tried, but he couldn't force himself to eat. His stomach was a massive knot.

"Has anything changed up in Maryland?" he asked Terry.

The detective seemed about to answer, then paused, dropped a nugget of sweet-and-sour pork into his box and picked up the radio headset. He flipped the switch for the speaker. "Lips, this is Clam, over."

"Lips here." It was Karen's voice this time. "Tell him nothing's happening and to finish his dinner."

"I'll tell him," Terry said. "What's she doing?"

"Taking coffee to the guys," Karen said. There was a slapping sound, and Karen muttered a curse. "Y'know, if you think a stakeout in a car is bad, try doing it in a forest. I have bites in places that aren't places."

Terry let out a tense laugh. "Grind up an aspirin tablet and add water to make a paste. Stops the itch."

"If I confiscated every aspirin tablet from every guy on the team, there wouldn't be enough."

"Well, let me make a note in the log," he said. He checked his watch. "Eighteen-twenty hours. Lips Two is taking coffee to the guys. Lips One is getting eaten by mosquitoes. Clam One won't eat dinner. And everyone's nervous as a wet hen."

"That's about the size of it," Karen said. "You know, if I didn't know better, I'd think there was a reason you suggested that y'all be 'Clam' and we be 'Lips.' Doesn't the department have sensitivity training?"

He laughed. "Sure. But considering the jokes I've heard about clams…"

"Don't even go there. Lips is bad enough."

Terry looked at Grant. "I'll tell Clam One to get a better teenage memory next time."

"You do that," Karen said. "This is embarrassing. Tell me he's not hearing this."

"You're on speaker."

"Shit."

"Oops," he said.

Her voice changed in an instant. "Stand by one."

"Standing by."

Grant sat forward in his chair. "What is it?"

Terry wrapped his hand around the headset microphone. "No idea. You're hearing everything I am, Senator."

"Sorry," Grant said.

He knew that tone in Karen's voice. Something was happening. But what? It was maddening to sit here, trying to choke down Chinese food, unable to do anything. He rose and paced the room for what seemed like the billionth time. His knee was already starting to throb, whether from the pacing or the tension, he couldn't tell. Reminding him that the arthroscopic surgery wasn't totally healed yet.

"Clam One standing by," Terry repeated.

"Target passed by the window," Karen said. "I swear he looked straight at me. He was talking on a cell phone."

"Do you read lips?"

"Not at three hundred yards. By the time I got my binoculars in place, he was hanging up." She paused for a moment. "Clam Three, call his home number."

Jerry nodded and dialed. The tension was evident in his eyes as he waited for the voice mail message to start.

"Put it on speaker," Terry said.

"What?" Karen asked.

"That was to Jerry. It's ringing now. Stand by, Lips."

"Standing by."

The same toneless voice kicked in. "Take the Metro to Union Station. Take the escalator up to the station. You will see a bank of pay phones to your right, at the top of the escalator. Go to the second pay phone from the left. You'll know what number to call. Come alone."

"Lips, we got the instructions." Terry relayed them quickly. "We're moving."

"Roger," Karen said. "Lips out."

Grant was already moving toward the door.

26

Terry stopped Grant before he made it to the door. "Slow down, Senator. You're not going anywhere without a wire. We'll hear whatever you say and anything people say around you. You won't hear us, though. The earpiece would be too obvious."

Grant nodded and tried to give a sheepish smile, wondering if it looked more a grimace. "I forgot."

"Take off your shirt. No reason this has to be obvious."

Grant complied and stood patiently while Terry taped the transmitter to the small of his back.

"Now," Terry said, "you're going to be watched every step of the way. I already have men at the locations on the list from Michaels' apartment. But Union Station isn't one of them. So as we go, I'm going to tell them where to be on the lookout next. I'll meet you at Union Station. I'll drive your car there. It's a rental, by the way. A Taurus. And it's got a GPS system. We're going to track you every step."

Grant nodded, then pulled on his shirt at Terry's direction.

"This thing has a sensitive mike," he said. "It'll pick

up a whisper. I'll have someone on the train with you to Union Station. We don't have time to tap the phone, so you'll have to find some way to tell us what he tells you. If he asks you to get back on the subway, stall for time so I can get someone aboard.''

Grant nodded.

''Okay,'' Terry said. ''Hang on to your cool. Do exactly what he says unless one of my people intervenes, and that will only happen if there's serious trouble. Which means you can be sure your daughters are still okay, because if anything at all happens at the cabin, we're going to pick you up immediately.''

Grant nodded again. Then said, ''Thanks, Terry.'' His face was somber, but there was no mistaking his sincerity.

Terry smiled at him. ''Trust me, Senator. There isn't a person on this team who wouldn't lay down his or her life to make sure you get your daughters back safely.'' He handed Grant the duffel bag. In it were stacks of cut newspaper, with a real bill wrapped atop each stack. It wouldn't survive a close inspection, but if Wallace or Michaels got that close, they would move in anyway. ''Here's the ransom. Off you go.''

''Tell you what,'' Art said, feeling more frazzled than he'd ever felt in his life. Usually these girls didn't trouble him at all, but today they were whiny. Bored. And Cathy Suzanne and her damn basilisk stare...

''When Belle and Cathy's dad gets here, we'll set up the tent outside for you girls to sleep in. How's that?''

It pleased them all...except Cathy Suzanne, of course. Her expression never flickered. There must be something wrong with that girl. Something wrong with her brain.

''So,'' he said, turning to the three younger girls,

"why don't you go roll up your sleeping bags and make a survival kit?'' Survival kit was the name he'd given to the tin box of cookies and treats they were allowed to take with them when sleeping outside. The three girls ran off happily, giving him a brief respite.

Except for Cathy. She just stood there looking at him.

He had to force himself to smile. "Don't you want to camp out?''

"When's Daddy coming?''

Art glanced at his watch. "A couple of hours.''

"Is that who you called?''

"Yes.''

Her mouth drew into a line. "Why didn't you let me talk to him?''

"Because he was busy. He only had a minute.''

Again her gaze never flickered. But, much to his vast relief, she said, "Okay.''

Then she went to pack for a camping trip.

It occurred to him that he didn't have to put up with her, that he could take her out into the woods this very minute and be done with the little bitch's attitude. The urge almost overwhelmed him.

But the other girls would get upset if Cathy disappeared, and he couldn't handle that. Besides, he assured himself, it would all get better once Grant was gone and they were out of here. Then Cathy would have no choice but to love him. No choice at all.

Karen was getting a headache from staring at the cabin, but she wasn't about to stop. A split second would be enough for things to erupt, for someone to get hurt.

Besides, she kept hoping for another glimpse of Cathy Suzanne. Moments later she was rewarded.

The girl appeared in the window where she'd been

that morning. Karen came to alert and tapped Miri on the shoulder. Both women raised their binoculars to look.

For what seemed a long time, Cathy Suzanne stood at the window, staring out toward the woods, not moving. As if she were waiting.

Then, almost as if she were absentmindedly doodling, she began to draw her finger over the glass pane.

Karen felt sweat beading on her brow as she realized the girl was drawing letters. She couldn't quite…was that a P?

Then Cathy started again. It was reversed to Karen, but this time she was fully ready.

Shock rippled through her, and she drew a sharp breath.

H-E-L-P.

Cathy Suzanne knew she was in trouble. And more, she knew they were out here.

The Washington Metro was widely regarded as the best subway system in the country, perhaps in the world. Clean, safe, easy to navigate and convenient, it often led D.C. residents to wonder why so many people drove cars rather than riding the train around town. Of course, Grant thought with edgy irony, most of those people did their wondering while they were sitting in traffic jams.

He didn't ride the Metro often, he thought as he fed a five-dollar bill into the vending machine that issued fare cards. It spat out a card with a magnetic strip, on which was stored his balance. He ran it through the reader at the turnstile and stepped onto the train. He opened his wallet to put the fare card away and was not surprised to find another card already there, frayed and stained around the edges. He'd probably put it there a year or two ago, the last time he'd taken the train.

Seats weren't too difficult to come by at this time of night, although the car wasn't empty, by any means. He scanned the faces around him, trying not to be obvious in doing so. He didn't see Michaels, not that he expected to. Nor could he spot Terry's assigned shadow. He supposed that was a good thing. It meant the shadow was doing a good job of blending into the scenery. Still, it would have been comforting to know who to turn to if something went wrong.

The white-tiled walls of the tunnel swept past in a blur. He was on the Red Line, traveling southeast into the heart of the city. At the Metro Center stop, a dozen or so passengers got off or on, transferring to or from the Blue or Orange lines. At the next stop, Gallery Place, more passengers exchanged with the Green and Yellow lines. None seemed to pay Grant any undue attention. None of those who had remained on the train throughout seemed noteworthy. Terry's shadow was very good.

Two stops later, Grant stepped off at the Union Station platform and looked for the escalator to the Amtrak station. At the top of the escalator, he looked to his right. As the voice had said, the pay phones were there. He glanced around quickly and saw Terry standing at a news counter thumbing through the latest issue of *U.S. News and World Report*. Grant walked to the second pay phone from the left and looked around the tiny phone bay. It was written in black marker on the metal grill that surrounded the phone: *For a good time, call Grant.* And a phone number. He dialed.

"You got started quickly," the voice said, suspicion evident.

"I want my girls back, you son of a bitch. I was calling that number every five minutes."

"Don't get cross with me, Senator. I'm in control of this. So just listen and do as you're told."

"I'm listening."

"Get back on the subway. Transfer to the Blue Line at Metro Center. Get off at Reagan National. Go to the USAir ticket counter. There will be a ticket waiting for you. Go now."

"Wait...."

There was a click, and the line went dead.

"Fuck," Grant said.

Terry glanced up quickly from the magazine, then went back to reading.

"Back to the damn subway," Grant said as he walked to the down escalator. "Sooner or later, I'm going to learn my way around this city. I'd be at the airport already if I knew how to read a map."

"You get used to it," a passing commuter said. She was a petite brunette, wearing a business suit and jogging shoes. "It takes a couple of days."

"Thanks," he said. "It's a confusing city."

She smiled. "Not really. North-south streets are letters, east-west streets are numbers, increasing as you move out from the Capitol. State-named streets are diagonals."

He nodded, trying to look as if he were soaking in the long-familiar information. "That helps," he said.

If she had any connection to Art or Michaels, it wasn't obvious. Just a friendly local commuter trying to help out a tourist. He didn't feel like socializing and was relieved to see her head for the northbound platform. He was headed the other way.

To Reagan National Airport and the next set of instructions. To his girls.

"My God, my God," Miriam said as Cathy disappeared from the window.

"I can't stand this." Karen pounded her fist once on the mossy, leafy forest floor. "That child must be scared out of her mind."

"But quick, very quick."

"Yeah. She must have seen someone move when she was looking out earlier."

"Probably. How old did you say she is?"

"Nine, I think. And smart enough to get herself into trouble."

Miriam looked at her. "What do you mean?"

"She's assuming we're not part of whatever Art is up to. Maybe she's even letting us know she's aware the cabin is being watched by cops. Either way, she's aware she's in trouble, and she might try something that could get her hurt."

"Lips One, Lips Three."

"Go ahead, Three."

"The vehicles are here."

"Copy."

The FBI convoy had left when they pinpointed the cabin, while Karen and the team had gone ahead on the helicopter. Now they had transportation. The net was tightening.

Terry wanted to smash something. The airport, like the train station, hadn't been on the list they'd found in Michaels' apartment. Something was wrong. Train station. Airport. On the one hand, it was easy to shadow Grant in public transportation facilities. Terry could have a dozen men on him and they would be invisible in the crowds. On the other hand, it was impossible to set up a phone tap in a train station or airport without being seen. That seemed to be the kidnappers' strategy. But sooner or later, they would have to send Grant out into the world. He couldn't get to the cabin by subway, and Terry would bet he wasn't boarding a plane. He would feel better once Grant was in the car.

He barked orders over the radio as he headed for the rental car. Jerry was waiting in the passenger seat. "Reagan National," Terry said as he climbed in. "I don't get it."

"Michaels is smart," Jerry said. "He's got a reason. We just have to figure it out."

Terry scanned the list of locations. All of them had been in the north and east side of the city. It had made sense this morning. Bouncing Grant all over the city, but always closer to Maryland. "There was a logic to this list. There has to be a logic to not using it."

He headed south, toward I-295. The highway would be the fastest way to the airport. Once he got to it. Minutes later, mired in traffic, he understood Michaels' logic. Maybe he'd expected the list to be found. He reached for the siren.

"All our people are on the wrong side of the city," he said. "No way will any of us get to the airport before the subway does. Unless Grant stalls changing trains at Metro Center."

"And there's no way to tell him to do that, because it's a one-way wire," Jerry said.

"Right."

"Shit."

"Right."

Grant got off at the airport station and walked to the

USAir counter. The woman behind the counter looked frazzled. "Long day?" he asked.

She gave him a tired smile. "They're all long. Can I help you?"

"Grant Lawrence. I'm supposed to have a ticket waiting."

She tapped away at the keyboard, nibbling on her lower lip as she waited for the computer to respond. She met his eyes and offered another smile. "The system seems to be tired this afternoon too. Oh, here it is. Yep. You're booked for New Orleans."

"New Orleans?" Grant asked, a bit taken aback.

"New Orleans?" Terry echoed, pressing the earpiece closer to his ear as he crossed the bridge, the airport off to his left, tantalizingly close but still several minutes away. And he was the closest of any of the teams.

"New Orleans," the ticket agent repeated. "Why do I think your boss surprised you?"

"He always does," Grant said.

"Damn right," Terry said, shuddering to a stop behind a mammoth SUV driven by a man who seemed more intent on his cell phone conversation than the road around him.

"Something's wrong," Jerry said. "There's no way they're in New Orleans. It's a setup, but why?"

Grant showed his ID and accepted the ticket. This was too well-planned not to have been thought out. But why?

"I'm headed for the security checkpoint and the departure gates," Grant said, hoping it looked like he was simply idly talking to himself.

* * *

Terry slapped a hand against the steering wheel. "Fuck. He'll have to lose the wire. The metal detectors."

"The mike will set off the metal detector," Grant said, pausing at the end of the line. "I'm going to have to take it off. I'm headed toward the men's room."

"Call the airport cops," Jerry offered. "They can cover him until we get there."

"They're too obvious. And we'll be there in ten minutes. Once I get past this idiot."

Grant stepped into the stall and stripped to the waist. He grunted as the tape tore away from his back, feeling like a trained animal jumping through hoops. But he would do whatever he had to to get his girls back.

"Bye, guys," he said into the mike. "I'm leaving it taped inside the third stall, in the men's room."

"Oh great," Terry said. He pulled the earpiece from his ear. "I'm not going to listen to people flush. I still don't see him getting on an airplane, though. That has to be a miss."

"We'll be fine once he gets in the car," Jerry said. "We'll be able to track him on GPS."

"Yeah," Terry said. "That's why we always have a backup plan." But his tone was ironic.

Grant made his way to the gate. A half-dozen business travelers were slouched in the seats, reading, noodling at laptops or staring out at the tarmac. Their faces all read the same. Another day, another flight.

He approached the gate desk and proffered his ticket,

trying to adopt the same tired, casual attitude he saw around him. Inside, his stomach roiled. The gate agent looked at the ticket, then looked at him.

"You're all set, Mr. Lawrence. Oh, wait. Someone left a message for you." The agent handed him an envelope. "Enjoy your flight."

"Thanks," Grant said.

"I hate not knowing what's going on," Terry said. They had finally passed the SUV, and he now swung on to the exit ramp for the airport.

"We'll find him," Jerry said. "Or we'll pick him up in New Orleans. I can get us on a government jet, if we have to. We'd get there before he does."

"Let's hope it doesn't come to that."

Leave the gate area and go to the Budget rental counter. There's a car in your name. Drop this message and your cell phone in the garbage can on the way out of the departure gate. You are being watched.

Grant cursed under his breath. He fought against the urge to look around and find who was watching him, to find them and slam them up against a wall until they gave up his daughters. God protect Art Wallace and Bill Michaels. Because if he found them, they would need divine protection.

He crumpled the note and dropped it and his cell phone in the trash can next to a water fountain. Fear battled with grim determination. Grim determination won. He headed for the rental car counters.

"D.C. Homicide," Terry said, flashing a badge at a startled curbside parking cop.

The cop nodded and wrinkled his forehead as the two men sped past him.

Jerry scanned the visual cacophony of signs, looking for directions to the USAir departure gates. "This way," he said, taking off at a run.

"I'm at the airport," Terry said into his walkie-talkie. "We're going to the gate. We'll signal Grant into the men's room or something. Find out what's happening and make plans."

"Copy that," Miriam's voice said.

"Michaels is one smart son of a bitch."

"You're smarter," Miriam answered. "Out."

"The airport metal detector was clever," Karen said, not taking her eyes off the cabin. "But they couldn't have known Grant would get started so quickly. He'll have to wait for the flight. Terry will get there."

"Yes, he will," Miri said. "Damn. I was sure they'd make the exchange here. Why New Orleans, of all places?"

Karen glanced up at the fading light. "Because we wouldn't have thought of it. We'd be saying the same thing if they'd put him on a flight to Boston or Memphis or wherever. Because it's anywhere but here."

"Lead us away from the kids. What if Michaels is going to pick up the ransom? Do we go in?"

"We have to," Karen said. "Art Wallace isn't going to give those girls up. This isn't about the money."

"I agree."

"We'll just have to see what Terry finds out when he catches up to Grant."

"Waiting," Miri said.

"Waiting."

Outside the airport there was a line at the Budget counter. Grant tried not to look as impatient as he felt. The woman at the front of the line wanted an SUV. The clerk was offering a minivan, all he had. She was holding out for an SUV. It looked like an unbreakable deadlock. He could be here all night.

"Lips One, Lips Five. The front door just opened."

Karen felt her heart slam. "Say again, Five?"

She could feel Miriam tensing beside her. Her voice crackled with adrenaline. "What's going on, Five?"

"Target is in the doorway. Repeat, target is in the doorway."

"What about the packages?" Miri asked.

"Negative."

"I see them," Karen said. "In the back window. All four of them."

She looked at Miri. "I can't believe he's going to leave those girls out in the woods alone."

"He's not," Miri said. "He just thinks he is."

Karen thought a moment. "What's going on, Five?"

"Target is out and closing the door. He has a long package under his arm. Looks like a rifle to me. I have a clear shot now. Repeat. I have a clear shot."

"Negative, Five," Karen said. "If he's separating from the packages, let him get farther away. Follow him. Once he's gone, we'll get the girls out and safe. Then you can take him."

"Copy that."

She turned to Miri. "I think we've got him."

27

Terry flashed his badge at the security checkpoint and nodded at Connally. "He's with me. Joint task force with the FBI."

The minor functionary at the checkpoint had a job to do, and he wasn't going to be deterred by what could be fake IDs and a high-sounding story. It was exactly the kind of lie a terrorist might tell.

"I need to call this in," he said.

Terry bit his lip. "This is a police emergency. There are four innocent lives at risk."

"I need to call this in," the security guard repeated. "Who is your superior?"

Terry handed him the walkie-talkie. "My superior is staking out a hostage situation. You're welcome to talk to her."

"That could be anyone," the guard said. "Who can I call at the FBI?"

This was beyond belief, Jerry thought. Trust airport security to be airtight at the worst possible moment. He felt his breathing quicken, his fists clenching.

Tyson raised the walkie-talkie to his mouth. "Clam Two to Lips Two. Agent Anson, I have a problem here."

* * *

"We simply don't have any SUVs," the supervisor said. "I'm sorry, ma'am. If you'd had a reservation, things would be different. We'd have one waiting. But those are very popular vehicles. I'm sorry. As the agent said, we do have a minivan."

Grant ground his teeth. *Take the minivan,* he thought. *Take a Yugo. Take a skateboard. Just take* something!

"Target is moving, Clam," Miri said. "Kinda busy here."

"What's your boss's number?" Terry asked. "Believe it or not, I'm having trouble clearing the security gate."

Miri rattled off the name and number, which Terry repeated to the gate guard, who in turn dialed a phone.

"Lips out," Miri said.

The guard paused a moment, phone to ear, then hung it up. "I'm sorry, but there's no answer. Just a voice mail. Now, if you'd like to leave your weapons and radio here, I can process you."

Jerry had had enough. The right cross connected solidly with the guard's jaw. Pain shot up his hand, but it was quickly followed by satisfaction as the guard sagged to the floor. Applause broke out behind them.

"Petty tyrants," he said, chasing after Terry, who was already moving as other guards set off the alarm behind them.

"Yeah, well, you'll probably get busted for that," Terry said.

"It was worth it."

"Maybe not. They're shutting this place down tighter

than a drum right now." Then he glanced toward Jerry. "But...you beat me to it by about three seconds. Now let's find Grant."

"Target is pulling away in the car."

"Copy that, Five. We're moving in now."

Karen ran across the meadow, ignoring the twinges as her ankles rolled over uneven ground. She would feel it in the morning. Right now, the girls were all that mattered. Miri kept pace beside her, snapping orders to the other team members, coordinating the net around Wallace's car. They had him. Once they got the girls, they had him.

"Do you have one of those new Volkswagens?" the woman asked. "They're cute."

Both the rental agent and supervisor looked as if manna had fallen from heaven. "As a matter of fact, we do, ma'am. Will you need collision insurance?"

Grant shifted impatiently, one foot to the other, as they completed the transaction. Finally.

"May I help you?" the agent said, smiling in relief as he approached the counter.

"Grant Lawrence. I have a reservation."

Once again the type-and-wait. Then, "Yes, here it is. You're in a Taurus. It's prepaid." She wrote the lot and space number on a paper key ring and handed him the key. Her voice brightened out of habit. "Enjoy your stay in our nation's capital."

He was already walking away.

Terry slowed to a walk as he reached the gate attendant and offered his badge. "D.C. Homicide."

The woman nodded. "How can I help you?"

"I'm looking for Grant Lawrence. He's booked to New Orleans."

Jerry looked around the gate area. Grant was nowhere to be seen. "Has he boarded already?"

She shook her head. "We don't board for another forty minutes. And he left."

"What?" Terry asked.

"Someone had left a message for him. He read it and left in a hurry."

"Do you know what the message was?"

"No," she said. "It was in an envelope. I didn't open it."

"Damn," Jerry said.

"Yeah," Terry agreed.

"Whatever it was, it upset him," the attendant said. "He muttered a curse and threw the note away. Even threw away his cell phone."

Terry's eyes lit up. "Where?"

She pointed. "In that can."

Jerry was already moving. He began to dig through the can. It hadn't been emptied in a couple of hours, at least.

"Fuck that," Terry said, hefting the can and tipping it over. "We don't have time to be neat."

"Check the door for traps," Miri said as they rounded the cabin. "Just in case."

"He doesn't know we're here," Karen said. "And he wouldn't risk his daughters."

"Check anyway."

They never got the chance.

Cathy Suzanne opened the door. "Are you here to take us to my daddy?"

Karen crouched and took the girl in her arms. "Yes, Cathy. That's exactly what we're here to do."

"Lips Five, Lips Two," Miri said. "We've got them. Take him."

"Copy that. Five out."

Grant climbed into the car. He turned down the visors, then opened the glove compartment. There it was. He opened the envelope.

Take I-66 west to Tyson's Corner Mall. There will be further instructions taped inside the lid of the trash can to the left of the north entrance to Sears. You have twenty minutes. This car has GPS. You are being monitored. Follow instructions exactly.

He pulled out of the lot and headed north toward Arlington and his assigned route.

"Found it!" Terry said, smoothing the message.

"What's it say?" Jerry asked.

"Lips Four, stop the target. Repeat, stop the target. Lips Three, cover."

"Copy that," the voices said.

Karen tried to listen to the messages passing over the radio, even as the girls babbled questions. Four hundred yards away, in the woods, someone had Art Wallace in the sights of a sniper scope. The girls were safe. It was over.

Terry's voice came over the radio. "Fuck fuck fuck fuck fuck!"

"Lips Three and Four, hold!" Miri said. "What is it, Clam Two? We have the girls and are ready to move."

"I've lost Clam One. He's left the airport in a rental car. I have no idea where he's going. He had to take off the wire at the security gate, and they put him in another car. He's gone. Fuck.''

"Cancel intercept!'' Miri shouted into the mike. "I say again, cancel intercept.''

"Lips Two, Lips Five. What's going on?''

"We've got the packages,'' Miri said, "but we've lost Clam One. I say again, we've lost Clam One. We have to assume he's being led to an ambush.''

"Five concurs.''

Karen looked at Miri. "Art's going to kill Grant.''

Miri nodded. "You were right. It wasn't the money.''

"Who's going to kill Daddy?'' Cathy asked.

"No one,'' Karen said firmly. She met the girl's eyes steadily until Cathy nodded.

"What?'' Terry asked, his voice crackling tensely over the radio. "What's going on?''

Karen took a slow breath. Everyone was on edge. This could get out of control very quickly. If they took Art now, Michaels might still be waiting at the ambush site. Two shooters would be better than one. And they had no idea where the ambush site was. Yet.

"Let the target go,'' she said. "Follow him.''

There was a pause.

"Did you copy my last, Lips team? Let the target go and follow him. We have to know where he's going.''

"We copy.'' It was Harrelson's voice. "Are you sure?''

"Just do it,'' Miri snapped.

Art drove on, unaware of the net that had settled around him. One more hour. Then Grant would be gone. Sixty minutes. Then a few seconds to settle his breath, let the sight settle on Grant's chest. Or his head. A half second to squeeze the trigger. A split-second as the high-powered rifle bullet flew through the air...

Grant pulled into the parking lot and stopped at the curb, ignoring the looks from startled shoppers as he dashed out of the car, leaving the door open, and attacked the trash can. The envelope was there.

Take the Beltway north to I-95, and I-95 north to Baltimore. Take the city bypass and go to the inner harbor. Leave the ransom at the entrance to the aquarium. You have forty minutes. You are being watched.

Forty minutes to Baltimore. It would be tight.

He climbed into the car and gunned the engine, tires squealing as he sped out of the lot and up the ramp to the Beltway.

"Just please, God, no traffic jams," he said. "Please. I need my girls back. Please, don't take them away from me. Please."

Karen had tucked the girls into the medevac helicopter, which had landed in the clearing behind the cabin. "You're going to ride to Bethesda Hospital," she told them. "It's a wonderful hospital. It's where they take care of the president."

The girls were scared, and she wanted to stay with them. But she also wanted, *needed,* to coordinate the chase. If anyone slipped up and Art Wallace saw that he was being tailed, he would skip. And Michaels would kill Grant.

Cathy Suzanne spoke quietly. "We'll be okay. Go find Daddy. I'll take care of them."

Karen blinked back a tear. The girl's eyes were mesmerizing. Seeing so much. Knowing so much.

"Go find Daddy," she said again. "Bring him home."

Karen kissed her cheek. "You bet I will."

She closed the door and patted the window to signal the pilot. Then she ran to the other helicopter. Miriam was waiting in the bay, listening to the radio chatter from the chase teams.

"I could have done this," she said. "You could have gone with the girls."

"I have to make sure," Karen said, her face grim against the rush of feelings that flowed whenever she thought of Cathy Suzanne's words. She wouldn't let that girl down. Ever. "I just have to make sure."

"I understand," Miri said, switching her headset to the intercom circuit. "Okay, pilot. Let's find this guy."

"On our way," the pilot said.

They lifted off into the growing darkness.

Grant wove in and out of traffic, having nearly rear-ended a Firebird on the interchange ramp to I-95. It was a straight shot from here. He had twenty-five minutes. Not enough time. He pushed the gas pedal harder.

"Wallace is headed to Baltimore," Karen told Terry over the radio. "We have a unit a half mile ahead of him and another a mile back. I have him in sight."

"He'll go downtown," Terry said. "It's the best place for an ambush. Lots of cover. Lots of escape routes."

"I know. Miri's on the line with Baltimore P.D. now, trying to get their help. Any progress on Grant's rental car?"

"We've got the information from the renting agent. The good news is that it's GPS equipped. We're setting up to monitor it from here." He paused. "Stand by, one."

"Standing by." She turned to Miri. "I think they've found Grant."

"Now if we could just find Michaels," Miri said. "He's the only wild card left."

Karen nodded. She put a hand over her ear. "What's up, Terry?"

"We've got Clam One's car on monitor. He's on I-95, just pulling into Baltimore now. Still on the highway."

"Where is he?" Miri asked. Karen told her. Miri thought for a moment. "I don't know this city. Where would you set up an ambush?"

Karen spread her hands. "I've never been here."

"Talking with Baltimore P.D.," Miri said.

"Right. Sorry."

"What's up?" Terry said.

Karen wished she had more than confusion to share. "Nothing yet. I'll let you know when we know something."

Jerry's voice came over the radio. "Just heard from the medevac. The girls are at Bethesda now."

Now if she could just get Grant home. For Cathy Suzanne. For herself.

Art wound through the city streets, following the route Michaels had scouted for him that day. As Michaels had said, the traffic was light. Not surprising, as the route wound through some of the worst neighborhoods in the city. Still, he emerged in the Inner Harbor area, and found the parking lot. It offered a clear view of the entrance to the aquarium. Two hundred yards. An easy shot, even in the dark. And Grant would be lit at the entrance.

It was perfect.

In the distance, he heard the *whump-whump-whump* of a helicopter. Probably one of those traffic monitors for a radio station, he thought.

He unpacked the rifle and popped the cover off the sight. There was a low wall at the perimeter of the lot. It was an ideal firing support.

Behind him, the *whump-whump-whump* settled for a moment, then faded into the distance. The night grew still. Quiet, save for the distant lap of water against the harbor seawall. Peaceful. Serene.

He settled behind the wall and leveled the rifle.

Grant pulled into the lot for the Inner Harbor aquarium. He'd taken the girls here once. Cathy Suzanne had loved the shark exhibit. Belle had preferred the seals. The memory jarred against the tension of the moment. Did anyone know where he'd gone? He hefted the duffel bag from the back seat, cursing the idea of substituting newspaper for real money. If Michaels or anyone else opened the bag here, Art would kill his daughters.

"Just let me bring them here one more time," he said, walking across the lot. "Let Cathy Suzanne see her sharks and Belle her seals. One more time. Please?"

The bastard was talking to himself, Art thought, watching him through the telescopic sight. Grant was looking upward, as if talking to God. Good. He could do it face-to-face in about twenty seconds, once he was out in the clear. Twenty, nineteen…

Miri pointed at the figure crouched behind the wall. Karen nodded. He was already in her sights. But they had to find Michaels first.

* * *

Grant walked between two vans with aquarium logos on their sides. Probably portable exhibits for schools, he thought. It was a good idea.

He was almost in the clear. Art's finger tightened on the trigger. Thirteen, twelve...

The gods were with him. Somewhere deep inside, he'd always known they were. Even when his mother was beating him. Even when Georgie was cheating. He'd always known the gods would come through. Eventually.

Nine...eight...

Michaels heard the crunch of a footstep on the asphalt behind him an instant before he felt the cold steel pressed behind his left ear. He let out a breath, released the rifle and raised his hands.

"We've got Michaels," Harrelson said. "Go go go."

Grant hesitated at the end of the fence. The entrance was deserted. Not even a security guard. Of course. That was why they'd chosen this place, and this time. The sign on the fence beside him announced the hours and admission prices. He walked toward the door.

Two...One...

"Freeze," Karen shouted, popping her flashlight on Wallace. "Put the rifle down, Wallace."

What? Art glanced over his shoulder. The flashlight hid the figure, but he recognized the voice. The lady cop from Tampa. What the hell was she doing here?

"Put it down *now!*" she shouted.

No. The gods wouldn't betray him. He'd spent his life being beaten and cheated on by women. Not again. Not this time. He turned and tried to fix the sight on Grant, waiting for the red retinal glow from the flashlight to pass. Ahh. There was Grant. Stopped. Facing him. That was the way it should be. Perfect.

Karen saw him turn and aim the rifle again. She already had her gun at the ready. Beside her, Miri grew still. Karen didn't feel her finger squeeze. The buck of the pistol surprised her. Her left ear rang with the report from Miri's pistol.

Art heard the reports a split second before the subsonic, nine-millimeter rounds punched into his back. The world reeled, then receded. Through his sight, he saw Grant crouch. He must have heard the shots. Art tried to steady the swaying rifle. He could still win. His finger tightened.

So intent was his concentration that he didn't hear the second pair of twin cracks, only felt the kick of the rifle butt against his shoulder as his finger tightened.

Then the world went black.

Karen saw the muzzle flash of Art's rifle an instant before his head snapped forward amidst a pink mist. Her second shot, or Miri's, had found its mark. But he'd fired first.

She ran across the lot. "Grant! Grant!"

"Target is down!" Miri called out beside her, as shadowy, black-clad figures emerged into the parking lot, guns leveled.

Karen hardly noticed. "Grant!"

There he was, in the parking lot. On his knees. Clutching the duffel bag to his chest. Not sinking. Not rising. Not moving.

"Grant!"

He sank onto one hip, then onto his side, his face contorted. She sprinted across the lot. "Get a medic!" she yelled. "He's down. The senator is down!"

She dropped to her knees beside him.

"Grant. Are you hit?"

He opened his eyes and met hers. "The girls?"

"We got them. They're fine. Are you hit?"

"Damn knee," he said. "Damn knee."

She looked down at his leg. The trousers were torn. And wet.

"Get a medic!" she screamed again. "He's hit."

"No," he said, wincing, gasping out words. "I heard shots. Crouched down. Knee gave out and I fell. Bee flew over my head." He let out a low groan. "Damn knee."

"Don't curse it too much," she said, relief surging through her. "It saved your life. If you hadn't fallen, that bee would have taken your head off."

He nodded and managed a pained smile. "Okay. Thanks, damn knee."

She smiled and touched his face.

"Yeah. Thanks, damn knee."

Epilogue

The woman's smoky voice filled the club as she built to the song's climax.

He really makes it hard for me to sing the blues....

Grant released Karen's hand and applauded. "That's cute," he said.

"I can appreciate the feeling," she said, meeting his eyes. They'd found a table this time. For four. "I can definitely appreciate the feeling."

"So can I," Miri said, squeezing Terry's hand.

He smiled, white teeth lighting up his face. "Yeah, well, I'm still gonna retire."

"Bullshit," Miri said. "Karen's going to need someone to partner with."

"Oh?" he said.

Grant turned to face her. "Is that so?"

Karen tipped her head. The past two months had been a blur. She'd flown back to Tampa to help Previn wrap up the paperwork, but Simpson had put her on administrative leave, pending the investigation of the shooting of Art Wallace. There was no doubt that she'd used justifiable force, but rules were rules. As it turned out, Previn hadn't needed the help. Paperwork was his element. His spirits had lifted since he'd talked to a lawyer. He was no longer a helpless victim of Linda's machinations, and while the breakup still nagged at him in quiet moments, he could see a light at the end of the tunnel.

The lab had matched the DNA from the saliva found around the bite marks on Stacy's body to Art Wallace. The official story was that he'd killed both Abby and Stacy, moving Stacy's body because he thought he might have been seen stalking her. Michaels hadn't been at the murder scene, so he couldn't contradict the story. It was, Karen thought, true in its essence. Art Wallace and Bill Michaels had created this horror from their own twisted motives. Whatever Jerry Connally had done, it had been done with good intentions. There was no reason to let Wallace and Michaels ruin someone else.

A thorough search of Wallace's house had turned up a journal. Wallace believed he was the father of Grant's girls. She'd asked Grant if he wanted a paternity test, but he'd refused. He'd raised them. They were his. Biology wouldn't change that. Ever. Karen agreed.

The girls were bouncing back...slowly. Belle still had nightmares sometimes. Cathy Suzanne kept her feelings to herself, except in fleeting, unguarded moments with her father. Then her fingers would tighten into his back as she hugged him, and a half sob would emerge before she caught herself. Someday, perhaps, she would talk to someone about what she'd seen in the early years when Georgie took her on trips to the cabin in Maryland. Or maybe she would work through it on her own.

She had, just once, kissed Karen's cheek, holding the contact for a moment, and whispered, "Thank you." It was a moment Karen would savor forever. The commendations Miri and Terry had forwarded to Simpson would never equal those two words.

She'd spent the last two weeks in Washington, staying with Miri. Seeing Grant when she could drag him away from the final wrangling over S.R. 52. Randall Youngblood had come to Grant's house to express his sorrow over what Michaels and Wallace had done. Professionally, he was still opposed to the bill. Privately, he told Grant he would back off if Grant would be responsive to the sugar growers in the aftermath. Grant had shaken his hand on the deal, a handshake between two men whose word was their bond.

The media was still abuzz with the kidnapping story. At a press conference the day after the rescue, Miri had made a point of mentioning that Grant had walked into that parking lot knowing the assassins must have had him in their sights, willing to die if necessary to protect his daughters. That story was also true in its essence, Karen thought. She'd had a gun and a bulletproof vest when she'd stepped into that parking lot. Grant had had nothing but his courage and his faith that he was doing what he had to in order to get his girls home. Karen didn't know if she could have walked out across that exposed parking lot in those circumstances. He had. If the American people judged him a hero, well, he was.

That, and Youngblood's tacit support, had made the difference. S.R. 52 had passed that afternoon—by four votes.

And tonight they were celebrating.

"Well?" Grant asked.

"Well what?"

He smiled. "So are you thinking of moving up here, joining the D.C. force?"

She could look at that smile forever. "I'm thinking about it."

He leaned forward and kissed her as the sax player began "What a Wonderful World."

They weren't looking for each other…
but the chemistry was too powerful to resist.

MARY LYNN BAXTER

A string of deadly warnings convinces Dallas mayor Jessica Kincaid to hire bodyguard Brant Harding. But as their personal agendas intersect, Jessica and Brant find themselves at odds, yet drawn to each other with a passion neither can deny. And when the threat to Jessica's life intensifies, not even Brant's best efforts may be enough to save her—or to buy them both a second chance.

HIS TOUCH

"Ms. Baxter's writing…strikes every chord within the female spirit."
—Sandra Brown

On sale February 2003
wherever paperbacks are sold!

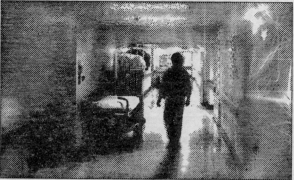

RACHEL LEE

66885	JULY THUNDER	___ $6.50 U.S.	___ $7.99 CAN.
66802	A JANUARY CHILL	___ $5.99 U.S.	___ $6.99 CAN.
66554	SNOW IN SEPTEMBER	___ $5.99 U.S.	___ $6.99 CAN.
66298	CAUGHT	___ $5.99 U.S.	___ $6.99 CAN.
66173	A FATEFUL CHOICE	___ $5.99 U.S.	___ $6.99 CAN.

(limited quantities available)

TOTAL AMOUNT $_____
POSTAGE & HANDLING $_____
($1.00 for one book; 50¢ for each additional)
APPLICABLE TAXES* $_____
TOTAL PAYABLE $_____
(check or money order—please do not send cash)

To order, complete this form and send it, along with a check or money order for the total above, payable to MIRA Books®, to: **In the U.S.:** 3010 Walden Avenue, P.O. Box 9077, Buffalo, NY 14269-9077; **In Canada:** P.O. Box 636, Fort Erie, Ontario L2A 5X3.

Name:_____
Address:_____ City:_____
State/Prov.:_____ Zip/Postal Code:_____
Account Number (if applicable):_____
075 CSAS

*New York residents remit applicable sales taxes.
  Canadian residents remit applicable GST and provincial taxes.

MIRA®

Visit us at www.mirabooks.com

MRL0203BL